Gail squared ... toward Hawk. "I don ... make you believe me ...

"That's how we Indians are, aren't we?" he said. "Stoic. Inscrutable."

She searched his eyes for something, a flicker of humor perhaps. But he might have been carved from the very mountain rock they stood upon.

"Oh, please," she said, "not the noble savage routine."

He gave her a hard stare for an uncomfortable moment, then turned away. But he turned back again and stared at her once more. "Gail."

It was the first time he'd ever used her name. He stopped in front of her, silent.

She waited. Tension crackled between them like dry lightning in a summer sky. For a long time they gazed deeply into one another's eyes. Finally, Gail dared to touch him. She slid both arms up over his and grasped the back of his shoulders. Then she pulled him close to her, resting her head against his chest.

She felt him stiffen, then slowly his hands came up to rest on her waist. Then his arms came around her. She lifted her face to him and closed her eyes. Their lips met and clung in a deep and wonderful kiss . . .

LOVE
AT LAST

GARDA PARKER

ZEBRA BOOKS
KENSINGTON PUBLISHING CORP.

ZEBRA BOOKS

are published by

Kensington Publishing Corp.
475 Park Avenue South
New York, NY 10016

First Printing: May, 1993

Printed in the United States of America

To
Brenda & Phillip Whiteman

Jimmie & Althea Little Coyote

People of the Morning Star
Northern Cheyenne Reservation
Lame Deer, Montana

The Busby School
Busby, Montana

Muta-wes-woomtet's — *Till we meet again*

Then Nature rul'd, and love, devoid of art
Spoke the consenting language of the heart . . .

— *John Gay (1685-1732)*

Chapter One

The afternoon sun streamed through the wall of windows in the guidance counsellor's office of the Riverview Private Residence School. Behind her desk, Gail Bricker leaned back in her chair wishing she could swivel around and lose herself in the dappled light on the lush early summer greenery along New York's Hudson River banks. Instead, she rested the entwined fingers of both hands on her crossed knee, and focused attention on yet another complaint from sixteen-year-old Chelsea Gotter who fidgeted in the tweed upholstered armchair opposite Gail's desk.

"That's the third leather bag that's been stolen from me this semester. My father is not going to be pleased to hear about this," Chelsea said.

"No, I imagine he won't," Gail responded in her usual calm tone, the one that always annoyed Chelsea. Gail had ascertained in Chelsea's freshman year that the girl enjoyed any scene she could create in which the adults around her were agitated or annoyed. And that same year Gail had determined she was one adult who would maintain her cool with Miss Chelsea Gotter.

"The security people at this place are lazy, if you ask me," Chelsea went on, knowing a dig at any member of Riverview's staff could aggravate an administrator as almost nothing else could.

Gail ignored the obvious ploy. "I'd rather ask you why you think your belongings are stolen so often."

"I just told you. The security people don't care. And besides, I have the most expensive things in this school," Chelsea sniffed, tossing back the satiny sheet of long blonde hair that had fallen over her shoulder, "and everybody knows that. I guess they just want to be as hot as I am."

"Could it possibly be that you may have misplaced the bags, and the number of other things you've reported stolen, yourself?" Gail pressed, hoping Chelsea would relent this time. "Or that you don't take care of your things? That you leave them out all over the place wherever you go?"

"Why should any of those goofy girls think they can just take my things?" Chelsea whined. "Why is it always me? They all hate me, that's why they do it." She let one tear slip dramatically from the corner of her blue-green contact lens tinted eye.

"Why do you think they hate you, Chelsea?"

Chelsea lifted her patrician chin. "And why do you shrink types always ask *why* about everything? It's pretty clear to me, and everyone else. I'm the prettiest and the richest girl at Riverview. They're all jealous, of course."

Gail sighed inwardly. Chelsea's words could be worn on a slogan tee shirt by too many of the young people at this school, boys as well as girls. Alternately ignored and indulged by their wealthy parents and various members of convoluted step-families, they resorted to all manner of tricks and trappings to get the kind of attention they desperately craved from adults. In the position of guidance counsellor she'd occupied for two academic years, Gail found Chelseas, different names but similar plights, in her office more often than she wanted.

She was searching her mind for a fresh approach to get at the truth about Chelsea's problem, when a knock came to the door.

"Madame Counsellor, I wish an audience with you—" Catherine Collings, a senior high history teacher and Gail's closest friend, peeked in, dark-rimmed half reading glasses perched on the end of her nose. She stopped at the sight of Chelsea slouched in the chair. "Oh, I'm sorry. I should have waited for an answer before I barged in. Hello, Chelsea, how are you?" Catherine smiled warmly at the girl.

Chelsea pushed out of the chair. "I was leaving anyway. As usual, I can't get any help from anyone in this place." She started toward the door, her bottom lip quivering, a frown pleating her delicate brow.

"I'm sorry you feel that way, Chelsea." Gail rose and came around to the front of the desk. Usually she stayed seated when a student came in to talk to her because, at almost five feet nine, she towered above all but the basketball players. This time she felt it necessary to let Chelsea feel her authority. "I'll report the theft of your bag as soon as possible."

"You bet you will. I'm going to call Daddy right away."

"I have an unclaimed L.L. Bean bag in my office you're welcome to borrow until yours turns up," Catherine volunteered,

"Forget it." Chelsea turned around, and raised her pointed chin a notch. "Alene is a Coach distributor, and there's a gorgeous forest green leather tote bag I'm just dying to have. I'll call her and she can Fed Ex it to me overnight." With a falsely triumphant smile, Chelsea walked out of the office leaving the door wide open.

Catherine dropped down into the chair vacated by the girl. She carried a compact grace about her. Not nearly as tall or long-legged as Gail, the impeccably groomed Catherine moved smoothly in her navy fitted blazer and matching

10

knee-length pleated skirt.

Gail noted with wry humor how she and Catherine closely followed the rules demanded by the school board, a well-turned out staff who blended with, not competed with or surpassed, the students and their families. They dressed fashionably, trendy without being faddish. Catherine in her classic feminine suits and dresses, and Gail in outfits like the one she wore today, a soft taupe silk shirt and matching draped trousers that tapered close to the ankle above taupe leather slender heeled shoes, epitomized understated elegance.

"Who's Alene?" Catherine asked.

"Her father's wife." Gail sat down again and stretched her arms high before settling folded hands behind her head. She removed round glasses with thin tortoise rims and rubbed the corners of her eyes.

"Ah yes, she's the third, right?"

"Fourth, I think, but who's counting?"

Catherine sighed. "So she'll call her father, and old Daddy Gottbucks will want some poor security officer's head to roll for this alleged theft, or else he won't send his hefty annual contribution."

Gail nodded. "And I won't be able to do anything about it."

"Not if you want to keep your job."

"Sometimes I wonder if I do. The kids don't

care and the parents don't care. Half the time it seems as if I'm the only one who does care."

"I know. These kids are so lucky, but they haven't been taught how to value what they have."

"The worst thing is, this latest episode won't help Chelsea at all. As usual." Gail rubbed her temples. "It's clear the only thing she'll come out of this with is . . ."

"One more Coach bag to go with the other two she's got stashed in the back of her closet," Catherine finished.

"Sometimes I wonder if I can endure this for the next three years until I retire." Gail said.

"Then what?"

"Beats the hell out of me. I don't want to stagnate then, but sometimes I feel that's what I'm doing right now. I wish I knew . . ."

Gail straightened the folders and papers on her desk. Sometimes she wished she could go back to teaching English and literature, and presiding over the photography club. Those endeavors had been much more interesting and rewarding than being the school's guidance counsellor. She rubbed her forehead where the rumblings of a headache grew stronger.

She was glad June was drawing to a close and the school year was almost over. Riverview seemed to be in the throes of every problem imaginable, and when those problems involved students and parents, they eventually landed in her office. That was her job, and she never avoided any of the accompanying difficulties, but sometimes the turmoil got her down. She felt hemmed in by it, restricted in her creativity to find solutions.

"I don't know why I thought I wanted this job in the first place, or why I even applied for it," Gail said at last. "Yes, I do," she answered herself. "This is the natural order of things, isn't it, a promotion of sorts? I can take advantage of early retirement at fifty-five. God, that's in three years. I can't believe it! How did I get so old so soon?"

Catherine threw up her hands in a gesture of futility. "I've asked myself that ever since I turned forty. Now I'm over fifty and sometimes I feel as if I've been sleepwalking through my life. You know, like I just woke up and wonder where a half century disappeared to."

"I know. I remember my Uncle John talking about retirement. It sounded so stodgy then, made him sound so *old* to be talking like that. Now I'm talking about it. I lived with them when I was growing up, and now I'm as old as Aunt Adelaide and Uncle John were when I thought they were *really* old!"

Catherine laughed. "I'm sure they felt the same way about their parents."

"Probably. But, from a practical standpoint,

I've concluded that this position, and of course the money that goes with it, is going to make my retirement package very attractive. Uncle John would be proud to hear me talk like that. If there's anything my Depression-era family instilled in me, it was to be security oriented almost to the point of panic if I wasn't planning for every future dollar. God!"

"What did your uncle do after he retired?"

"Watched television, went fishing once in awhile. Argued with Aunt Adelaide a lot. Then he died. Then she died." Gail shook her head. "I may not have a husband to argue with, but I do have other options . . . I think . . . I hope."

Catherine's gaze went over Gail's shoulder and out the window. "I've never thought I had any other options. No family, no real hobbies. I hate hobbies anyway. I'd much rather be doing something productive. If I'm forced to retire, I haven't any idea what I'll do with my time."

"If we only played golf!" Gail laughed.

Catherine made a face of distaste.

"Anyway, what did you want to talk to me about?" Gail brought the conversation back to the moment.

Catherine thought for a moment. "Damned if I know!"

"Girls, I've got a great idea!" Sheila Watson breezed in and dropped her plump form into the other chair facing Gail's desk. Her round face was more flushed than usual, her recently bleached permed curls bounced, and her brown eyes sparked with excitement. "A group vacation!"

Gail and Catherine let out a collective groan.

"What's your idea this time?" Gail asked. "So far you've suggested white water rafting down the Colorado River for Thanksgiving, mountain climbing in Alaska over Christmas, and a deserted island survival course in August. None of which produced any takers. So what is it this time? Bungee jumping into the Grand Canyon? Hot air balloon rides over Old Faithful?"

"Hey, you were all a bunch of faint hearts. Those were great ideas!" Sheila leaned forward and inched herself to the edge of the seat. "This one is it. I mean it. America's Adventure Tours is offering a six week motor coach trip to the wild and wooly west! Real cowboys and Indians!"

"Motor coach? That's just a fancy name for bus, isn't it?" Catherine's voice cracked.

"Singles only, men and women!" Sheila said.

"Bus?" Gail echoed in a whisper. "Six weeks?"

"See America at eye level," Sheila said, waving her palm over an imaginary panorama. "See single men up close and personal. Two weeks out and back, and two weeks on a real working ranch in Montana. Cowboys in wide open spaces and tight jeans. The West, where men are men and the women take advantage of them. This is such

15

a glorious country . . . God! It'll be like Club Med on wheels!"

"Sounds like Club Dread to me," Catherine muttered. "Twenty-eight days on a *bus!*"

"We'll stay in the best places on the way," Sheila rushed on, "eat good food, drink good wine, and ride in comfort on a luxury motor coach . . . okay, bus."

"Luxury bus is an oxymoron," Gail said, replacing her glasses and scrutinizing Sheila's face.

"What do you mean?" Sheila stared at her. "It's air-conditioned and rest-room equipped!"

Gail and Catherine laughed.

"C'mon, girls," Sheila pleaded. "Prudie and Bethanne said they'd go if you'd go."

"Prudie said she'd go?" Gail's voice registered the honest surprise she felt.

"Can you imagine?" Prudie responded, stepping inside the door. "But, yes, I want to go on this trip. I could use something in my life as good as the books I read."

As long as Gail had known Prudie Chase, the school's librarian three years her junior, she had looked a decade or two older, and she'd always lived with her mother. She was thin and angular. She had small gray eyes and wore silver wire-rimmed spectacles that rested over her gaunt cheeks, or dangled at the end of a black cord that brushed the shoulders of the high-necked charcoal, straight-to-the-ankle dresses she wore

16

year round and was wearing now. Her gunmetal gray hair was pulled back in a bun. The whole look was assembled, Gail figured, in order to scare the students. But instead, behind her back they ridiculed her looks and her vocal hypochondria. Thinking of her dressed like Annie Oakley out in the Wild West made Gail's lips quiver in a suppressed smile.

"Are you talking about the trip?" a breathless Bethanne Proctor said, a wave of musky perfume following her. She pushed into the room and took a place in front of one of Gail's low bookcases. "Let's do it! There'll be so much I can learn about rocks and plants. And of course, the *men!*"

Bethanne, a junior high science teacher, was always concerned about her makeup. She wore too much most of the time, an overload of perfume, and so much hair spray on her dyed jet black bouffant that it was stiffened to an unmovable mass. Gail had once seen Bethanne apply four coats of black mascara after painting on a thick stripe of black eyeliner. The rouge, heavy lipstick, and dark foundation on her light olive skin gave her face a look of being masked. Gail suspected Bethanne had difficulty with her own image, not wholly unattractive, and preferred to paint on a new one.

"Why do you want this vacation so bad?" Gail asked Sheila.

17

Sheila entwined her fingers and stared at her ringless left hand. "I'm going to be fifty years old next month. I've been teaching math for the last twenty-seven of those. I finally got up enough nerve to dump Lennie after thirty. I've never done anything exciting in my life. I want this vacation so bad I can taste it. And I want to share it with my dearest friends. And . . . ," her voice lowered, "being with a cowboy has always been my . . . fantasy."

"You . . . fantasize?" Prudie asked, surprise and curiosity genuine in her voice.

Sheila's neck showed a patchy flush. "Well, sure, don't you?" When Prudie jerked her head around and stared out the window, Sheila recanted a little. "I suppose that's bad of me, but . . ."

"No, it isn't," Gail said, "it helps to have a rich fantasy life. The best of fantasies live on library shelves, don't they, Prue?"

The librarian showed the most color in her face Gail had ever seen.

Catherine grinned sheepishly at her friends. "Well, I guess I can tell you I was always partial to playing cowboys and Indians with my brothers."

Gail leaned back in her chair. "Six weeks, huh?"

Seeing Sheila's face so earnest tugged at Gail a little. She'd been friends with Sheila for a good many years. They'd spent an evening together or a shopping day in the city once in awhile, that is, when Sheila's husband Leonard would allow her out of the house. Sheila was always bubbly, at least on the outside. But Gail suspected inside she was sad and unfulfilled.

Gail craved adventure and excitement, too, but at fifty-two, she was still doing the responsible things she'd been taught to do. She'd thought she'd have plenty of time to do what she wanted later, when she wasn't working. She'd *always* done that. Postpone things. She'd probably keep doing it until she retired. She hoped she was still as healthy then as she was now. Then what? What, even for this summer? The usual. Share her brother Dane's summer house at Cape Cod with his family. Gail loved her two nieces and her nephew, and they adored their unmarried aunt because she was never too busy for them, always willing to play a game or romp on the beach. Beautiful, fun . . . but definitely lacking any new adventure.

"Count me in," Gail said to Sheila, and surprised herself as much as she did the others at her quick answer.

Catherine's longish face dropped even longer. "Well . . . if Gail's going, I guess I'm going, too. Where do I sign?"

Sheila's face lit up and she looked as if she'd just come from a tryst with a great lover and had enjoyed every moment of it. "I'll take care of everything. You won't have to do a thing except pack your bags!"

"Great!" Gail laughed. "I've always hoped someone would hand me an all-expenses paid vacation."

"Pack . . . and pay," Sheila added quickly. "We leave July 20, and we'll be back in time for fall semester orientation week in September. Yee ha!"

That evening in her garden apartment, after listening to the messages on her answering machine including one from Chelsea Gotter's father which she decided to ignore, Gail sipped a glass of chardonnay and contemplated the approaching vacation. She'd made the decision to go pretty quickly. That wasn't her style. She usually took her time making decisions. Sometimes too much time. This was not the kind of vacation she would have opted for on her own. She was more the sand beach in Hawaii kind of vacationer, one who liked to read, shop, sample interesting food, maybe take in a cultural museum or art gallery. She definitely was not a month-on-a-bus-and-two-weeks-on-a-dude-ranch-during-the-hottest-days-of-summer kind of vacationer.

She wasn't looking for a man either, questing for one in every circumstance like so many of her friends. Not that she'd chosen to be without one, exactly. She'd lived with Hank Anderson for five years. He'd even asked her to marry him. She hadn't. She had, however, tried working with a dating service. Disastrous results. She shuddered now thinking of the seventeen responses she'd received. But she *had* chosen to be celibate after her relationship with Hank ended. It simply wasn't worth the risk of disease for one night of sex, no matter how great. Although . . . a night of great sex could be good . . .

While it didn't depress Gail that she was without a man right now, and though she liked her life for the most part, there was something missing. She knew that in her gut. Something . . . or someone, the sharing with someone special and close.

What was being in love anyway? Lust? Biological urges? Her mother had once told her love was a tickling sensation around the heart that couldn't be scratched. Maybe, in that simplified way, her mother had been right.

Bringing herself back to the impending adventure Sheila had promised, Gail thought about the clothes she should pack. She hated schlepping a lot of bags anywhere, so coordination was the key to getting everything in one. Travelling clothes should be light and comfortable, something that wouldn't wrinkle easily. Then there was this dude ranch fortnight to think about. She'd get her two pairs of Gloria Vanderbilt jeans from the dry cleaners. She'd bring that all important item, her great Donna Karan white shirt with French cuffs. That would be ideal. She had a nice pair of black leather western boots, and that was about as far as she would go as far as a costume of any kind went.

Organization was one of her strongest assets and, great list-maker that she was, Gail listed everything, deciding on black and white combinations of skirts, pants, and jackets, with teal accents like her scarf and silk tee shirt. That way she could mix and match. She'd need a facial and some new makeup from Georgette Klinger's salon, her hair trimmed and the color refreshed at Sassoon's, and her nails silk wrapped earlier than usually scheduled. And she could still get in a week at least at the summer house with her family.

The planning finished, Gail took a long bath enhanced with aromatherapy salts, then turned on the Jacuzzi jets and settled into a soaking massage. Relaxed, she popped a frozen health dinner into the microwave, a video into her VCR, and settled down. While the dishwasher was running with a load of three days worth of dishes, she figured some finances on her computer, then did two loads of laundry in her automatic washer and dryer, and made a few phone calls.

She enjoyed the creature comforts her career afforded, something her Depression-era family hadn't allowed themselves to do. She was glad she didn't feel guilty about spending money on herself. Her life was vastly different from theirs, no spouse, no children. But she wasn't complaining. She liked the ordered, neat, clean way of it.

It was comfortable. Predictable.

And fairly boring at times.

Maybe Sheila's idea of adventure was, after all, just what she needed. But on a bus?

". . . traverses gently rolling farmlands noted for poultry, dairy, wood, sugar beets, diversified feed and grain products," Helene Matthews, their American Adventure tour guide, was saying over a PA system when Gail came out of her doze.

"Where are we?" she asked Catherine who sat next to her in the rolling bus.

"We've just crossed the Big Sioux River into South Dakota. Listen."

". . . fertile, diversified farmland, from which corn, sorghum, and small grain are produced," Helene droned for at least the twentieth time.

"She said that about Central New York, Pennsylvania, Ohio, Indiana, Illinois, Wisconsin, and Minnesota," Gail said, rolling out the kink in her neck. "But the scenery has been wonderful."

"If you like cornfields and hog farms," Catherine said.

"The only adventure has been the wait in line

at the rest room when the driver wants to make time over the road," Prudie whispered, leaning over from the seat behind. "My kidneys can't take this constant traversing, and I think my bladder has a cramp in it. I'm on diuretics, you know."

"I hope Sheila's having a good time," Catherine said, and Gail knew she was sincere. Sheila hung on Helene's every word, now and then turning to watch her friends to see if they were as into it as she was.

"I hope so, too," Gail said. "She deserves to."

Gail had the feeling Sheila was trying to hide how disappointed she felt. She'd wanted everyone to have a good time, and so far it was pretty obvious most of them weren't. The tour had turned out to be less than adventurous, no matter what Helene had promised. The group consisted of six painfully shy men from an eastern based insurance company — the teen-aged girls at Riverview would have deemed them dorks — who kept to themselves. So much for fun with single men. The rest of the bus was filled with women who all seemed to be in one lovelorn stage or another. The high anticipation shared in the beginning had gradually spiraled down, and most of them had ridden along glumly watching bugs commit suicide on the bus's windshield.

Gail saw Sheila turn back to look at her now. "I've been getting some great photos," she said brightly, watching a small smile light her friend's face. "I feel I've missed a lot of wonderful country by flying everywhere up to now."

"At least flying made it less time between bathrooms. I can't believe I'm actually travelling on a *bus*," Prudie intoned before settling back in her seat.

Route 90 stretched across the vast expanse of western prairie, crossed the Missouri River, and headed toward the Black Hills which crossed dark and shadowy across the horizon, jagged like the back of a dragon. The divided highway looked to Gail like two strips of fat bacon sizzling in the heat on a cast iron griddle.

Gail chuckled to herself. The words to the old western song, "Don't Fence Me In" echoed through her head. While the states they'd crossed at first now seemed compressed to her, she'd begun to feel a sense of emerging expansiveness as the West spread wider before her. Days spent in the cramped bus might contradict that thought. And then there were the nights spent in some very much less than the promised luxurious accommodations. Faulty air conditioning, noisy patrons returning from some late night revelry, tepid water and low pressure from the showers, rattling exhaust fans that disturbed sleep, and the general feeling of discomfort and restlessness which ran through the group contributed to their overall cheerlessness.

Then there were the fat and cholesterol-heavy breakfasts accompanied by sugar and thin coffee served up at Aunt Mabel's Cock-a-Doodle-Doo Houses across the country. Vaguely Gail remembered reading somewhere that America's Adventure Tours owned an interest in the restaurant chain. She surmised that "rolling farmland" meant they traversed right onto the exit ramp to Aunt Mabel's.

Advertising on signs or tractor trailer boxes was everywhere now, breaking up the vast stretches of green and brown rangeland. The bus stopped at every one of Helene's points of interest beginning with a famous drug store the size of a city block in the town of Wall.

They stopped at Mount Rushmore and watched a film about Borglum, its sculptor; on to the evolving sculpture memorial to the warrior Crazy Horse; bought some Black Hills gold jewelry; strolled Deadwood and spent a little time in its recently built casinos and gambling houses; stopped at museums, recreated western towns, reptile gardens, and several sales outlets for fireworks.

Nursing a headache the thirteenth day into the trip, Gail leaned her head against the bus window and watched the rolling prairie pass. A thought that had been whispering in the back of her mind came forward, shouting loud and clear to her consciousness. *I wish I'd come West alone!*

She wished she'd had the courage before now to take a vacation on her own, to do some of the things she'd longed to do and never did. She wished she could linger in some of the places they'd touched on this trip, and skip over others. This stopping at national monuments or museums on schedule was beginning to drive her to distraction.

Maybe she was learning something about herself, Gail finally decided. Maybe doing this was a good thing, this being on a bus tour that hopped across America like a frantic frog. At least she knew what she didn't want. Maybe she'd gain new courage from this. Next time, maybe she'd have the guts to strike out on her own and pursue what interested her at the moment, any given moment. Maybe.

In the corner of Wyoming they drove through, Helene told them, without taking her eyes from her script, that they were "traversing rolling rangelands devoted to livestock, dotted with working oil wells and coal mines."

"Look at that!" Gail leaned forward, having forgotten her headache by losing herself in her thoughts. "The deer and the antelope really *do* play out here!" A trio of muledeer ran along a rangeland fence. On a craggy stone hillside three antelope doe scampered up a steep climb while their pronghorn buck peeked from behind a jagged pale rock formation. "Look at those! That buck is actually flirting with us!"

"Well, at least *something* is," Sheila said, straining to see the pronghorn.

"And the buffalo do roam, too!" Prudie exclaimed, pointing to a pair of buffalo cows lying on the ground shaking their massive shaggy heads to loosen flies. "They're probably mangy and infested with fleas and parasites. I'm glad I didn't eat any of that back in the Badlands." She gave an audible shiver.

"This country is so vast I feel like I'm on a bus ride to the twilight zone," Catherine said to Gail.

"And with Helene as a tour guide. I'm sure she will tell you the road to the twilight zone 'traverses gently rolling rangeland where invisible cattle . . .' "

Route 90 crossed into Montana. "We are now traversing rolling hills and rangelands," Helene announced, "a dominant portion of which lies in the Crow Indian Reservation. Oh, yes, and a little in the Northern Cheyenne Reservation. Cattle and other livestock are the mainstay of the region. Little Bighorn Battlefield National Monument, formerly known as the Custer Battlefield, is next on our agenda."

Montana rolled lazily ahead, around, and then behind them. Gail felt oddly that her senses were absorbing more and more as they went deeper into the country. Clumps of blue sage sprung up everywhere in dusty patches. Cottonwoods outlined streams, and cedars pointed dark against a big azure sky. Cattle of varying colors and breeds, whiteface, black Angus, rusty Herefords, and pale tan Charolaighs dotted the range.

Gail silently enjoyed the passing West outside her window. Like pages from a magazine the pictures flipped past her vision. Quarter horses with visible brands grazed beyond long fences. Now and then what looked like a driveway entrance appeared, a sign overhead naming the cattle company or family whose land they were crossing. Ranches nestled among cottonwoods in far off rolling terrain like little communities unto themselves. Everywhere windmills turned, churning up water to fill huge troughs for the roaming cattle. Gail felt oddly moved by the windmills, and took many photographs.

Somewhere along the way, their luxury bus had developed a glitch in the air conditioning system which turned it into a refrigeration system. The frigid air pouring into the coach now kept them all bundled in sweatshirts and turtlenecks, forced to keep windows open, allowing very dry air and dust to fly in. The women slathered their faces with moisturizing creams, and those who wore contact lenses were compelled to remove them as specks of dirt got under them and irritated their eyes. In high states of irritation, the men snapped at each other and glared at the women, and some of the women grew downright whiny. It was a miserable lot travelling across the country together.

"We'll be at the ranch in about one hour," Helene said loudly, as the bus turned off the main route onto a two-lane narrow road.

"I'm sure I'll be just another experiment in cryogenics by then," Bethanne announced, slipping the top of her turtleneck up over her bright red nose.

If nothing else, her quip brought a round of light laughter.

Just outside of the small rundown town of Lodgepole, the road wound in serpentine fashion. The bus slowed as it neared a dirt side road marked with a sign straddling it, *Kincaid's Triple or Nothing Ranch*. The driver turned the bus onto it, and over the next twelve-and-a-half miles of rutted unpaved road it bounced and lurched, pitching the passengers around like stiff beanbags.

Turkey vultures, buzzards to tenderfoot visitors, circled the sky searching for weak or dead wildlife.

"Oh, God," Prudie moaned. "I'm getting motion sick. I knew it, I just knew it. I'll be buzzard prey for certain. Of course, as cold as I am, I can only hope they break their beaks on my frozen body." She stood up and, hanging onto seat backs, meandered toward the rest room.

Gail pulled her jacket around her and nodded

off. The bus hit a rut and jounced her enough to knock her head against the window. She opened her eyes wide. A few hundred feet off on the horizon where the rangeland met the sky, she saw a horse and rider. At first she thought she was dreaming. The duo looked like something out of an old Western movie, and since she couldn't hear over the roar of the bus engine, she felt strangely as if she were watching a silent film.

She sat up straight never taking her eyes off the scene outside her window.

The horse was palomino, golden with pale cream mane and long sweeping tail blowing out in the wind. His strides were long and smooth. The rider was a bronze wild streak with a naked torso, soft fringed leggings and what looked like knee-high brown boots or laced moccasins. But it was his hair, long, black, flying out past his head that made him look free, a wild thing from a wild time. He was Indian. Native American. She didn't know which was politically correct, as the saying went, and at the moment it didn't matter. All Gail knew was that she couldn't take her eyes off him, couldn't speak for the spellbound awe in her mind, afraid to blink for fear he'd be gone in the split second it would take.

He was beautiful, thrilling to watch as he rode the palomino bareback, held the reins in his left hand, the other arm flung back straight from the shoulder. A chill ran over her own arms that had nothing to do with the temperature inside the bus. She saw the horse stretch then to a full-out gait, making clouds of dust from its pounding hooves, and soon the two disappeared over a rise leaving nothing but a trail of dust.

Gail kept watching as the bus dragged her gaze past the dissipating dust cloud. She felt strangely moved by the scene it seemed only she had witnessed. She looked at Catherine whose gaze was fixed on the windshield, and the others locked in their travelling misery. Somehow Gail didn't want to say anything to anyone, wanted to keep the scene and the memory to herself.

She leaned her head back against the window and rode in silence.

Chapter Two

"Here we are!" Helene announced. The bus door rattled open and a blast of searing hot air rushed inside.

"Here we are where?" Prudie asked, as she emerged from the rest room ashen-faced, a towel draped around her neck.

"If it's Tuesday it must be Yellowstone, according to my notes," Catherine said, yawning. "Or is it Yosemite? We saw Mount Rushmore, didn't we?"

"If we didn't," Gail said, shaking her thoughts and trying to inject a little humor into the moment, "then those hook-nosed guys were all part of a bad dream about the last four dates I had from that dating service!"

"All right fun devils and thrill seekers," Helene announced with uncustomary cheeriness in her voice, "all out now! This is your home away from home for the next two glorious weeks! Have a fabulous time, and don't forget," her voice dropped to an intimate hush, "I'm here for you whenever you need me, for any little problem you may have, day or night." Gail thought she made it sound as if she anticipated problems.

Sheila grinned and peered through the bus window, looking around at the adventure she'd organized for the Riverview School single faculty. Several good-looking men in western hats, boots, and jeans gathered around the bus.

Sheila winked at Gail. "I think we're gonna like it here, pardner!"

Gail was glad her friend's spirits had gone up a few notches, and in spite of her rapidly thawing cold and perspiring discomfort in the layers of clothing she wore, she gave Sheila a delighted smile. "To paraphrase a comment I believe you made before we left on this trip — yee ha!"

"We've landed!" Sheila said. "This is where the men are men and the women are thrilled!"

"And my butt is grateful," Bethanne said.

"And my bladder will be relieved," Prudie said. Suddenly she realized the pun she'd come out with, and an embarrassed smile spread over her lips.

Amid tired groans, America's Adventure Tour guests piled out of the bus and gathered behind Helene at the foot of a set of six wide stairs leading up to a long covered porch. A blast of arid Montana heat carried in on a gusting wind hit them all with almost knee-buckling results. Sweatshirts and sweaters were swept over heads at once as if choreographed by the tour guide.

Gail looked up and shaded her eyes. They were standing in front of a white painted ranch house that from the architecture and detail looked to be a century old or more. It was in such well-preserved state it appeared almost as perfect as those of wealthy ranchers in movies. The men in western dress who had caught Sheila's eye before she was even out of the bus, hurried to collect luggage from its gaping undercarriage, and carried them up through the oversized screen door.

"Welcome, welcome lovely ladies!" A medium-height man with a thick girth and shoulder-length faded yellow hair burst out onto the porch doffing a high-crowned white Stetson. "Well, now, we have a particularly lovely bevy of beauties this time, Helene," he gushed, giving her a bear hug she seemed to enjoy.

The women groused among themselves, self-consciously smoothing locks of flyaway hair, and blotting their temples with tissues. "Oops," the man said seeing the wilting male contingency stepping off the bus, "almost missed the few gentlemen mixed in with all this feminine pulchritude." Gail grimaced. She'd always hated that word. "Welcome to Kincaid's Triple or Nothing Ranch where we guarantee to triple your pleasure in everything we do!"

"Now there's an idea whose time has come! If you catch my drift," Sheila whispered to anyone who could hear.

"I'm Kenneth Kendrick Kincaid the Third, but my guests call me Trey. I'm your host," he boomed, "and the friendliest of the Kincaids, in any event. If you'll follow me, we'll soon have you settled comfortably. We have another tour group with us from Minnesota."

Trey Kincaid wore a light blue fitted western-cut sport coat with navy blue suede shoulder patches that strained over his ample middle. His dark blue trousers showed perfect knife-creases that flared slightly at the appropriate length to show off his pointed-toed boots that Gail noticed were of gray ostrich and looked brand new. He certainly dressed and acted the part of a wealthy cattle baron as portrayed in television shows. The other guests seemed taken by it, but Gail found his role-playing rather obnoxious.

Helene was the first of the group to follow Trey up the steps for official registration at the front desk. Gail stepped up behind her, tugging on the neck of her black silk turtleneck shirt. It clung to her, as did her cotton trousers, damp with perspiration. A wave of dizziness swept over her as she walked, and a headache gripped her. Must be the dry, hot air and the need for water, she thought.

"I leave you in good hands now, ladies and gentlemen. I'll meet y'all later. Welcoming cocktail reception begins at five thirty in the back parlor, bar-be-que supper at seven in the pavilion down by the swimming pool." He doffed the white Stetson again and gave an intimate wink at Helene, then headed into the house.

It felt good to Gail to step inside the lobby and get out of the blast of heat that was too sharp a contrast to the frigid air in the bus. The room was cool, and she decided it was not from air conditioning, but rather a natural cool from the wood structure and the stands of leafy cottonwoods that surrounded the house. The room smelled fresh with the outdoors, yet offered relief from the drying wind.

Registration began smoothly, owing to the efficient young woman behind the desk who'd clearly been through it many times. Gail stood back and surveyed the ranch house's lobby as the others took their turns. Irregularly hewn beams overhead with almost hieroglyphic carvings in them intrigued her. They looked to be real, not some interior decorator's concept of early western decoration.

One particularly interesting beam stretched across the width of the ceiling, through a door casing and into a room just off the lobby. Gail could see a partial wall of books visible just around the slightly open door. It must be a library or study. She hoped it was available to guests, for the idea of simply sinking down into a chair with a good book and some blessed peace and quiet tantalized her thoughts amidst the chatter and laughter at the registration area.

She edged away from the crowd and stepped into the study. It was even more blessedly cool than the lobby. The light was subdued with half drawn shades, and the room smelled of . . . incense, she guessed. She took in a deep breath. It was different, soothing, but something she couldn't identify. She uttered a sound of appreciation and wished she could strip off the constricting turtleneck and pants and allow the coolness to bathe her skin.

Gail let her gaze skim over the first wall of books, to an earth-colored woven wall hanging, to a round doeskin shield decorated with the silhouette of a buffalo and long hanging strands of combed white yarn and black-tipped eagle feathers. She let her fingers skim over the brown leather plump couch and chairs, and then walked to a window and shifted her gaze outside over the rolling rangeland beyond the house. A photo in a wooden frame sat on a low table in front of the window. She bent down for a closer look.

In an outdoor setting, an Indian woman and lanky boy with long wild hair stood next to an imposing white man and a smallish white boy with light hair. Intrigued, Gail picked up the frame and held it in the brighter light of the window so she could get a closer look. Her eyes shifted back and forth between the pairs, noting the space between the adults, and the plain wood house behind them. The photograph was interesting enough to have a story behind it. Gail wondered who the people were. She set down the photograph and moved on.

Between two windows on the far wall hung a large painting in a rustic, aged wood frame which drew Gail toward it. Colorful figures of Indians in flowing headdresses riding hard on pinto ponies and black horses, some carrying lances, some with bows and arrows, filled a kind of semi-circle in the top left third of the painting. In the lower right third a troop of white, blue-suited soldiers on brown horses, rifles drawn, charged toward the Indians. The distant landscape showed snow-capped mountains, a herd of buffalo with their heads raised

39

in alarm, and green rolling plains all around the figures. It was done in primitive style, but there was no mistaking the individual expressions in the faces of the Indians.

A noise out by the registration desk disturbed Gail's scrutiny, and she turned around.

Then she saw him, a tall, very dark man stood in the far corner at the end of a massive stone fireplace watching her. Startled, she jumped.

"Excuse me," she said, her voice a little shaky, "I didn't know anyone was here."

He said nothing. Almost rooted where she stood, Gail was held by his sharp black gaze and the sheer magnitude of his person. He stood well over six feet tall she guessed, but looked even taller in black leather boots, indigo jeans, and dark blue cotton shirt with cuffs neatly rolled, revealing dark brown forearms. Over the shirt was a black leather vest decorated with two silver conchas on the front from which long leather thongs hung to his waist. A silver buckle on a black leather belt was visible.

His head seemed massive, with chiseled facial features, black hair with silver threads running through that fell below his shoulders. But it was his piercing black-as-night eyes that rendered her motionless and somehow feeling guilty, as if she'd entered someone else's territory uninvited.

Without speaking, the man closed the book he held without so much as a whisper of the pages, then turned and left the room soundlessly.

Gail watched his imposing visage disappear. She frowned. For a moment the scene of the rider she'd seen earlier tearing along the horizon lit in her mind the way a photograph taken with flash might. Could it be?

"Gail! There you are!" Sheila called from the lobby. "We've been assigned to our rooms."

Gail turned and started out of the study, stopped at the door and took one look over her shoulder, then entered the lobby.

"You're with Catherine," Sheila continued, "I'm with Bethanne, and Prudie has the room next to us with a bath of her own. The four of us are sharing the bathroom just down the hall. Oh, we're on the second floor in the back. They tell me it's a wonderful view of the pasture. I mean, range. Great huh? Yippee aye oh kay yay!"

Gail didn't respond. Sheila nudged her.

"I'm sorry, did you say something?"

Sheila eyed Gail with amusement and took advantage of her friend's blatant distraction. "I said you and I are lodged in the bunk house with twelve love-starved buckaroos, and aren't we lucky?"

"Very," Gail said absently, following her luggage and Catherine's in the hands of a muscular young cowboy named John. He waited at the foot of the polished dark wood stairway to the second floor.

Sheila laughed. "This from the woman who has professed not to care if there's a man in her life or not. Should be an interesting couple of weeks!"

"What did you say?" Gail turned to look over her shoulder at Sheila.

"Are you suffering from heat stroke or something? You've been acting peculiar since we checked in."

Gail stared at Sheila for a moment, then brushed up the front of her hair with her fingers. "Just tired. Where's Catherine?"

"Right here." Catherine caught up with them looking almost as fresh as if she'd just stepped out of a shower.

"You are hateful, Catherine, do you know that?" Sheila pushed her damp hair up off her face. "Why aren't you dripping and sweating like the rest of us greenhorns?"

"Listen to Calamity Jane, would you?" Catherine laughed. "I don't sweat. Before you give me that business about always looking perfect, let me just say my mother always said that animals sweat, men perspire, and women effervesce. I love the heat, so I guess I'm effervescing!"

"God, that's disgusting!" Sheila said. "I'll meet you at the cocktail party after I've had a shower and a total makeover from my bus look." She climbed the stairs behind a cowboy named Marcus who was carrying her luggage.

Gail and Catherine followed John, their own cowboy. He stopped at a door at the end of a long hallway and set their bags down.

"Here you are," he took a white card from his breast pocket and read it, "Miss Bricker and Miss Collings." He unlocked the door and ushered them inside. "I think you'll be comfortable here. Any problems, give us a call. I'm sure I'll be seein' you on a trail ride or somethin'." He stepped into the hall to retrieve their bags.

Gail sniffed. There was that intriguing scent again. "What's that aroma?" she asked. "Is it incense of some kind?"

John sniffed. "Oh, that's blue sage," he replied, setting the luggage down on a long low dresser. "And cedar. I guess you easterners would call it incense. Mrs. Kincaid burns a little in pots now and then. It's special to her."

"Trey Kincaid's wife?"

"Nope. His stepmother. She's Cheyenne."

"Cheyenne," Gail said. "How interesting." She sniffed the air again and closed her eyes, making a memory of the scent.

"Yes, ma'am," John said, heading for the door. "Y'all have a great stay with us. I'll be seein' ya'."

Early the next morning, Gail left the noisy breakfast preparations in the dining room, a spacious area with French doors that opened onto a wide covered patio that could accommodate as many people as the main room. She requested a mug of black coffee, then headed toward the front of the house. Big gatherings were not something she enjoyed usually. She'd managed to get through the welcoming cocktail party and bar-be-que fairly well. She simply couldn't face another one this early in the morning.

She was surprised to realize how well she'd slept the night before. For the first time since she'd left home, she was able to open a window before retiring. The night air was surprisingly cold, and sinking down into the feather bed under thick quilts offered cocoonlike comfort. An impromptu symphony performed by crickets and owls had relaxed her as she read a couple of chapters of a novel she'd started on the bus. Upon awakening she was aware she'd had several dreams, but couldn't recall them in any detail, just a series of unrelated images.

Now she wandered through the lobby, knowing full well she meant to go back to the study where she'd seen the intriguing tall dark man the afternoon before. Even if he wasn't there, especially if he wasn't there, she hoped to sit down in one of those leather chairs and just relax in the quiet coolness.

Gail was feeling almost desperation to be alone to think. The trip thus far had afforded no moments for any real thinking, what with being stuffed together in that sardine can of a luxury bus, spending every meal and every tourist stop together, and then doubling or tripling in small motel rooms at night. She wasn't even sure what it was she wanted to think about, but something kept nagging at her to manifest itself, and she wanted to give it the chance.

The door to the study was closed, and Gail felt a twinge of disappointment. She started to knock, then held her knuckles poised when she heard voices behind it, a man's deep one, and then that of an older woman. She couldn't make out the words. Maybe it was because of the thickness of the door. She felt compelled to lean closer and try to discern what was being said. She could hear the two people more distinctly, only to discover they were speaking in a foreign language. She'd had exposure to several languages in school and while traveling abroad on occasion, but this seemed to have none of the basic derivatives found in many of the world's languages. And it sounded as if they were arguing. The voices rose and fell, yet there was an element of respect in each.

The voices came nearer, and Gail felt an anxious moment when she realized they might be coming out of the room. She headed toward the front door and stepped outside. The sun was starting a slow ascent in the eastern sky, sending gold and blue streaks across the porch. She stood sipping her coffee and scanned the porch up one end and down the other where it wrapped around one side of the house.

Paned windows in the lobby end were set off with black painted shutters and sills. Dark green wood tables and armchairs and rush-seated rockers were grouped along the porch's length. Swaying yellow blooms that resembled miniature sunflowers, and clumps of cedar and Montana blue sage softened the hard line of the wood railing and offered a fleeting pleasant aroma as breezes played through them. At the far end, two chestnut brown horses with black manes and switching tails were tied to a black iron hitching post fashioned by a chain of linked and welded horseshoes. Beyond the front of the house, across a horseshoe-shaped gravel drive and over a split rail fence, a dozen or more horses grazed on a shrub and wildflower studded green and rocky range.

Gail settled down in a high-backed rocker with arms. She wasn't certain if she viewed with a sense of disappointment or relief that whoever was in the study did not come out. She sat rigid in the chair for a few moments, then let out a breath of ensuing contentment. After a time, she breathed in the still warm air that carried the scent of hay and coffee and bacon and horseflesh. The hum of a bee in a stand of yellow and orange wildflowers at the base of the porch was pleasant accompaniment to the quiet. Beyond where the horses grazed, the rangeland sloped then rose to a rocky ridge so far away it appeared to Gail's vision to be lost in a haze of purple cloud.

So this was home on the range. Not bad. Fun at her brother's summer house on Cape Cod, and the smell of the ocean and fish were things she never failed to enjoy. But this country, this West was something new and very different from anything she'd experienced before. A woman could get lost here. Or found.

She heard a rustling sound, a whisper of something at the end of the porch that curved around the side of the house. She looked and waited for someone to appear. There were no footsteps. Nothing. Maybe it was just an errant breeze in the cedars, or the whispering of the cottonwoods as morning dawned bright and clear.

The rustling came again, louder, closer. Gail leaned forward in the rocker and strained to peer into the bushes. She caught a glimpse of something pale blue, like a piece of fabric. She lifted her body as soundlessly as possible out of the chair, then inched forward. The pale blue moved beyond a thick cedar, and a small dark head emerged and turned. Gail stopped, stunned by the enormous startled dark eyes of the child that stared up at her.

"Hello," she said quietly.

The child froze like a rabbit in a car's headlights.

"Hello," Gail said again, softly as before.

The child scampered from the bushes, clutching a rolled magazine. The magazine fell into the gravel drive. The child stopped and turned around, panic registering in the dark face, and desperation to retrieve the magazine. Gail came quickly down the stairs to help.

"Wait a minute. You dropped your magazine. I'll get it for you."

The child's face contorted in pain. Then he — or she, Gail couldn't tell by the ragged pale blue shirt and frayed short green cotton pants — ran away on swift bare feet.

"Wait!" she called, walking quickly in the direction of the retreating slight form. "I won't hurt you."

The child kept running and soon disappeared around a shed. Gail stopped. Well, that was curious, she thought. She looked down at her feet. The rolled magazine that had only moments before been clutched in a little fist lay with its pages lifting slightly by a breeze. She bent down and picked it up.

Most of the pages were missing, it was torn and dirty, and the cover and a few other pages were turned back. Gail looked at it.

"For heaven's sake. This is an antique!"

It was an issue of a no longer published movie star magazine from the late Fifties featuring the screen legend, Kim Novak. There she was in all her ethereal, mysterious blonde beauty. Only now she had a film of aged dirt all over her famous face and bared shoulders. Her crop of pale blonde hair had been outlined with a yellow crayon. But it was something else that stirred inside Gail. In black crayon letters crudely scrawled across Kim Novak's back was the word "Mother."

* * *

Just beyond the enormous swimming pool, the crowd of tourists was queuing up for supper under the bar-be-que pavilion. Gail found Catherine and slipped into the line with her. She'd brought the magazine to show her over supper.

"What'd you do today? You missed an . . . I guess I can say *interesting* time," Catherine said. "Helene herded us all into Billings. We ended up in this western clothing emporium. Several floors of jeans, and boots, and hats, and you name it. If it looks remotely western or is made of rattlesnake skin, they have it."

"Did you buy anything?"

"Check me out," Catherine said, spinning around. "You may have noticed, Wranglers are the jean of choice by the locals. I don't look too bad, I think."

"You look great. I didn't know Wranglers could fit that well." Gail meant that. Catherine's twenty-four hours in Montana seemed to agree with her. She looked more relaxed than she had since the beginning of the trip.

"So what did you do?"

"I just wanted to find a few hours by myself. I wouldn't want Sheila to know this, but for the last two weeks I've felt like I was on the bus from Hell."

"I know exactly what you mean. This isn't bad, though. In fact, it's wonderful. Our room is great, nothing like those roach motel accommodations. And supper certainly smells wonderful. If it's as good as it looks . . ."

Sheila, Bethanne, and Prudie called to them from a long red and white gingham covered table on the other side of the pavilion. They'd met a lively bunch from the Minnesota group and were already escalating into a rowdiness Gail had never seen among the three.

She and Catherine picked up white plastic plates and a bundle of flatware rolled in red and white checked paper napkins. Gail tried to find a convenient place to put the magazine, and ended up with it clutched under her arm.

"I think I'm overdressed," she whispered to Catherine. She'd thought a teal wide vee-necked tee shirt with shoulder pads, black linen shorts, and gold strappy sandals was a casual outfit for supper *al fresco*. But Catherine's outfit of dark blue Wrangler jeans, yellow linen camp shirt and slip-on black canvas shoes fit in with the rest of the guests in their pseudo-western costumes right down to bandanna neckerchiefs or bolo ties with turquoise-laden slides.

"You look fine," Catherine whispered back. "The dirty rolled magazine is just the right

51

touch. I'm jealous. Where did you ever find it?"

Gail laughed. "It found me, I guess."

Gail held the magazine close to her side with one arm, and tried juggling the plate laden with bar-be-qued chicken, salt potatoes, corn on the cob, and thickly sliced tomatoes, and balancing a can of cold Coors Light beer snatched from a huge barrel filled with ice by a young server. She reached the end of the food line and was searching for a table to set everything down on, when she saw him.

Outside the pavilion, leaning on a length of split rail fence, was the dark man she'd seen in the study. She stopped just as still as she had before, caught up in the fierceness of his dark gaze. His face was lost in the gathering shadows of night, and his head and length were chiseled in the grays and purples against the striated sky. There was a contained wildness about him.

He shifted away from the fence, appeared to send Gail, and Gail alone, a look she didn't understand. Then he walked away with long and smooth open strides. Gail's body quivered. The magazine fell to the ground.

Catherine hadn't noticed the man outside the pavilion. When she bent to pick up the magazine, another hand shot out and caught it first.

"Here you are," a dusky voice said. Gail snapped out of her thoughts, and she and Catherine both turned. Their eyes traveled up over high-heeled doe-colored boots, soft faded jeans, a blue chambray shirt, and a tanned hand holding the magazine, to the face of a tall wrangler.

"Thanks, Mister . . ." Catherine said.

"You're welcome, ma'am. Just call me Jerrie," the warm voice said. The other tanned hand decorated with an intricate silver and turquoise ring swept up and removed a black Stetson. A long mane of straight jet black hair fell out from under the hat, and a pair of eyes as blue as the Montana sky crinkled at the corners as the full mouth smiled showing small white teeth.

A woman!

Gail and Catherine stood there mesmerized. Jerrie was even taller than Gail, and she had a strong look about her, flawless skin the color of coffee with cream, and expressive hands as she brushed off her hat and swept her hair back off her shoulders.

"Uh," Catherine began, at a loss for words.

Gail set down the can of beer, stepped out of line, wiped her hand on a napkin, then held it out for a shake. "Thanks. I'm Gail Bricker and this is my usually articulate friend, Catherine Collings."

"Pleased to make your acquaintance, ma'am," Jerrie came back, grasping Gail's hand, "and ma'am." She released Gail's hand and held it out to Catherine.

Catherine, too, stepped out of the food line and struggled with her plate, utensils, a beer, and managed to stick her cold damp hand out. Jerrie trapped it in a strong grasp and held onto it an extended moment. Jerrie smiled. Gail noticed how Catherine nervously extracted her hand, and how she couldn't seem to take her eyes off the striking woman.

"I . . . I'm sorry. It's just that . . ." Catherine colored and searched for more words, but found none.

"You're surprised I'm female. I know. Happens all the time. If you want some fun, just watch the men's reactions! I love it!"

Catherine's eyes were fixed on Jerrie's face. She appeared totally captivated by her. "Are . . . are you a tourist . . . too?" she tried again.

This is curious, Gail thought. *Catherine is always in control, right now she's acting like an inexperienced teen-ager.*

"Worse than that," Jerrie said, laughing. "I own the place." Catherine colored again, and Jerrie continued. "I should say I own one third, with my brothers. I'm Jerrilyn Kincaid. Trey won't admit I'm his sister. His pride gets in the

54

way, not to mention his lily-white hands. Now mine, on the other hand," Jerrie held out the hand bearing the turquoise ring, "are earth brown and rough from work. I'm a horse wrangler, and that's just the way I like them."

Regaining control, Catherine hung her head in mock shame. "Oh God, I've just insulted our host by calling her a tourist."

"And your sentence will be another two weeks on the bus from hell!" Gail said mimicking a judge.

Catherine groaned.

"Thanks for catching it," Gail said to Jerrie, holding out her hand for the magazine. "I'm afraid I'm not used to playing a balancing act." *Nor having unsettling encounters with dark, mysterious men.*

"No problem." Jerrie took a real look at what she was holding. "I'm surprised you were able to get close enough to Willow to steal this from her."

"Steal it? I didn't . . . Willow? That child is a girl?" Gail was genuinely interested.

"Having a bit of trouble this evening with gender identification, aren't you?" Jerrie teased with good nature.

Gail gave her a tenuous smile. "Who is Willow? I found her hiding in the bushes this morning, and when I went to talk with her she

55

dropped this, and took off like I was some kind of monster."

"How to explain little Weeping Willow," Jerrie mused. "Grab that table over there," she said, pointing to a gingham covered picnic table at the end of the pavilion, "and sit down and eat your supper before it gets cold. I'll join you in a couple of shakes, if you don't mind, and tell you."

"That would be great," Gail said, "wouldn't it, Catherine?" She nudged her friend.

"Yes, of course," Catherine said at last.

"What is going on with you?" Gail said low, as they set the plates and things on the table and sat down on the benches.

Catherine shook her head and busied herself settling at the table. "I should ask the same of you. What turned you into a zombie at the end of the food line?"

Before Gail could even attempt an answer, Jerrie came to the table carrying a tray laden with a plate of bar-be-que, utensils, and three cans of ice cold beer. She sat down next to Catherine. "You forgot your drinks." She popped the cans and slid two of them to Gail and Catherine, then lifted hers and clinked against theirs. "Welcome to the Triple or Nothing. I hope it's an unforgettable vacation for y'all." She took a long slug while Gail and

Catherine sipped. "You take a good look at that magazine, Gail . . . is it?"

Gail nodded in response to her name. "No, I haven't really looked at it other than to notice it was pretty old and very dirty. And someone's been enhancing Kim Novak's looks."

"Yep. That's Willow. Notice anything else about Kim?" Jerrie picked up a bar-be-qued chicken breast in both hands and took a bite. She looked at Catherine. "You like mesquite? We get the chips specially for these bar-be-ques. Most people like the flavor."

"It is wonderful," Catherine answered quietly.

"Mm-hm," Gail answered, savoring the chicken herself, and studying the magazine. "The word 'Mother' is written across her back."

"Yep. But there's somethin' else now. I can see it. I'll bet you can, too, Catherine." Jerrie slid the magazine toward her.

Catherine brought the magazine close for a better look. She looked up at Gail then back at Kim Novak. *"Gail looks like her.* Is that what you think?"

"Whoa! *I* look like Kim Novak?" Gail coughed over an ear of steamed sweet corn. She grabbed Catherine's beer can away from her. "That's it for you. No more alcohol!"

Jerrie laughed. "Catherine's right. At least to Willow, you probably do. Your hair is the most noticeable thing, blonde, short and swept back like Kim's."

"But," Gail shook her head, trying to comprehend, "why would an old magazine with a movie star in it that a child that age wouldn't know a thing about be so important to her? How old is she, anyway?"

"Somewhere around twelve or thirteen, I think," Jerrie said.

"She's so little. She looks much younger than that."

"She doesn't eat much. Been on her own since she was a pup. She's half Cheyenne."

"Nobody takes care of her?" Catherine was now caught up in Willow's story.

"Nope. Nobody can get near her. She's wild, and I guess she wants it that way."

"What happened to her parents? And why is Kim Novak so important to her?" Gail pressed.

"The way I got it, somebody once told her that her mother was white with short yellow hair. Heard her father was a drunk and somebody killed him in a bar."

"How awful," Catherine said.

"The kid hung around a dump and some abandoned buildings down in Lodgepole for a while. It's my guess that's where she found that old magazine. Wouldn't part with it. Police picked her up off and on. A couple of teachers at the Medicine Wheel School took her in and tried hard to keep her and teach her, but she kept running away. We tried to keep her here on the ranch, but she won't live inside. So we let her be. It's the Cheyenne way, her own way."

"That's so sad," Gail said, setting her fork down.

"Are there a lot of Cheyenne Indians around here?" Catherine asked. "Or should I say Native Americans?"

"You're sittin' just outside the Northern Cheyenne reservation. And you can say either one. We go with the flow. It's not our argument over what's politically correct. We simply say The People."

Catherine leaned across the table and took a closer look at Jerrie. *"We?"*

"Yep. You're sittin' next to an Indian, or Native American, if you prefer. Does that make you want to hold onto your hair a little tighter?" She smiled.

"You're Cheyenne?" Gail asked.

"Half-blood. My mother's Cheyenne. My father was a white man. A rich white man. He died five years ago. Ask Trey about him. He's my half brother actually. My father lost his first wife."

"You're as much a story as Willow is," Catherine observed.

"I never thought so. Never wondered. That's the Cheyenne way, too." Jerrie cleaned up her plate, drained her beer can, then stood and picked up her hat. "Well, ladies, I must say my goodnights. My day starts mighty early."

"Thanks for telling us about Willow," Gail said. "Is there some way I can get this magazine back to her? If it's that important to her, I want her to be sure to have it."

"If you can catch her, ma'am," Jerrie said. "I have a feeling she'll come looking for you. Do you know about the Cheyenne and the morning star?"

Gail shook her head.

"You'll find out."

Gail looked up at her and blurted out what she'd been wondering about since she'd arrived. "I've seen a strange man around here, well, strange to me."

"You're gonna see a lot of that, I'm afraid!" Jerrie laughed.

"Maybe he's a guest. Or he works here. He's . . . Indian. Very tall." She gestured with her hands toward her shoulders. "Long straight black hair, a few strands of gray. I saw him earlier in the study, and then just a little while ago outside the pavilion. He didn't speak either time, but his eyes made me feel, I don't know, like an intruder, I guess, like he didn't want me here, although I don't know how that could be."

"Hawk." Jerrie said matter-of-factly, and fit her black Stetson over her fall of black hair. "Well, I'll be seeing you on the breakfast trail ride tomorrow."

"We haven't signed up for that yet," Catherine answered.

"It's not too late," Jerrie said, holding eye contact with Catherine. Then she turned to Gail. "By the way, I wouldn't wear those gold sandal things you've got on. No protection from rattlesnakes. G'night." She picked up her supper things, and strode off with a long-legged gait.

"Rattlesnakes!" Catherine called. "You've got rattlesnakes here?"

"Who's Hawk?" Gail called.

Jerrie just waved and kept walking. Then she stopped and turned around. "My brother!"

Catherine stared after her. "Fascinating . . . person," she said quietly.

"Yes, he is," Gail said, her voice underscoring the distraction she felt.

Catherine tilted her head toward Gail. "I meant Jerrie. I've never seen your mysterious man."

Gail felt the heat of embarrassment rise over her face. She fingered the pages of the magazine, then eyed Catherine whose eyes lingered in the direction Jerrie had gone. "Do you know her, or something?"

Catherine turned back. "Of course not. Where would I have ever met Jerrie Kincaid?"

"I don't know," Gail said thoughtfully, "but I had the feeling you knew her somehow."

Catherine rose and picked up her plate and utensils. "Never met her before." She picked up the beer can and drained it. "What do you think about signing up for the breakfast trail ride?"

Chapter Three

"I haven't been on the back of a horse since my uncle let me ride a pony at the State Fair," Gail said with a hint of nervousness. She grabbed the saddle horn with her left hand and the cantle with her right, then labored her left leg up to stick the toe of her boot into the stirrup.

"Just like ridin' a bike, ma'am," the wrangler drawled, giving her a careful boost with one hand on her waist and the other under the back of her thigh. "The seat's a little wider is all. This guy here is called Mojo."

"Hello, Mojo," Gail greeted the chestnut-brown quarter horse. She shimmied her buttocks, trying to find her most comfortable seat in the saddle, while the wrangler adjusted the stirrups to fit her feet comfortably. The morning was chilly, and she was glad she'd put on gloves and her short leather jacket.

The other brave souls who, with Gail, ventured out at six in the morning numbered four, all women, and all from the Riverview School. Sheila proclaimed them a hearty lot, and only once mentioned the fact that all the men on their tour bus were less social than she'd hoped. Maybe the Minnesota contingency was only a night-time sociable group.

They stood along a corral fence that was over six feet high watching the saddled horses being brought out by a young man in western clothes so crisp and sharp they could have been brand new. The horses stood obediently quiet, now and then breathing out through their noses. In the brisk early mountain morning, their double columns of exhaled breath shone like thick white straws with puffs of smoke at the ends. One by one each of the women was boosted into a saddle and given the name of her mount.

"All right, little gals, let's move 'em out!" the wrangler said. He secured his left foot in a stirrup then leaped into his saddle as if he were a feather on the wind, even though Gail guessed him to be somewhere near her age. "Name's Skeeter Davis, and I'll be your wrangler and guide this mornin'. There's a few rules to ridin' these here horses. First, you trust 'em to know what they're doin' cuz they done it a hunnert times. Second, don't trust 'em too much cuz they got other things on their minds."

Skeeter drew his soft gray speckled Appaloosa around, and pulled his battered high crowned tan hat down over his forehead. He was a lean and wiry man, and looked almost all legs in his worn leather narrow chaps with zippers hidden behind the fringe. Only his jeans fly and rear pockets were visible above the chaps. His tan canvas range jacket with brown corduroy collar and cuffs drifted loosely over a dark blue denim shirt. He sported a long and full sandy brown mustache.

"As I call out the name of your horse, which I hope you all remember, pull 'em up here in line." Skeeter motioned toward the corral gate. "We do that cuz they travel better that way."

He called out the list. First, Prudie. In her slim jeans she resembled the wishbone of a chicken perched atop a quarter horse named Cutter.

Next, Skeeter called Mojo. Gail pulled him into line, feeling pretty good about accomplishing the feat.

Sheila was called up then on a buckskin called Puddin' Head, followed by Bethanne on Vixen, a name she hoped had nothing to do with the horse's personality, and Catherine on

Gambler, the last two half quarter horse and half Percheron in varying shades of brown with dark manes and tails.

They'd all been instructed to dress in layers so they could adjust to the changing weather. The last three women proved they'd shopped together the day before, for they sported the requisite Wranglers, denim jackets with embroidery and fringe, flat crowned black hats with chin straps, and cotton ribbed turtlenecks in red, green, and yellow.

"Keep just the toes of your boots in the stirrup. If you get thrown, you could get caught by your feet if your whole foot is stuck in there. Hold your reins loose in one hand near the saddle horn. To go right, tip your hand to the right, go left, hand tipped to the left. Give 'em a little nudge with the heels of your boots and lift the reins to go forward. Pull back to stop and say 'whoa.' Don't pull the reins too tight, they don't like that bit cuttin' into their mouth and neither would you. Don't let 'em eat along the way. Keep your clothes on till we get to the breakfast place. The horses are curious and they'll wanna know what you're doin' behind their heads if you start tryin' to take off clothes. Any cameras here, if they got automatic rewind, don't use 'em. Horses think they're rattlers and they'll bolt and dump ya' or worse. Speakin' o' rattlers, if you see one, let me know. Horses get spooked by 'em. Any questions?"

"Rattlers?" Catherine asked tentatively from the end of the line.

"Okay then, let's move 'em out."

Skeeter motioned for Prudie to start down the trail while he waited to close the corral gate behind the line. She didn't have to say anything to Cutter because he started without any urging from her. She turned her head over her shoulder and stared at Skeeter, pure terror in her widened eyes. He waited for Catherine to get out of the corral, then pushed the gate shut, bent over his horse and latched it. Then he trotted up the line and took his place in front of Prudie.

The horses did indeed know what they were doing and where they were going it seemed. Through no direction by the inexperienced riders, they followed a narrow path behind Skeeter away from the corral and up an incline. Gail relaxed in the saddle once she found the place for her sit bones, and isolated her ribcage above her waist and hips as she'd been taught in yoga class. By some miracle, the bottom half of her body rocked gently with Mojo's gait, her upper half left to ride smoothly so she could simply enjoy the passing scenery and listen to the mutterings and grunts of the others.

Except for Catherine. When they rounded a horseshoe bend, Gail looked back and was struck by how content Catherine appeared, except for the shifting of her eyes around the low clumps of prickly pear cactus, yucca spikes, and blue sage. No doubt she was keeping an eye out for rattlers. Though what Catherine would do if she saw one, Gail couldn't guess. She couldn't guess what she herself would do, for that matter.

Dawn faded up like the lights in a theater, cool to hot, gray to bright, and spread a backdrop to the canyon in deep rose to pale blue with streaks of mauve. Somewhere around them coyotes howled and were answered in kind.

"Herd of mule deer up left," Skeeter announced.

As their band drew near, the gray-brown mule deer took varying stances of lookout, their means of escape clear. Gail counted nine, and watched their large, black-rimmed mule-like ears twitch with vigilant caution. She breathed in the experience as much as she did the crisp morning fragrant with sage.

A nonvisible coyote yip-howled in the distance followed by the childish high-pitched howls of her pups. Gail felt more and more . . . what? An *attachment,* she guessed, with the land, the sky, the air, the horses, and her women friends. She didn't want to say *communion* because that sounded somehow spiritual, and she didn't think she'd recognized a spiritual part of herself ever. Except for those friends, Riverview School and all its problems seemed a forever away.

In front of Gail, Prudie's horse broke wind. In the still crisp breeze the odor was carried up to waft over Gail's face and wash behind her. She groaned.

"Cutter, really, you should excuse yourself!"

Sheila coughed. "Hey Gail, you eat prunes this morning or what?"

Prudie twitched uncomfortably in her saddle. "Isn't it time to get down now?" she asked weakly.

"You have nothing to complain about," Gail called to her. "You're not at the business end of your own horse."

"You should talk," Sheila came back. "Your horse just let one I could hear over the coyotes!"

"Well, it's catching!" Bethanne said behind Sheila. "Yours actually lifted his tail so I could be sure to experience the full impact!"

"And all this before the first cup of morning

coffee," Sheila groaned.

Catherine laughed at the end of the line.

"What's the matter back there?" Gail called over her shoulder, laughing herself. When Catherine was laughing too hard to respond, she called again. "Looks like Catherine's the first casualty of the trip. She's been gassed!"

"Well, I don't think I can go another step," Prudie whined. "I should have had some orange juice before I left. I'm feeling a terrible sugar low."

Skeeter looked over his shoulder at her, but said nothing.

Magpies chattered past them in black and white swoops as the horses picked their way down narrow steep terrain. The clop of metal against stone as their feet hinged over rocks and roots, the squeak of leather saddles with the rhythm of their gait, and the blowing and shaking of their heads to rid their eyes of gathering flies were a collection of sounds that Gail selected individually and enjoyed moment to moment.

"Into the corral, ladies, and wait for me to help you dismount," Skeeter said as they drew along a fenced square in what looked like the middle of nowhere.

They dismounted in the succession in which they'd mounted, then stretched their legs, lifted their knees, and rubbed their butts as they eased on shaky limbs out of the corral. A few hundred feet away a fire was smoking, and Jerrie was wielding a blackened gallon size coffeepot while another wrangler was unloading crates from a battered brown pickup and setting them on wide flat rocks.

"Mornin' all!" Jerrie called, as the band trudged up the reddish rocky canyon slope toward her. "Great day for a ride! Everyone sleep all right last night?"

"Great!" Sheila said. "I never heard a thing from the moment my head hit the pillow until the alarm this morning. Amazing. I never sleep like that."

"Why is it so cool, almost cold, at night and so hot during the day?" Bethanne said, stripping off her jacket, and rolling down the top of her turtleneck.

"No humidity," Jerrie said, "and no trees to hold the warmth."

The women gathered around, marvelling in the feast that was being prepared for them. In one crate were blue and white speckled enamelware plates and mugs, and a plastic jug of forks and knives. In another was a jug of milk and a box of sugar packets. In a solid built square of rocks was a hot wood fire over which a heavy black iron grate was stretched.

A long black griddle was warming at one end, and the coffeepot occupied a corner. A big basket of raisin bran muffins sat on the ground next to the fire square.

Skeeter joined Jerrie and hefted the pot. "Pull up a rock, gals, and grab a mug." He opened the coffeepot and poured a cup of cold water inside.

"What does that do?" Gail asked.

"Settles the grounds besides takin' the edge off. Lost a lot of spoons 'fore I learned that. Turned 'em right into nubs."

"Same as it did Skeeter's brain," Jerrie said, winking.

Skeeter opened and peered into the coffeepot. "Done," he pronounced, replacing the top and picking up the pot by the handle with one hand, balancing it by the bottom with a towel in the other hand.

"How can you tell?" Sheila asked, brushing the dirt off a rock and groaning as she bent to sit.

"Wal, it's simple. You just drop a horse shoe in it. If the shoe falls to the bottom, coffee's too weak. If it floats, coffee's just right. If the whole horse floats it's too strong!"

The women laughed, sat down on varying heights of rocks, and gratefully held out their mugs.

"You gonna introduce me or what?" the other wrangler said to Skeeter, straightening up and rubbing the small of his back.

"I guess I got no choice now," Skeeter said, feigning distaste for the job. "This here's William Williams. One of our smart college kids says his name's redundant, whatever that means, so he's just called Wills."

Wills shifted his bottom lip left to right. "Now you be careful, Davis, or I'll tell 'em how you come to get your name."

"Not if you value livin', you won't," Skeeter warned, opening a package of steaks and slapping them on the grill in a line.

The women said their names and their good mornings to Wills, who stripped off his tan pointed crowned quarter horse hat with the curled brim and smoothed his damp brown hair. He was a slight wiry man probably somewhere in his forties, Gail guessed, with bowed thin legs in worn jeans. He politely repeated each name with a slight bow, but his bright small brown eyes lingered appreciatively on Sheila. Her cherublike round face broke into a brilliant smile.

"How d'ya like your steak and eggs?" Wills asked, looking at no one but Sheila.

Orders of rare, medium, scrambled, and sunnyside went around the group. All but Prudie responded. She fixed a haughty glare on Skeeter.

"I hate to mention this, Mr. Davis, but you failed to wash your hands before picking up those steaks."

"Sure I did. You just didn't see me. Did it 'fore we left this mornin'."

Prudie grimaced. "Is there a rest room someplace?"

Jerrie had swiftly cracked and snapped open with one hand a dozen and a half eggs as fast as if she were dealing cards. She looked up, a black spatula in her other hand. "Blue flowers over there," she used the spatula as a pointer to her left, "and pink flowers back there." She pointed beyond a stand of box elders.

Jerrie's rest room directions received a round of good-natured laughs from the women, except for Prudie who made it clear with facial expression that she found the entire exchange distasteful. She reached into her anorak for a tissue and used it to pick a muffin out of the basket.

Gail and Catherine watched Jerrie. There was not a wasted movement as she worked over the griddle full of eggs and the grill lined with rib steaks. Her long body was lean in her jeans and boots, and she wore a pale tan cotton shirt with pearl snaps and chest yoke corded in rich brown. A brown hand-tooled leather belt with a heavy sculpted silver buckle circled her trim waist. Her black hair was pulled back this morning, trailing down her back in one long braid.

"She's fascinating, isn't she?" Catherine said to Gail as they stood on the sidelines. "There's almost a cougarlike grace about her. She practically emits strength and agility."

"Mm-hm," Gail responded.

"Watch her hands." Jerrie's hands seemed to fascinate Catherine the most. She couldn't take her eyes off them. "They're so . . . expressive, I guess is the word."

"She's very strong," Gail added.

"But capable of great tenderness, I suspect." Catherine looked a bit unsettled at her own comment. She turned away quickly.

Jerrie flipped some eggs and moved some others on the griddle, and then motioned for them to come and get breakfast. With plates and mugs filled, one by one the group settled back in the warming air drinking coffee and exclaiming over the steak and eggs. Except for Prudie. Forks and knives clanked against metal plates, and the group fell silent, obviously appreciating the breakfast as if they'd never had one in their lives.

Gail moved away from the group, took off

her jacket and put it down on a rock, and then sat down. She sipped the strong coffee that had moved to floating-horse strength, rested her elbows on her knees, and let her eyes skim the edge of the canyon. High above the rock rim glinting with crystals in the sun, sat a rider atop a golden palomino. The horse's tail moved lightly in the sun, but the rider seemed motionless. Gail squinted.

She knew who it was.

His stature, his black hair moving imperceptibly in the stirring morning breeze under a black hat told her it was Hawk, the imposing man in the study, the neatly dressed man watching from a distance near the pavilion, and the wild-looking, half-naked man on the running horse the day she arrived at the ranch.

Catherine, a plate of food in one hand and a mug of coffee in the other, inched her way over the rocks and sat down next to Gail. She followed her friend's gaze to the canyon's rim.

"Your mystery man?"

Gail nodded.

"Like something out of an old novel."

Jerrie came over and squatted down near them, digging into a pile of scrambled eggs on her plate.

"Why doesn't he come down?" Gail asked her, her voice barely above a whisper as if, somehow, Hawk might hear.

"Hawk?" Jerrie said, not even looking up toward the canyon's rim. "He can't."

"Why not?" Gail held her gaze fixed on horse and rider.

Jerrie swallowed some coffee. "Well, don't misunderstand this, but Hawk doesn't want you here."

Gail dragged her eyes to Jerrie's face. "You don't mean me, personally?"

"Yes and no. He doesn't like the guest ranch part of things. Trey dreamed that up when money got tight. Hawk wants the ranch to be just that, a working ranch as it's always been. It's tough. He's struggled, fought tooth and nail to keep it going. But Trey enjoys living the easy life. The guest ranch is what helps keep the rest of the business going. Hawk resents all that."

"Then why does he come around the bar-beque pavilion, or do that?" Gail motioned with her head toward the canyon's rim. "Is he trying to scare us away?"

"I've never seen him follow the trail ride, so I don't know why he's up there now," Jerrie said, shaking her head. "He's never tried to scare the guests away. He has simply avoided being a part of anything when they're here. He's just . . . different."

"What about you? How do you feel about all this?" Catherine asked.

Jerrie stood up. "Me? Whatever works. I like both. I like the work, and I like the people who come as guests. I love this place, and I don't ever want to leave. So I guess I'm like both my brothers."

"Is it too personal to ask how the three of you became . . . ?" Gail began. She lifted her eyes back to the canyon's rim, but Hawk and his horse were gone.

". . . a family?" Jerrie finished. She laughed. "I guess we don't exactly look like identical triplets, do we? Let's see. My father lost his first wife, as I told you. He had Trey then. He met Ada Little Fox, my mother, when he was trying to buy land from the Cheyenne reservation. She was a widow with a young son, Lone Hawk. She was struggling. Her husband had been a Crow, and sometimes the Crows and Cheyennes still feel old hatreds, old rivalries. Hawk was always in fights in school with both the Crow kids and the Cheyenne kids. He didn't fit anywhere. Long story short, Trey's father and Hawk's mother got married. The boys hated each other right from the beginning. Mr. Kincaid had money, and he sent both of them away to school. And then there was me. I always called him Mr. Kincaid because that's what my mother called him."

"Do they still hate each other, Hawk and Trey, I mean?" Gail asked.

"Hawk hides it fairly well, if he does. Probably for our mother's sake. Both of them came back from school civilized, Trey more than Hawk. Hawk keeps to himself most of the time. He reads, listens to classical music. And he thinks. Too much, sometimes. I think he wishes he could live in the past, the time before the settlers and the railroad came."

"What do you feel about that?" Catherine probed.

"Me?" Jerrie laughed freely. "I'm a little of both, Cheyenne and white, so I live both."

"That must be difficult," Catherine said, watching Jerrie's eyes.

"Sometimes. There are worse things."

"How do Trey and Hawk feel about you?" Gail asked.

"I'm closer to Hawk than I am to Trey. But you know how it is with little sisters." She took their empty plates and headed back toward the others. Catherine and Gail followed.

"Tell us how you came to get the name Skeeter," Sheila was saying as they approached. They set their empty mugs in a crate for soiled dishes.

"Don't think so," Skeeter said, scraping the

79

leavings from the griddle into a plastic bag.

"Skeeter Davis is a famous name, you know," Catherine said.

"Yeah, I know," Skeeter muttered.

"There's another Skeeter Davis?" Bethanne stood up and stretched.

"Yes," Catherine answered, "she's a famous country singer."

"How do you know about her?" Jerrie sounded honestly curious, and sort of impressed.

"I grew up listening to country music. My mother wanted to be a country singer. She used to play records all day long. Patsy Cline, Kitty Wells, Wilma Lee and Stony Cooper, and later on, Skeeter Davis. I loved her voice." Catherine's gaze drifted into space remembering.

"Betcha she didn't get her name the way our good ole boy, here, did," Wills said, clamping a hand on Skeeter's shoulder.

"That's a fact!" Jerrie said, laughing.

"Well, how did you?" Prudie asked, finally getting caught up in the fun.

Skeeter started off for the corral where the horses waited. "When you're through havin' your fun, I'll be waitin' to head back." He stomped away.

"It seems," Wills said, taking on the demeanor and voice of a born storyteller, "that one day Homer Davis . . . he musta been about fourteen give or take . . . he was ridin' the fence line on his daddy's ranch with me when he had to, well, to go to the blue flowers, if you get my meanin'." He paused and let his gaze travel over the faces of his audience. When he was certain they had indeed got his meaning, he continued. "So off he goes into the woods, and the next thing I hear is him screechin' an hollerin' like a stuck pig. I says, 'what's the matter, Homer?' and he says 'goddam'—sorry ladies, I'm quotin' here—'goddam skeeter just bit me on the peter!' Well, I never laughed so hard in all my born days! His poor little thing just swelled all up . . . Oh, I am sorry for that one. Anyway, you can guess just how natural it was to call him Skeeter after that, and I guess it just stuck!" Wills laughed until tears formed in his eyes.

"Well, no wonder he's embarrassed," Prudie said. "Poor man ending up with a name like that. I'm sure he's been ridiculed all his life."

Jerrie chuckled as she cleaned up dishes and food from the breakfast. "That's kind of how Indians are named."

Both Gail and Catherine looked up from their cleaning chores and stared at her.

"Maybe not quite that blatant," Jerrie said

when she saw their faces. "The old way was, if something significant was seen soon after birth, like an animal or a bird, the baby received the name."

"Like Hawk?" Gail asked. "Did your mother see a bird when he was born?"

"As I understand it, she saw one lone hawk circling overhead a few days after his birth. She told me it was his eyes that made her choose the name, though. She said right from the beginning Hawk had searching eyes. He was always looking for something. She never knew what, and said only he knew in his heart what he searched for. Sometimes when I look at him I see the eyes of a hawk in his, sharp, seeing all. But in Hawk's case I don't agree with my mother. In my opinion, he doesn't know what he's searching for, and he doesn't know what he's seeing when he sees it."

Gail wasn't sure she understood what Jerrie meant by the last. She also didn't understand why she wondered so much about Hawk in the first place.

"What did your mother see when she named you?" Catherine asked, a grin on her face.

"A buxom registered nurse wearing a plastic name tag!"

"Named Jerrilyn of course," Catherine came back.

"No, but it was the first time my mother had ever been in a hospital. She was surrounded by white everywhere, walls and uniforms and people's faces. My father named me for his parents, Jerred and Carolyn. My mother didn't like it, so she gave me her name, Little Fox, and when I was old enough to know, she told me never to tell him. Secretly she always called me Fox, and still does."

"See?" Wills choked, still laughing over his own story about Skeeter. "Homer is a pretty bad name, come to think. Skeeter's much more fittin' when you consider the circumstances!"

"That's disgusting," Prudie snapped, and started off for the corral.

"Well, now, what do you make of that?" Wills doffed his hat and scratched his head with the same fingers.

"Unless I miss my guess, Prudie's having a biological attack brought on by the presence of a certain male of the species," Bethanne said knowingly.

"I'll bet it's the first time in almost fifty years!" Sheila came back.

"Don't be unkind," Catherine chastised her with good nature.

"Just being truthful," Sheila responded, bending her elbows and opening her palms toward the sky.

Smiling, Gail started for the corral. She marveled at the expansiveness developing in her thinking and feeling since she'd arrived in the West. And one good thing about this trip was the way her women friends were growing together, adding another dimension to their friendship. She liked that. Starting a half century didn't mean women's relationships with friends, or lovers if they had them, had to be stuck in a time warp.

Leaving several articles of clothing in Jerrie's pickup for her to bring back to the ranch house, the group joined Skeeter in the corral, mounted up and headed along a different route back to the ranch house. The sun was high in the clear blue sky, warm and shining bright on blue sagebrush, purple elephant head weed, and buckbrush that Skeeter called mountain mahogany. They meandered along a trail, and the flies seemed to grow more abundant and persistent. By the time they returned to the ranch corral, they were all ready for a shower and a rest.

Gail took her shower before Catherine, and when she came out of the bathroom she noticed her friend staring out of the window over the rangeland.

"This is some place, isn't it?" Gail said in more of a statement than a question. She went to the bureau for her brush and hair dryer. The brush wasn't where she thought she left it, and she started looking around the room for it.

Catherine waited a long time before she spoke. "Yes it is, but I'm ready to be home," she said quietly.

Gail was searching her cosmetics bag when Catherine spoke her surprising words. "You'll have a long wait. We're over two thousand miles from home." Not finding the brush in the bag, she opened one of the bureau drawers and started searching among her clothes. "Where did I put that brush? Have you seen it?"

Catherine didn't answer.

Gail stopped searching. "What's the matter, Cath? Aren't you having a good time here? Don't tell me you'd rather be on that Bus from Hell!" She went on her brush search again.

Catherine turned around then, a wistful look on her face. She focused Gail's questions away from herself. "I thought I saw your brush on the bureau before we left. Yes. You brushed your hair and dropped the brush on the bureau because we were late." Catherine stared at Gail.

"That's what I remember, too. It must have sprouted legs while we were gone and walked away." She lifted her eyes and caught Catherine's stare. "What are you looking at? I know my hair's a mess from the shower. That's why I want my brush, so I can dry it."

"You really do look like her right now," Catherine said, a strange tone of recognition in her voice.

"Look like who? Medusa?"

"Kim Novak. With your hair damp and pushed back like that, you do resemble her. Where's that magazine?"

"Over there." Gail turned to go to the night stand. All that was on it was a lamp and a clock. "Or at least it was." She looked around the floor and under the bed. "But it's not here now."

Catherine searched for a few moments, then stopped. "You know what I think? I think your mysterious child, what's her name? Willow? I think Willow got in here somehow and took back her magazine. And your brush."

Gail watched Catherine walking slowly around the room. "How could she get in here? The door was locked." She walked around the room slowly, too. "I can see why she'd want that magazine back. It seems so important to her. But, my brush? Why on earth would she want that?"

Catherine stopped. "Your hair. That's why.

Your hair. I know it sounds pretty wild, but I think Willow thinks she's found her mother. She has her magazine back, and she has your brush with strands of your hair in it. She thinks you're her mother!"

Gail's mouth dropped open, and she instantly closed it. Then, she thought a moment before speaking. "You're right. That is pretty wild. A child's mind would have to be pretty confused . . ."

"You heard what Jerrie said. The kid is on her own, alone most of the time. She's probably pretty unhealthy. And who knows how her mind works? Somebody told her her mother was white and had short yellow hair, remember?"

"I remember," Gail said, barely above a whisper.

"You found her spying on you from the bushes."

"I found her hiding, Cath. I don't know that she was *spying*. This is a ridiculous idea."

"I don't think so."

"If that's what happened, then I have to find that child. She must be terrified, confused, and hurt."

"Of course she is."

Gail sank down on her bed. "Remember the leather bag episode with Chelsea Gotter at the end of last semester?"

Catherine nodded.

"If what we're thinking about Willow is true, if we thought we hadn't helped Chelsea with her problems, how the hell are we going to help this little girl?" Gail ran her hand through her damp hair in frustration. "This is . . . I don't know what this is. If Willow did take back the magazine, and my brush, how am I going to know how to handle it?"

Chapter Four

By the end of the week, Gail had experienced enough concentrated staged Wild West experiences to last a lifetime. The campfires and cookouts and singalongs had been good times, the square dancing less of a good time owing to a couple of the male Minnesota contingency and their exuberant allemande lefts and do-si-does. One evening Prudie was certain her shoulder had been dislocated. If it hadn't been for Skeeter's expert examination, and his prescribed banana split at the ice cream social later that evening, she might never have believed it wasn't.

The ghost town tour was most interesting and thought-provoking to Gail, as well as to Sheila. Helene and Trey insisted that everyone don bits of costumes and play parts. Gail dressed as an early settler, and kept thinking about those people arriving there, hopeful about their future. And she thought about the Indians who wanted only to keep their land and way of life.

Sheila, on the other hand, fantasized about being a dance hall girl and having all the cow punchers lusting after her when they rode into town after a long, arduous trail drive. Gail noticed Wills was only too happy to play act the part of a lusty drover to Sheila's upstairs girl with a heart of gold. They both seemed quite adept at bringing realism to their parts.

A trail ride out to a cattle branding site had been fun for most of the group. Some turned their faces away as a red hot iron with the KKKO brand was firmly planted on living horse or cattle flesh. For Gail the actual branding was an experience in memory as well as newness. The smell of hot branding iron against hair and flesh sent up an odor rather like a combination of burning baling twine as she remembered smelling on a visit to a farm in Central New York, and fresh bar-be-qued beef steak over mesquite coals as they'd been smelling on the ranch all week.

Gail noticed some of the horses and cattle took the branding stoically, while others reacted like cats with their tails trapped in a screen door. When she'd asked Skeeter why they still branded the old fashioned way, he'd retorted, "You mean they got electric brandin' irons with twenty mile long extension cords now?"

Every day she saw Hawk, always from afar. She didn't want to think he singled her out for his unsettling scrutiny, but there were times when she was hard-pressed not to think so. He had a way of looking at the group as if they were a blight upon the land. And so many times she thought she could feel those eyes boring through her, no matter where she was, in or apart from the group.

Gail caught sight of Willow, on two mornings when she was alone on the porch or down at the corral by the horse barn. Both times the child was crouching in bushes or behind a shed, still clutching the rolled magazine. Gail tried calling to her once, but she scurried off like a frightened chipmunk. The second time the child appeared, Gail decided on another tack. She pretended she didn't see Willow at all, and the child stayed longer, just watching her. She tried to see if her hairbrush was visible in the little girl's hand or in a pocket, but she couldn't tell. The brush had never turned up in her room. No amount of searching was of help in finding Willow. The child simply found her. Gail marveled at her craftiness, at her secretiveness. And at her enormous eyes.

As the week drew to a close, Gail grew more and more restless. Her gaze would drift toward the snow-capped Big Horn Mountains in the far distance, and drew her mind along with it. And then she'd feel a kind of longing. It wasn't that she wished she was back in her own apartment. That wasn't it at all. But she was wishing for something. It wasn't to go back to work at Riverview, either. It was . . . hell, she didn't know what it was. But she couldn't sit still for long, and she definitely couldn't go on another trek with a busload of people.

Saturday evening, by the time the nighthawks were busy out hunting insects, and dusk had turned to evening, Gail ambled back to the ranch house from a long walk along a fence line. She'd been thinking, or rather letting her mind travel where it would on its own. Someone had told her once that up in the mountain's altitude dreams were more vivid, scarier, but more telling about one's real thoughts if one paid strict attention to the detail in them. She had an inkling every morning that she'd been dreaming important things, significant things, though she couldn't remember what the dreams had been about. So much for learning from her subconscious.

Her daydreams, or duskdreams however, were very confused, very convoluted. She'd been thinking about herself, her life in even greater breadth. Maybe it was from worry about things that were out of her control. That was frustrating. She was growing older, nothing could stop that. She had her work, and if she wasn't doing it, someone else would be in her position and doing the job probably quite easily, and most likely making more money. No one was indispensable, she knew that. The thought continued to nag her as she neared the porch. *Is this what I do until retirement doth part me from Riverview?*

She was set for life. She had a good job, no doubt about it. Good pay, wonderful benefits, and she had a very pleasant place to live, could afford a good vacation now and then, or a cruise. Gail had never thought of an America's Adventure Tour before, and up until this evening she'd figured she knew exactly why.

Now as she slowly climbed the steps toward the front door, she began thinking that, if nothing else, that blasted bus had brought her to a place where she could let her mind roam free. She had the strangest feeling that she was on the brink of something, a new thought, a new idea, a *eureka!* of sorts that would send her off on a new road to . . . what? Adventure? Satisfaction?

Inside the lobby, Gail started toward the stairway. She remembered then that she'd finished the novel she'd brought with her, as well as the magazines that had accumulated in her apartment over the last two months. She looked toward the study door and saw that it was slightly open. There was a light on in the room. Maybe she could just step in and, if anyone was there, she could ask to borrow a book. She had to admit, she hoped someone was there. Hawk. But anyway, if no one was there, maybe she'd get that chance after all to sink down in one of the leather chairs and read a book from one of the shelves.

She opened the door and looked in. Over by one end of the fireplace a woman was bent over a large open carton. Two long gray braids fell over the front of her shoulders. She was talking softly to herself. Gail waited a moment, started to leave, then decided to stay and see what might happen.

"Excuse me," she said quietly.

The woman straightened slowly, then turned around. Gail could see she was older, and Native American. Her deep tanned face was lined, showed years of worry, yet her dark eyes sparked with life. She wore deep blue cotton pants and a white loose shirt, and on her feet were beaded doeskin moccasins.

Gail took a chance. "Mrs. Kincaid?"

The woman smoothed her steel gray hair where it was parted in the middle. It curved loosely down over her ears and ended in the two long braids. She seemed to be reading Gail's face for a long moment.

"Yes," she said finally, her voice surprisingly strong for someone who looked to be in her seventies.

"I'm a guest here this week. My name is Gail Bricker."

"I know who you are," Mrs. Kincaid said. She looked as if she wanted to say more.

She waited and, when Mrs. Kincaid spoke no further words, Gail ventured into the center of the room. "May I come in for a few minutes?"

"If you want to," she said evenly.

She bent over a low table and picked up three books, then set them down in the carton. She straightened, then reached high on a shelf and picked up two more, heavier than the first, and started to lower them toward the carton, when one of them slipped out of her hand. Gail rushed over and picked it up.

"May I help you with those?" Gail pointed toward the books on the high shelf. Mrs. Kincaid nodded. "Are all of these on the shelf going into the carton?" Mrs. Kincaid nodded again. Gail reached for two more and pulled them down, turned them over and looked at the spines. "Rudyard Kipling. Shakespeare's plays. I remember when I first read these. Must have been in junior high school, I think. Seems like a hundred years ago."

She smiled at the older woman who took the books from her and set them down into the carton. Gail noticed that the skin on Mrs. Kincaid's hands was rough from work and she marveled at that, thinking how a grand house like this, a ranch of over seventy thousand acres, well, there must be money enough for servants, or at the very least a cleaning woman.

"This is a wonderful room," Gail went on, trying to make conversation. "I noticed it the first moment I arrived. It's so inviting, so comfortable. I hope you're not planning to remodel it." When Mrs. Kincaid was silent, only taking more books out of Gail's hands and giving her a questioning glance, Gail went on. "I don't mean to pry, but I just guessed you might be planning to paint since you're removing all of these books."

Mrs. Kincaid straightened the books inside the carton and then stood up. "No. Only some of them are going." Again her voice seemed even, yet carried a hint of a lilt Gail didn't recognize.

"Going? You don't mean you're discarding them?"

"They're going to the school," Mrs. Kincaid said in an articulate monotone.

"What school?" Gail grabbed two more

books from the shelf and lowered them to the older woman's hands.

"Medicine Wheel."

"Where is it? What kind of school?"

Mrs. Kincaid pointed to the shelf above and four books on the far end. Gail reached for them. "All years. It's a reservation school in Lodgepole."

"Really," Gail was genuinely interested. "Are they expanding their library?"

Mrs. Kincaid let a wry smile tip one corner of her mouth. "They've converted a corner of the cafeteria to start one."

Gail felt surprise. "Start one? Is it a new school?" That seemed like an illogical question when she remembered how the village of Lodgepole had looked sparsely populated and very poor.

"The building is over a hundred years old. It was a school a long time ago, until the priests started theirs. Now some people want a native school without outside religion."

"How many students are enrolled?"

"Depends what week it is." The answer surprised Gail, and she started to ask another question, but Mrs. Kincaid cut in. "They have a modular building now for the cafeteria, so the old one will be used for other things. One end is leaky and the plaster is falling, but the other end will have shelves for library books."

Gail was further surprised. Up to that moment, she'd seen this woman only from afar, and up until a moment ago Mrs. Kincaid had spoken to her only in clipped sentences. Now she seemed almost animated talking about the school and the library. And Gail had a clear picture in her mind of the reservation school, or at least its library. Poor, rundown, sadly lacking in so much.

"When I think," Gail mused aloud, as she picked up the last two books on the upper shelf, "of the number of books Riverview throws out in one year alone to make room for the updated and new ones . . . they could fill the entire cafeteria at the Lodgepole school."

Mrs. Kincaid's face took on an unreadable expression. "Riverview?" she asked quietly.

"Yes. It's a school in New York State. I work there."

"Do you teach?"

"I used to teach English. And I was advisor to the photography club. Or at least up until two years ago. I'm the guidance counsellor now. I try to help the students decide things like a course of study in college, and . . . ," *listen to them report things like stolen leather bags that cost more than a roomful of books for this school.* The thought hit Gail hard.

"Many of our children never make it through high school. They don't think a lot about college." Mrs. Kincaid gave her the benefit of her full gaze for the first time. Gail saw depths in the dark eyes she couldn't read.

"Why not?"

"They're too busy worrying about finding work so they can help feed their families," a gruff male voice came from behind.

Gail jumped visibly, and turned around, her heart pounding in her ears. Mrs. Kincaid went on working as if she hadn't been startled.

There he was. The man on the horse. The man in the study her first day there. The man at the rim of the canyon.

Hawk.

"You . . . you gave me a scare, Mister . . ." Gail waited for him to do the polite thing and respond with his name, introduce himself.

"I'll take care of this," he said again, not moving from his place just inside the door by the fireplace. His eyes were leveled on the carton of books.

Gail watched him warily. He did not make eye contact with her this time. She didn't know if she was grateful or not. The last time she'd seen him in this room, she felt his eyes bore through her, felt herself to be an intruder.

"I'm glad to help," she said at last.

"No need," he said.

"Really, I don't mind. I never could be on vacation for too long. I get bored if I'm not doing something."

He moved between her and his mother. He was taller than she originally thought. Maybe it was the fact that he was physically closer to her now than before. Or maybe it was because, except for his beaded soft brown deerskin moccasins, he was dressed all in black, black jeans and black shirt, and his black hair grazed his shoulders. Gail thought she saw a sneer around his lips, but upon looking more closely she thought she could be wrong, and she saw that his face offered no hint of what he might be thinking.

He touched his mother's shoulder and said something to her in a language Gail guessed to be Cheyenne. His voice held the fascinating lilt of his mother, and it was then she realized it had been the two of them she'd heard arguing behind the closed door of the study that first evening. Mrs. Kincaid raised from her work. She nodded a brief good night to Gail, and silently left the room.

Gail felt genuinely sorry to see her go. "I . . . I hope I didn't . . . make her feel uncomfortable. She didn't have to go."

"What do you want?" Hawk asked, picking

up the carton and setting it in a corner. There was not a friendly spark whatsoever in his words.

Gail swallowed, again feeling as if she'd intruded on someone's private territory. "I'm sorry if I've somehow offended you, or Mrs. Kincaid. I was just being friendly." She took a breath she hoped would relax the constriction she felt in her throat muscles. "We haven't formally met. I'm Gail Bricker." She held out her right hand. When he ignored it, she let it fall slowly to her side. She tried again with friendly conversation. "I hoped I might either borrow a book from your library, or with your permission sit in here and read one. It's such a comfortable room. Is it available to guests, or is it private?"

"Would it matter to you?"

Gail stepped back as if stung. "Of course it would. I wouldn't think of walking into someone's private room."

"Haven't you already done it?" He turned around and gave her the full force of his dark penetrating gaze. Sharp though it was, for a fleeting moment Gail thought she read something else. Pain, perhaps, or loneliness.

"I . . . I'm sorry, I wasn't certain if this was a private room or . . ."

"This is a private *home.*"

"I know that, but you do offer it as guest lodging. I'm here as a guest."

"Whose? Not mine."

"Well, Mr. Kincaid's I assume. Your . . . Trey Kincaid." When he let out a sharp small breath through his nose, Gail started to lose her apprehension.

"You're not welcome here," he said.

"Me, or all of these people?" She asked it, but still couldn't for her life figure out what he might have against her personally. They'd never laid eyes on each other before.

"Take it however you wish."

She took in a deep breath. "Well, I'm not taking it well at all . . . Mr. Kincaid. I've paid dearly for this vacation, this America's Adventure Tour, and the Triple or Nothing Ranch is part of the tour, part of the accommodations provided. None of us would be staying here if we hadn't been invited, if the house hadn't been opened to us. If you don't want us here, why do you make your ranch available to the public?" She suddenly felt as if she were in an argument with herself.

He turned and started to leave the room.

"Just a minute, Mr. Kincaid. You're being rude to me, and I don't think I deserve that treatment. I've tried to be polite, be friendly and helpful, ask permission to borrow a book, or ask about the use of this room. A simple response will do. Is this room, or is it not, available to guests?"

He stopped at the firm sound of her voice. "Unfortunately, it is. Take it over. That's what you do best."

"What does that mean?"

He left the room this time without pausing or looking over his shoulder.

Gail stood there bewildered. What had she done to provoke this man? Nothing that she could think of. Was he scrutinizing her in particular, singling her out with his intimidation?

Now she was being paranoid. She understood now what Jerrie had said at the breakfast trail ride. Hawk didn't want any "guests" on his ranch. People who poked, and pried, and prodded, and probably stole towels and whatever looked like it had been placed in a room for the express purpose of being taken.

She didn't want to think about a hundred and twenty year old offenses, but one fact remained. She didn't have to be an Indian to notice that all the guests who filled the ranch's rooms to capacity were white. Was Hawk condemning her today for yesterday's crimes?

On Sunday night Gail begged off of the hayride, even though Helene hinted that some of the Minnesota men would be going and one in particular had mentioned that he hoped "the engaging Miss Bricker would be going, too." Helene had latched onto Trey Kincaid in a familiar way, and Gail guessed it wasn't the first time they'd been on this hayride side by side on the same pile of hay.

Gail feigned a headache, and lingered on the pool patio until the wagon with the rowdy group perched atop hay bales had been hauled away by a pair of lofty draft horses.

"I see you got out of the hayride, too," Catherine said, ambling along the pool's edge.

"Yes," Gail said. "I have to give my mind and jaws a rest. Did everyone else go?"

"All but Prudie. Last time I saw her she was in search of yogurt, I think."

"Ah yes. I think I heard her muttering something about eating red meat at both ends of the day sending her cholesterol count soaring."

"Yeah." Catherine gave a small laugh. "You haven't found Willow yet, have you?"

Gail sighed and sat down along the edge of the pool. She took off her shoes and dropped her feet into the water. It was still warm from the sun. They didn't need a heater in it, or at least they never used one, she noticed. "No.

But she's found me. She won't let me near her. And, anyway, I don't know what I'll do if I do get near her."

"It bothers you, doesn't it?"

"Yes. I don't mind admitting that. God, Cath, this has been the strangest vacation."

"You're telling me."

Gail watched her friend strolling up and down the far side of the pool. "Everything okay with you? You seem bothered by something, too." She remembered a snippet of conversation from the night before. "Still feeling like you wish you were back home?"

Catherine kept walking. "I don't know. I'm out of sorts, or something." Her voice sounded hollow across the expanse of pool water.

"I know the feeling. Sometimes I feel out of sync, like the world's spinning as usual, but somehow I've lost my toehold and can't keep my equilibrium. Maybe you're just feeling out of your element. Sometimes it's hard to be away from familiar surroundings. It makes us feel insecure or something."

Catherine came around to Gail, sat down and put her feet in the water next to her. "You said it well, about the equilibrium thing, I mean."

The two swirled their feet in the water and didn't speak for several minutes.

"You ever been in love, I mean what you knew was really in love?" Catherine was first to break the silence.

Gail looked over at her, wondering what brought on this train of thought. Catherine was staring into the water, and Gail knew she was serious. As often as they'd spoken about love, or relationships, or the lack thereof for both, they'd ended up dissolved in laughter over the fictional liaisons they'd construct for each other. But, since they'd both turned fifty, they hadn't talked quite like they had before, at least not about love and relationships. It was as if they both felt real love would never happen to them now.

"I thought I was, off and on," Gail said at last. "Afterwards I'd always decide I wasn't. You?"

"Same thing, I guess. I don't know. How was it with Greg? I guess people thought you two were going to get married."

"I guess I thought we were, too, for awhile at least," Gail said.

When Greg Anderson asked her to marry him after five years together, Gail took three years to decide not to. He married someone else a month later.

"I'm glad for Greg," Gail said. "I don't believe I was ever truly in love with him. He found someone who was. You know, I heard the other day he has two children, young teenagers. I don't know if I could handle *that!*"

Catherine laughed lightly. "I couldn't. I like going home the end of the day and leaving all the little darlings back at school." She swirled her feet again. "Ever wish you got married? If not to Greg, then to someone else?"

"Not very often. Marriage is hard. I think you have to be completely in love with that person and he with you in order to survive marriage." Gail looked over at Catherine. "What about you? You were married once. Do you want to be again?"

Catherine lifted her head and sighed. "Funny, I never thought I wanted to be married, then or now."

"Why'd you do it, then?"

"Oh, you know. We were supposed to do that back then, get married, have kids. One thing we weren't supposed to be was promiscuous. Remember that word? Well, I was that, personified."

Gail searched her friend's face. "You?"

"Me. Surprised, aren't you? I fairly reek with decorum now, don't I? I was searching, I think."

"Did you think you found what you were looking for in . . . what was his name?"

"Mike. No, I know I didn't. But my parents did. And they wanted grandchildren, and when you're an only child there's a subtle—in my parents' case, not so subtle—pressure applied. I thought I might be good with children, but I wasn't sure I could be a mother. Maybe that's why I became a school teacher. I didn't think I could be a good wife, and I was right about that. None of it was Mike's fault. He was a good man."

"What about love?" Gail asked softly.

"Yeah, what about love?" Catherine came back with a wistful note in her voice. "I've always wanted to be in love. I've even tried to be with some people I thought would be right. No one ever was."

Gail looked directly at Catherine. "Are we too fussy?" She thought a long moment during her friend's silence. "Well, God, we *should* be selective, shouldn't we? It's easy to get married, and hell to get unmarried, right? And if people stay together, it must be worse hell if they don't love or care about each other. I'd rather be alone than go through what I know some women have been through."

"Amen. And no, I don't think we're too fussy. I think we . . . know ourselves well, I guess," Catherine answered.

"Sometimes I think people come together,

and stay together, out of pure dumb luck." Gail laughed lightly. "Maybe you and I have just been too smart for our own good."

Catherine nodded.

"What brought this on anyway?" Gail asked her.

"Oh, I don't know. Maybe it's Sheila and Bethanne both looking for male companionship. Even Prudie seems to be caught up in it. They all seem so desperate to me. Yet, in some ways I wish I could feel like they do. At least they're vigilant, and maybe love will come to them because they are. Me, on the other hand . . ." Her thought trailed away.

"You are a lot like me. We don't go looking. If love comes, fine. If it doesn't, well, maybe that's the way it's supposed to be for us."

"Maybe. But don't you wish sometimes . . ." Catherine's voice trailed off.

Gail lifted her legs and let the water drip off. It made little tinkling sounds in the pool. "Yeah, I wish sometimes . . ."

Monday morning, Gail brought her coffee out on the porch again. She felt weary. She hadn't slept very well, that was probably it. She kept seeing Hawk's accusing eyes when she closed her own, heard his disdainful voice echoing in her head. His specterlike presence disturbed her sleep, dominated her dreams, at least those she remembered this morning. She woke up feeling . . . guilty, she guessed. But she had no reason to feel guilty. It wasn't her fault what happened several lifetimes in the past. Nor, she added, was it his fault either.

She pushed her hair back along the sides of her head, but it didn't stay the way it used to. She probably needed it trimmed. This outdoor high altitude air seemed to stimulate its growth. Or maybe it was that cheap hairbrush she found in a discount store on one of their last outings. It wasn't one tenth the quality of brush her other one was. She was more than convinced in her mind that the child, Willow, had taken it when she retrieved her magazine.

Gail decided now that perhaps if she sat in the rocker as she had on that first morning, Willow would come again. This time, if she did, Gail meant to catch her, even if it meant scaring the girl. She needed to have a conversation with her.

Gail didn't see Willow, but she did see the wrangler Wills loading the back of an old dark green pickup truck with several cartons, a broom, a mop, and a crate of cleaning liquids and powders. Wills brought another crate with loaves of bread and wrapped food packages, and a long red cooler. A moment later she saw

Mrs. Kincaid come around from behind the house. Wills assisted her into the driver's side of the truck, closed the door, then conversed with her through the open window.

Gail watched, curious. Where was the elderly but tough Mrs. Kincaid off to with all that paraphernalia? Then it came to her. The school. Of course. She'd talked about it last night. She was going to the Medicine Wheel School in Lodgepole. Whatever took over Gail's mind and body at the moment was indefinable, but she rose quickly and ran down the steps two at a time.

"Mrs. Kincaid?" Breathless, she reached the truck. "May I go with you?"

"Mornin' ma'am. Miz Bricker, isn't it?" Wills tipped his battered hat. When Gail nodded, trying to catch her breath and calm her racing pulse, Wills spoke. "Mrs. Kincaid has business in town, ma'am. She goes alone."

"Thank you, Wills," Gail said, swallowing. "I appreciate that." She turned to Mrs. Kincaid. "Would it be all right if I went with you."

The older woman looked into Gail's eyes a long time. "I think it would be all right if you came."

Gail didn't need further invitation. She ran around the side of the truck, opened the door quickly, climbed in and slammed it securely.

With a snap she drew the seatbelt around her.

"I'm ready," she announced.

Wills looked into the truck past Mrs. Kincaid. "I rather doubt that, ma'am, I rather doubt that." He turned and walked away.

Mrs. Kincaid's movements might have been slow, but Gail noticed she drove the pickup as if she'd been in the driver's seat all her adult life. They drove over the gravel road to the main road, and turned east.

Beyond a barbed wire fence that ran along the side of the road, cattle grazed on either side. Mrs. Kincaid turned the truck onto a side road that seemed to run down the middle of the open rangeland. At the head of the turn was a metal grate stretched across the width of the road. The tires made a hollow whirring sound as they passed over it. When Gail asked what that was for, Mrs. Kincaid told her it was a cattle guard. She explained that roads like this ran over leased land and had to have gateless access from the main road. There had to be openings in the fence. Cattle would not step on the metal guard grates, and would stay contained within their range. A clever device, Gail thought, but one that worked because it capitalized on a basic fear in cattle, that of walking over open mesh constructions. It was the human mind that knew how to manipulate fear in other creatures.

Gail watched as they passed trailer houses sporadically situated among dirt and stones. No trees protected them from the relentless sun. Children played around them, some in ragged clothes and some dressed fairly well. There were usually at least two cars and a couple of dogs near each trailer. Sometimes adults were visible and sometimes not. Gail kept her camera inside the pickup. She didn't need to take a permanent photo to remember the picture of poverty and hopelessness she saw among the Northern Cheyenne.

Then they passed a magnificent stone church, a huge iron cross poised at the peak of the roof, surrounded by manicured lawns and tended gardens. Gail marveled at such a well-cared for place out in the middle of such desolate country. She saw a posted sign, "Mission of Salvation School" at the end of a paved sidewalk, and the name of the architect inscribed at the bottom. Compact modular houses with trees and flowers around them dotted the grounds. Gail noticed that Ada Little Fox Kincaid did not look at the mission school as she passed. She kept her eyes steadfastly on the road in front of her.

A turn down another road brought them into the village of Lodgepole from another direction than that which Gail had seen on their way in to the ranch. Several dogs came from seemingly out of nowhere to bark and chase the truck. Two Indian men lounging against the stone wall of a convenience store waved. Ada waved back. A woman in a dirty pink sweat suit carrying a black-haired baby walked along the edge of the road. She waved without looking as they passed. Gail saw several wooden beehives surrounded by a white picket fence that gave them the look of a small cemetery. Beyond that was a wooden sign stuck low to the ground, crudely painted with yellow letters, "Medicine Wheel School," and an arrow pointing up left.

They turned into a drive leading to a building that was wood at one end with white paint chipping off, and cinder block at the other, not painted at all. A row of small square windows lined it. Beyond that were two modular buildings, one marked with a sign designating it as an office. Ada pulled up to the one marked "cafeteria." Several cars were parked in a narrow lot behind it.

Gail looked at the school. This was a long way from Riverview's brick walls with lush ivy clinging to them, the perfectly shaped hedges that were trimmed once a week by two gardeners, and high windows that let in streams of bright sunlight and a view of the Hudson. And it was a long way from the mission school just down the road.

Ada got out of the truck and opened the tailgate. She grabbed a crate of food. Gail followed her and tried to pick up the cooler. It was too heavy, so she took one of the boxes of cleaning supplies.

"Ada! Good morning!" A thin woman, almost thinner than Prudie, with a bright smile and a blue headband in her straight brown hair pushed through the double doors and hurried down the walk. "How wonderful to see you again! Oh, I see you've brought a friend."

"Hi," Gail said. "I'm Gail Bricker. Just visiting."

"Come on in. I'm Carol Madison. I teach fifth grade here." She held the door. "Let me get the Two Bulls brothers to help with the heavy things."

Gail followed Carol and Mrs. Kincaid down a narrow hall and turned into a dark, dank-smelling room. "This is going to be the library. We'll start here," Mrs. Kincaid said.

Gail turned around and set the carton of food down on a wooden chair. "Start what?" The place was a closed-in cavern. Gail couldn't imagine doing much in here except perhaps mine coal.

"Cleaning."

115

"Cleaning?" Gail turned to look at her hostess.

"School starts next week here," Ada Kincaid told her. "They've only these few days to ready the school for the children. The library will be a wonderful surprise for them."

"They have to clean the place before they teach in it?" The surprise in Gail's voice was extremely evident.

Ada said nothing. She pulled out a mop pail and a plastic bottle of disinfectant cleaner. Gail peered into the gloom. *If this place is going to turn into a library in one week, the children aren't the only ones who'll be surprised.*

Carol returned, followed by two Indian men carrying the cooler and a carton with plastic drop cloths, paint brushes, roller pans, and turpentine. It was easy to see they were brothers, Gail thought. They were short, with large round faces and large round bellies that drooped over their belts. They both had thick black hair that fell just to their collars and showed slight waves in it. They looked to be somewhere in their forties. The only difference in their looks was that one had a big bulbous nose and the other had a big hooked nose.

"This is Vernon and Burt Two Bulls," Carol said. Vernon was the one with the hooked nose. "They help us out here once in awhile with the

116

heavy work. Vernon drives a van during the year and picks up the children, and Burt cooks the hot lunches when we can get the provisions. This is Gail Bricker. She's Mrs. Kincaid's guest."

"Tourist," Ada Kincaid corrected Carol.

Gail felt a prickle of disappointment. Aside from all the activity of the last few days on and off the ranch, she'd stopped feeling like a tourist. She'd been feeling like a . . . visiting friend.

Carol started spreading drop cloths over the floor. "It will be so good to see those old walls painted," she said. "I can't wait to see the shelves go up. This place will be so much brighter and cleaner."

"Let me help," Gail said, grabbing a dust mop and raising it to clean cobwebs from the room's corners and over the two windows, both on one side. "When will the other workmen be here to start repairing the walls and building the shelves?"

"There's only one," Carol said, dragging the carton with the paint equipment in it. "He worked all night preparing the walls, and now he's out mixing the paint."

"He sounds dedicated," Gail said, brushing under her nose as dust flew out of her mop.

"Devoted is more like it," Carol said.

The Two Bulls brothers went out and came

back in with ladders and paint rollers on long handles.

"I'm ready when you are!" a deep male voice called from a place beyond the room where they stood. It sounded friendly, enthusiastic.

Gail turned around and her jaw dropped. The majestic and impervious demeanor of the wild man on horseback, the inscrutable man outside the bar-be-que pavilion, and the man she'd seen twice in the study, had undergone a transformation in the twelve hours since she'd last seen him.

Hawk Kincaid strode into the room. He wore white painter's coveralls, a paper billed cap on his braided black hair, and bare feet. In one hand he held an open gallon can of white paint, and in the other a wide pale bristled brush. He looked *touchable* to Gail somehow, much more approachable than he had in, or out, of his regular day clothes.

On Hawk's face was a look of contentment. Gail marveled at the sight. But his expression was quickly replaced by shock the moment he saw her.

Chapter Five

Hawk didn't move. Gail knew he was wondering why she was there. She wondered if he'd be pleasant to her for the first time, or if he'd continue to show his distaste for tourists. Tension hung in the air between them.

"Hawk, I'd like you to meet . . . ," Carol began.

"We . . ." Hawk interrupted.

". . . haven't been formally introduced."

Gail cut him off, knowing he was about to say they'd already met. She'd been bothered by her accusation of his rudeness of the night before. He was, after all, one of their hosts. With other people all around them, this seemed like the right time to cut through some barriers. Impulsively she crossed toward him, her right hand outstretched.

"I'm Gail Bricker. It's a pleasure to meet you at last."

A heavy moment passed. Hawk set down his

paint can, took her hand for the briefest of seconds, and nodded. Gail believed it was a polite concession on his part, yet she felt a lingering current of warmth when he withdrew his hand. He turned and settled his paint equipment near the far wall.

"So what brings you out here?" Carol asked Gail, and busied herself preparing the area for painting.

"I'm on vacation," she answered.

"Oh," Carol said, nodding, and smoothing the drop cloths, "on one of those America's Adventure Tours."

"You guessed it."

"It wasn't hard. I just never would have expected one of you people to show up at Medicine Wheel School. This isn't usually on the itinerary."

"Actually, I'm a teacher, too," Gail said. "Your school interests me a great deal, and I wanted to take the opportunity to visit." She explained about Riverview, its students, and what her position was there. She thought she noticed Hawk listening, even though he appeared to be engrossed in the work at hand.

"Sounds very difficult," Carol said. "I don't think I could understand children like that enough to be a good teacher to them."

"It is difficult sometimes," Gail said, "but

120

you could manage, I'm certain. You must have your own set of difficulties with these children, too.

"That's for sure. Sometimes we don't know from day to day what we'll be facing." Carol turned toward Mrs. Kincaid. "Did I tell you Sandra won't be back this year? Her mother was taken very ill and needs constant care. Sandra's the only girl in the family, so she had to go back to Iowa to care for the family."

"I'm sorry for her," Mrs. Kincaid said with real sympathy. "Looks like you'll be doubling up again." Her last words sounded to Gail to be filled with even more sympathy.

"It's not like we haven't done it before," Carol sighed. "The worst is, Joe Bearpath won't be back either. He's gone home to his people in South Dakota."

Mrs. Kincaid shook her head. "You and the others won't be able to take care of all the children. They'll have to go to the other schools."

"We can't let that happen. They've got to come here. We're so close to getting some playground swings and the computer equipment we need. If the numbers don't stay up this year, we won't receive enough money. And we're so close." Carol's voice escalated slightly.

Gail thought Carol's voice sounded as if she

might be heading to the brink of despair. She listened closely, but wasn't certain she understood. "Do these children pay tuition to come to this school?"

Carol looked at her, not quite understanding Gail's question. "Oh no. We get funding from the federal government based on the number of children present during count week."

"You mean you don't have the same number of kids in school most of the time?"

"No, I'm sorry to say. If parents are upset with us for one reason or another, or they get some notion in their heads, they take the children out of here."

"And put them in other schools?"

"Sometimes. Sometimes they don't even see that they're in school. And then when we have to double up on classes, we can't always see to the needs of every student, and some of them just get lost in the shuffle. It's very discouraging." Carol's hands dropped limply to her sides. Suddenly she turned and quickly scanned the room. "Isn't it going to be great in here when we're finished?"

It was clear to Gail that Carol wanted to change the subject. But she pressed further anyway. "Can you get another teacher so quickly to take the place of the one who's going to South Dakota?"

122

Carol laughed lightly. "I'm afraid not. School starts next week here, much earlier than I imagine you do, and while I'm sure you haven't noticed," she said with a light joke in her voice, "this isn't exactly like working in a palace."

Gail was astounded at what she'd heard. "But, how will you manage? You can't work this way, never knowing from one moment to the next if you'll have money enough for your programs, or even students . . ."

"We have to manage. We can and do work this way. Everybody pitches in, even the superintendent and the principal at times."

Gail looked around the dismal room. The Two Bulls brothers had fastened extension poles to paint rollers and were painting the ceiling bright white. One was whistling as he swept the roller above his head. Hawk already had a quarter of one wall finished. He seemed to be painting with a vengeance, wielding his roller like a weapon. Carol turned on more lights and masked the windows.

"I think this is going to be a popular room when we're finished," she said, standing with her hands on her hips and surveying it from one end to the other. "Over there and there," she gestured to two walls at the far end of the room, "will be bookshelves. Of course, we won't be able to fill those shelves all at once, but we've got a good start. And at this end will be a kind of reading nook, I hope, a quiet activities corner, too. We need a lot, but we'll get at least some of it little by little. It will be wonderful, don't you think?"

Gail couldn't visualize Carol's dream room, no matter how hard she tried. Back at Riverview a building like this would have been demolished and a brand new one constructed in its place.

Ada Kincaid picked up a carton of food and headed out the rear door. Grateful not to have to answer Carol, Gail followed. She stopped near a classroom as Ada went out another rear door toward the cafeteria building. Gail looked into the classroom. Wooden chairs were set upside down on low round tables, and the carpet smelled damp and recently shampooed. A bulletin board on one side of the room was devoid of pictures, but dotted with silver thumb tacks. A name tag fashioned of red construction paper letters mounted on yellow poster paper said "Mr. Bearpath." She wondered what was going to happen in Mr. Bearpath's room now that he wouldn't be here.

She walked on, and in another classroom she saw a woman in denim shorts and a plaid shirt on her hands and knees using a sponge and pail of water to wash book shelves. She stood up and started on the heating units. She was heavyset, with strong arms.

"Hi," Gail said, stepping into the room.

The woman turned around quickly, and pushed an errant lock of dark hair out of her eyes. She had a pleasant round face, and expressive large brown eyes. "Hi. You lost?"

"I guess I am. I'm visiting the school with Mrs. Kincaid, and I guess I've been so busy looking around she got away from me."

"Ada's here!" The woman was genuinely excited to hear that. She dropped the dirty sponge in the pail.

"She went out to the cafeteria, I think."

"Well, I've got to see her. It's been awhile since she's been out here. She was sick all last spring." She grabbed a roll of paper towels, snapped one off, dried her hands, and introduced herself. "Name's Ang Carinci. I teach sixth grade."

Gail introduced herself in return and mentioned Riverview.

"Always wanted to work in one of those ritzy schools," Ang said, finishing wiping her hands on her ample buttocks. "They probably have janitors who do the cleaning. Or do they call them sanitary engineers there?"

Gail smiled. "Working in that ritzy school,

125

as you call it, has drawbacks, too."

"Like what? Thinking up ways to use up all the grants in aid they get? Or what you'll do on your next vacation? Or how you'll spend your big fat retirement bonus? I suppose it's a nasty job, but I'd be willing to sacrifice all this," Ang gestured toward the pail of dirty cleaning water, "and give it the old college try."

Gail stared at her, speechless at how uncannily close to the truth her words were.

Ang softened. "Hey, don't mind me. I took an overdose of bitter pills with my coffee this morning, and I'm having a bad reaction."

She tried to open a window. It wouldn't budge. She picked up a screwdriver and ran the edge along the sill under the window frame. She tried again. Stuck. Gail saw the frustration vibrating in Ang's muscles.

"Here, let me help. Maybe an extra body can make it work." Gail grabbed the screwdriver, ran the edge again along the sill, tipping it under the window frame.

A sick crackling sound came from the frame. Gail stopped and looked at Ang. They both laughed. Together they braced the heels of their palms on the upper edge of the window frame and lifted. It gave, and they slid the window up, letting in fresh dry air.

"You're right," Ang said, "an extra body can

make things work. Thanks, pard!" She stuck out her right hand.

Gail shook it. "You're welcome, pard! Anytime."

"I'll remember that this winter when I can't get the damned thing closed. I'll call you at River-whatever and you can phone in your help. Or, in your case, fax it!"

"Ooo, that stung," Gail said, wincing with good nature.

"It's those damned bitter pills again. Sorry. Did you say Ada went to the cafeteria?"

"I think so. Is that the building out back?"

"Was it marked Hyatt Regency West?"

"Uh . . ." Gail tilted her head and looked at Ang.

"That's the one. C'mon, I'll buy you a cup of coffee. That's double the wages I usually pay for window prying."

"I accept," Gail said, "even though that is, of course, only about one-tenth what I'm paid for calling a sanitary engineer to do the actual prying." She added that as a friendly joke, and Ang broke out in a grin that told her the joke had been accepted in the spirit in which it had been given.

Ada Kincaid stayed all day at the school. Gail noticed she sat down for a rest only once, and then for not more than fifteen minutes.

Ada kept coffee going, set out a lunch of bread, fruit, cheese, and cold chicken, and a big jug of lemonade.

Gail had remembered, fortunately, to bring her camera, and lest she look like an annoying tourist to them, asked permission to photograph school rooms, the cafeteria, and all of them at work. She promised to develop the pictures and give them to them as a pictorial memento of their work in progress.

Everyone worked, and worked hard, and Gail got caught up in it herself, doing the fine work that no one else wanted to do like painting around windows and panes. Her Gloria Vanderbilt jeans now were streaked with bright white and sun yellow, and her bare arms and black tee shirt were sprinkled with tiny white specks. She brushed a fly off her face once and was positive she'd managed to streak her chin with yellow. The fleeting thought jumped through her mind that she probably looked decorated with war paint. She didn't say it out loud. The Two Bulls brothers might take the joke well, but Hawk Kincaid would not. That she knew instinctively.

She and Hawk did not exchange words all day. If she was in the cafeteria, he was not. If she was on one side of the room working, he was on the other. Once she thought she felt his hard stare on her back, and when she turned around, she saw him turning as well, toward the wall he'd just finished.

She found herself stealing glances at him now and then. He looked so different in those coveralls and that paper paint cap, like a real person, down to earth, a breathing part of life rather than the almost unreal detached figure she'd imagined him to be.

By mid-afternoon, she'd leaned over near a window frame and got white paint in her hair, and backed up for a long shot with her camera into a wall and ended up with what she knew was a round yellow spot centered on her backside. She saw Hawk catch that encounter. She'd let out an expletive, and that turned him around. If he hadn't looked away so quickly, she might have confirmed that a smile had threatened to break out.

Gail then had an almost overwhelming urge to take his paint roller, start at his bare feet, and run it right up his coveralls over his face and stop at the top of his head. Now that was one bratty thought! Put a paint brush in her hand inside a school and she turned into a kid with a nasty streak!

By late afternoon, the group had tired visibly, and Gail along with them. She wasn't used to such strenuous manual labor. Wearily, they cleaned up their tools, folded drop cloths, washed paint brushes, and helped Ada gather up the food and tidy the cafeteria. They loaded her pickup with everything, except the paint things which went into the black pickup at the rear of the building which belonged to Hawk. Then they all flopped down on the grass and finished the last of the lemonade. Vernon and Ang smoked cigarettes and leaned against a tree.

"I'm wiped," Carol said.

"This grass needs cutting," Burt said dully

"It's August. It's supposed to be dead," Ang said, letting out a smoke cloud along with a sigh.

They were all quiet for several minutes. Ada sat cross-legged in the shade, and Gail wished she could sit like that. Her back wasn't very flexible, and her knees would have snapped for sure. Hawk came over. He'd removed the coveralls and put a pair of moccasins over his bare feet. His soft jeans outlined the power of his strong thighs and the leanness of his slim hips. He wore a cream cotton shirt open at the neck that was in sharp contrast against his bronze skin. He stood silent, thoughtful.

"The library is going to look great," Gail said, "if you don't mind the opinion of an outside observer. I never would have imagined such a transformation when I first walked through the door."

"There's a lot more to do," Carol said, rubbing the back of her neck. "If you haven't anything planned tomorrow and you feel like coming back, we can use another pair of hands. Right, Ada?"

Ada watched her son, his gaze fixed on something in the far distance. "Yes, that's right," she agreed, softly, "if you'd like to come."

Gail was pleased she'd been asked by Carol, and doubly pleased by Ada's support of the invitation. "I'd like that very much. Is there anything I can bring, anything in particular you'd like me to do?"

"Just your able body," Ang said, looking over at Gail through half-closed eyes, "and maybe some real work clothes."

Gail smiled and took the subliminal teasing to herself with good nature. "Whatever do you mean, Ang? This is what all the society ladies are wearing to their volunteer services these days."

"What do they do with their fingernails?" Ang came back, waving her own in the air.

Gail took a close look at hers now. The fuchsia polish was chipped and ragged, and her nails had seemed to suddenly get an uncustomary growth spurt. "I think they'd race with unchecked speed to have a new manicure. I, on the other hand, so to speak, shall plunge mine into paint thinner and take a file to them. Will that meet with your approval?"

"But of course!" Ang laughed. "For a society dame, you're probably okay. Of course, out here in Cheyenne country, we tend to reserve judgment with newcomers, especially easterners. That right, Hawk?"

Hawk turned and headed for his truck.

"See? He agrees with me," Ang said, not the least bit unnerved by Hawk's abrupt departure. "If you're coming in with Ada, we'll see you at daybreak."

The following daybreak Gail bounced along in the green pickup beside Ada, holding a cup of coffee as steady as she could. The others, all but Catherine, were on their way to a rodeo and flea market near Crow Agency. Catherine had been invited on a calf roundup with Jerrie, and she was as excited as a kid going to a circus.

Skeeter had rounded up a worn pair of jeans for Gail, and Wills had donated a shirt. She'd brought a pair of white lightweight sneakers and a pair of white cotton socks. She'd threaded a teal and black printed scarf through the belt loops on the jeans to hold them up, and pushed a black velvet headband up to keep her hair off her face. There hadn't been time for makeup, but she had made a point to remove all traces of fuchsia from her nails, and file them to a rounded short length.

At the school, Gail noticed that all the cars were there from the day before, including Hawk's black pickup.

She'd brought her camera again and found the group more eager than ever to mug for her lens, and point out areas for her to see. They also pointed out windows she could wash, curtains she could take down and put in the washing machine in the boiler room, and classroom shelves she could dust. Gail followed orders, mostly from Burt Two Bulls, and through it all enjoyed their interest, their banter, and their questions of how her own school operated. As the morning progressed toward noon, she felt an easy rapport with the group, as if she'd been working with them for years.

Hawk stayed in the library, and Gail didn't see him till lunch break. She helped Ada and Carol bring food out to the picnic table in a stand of cottonwoods behind the cafeteria, and the Two Bulls brothers were the first in line. Everyone fixed a sandwich and grabbed a cola or lemonade or iced tea and sat at the table or lounged on the ground next to the trees.

"Do any of you know a little girl named Willow, or I guess Weeping Willow is her full name?" Gail asked as they settled into lunch.

"Ah, Willow," Carol said. "Yes, indeed. My biggest, or at least one of my biggest challenges since I've been at Medicine Wheel."

"I think she's been a challenge to every teacher here," Ang put in. "She's probably even what drove Joe away!"

"That's not fair to say," Carol chided her, "but Willow is . . . well, difficult. How do you know her?"

"I don't," Gail said, "but I wish I could. She seems to have made a connection with me from a distance, and I don't know how to handle it."

"Connected with you how?" Carol leaned across the picnic table and looked at Gail with great interest.

"Well," Gail started, "I'm not even sure I should say 'connection.' I've caught her watching me from a safe hiding place in shrubs or around the ranch house a couple of times. Once I spoke to her, but she ran off. She dropped a magazine."

"Oh yes," Ang said nodding, "her precious magazine. I don't know what's holding that thing together. I'm surprised she let it slip from her hands for even a second."

"I could tell it pained her to drop it. And I think it pained her more that I picked it up. She ran like a scared rabbit."

"You picked it up?" Carol seemed genuinely surprised.

Gail turned toward her, and noticed Ada on the other side of the table intently watching her. "Yes, but only to return it to her. She wouldn't let me, and I couldn't find her after that."

"Don't worry, she'll find you," Ang said.

"She already did. She got into my room the morning we went on the breakfast trail ride . . . at least I think this is what happened . . . and she took back her magazine. Unless I've become forgetful in my advancing age and have started losing things, she also took my hairbrush."

"I saw the hairbrush," Ada said in her soft lilt. "I didn't know she took it from you."

"You saw it?"

Ada nodded toward her. "And she has the magazine back."

"Where does she go at night? Where does she live?"

"Wherever," Ada said.

"We've tried to keep her in school," Carol said. "She's intelligent, but I'm certain she has ADS, attention disorder syndrome. She shows

135

all the signs of it."

"Jerrie told me her mother was white and her father Cheyenne," Gail said.

"That's what we understand, too," Carol said. "They met in a bar someplace, and far as I can tell they lived in the bar until the mother disappeared and the father was killed. Willow was about four, I think. Got pushed around here and there, till she finally took off on her own. Every now and then some family takes her in, and she stays awhile, and they make her go to school. Eventually she just takes off."

"I wish I knew what to do. I'd like to help her if I can," Gail said. "Any ideas?"

"You won't be here long enough to be of real help," Ada said. "She doesn't want anyone to help. She's gone wild, like a neglected cat."

"But she's not hopeless. You're not saying that."

"No. It would take a lot of time, a lot of patience, a lot of repetitive work with her. That is, if you could catch her and hold her long enough to even begin." Ada's voice sounded sad. "She's not the only one."

"How do you teach these kids?" Gail was truly interested in what methods these teachers used. "I understand about lack of attention on the part of students."

"Not this way, you don't," Ang cut in. "Your kids have a whole other set of things that takes their attention away from school-work. They're bored, or they are rebelling against their parents, or they have too many material things to take their attention. These kids . . . it's just not in their mental power to concentrate for long. It has to do with the consumption of alcohol during their mother's pregnancy, and all that follows afterward, neglect, abuse, lack of direction and discipline . . ." she shook her head, and threw up her hands in futility.

"So what do you do? How do you get them to focus even some of the time?"

"Well, you have to do this one at a time," Carol told her. "Each one is different. You try to find something they're good at and focus on that long enough to get them involved. Of course, you repeat this and repeat this, because they forget what they've learned or part of it, and then you start all over again."

Gail looked at them in amazement. "How can a teacher possibly do that with the number of kids in a class that you have? Especially now that you're doubling up. That's impossible."

"Yeah, but we do it anyway," Ang said. "Who else is going to do it? We have to keep trying."

"What makes you keep trying?" Gail recalled the bitching and moaning, as Catherine called it, of the teachers at Riverview over what they deemed poor working conditions. Twelve students in a class, paid holidays off, long vacations, good pay and benefits, and still they wanted more. "Don't you get frustrated and want to just quit and run away?"

"Almost every day!" Ang replied.

"They're not all like that. Some of these kids are real smart and real interested. And then there are some days when you've had a breakthrough with a particularly tough kid, you go home and feel satisfied. That is on those rare nights when I, for one, don't go home and have a good cry." Carol cleaned up her lunch things and stood up. "One year, I didn't come back. I thought I was through, couldn't take it anymore. You get some real burnout here. But the following year I wanted more than ever to be back at Medicine Wheel. They need me here. I can't let these kids continue to live like weeds on a barren mesa. Somebody's got to be here for them, and for the families that do care."

"Back to work," Vernon Two Bulls announced. "You just can't get good help these days," he teased. "Let 'em have five minutes extra at lunch and they take a half hour jabbering."

Gail looked at her watch. "You're right," she said with surprise. "The time just flew by and I've barely touched my sandwich."

"Well, don't waste it," Burt Two Bulls told her, "but don't take all day nibbling either!"

"Yes, captain," Gail said, smiling.

She liked these people, all of them. Even Hawk. While he didn't contribute to the conversation, she noticed he listened closely, and his facial expressions told her how involved with it he was. He made eye contact with her on a couple of occasions. Once she thought she saw a hint of approval in his swift gaze.

On her way inside from the picnic area, Gail stepped again at the open door to the classroom vacated by Joe Bearpath. Cobwebs hung from the light fixtures, dust dimmed the windows inside and out, and the room smelled musty. She stepped into the room and scanned some of the books on a dusty bookshelf. English grammar, drama for junior high school, writing, poetry. She smiled. Some of this was very familiar to a former English teacher. When she'd first been a student teacher it was in a small school in Hamilton, New York, and she remembered the English teachers doing a little of everything, including directing plays. Joe Bearpath must have had his hands full here.

It hadn't been Joe's classroom she meant to go to when she returned to the school. She meant to go to the library, not only to photograph the progress of refurbishing, but also to see Hawk. She knew that now. For some reason it was important to her that she try to get him to talk to her. She had no difficulty conversing with his mother or with the Two Bulls brothers, and certainly not with Carol or Ang. In fact, they seemed to genuinely like her and enjoy her company.

So, what kept Lone Hawk Kincaid from being friendly, too?

Gail stopped into the library, and stopped sharply at the door. Hawk was up on a ladder at the far wall. He was painting, not with a roller this time, but with several brushes and a masonite palette smeared with bright paints. On the ladder's small platform was a small can of black paint and another can with varying thicknesses of pale tan brush handles sticking out of it. And on the wall was the beginning of a mural.

He was so engrossed in his work, he didn't notice she was there, or at least didn't acknowledge her presence. She wanted desperately to take a photograph of that first picture she saw when she stepped into the room. Should she do it and suffer the consequences of his possible anger from the moment he heard the shutter click? Or should she ask his permission to take his picture? If she asked his permission she'd lose the spontaneity of the moment of impact, of his unknowingly being observed.

She'd take the risk of his anger. Gail focused the camera lens, and pressed the button. Click. She lowered the camera as quickly as he turned around.

"What are you doing in here?" he asked, low and sharp.

Gail cleared her throat. "Just following orders. The others want photo-documentation of the work on the school right now." Her calm voice belied the quickening pace of her pulse and the little clutching in her stomach.

He turned back to his work and said nothing more. Gail moved into the room. It was a stark contrast to the room she'd stepped into the morning before. The white walls and ceiling reflected the sunlight streaming through clean, yellow-trimmed windows. On the ceiling over the area where the reading nook was to be set up, Hawk had painted a bright sun, pink-tinged clouds, and a flock of birds. A fanciful brown and tan tree trunk was painted into the corner, its leaves in varying shades of green spreading onto two walls. There was even a bird's nest painted into the top of it.

But it was the mural on the far wall Gail was fascinated by, the one he was working on right now. She walked closer. This work resembled the painting in the study back at the ranch house. Mountains loomed in the background, colorful Indians on horseback raced across the plain. She watched as he swiftly painted dark fanciful objects, and marveled as they magically emerged into buffalo. This was a Cheyenne buffalo hunting party. Fascinated, she watched him with minimal brush strokes add arrows in the backs of a couple of the buffalo.

She'd never seen an artist quite like this one at work. Hawk was spare in his approach, didn't waste a stroke, and the objects took shape as if they'd been born in his hands, waiting only to be freed on his choice of canvas.

Breathless, almost awed, Gail watched him. "I'd like to take a photograph of your work. That is, if you don't mind."

He didn't look down from his lofty position on the ladder. "The work isn't finished."

"I know. But, it's wonderful," that seemed like such a feeble word to describe what she was seeing in the mural, "and a photograph of it in progress will be important to . . ."

"Wait till I'm finished, please. Then you can

take the picture." Hawk's words sounded like a reluctant concession.

"Look at this!" Vernon stepped into the room, startling Gail. "We've made two tables out of it." He and Burt rolled a huge wooden wire cable spool to the door, then shimmied the round top of it and inched it into the room.

Gail grinned widely and took a photo. They'd taken the spool and cut it in half through the cylinder part, put four braces on each of the two cuts, painted them bright yellow enamel and set them up in the reading nook.

"That is fantastic!" Gail whooped. "What a great idea!"

"Thanks," Vernon said. "We've been working on these most of the summer. Took a while to get the spool out of the hands of the electric company, but we did it. Now all we need are some chairs. For now, they'll just have to stand or kneel around them."

Gail set down her camera and helped the brothers move the tables into the reading nook. She directed them to move them here, move them there, together, apart, until finally they seemed to look just right flanking Hawk's tree. Gail grabbed her camera again, and took another shot.

"These are terrific. You two are geniuses! What kids wouldn't think they'd entered a wonderland when they come in here?" Gail took a photo of the Two Bulls brothers admiring their own handiwork. "All you need now are some plants around the place to decorate it, and . . ."

"Plants?" Vernon said as if she'd said something vile, "I'm not going to be responsible for plants. I'm no gardener."

"Well, if I were here," Gail said, "I'd bring in the plants and I'd take care of them."

"If you were here, Missy, you wouldn't have time to take care of no plants," Burt told her. "You'd be too busy taking care of these kids and yourself. The plants would be dead inside of a week, if you didn't keel over first." He laughed lightly to let her know he didn't mean an insult.

"Oh yeah?" Gail challenged.

"Yeah," the brothers said in unison.

"You think I'm some soft greenhorn, or whatever these cowboys call us out here. Tenderfoot, that's it. Don't you? Admit it, you guys, you do, don't you?"

The Two Bulls brothers just grinned.

"Well, if I had the opportunity, I'd show you how wrong you are."

"And since you won't, then we know we're

144

right," Vernon teased. "No offense, ma'am, but this ain't no easy job. Even I couldn't do it, be a teacher."

Gail tilted her head in agreement. "I'll grant you that this ain't no easy job. But they seem to love it."

She stood in the center of the room thinking. She didn't want to admit it out loud, but to herself she did — she wasn't sure she would have the mettle it took to survive in this environment. Did that make her less of a good teacher, or less of a good counsellor? Suddenly she didn't know, couldn't appraise her own performance the way she had before, in her own element. Had she become too complacent at Riverview? Was that what her feelings of restlessness were all about?

"This is making you think, isn't it?"

"What?" Startled by his voice, Gail turned around and saw Hawk coming down off the ladder.

"Things aren't always what they seem," he said.

"What do you mean?"

"The kids seem like lost causes, but these teachers love their work with them. This room was a lost cause. Now it's a library." His voice was gentle, softer than she'd ever heard it.

Gail couldn't take her eyes off him as he

folded the ladder and set it against the far wall. He walked back toward her and stood a few feet away, facing her, looking at her long and hard.

"And you're not what you seem either." He lingered a moment, watching her face, then he walked past her and left the room.

Gail wondered if his words were meant to be a compliment, or an apology. But were they also a suggestion?

Chapter Six

"So now you know what a calf roundup is all about," Jerrie said to Catherine as they dismounted in the corral.

They'd returned after a long, often frustrating day of locating and bringing in the youngest of the young stock. Not knowing the exact number was frustrating to Catherine. How did they ever know when the last one was caught?

She had to admit, though, she'd had fun watching the antics of some of the young wranglers as they roped or tackled a calf, only to have it slither out of their hands like a greased pig and gambol away, tripping over its own knobby knees and wobbly legs.

"I'm weary to the bone, but I think half of it is from laughing so much." Catherine rubbed the back of her neck.

She watched Jerrie lift a coiled lariat from her saddle horn, and twist it into a figure eight with the metal honda rings in the middle, then loosen the cinches around the horse's belly.

"It is a little like watching a comic rodeo with that bunch!" Jerrie finished unsaddling her Arabian. She reached up and clamped both hands in the curves of each end of the saddle and lifted it off the animal's back. She carried it to a split rail fence along the barn and flipped it over so it straddled the top rail with the stirrups dangling.

Catherine continued to watch her. Everything Jerrie did fascinated her. Jerrie was strong, capable, knowledgeable, and seemed to use that knowledge effortlessly in her work. She was as good with a lariat today as any roper Catherine had ever seen in movies or television. Now she watched her heft the saddle like a sack of feathers and fling it over the fence. Just like a cowboy in an old western movie. She wished she could do that. But as her mother had often told her, wishing wouldn't make anything happen. *Doing* was what made things happen.

Catherine decided to *do*.

"I'd like to know how to do that, unsaddle a horse. Would you teach me?"

"Why, shore thing, tenderfoot," Jerrie drawled, purposely elongating the words.

"Start whenever you-all are good 'n ready."

Catherine thought Jerrie seemed pleased that she wanted to learn. Jerrie watched her work at the latigos and cinch rings, guiding Catherine's hands when it looked as if she was becoming all fingers and thumbs. When the cinches were open, Catherine smiled wildly, pleased with herself. Jerrie smiled back, proud of her student's first try. She grabbed her Arabian's bridle and started for the barn.

Catherine, feeling more physically capable than she ever had, reached up and grabbed both ends of the saddle as she'd seen Jerrie do, and yanked hard. The saddle slipped, the horse jumped and moved away, and Catherine fell flat on her back in the corral muck, the saddle landing on top of her. A column of air whooshed out of her.

Jerrie was back to her side in three strides. She hunkered down over her. "Are you hurt? God, what happened?" She picked up the saddle and moved it away from Catherine.

"I . . . don't think so," Catherine said. "I was pulling on the saddle one way and the horse went the other, and the next thing I knew I was down here!" Gingerly she tried to push herself out of the mud and manure, using her elbows.

149

Jerrie's face creased with concern. Then it smoothed, and she started to chuckle. Then the chuckle turned to a controlled laugh, and finally broke into a guffaw.

"Well, what . . . ," Catherine tried to sit up. Her boots kept slipping in the muck, and her jeans were soaking through. The futile act of attempting to stand, and the fact that Jerrie just stood there laughing, were frustrating her. ". . . is so blasted funny?"

Jerrie stood up, laughing so hard she could barely speak. "You . . . are!"

"What?! How can you say that? I've nearly been crushed by a saddle that weighs as much as a person, I'm lying in horseshit up to my rib cage, and you think I'm funny?"

Jerrie laughed uncontrollably. "Damned funny!"

Catherine struggled harder and seemed to go down farther, as if caught in quick sand. She pushed to one side with her elbows and heard a sickening sucking motion as one boot filled with the soupy corral fill.

"You have a sick sense of humor, Jerrilyn Kincaid!" she spluttered, then grimaced when she caught a taste of what had splashed up onto her face.

"Well, if you could . . . see yourself . . ." Jerrie laughed uproariously then, "you'd laugh, too! You're working so diligently with your elbows trying to push yourself up, your backside is hip deep in muck, you're covered with it the length of your body, your face is splattered, your hair's full of it, and you're . . . you're doing everything you can to keep your hands from touching it! You're the funniest sight I've ever seen!"

Catherine stopped struggling and looked down at her hands. Jerrie was right. She was a mess toe to head, but there she was, her hands elevated and absolutely spotless. She watched Jerrie, tears running down her face, so weak with laughter she hung like a rag doll on a peg.

Catherine started to laugh from somewhere down deep. "Well, I'm sure glad I was able to provide entertainment for you at the end of a long day!"

"You did that, that's for sure! Whoo!" Jerrie ran the back of her hands over her eyes.

"The least you can do is take one of these clean hands and help me up out of my predicament." Catherine raised one arm toward Jerrie.

Jerrie's laughter subsided. "Oh, all right. I suppose it wouldn't do to let a guest sink out of sight at the bottom of an old horse corral now would it?"

"Think what the *Michelin Guide* would do to you." Catherine lowered her arm. "They'd be brutal."

"Right. I hadn't thought of that. I don't think we're even listed in the *Michelin Guide*." Jerrie stepped one foot forward to brace herself, and put out a hand toward Catherine.

Catherine grabbed Jerrie's hand, but not before she grabbed two handsful of dirt and manure. She slapped one handful into Jerrie's and yanked hard. Taken by surprise, Jerrie lost her balance and fell into the dirt beside Catherine, who in a swift movement she didn't know she was capable of, painted Jerrie's face with streaks of dark brown. Then she pushed to get away. Jerrie caught her belt and pulled her back down, and the two lay side by side and hand in hand in the horse manure, dirt, and straw, laughing and coughing.

And then Jerrie wasn't laughing. She pushed herself up with a powerful pitch, and got to her feet. Almost in a heartbeat she was behind Catherine, placed strong arms under her shoulders and pushed her up.

Catherine watched as Jerrie stomped toward the barn, an angry set to her shoulders and gait. Catherine was confused. She'd thought it was all a joke. She hadn't meant anything by causing Jerrie to end up wallowing in the mire as she'd been doing. After all, Jerrie had found it enormously amusing. Couldn't she take it when the joke was on her? That notion confused Catherine all the more. She'd thought Jerrie was laid back, a woman who took things as they came, and stopped, dropped, and rolled away from the heat.

"I'm sorry, Jerrie," she called to the retreating back.

Jerrie kept walking. She slapped her horse on the rear to get it to move out of her way. "Better get in here so I can hose you off," she yelled angrily. "Can't go in the house in that state."

Catherine followed her. Without looking at her, Jerrie took a hose and sprayed Catherine's boots and pants, then up to her shirt. The water was cold, and in the waning afternoon light, it felt even colder on Catherine's skin as the air current picked up. She could only wait silently as Jerrie hosed herself off. Catherine noted she turned up the pressure on the nozzle, and fairly blasted the mess away from her own body.

"Jerrie," Catherine started.

Jerrie turned off the water and made a big production out of recoiling the hose, grabbing a broom, and sweeping out the end of the barn.

"We left a rope out by the fence. I'll get it," Catherine said, and slowly walked outside. She stopped near the split rail that was holding the saddles. She turned back a moment and looked at Jerrie who seemed to be loosening her belt and attempting to slide it out of the wet loops on her jeans.

"I'm really sorry if I made you angry," Catherine said. She hated this. What had happened? Why had Jerrie changed so quickly?

Jerrie looked frustrated trying to pull the damp leather through the even damper denim. Why she was doing such a thing, Catherine couldn't guess.

"I thought it was a joke on both of us, really," Catherine went on. "I was just trying to show you I was a good sport, and not a tenderfoot anymore." When Jerrie stayed silent, she turned and started to walk on.

"Don't move!" Jerrie commanded through clenched teeth, making her voice sound like a whispered growl.

Catherine stopped dead. Jerrie's tone and words startled her, then froze her mind. She heard the slap of leather against wet denim. And then something flew past her like a knife blade and connected not more than six inches from her boot. She let out a small scream and stepped back.

Jerrie ran to her, grabbed her arms, and dragged her into the barn. "You okay? You okay? He didn't get you, did he?" Her breathless voice sounded frantic.

Catherine's heart was pounding so loudly in her ears she hardly heard what Jerrie said. "What . . . what was that?"

"Stay here," Jerrie commanded, grabbed the lariat with a metal honda from a peg, and walked out toward the fence.

Catherine followed her. She saw Jerrie's arm go up with the lariat, and come down with a hard strike. She heard the honda connecting with something, emitting a dull thud. Catherine was almost to Jerrie's side when she stopped cold. At Jerrie's feet lay a snake, its body in a pile of loose loops like the lariat had been before Jerrie coiled it. Jerrie's belt was strung out beyond it.

"Oh, my God!" Catherine gasped.

"I . . . told you to stay put," Jerrie said, and her voice was hard. She pulled back the honda, loosened the rope to a small loop, and slipped it over the snake's head. Then she stepped on the snake's body and pulled on the loop hard. The snake's head snapped clean off.

"Oh my God!" Catherine shuddered. "That's a . . . a . . . you just . . ."

". . . beheaded a rattler," Jerrie finished for her. "Only way to take the bite out of them."

"A . . . a rattlesnake." Catherine's knees felt filled with water.

"Didn't you see it?" Jerrie asked, sharply.

"No! If I had, I would have jumped right out of my skin!"

"Well, that would have made two of you," Jerrie came back, her voice lighter. She started to laugh.

"This! This you think is funny now!" Catherine stepped back. "You . . . I . . . you seemed so mad at me for pulling you down in the muck." Her frustration mounted. "And now you can stand here laughing when . . . when I could have been bitten by that . . . that *thing?"*

"I told you not to move, didn't I? I gave you fair warning," Jerrie leaned down and shook the honda away from the snake's head.

Catherine uttered an audible shudder. "I thought you were just being nasty."

Jerrie picked up the snake's body and strung it out. She seemed to ignore Catherine's words. "Must be a good forty inches. Look at those rattles. Must be . . ." she coiled the snake around her arm and ticked

156

off the rattles, ". . . eight, nine, ten, eleven rattles. He's a good one. Beautiful, too. His skin's going to make somebody a fine belt." She turned and faced Catherine. "Shows you, doesn't it?"

"What?!" Catherine felt wound tighter than an eight day clock.

"What you see on the outside isn't always the way it is on the inside. Be careful what you grab for next time." Jerrie turned and walked back toward the barn.

Catherine shuddered again, from the cold as much as from fright at the sight of that headless rattler coiled around Jerrie's arm. Or was it from Jerrie's words? She wasn't certain what Jerrie had meant by them.

Suddenly she wanted to be as far away from that dark corral, and the lighted barn, as she could possibly get. Shivering, she turned and trudged toward the house.

"What happened to you?" Gail blanched when she met Catherine coming in the front door of the ranch house. She was just starting to drag her weary legs up the stairs to their room.

Catherine looked up and the frustration in her face melted at the sight of her friend, decorated in a fresh paint job of yellow and white. "What makes you think *you* can ask that question?"

Gail looked down. "Oh. I guess you're right." She leaned toward Catherine, and sniffed. Her nose wrinkled. "I think the fact that you smell ungodly, much worse than I do, gives me the right to ask that question."

"Let's get out of the most public place in this house, and I'll explain. Or at least try to. But I'm expecting the same from you."

"You'll hear it, I promise." Gail stepped up to the first stair. "If it takes all night, I'll try to explain."

"All night I got. I'm so tired, all I want is a shower and bed."

"Hey!" Bethanne came through the front door and let the screen door slam behind her. "You two better come to the dance tonight. Sheila's bothered. She says you two haven't been sociable since you got here."

Gail yawned. "I don't know," she said, "I'm pretty beat."

"Me, too," Catherine said.

"You, are more than beat," Bethanne said, sniffing near Catherine. "Where have you been, in a pig sty?"

Catherine pushed a lock of damp hair up off her forehead. "It looked like a horse corral, but what do I know? Things aren't always what they seem, or so I've been told lately," she snapped.

"What does that mean?" Bethanne put up her hands. "Never mind, please don't tell me. What do you two do all day long while the rest of us are out having a good time? Anyway, there's an ox roast first, though why they call it an ox is beyond me. Just like when it's called a steamship of beef. How can there be a steamship made of beef? It's just a big side of cow. Anyway, that's first, and the dance is in the long barn. They've got a live band and everything. What do you say?"

"I'll think about it," Gail said.

"We do have to eat, I guess," Catherine said, injecting a note of reality into the conversation for Bethanne's sake.

"Be there," Bethanne whispered, leaning close to them. "You've been missing some bits of drama among our group."

"Drama?" Catherine asked, a tentative note in her voice that Gail noticed.

"Yes. Prudie is smitten with Skeeter, I'm positive. Sheila had a crush on Trey, but Helene's already got him sewed up. But Wills, Wills has got it bad for Sheila! She doesn't even know it! It's hysterical! That long drink of water, as they say out here in the wild and

159

wooly west, and our little butterball of energy! Can you believe it?"

"Opposites attract, or so I've been told," Gail said, interested in Bethanne's story. "What about you? Are you withholding news of your own little drama?"

Bethanne colored. "Ha! What drama? I've stayed three steps ahead of the Minnesota Madman from the other group, and that's enough for me. How he has the nerve to chase after every woman on the Triple or Nothing is beyond me. Anyway, you know Helene. She's dying for Sheila and Prudie to tell all to her, and they won't give her the satisfaction. I think they're actually having a good time with this!"

"I just hope neither one of them gets hurt," Catherine said. "Vacation romances are what you make of them, a fling, or a heartbreaking experience. You have to be careful, or avoid them altogether."

Gail and Bethanne looked at Catherine a long moment. Finally Bethanne spoke in her scrutinizing manner. "Speaking from experience, my dear?"

Visibly coloring, Catherine started upstairs. "I'll see you at the, uh, ox roast, and I'll probably be at the dance. Maybe I can protect you from the Minnesota Madman."

"Me, too," Gail said. "Only you can have Mr. Minnesota." She followed Catherine up the stairs.

"Check your itinerary," Bethanne instructed, her voice following them up the stairs. "Tomorrow we go to a recreated Indian village to see how they used to live. There's a trading post there. Good place to buy souvenirs. And a big pow wow tomorrow night."

Gail grimaced. She wasn't sure she wanted to see that. Modern Indians playing the parts of their ancestors for the white tourists. Not after listening to everyone at the school talk about how they were living today.

"Somebody warned me about that trading post," Bethanne called to them. "You have to check things over carefully. Some of those authentic genuine Indian artifacts are made in Taiwan!"

"How was your day?" Catherine asked when they were inside their room with the door closed.

"Interesting, very interesting," Gail answered.

Her mind was distracted. Her last two days at the Medicine Wheel school had been filled with hard physical work, and an emotional labor she hadn't expected. Being around Hawk made her tense. The reason escaped

161

her why she felt like that when she was even in the same room with him. She was rational enough to know that another person couldn't make her feel a certain way if she didn't want to. Not that she wanted to feel tense in Hawk's presence. Something about him . . .

She went to the side of the bed. "How was yours?"

"Same." Catherine sounded distracted.

"Look at this!" Gail jumped up.

"What?"

"My hairbrush! It was sitting on the nightstand!"

"You're not going to say it was sitting there all along, are you? We're not that senile yet."

"No, of course not. Willow has returned it. I'm sure of it." Gail ran her fingers over the bristles. Her nails caught some strands of her own short blonde hair, and a few long black ones. She held them toward the light. "And she left a couple of subtle reminders."

Catherine came around the side of her bed and sat down so that she and Gail were almost knees to knees. Then she sprang up quickly, remembering the state of her clothing. She picked up the hair strands and ran two fingers down their length.

"I'd say that child was a lot smarter than anyone realizes."

162

"What do you mean by that?" Gail asked.

"She's saying a lot to you with this whole hair brush episode. She wants to get close to you but she's afraid."

"I see. I think. What do you think?"

"Well," Catherine went on, "it was your hair and Kim Novak's that drew her to you in the first place. Whether she honestly thinks a movie star is her mother, I couldn't say, but she is attaching herself to you as if you could be her. She brushed her own hair with your brush. See? There're some strands of blonde in here. She's mixing those parts of herself with you. And she's telling you how she feels by returning the brush."

"I don't know," Gail said distantly. "And maybe she just had an attack of conscience and returned to the scene of the crime to replace the stolen item."

Catherine laughed. "That's pretty wily. I'm not so sure a kid her age would think that way."

"You said she may be smarter than we think."

"Maybe."

"Maybe we're all smarter than we think," Gail said, rising and going to the chair by the back window. She gazed out over the barbe-que pavilion toward a far corral.

"What do you mean by that?"

"As soon as I know I'll tell you."

Catherine left for the bathroom to take a shower. When she came back to the room hand drying her hair, Gail was still at the window. This time she wasn't simply gazing out the window. She was focused intently on something.

"Ready to tell me what you're thinking about?" Catherine asked. "What's on your mind?"

Gail spun around. "Stools!"

"Stools?"

"Stools!" Gail stood up quickly.

"Stools." Catherine dropped down on her bed. "Reminds me of the afternoon I spent in the corral," she said to herself.

"It's brilliant!" Gail exclaimed. She spun around and clapped her hands.

"Care to elaborate on that?"

"Not right now, but give me a few days and I should be able to show you what I mean."

"We don't have a few days. We're getting back on our luxury motor coach and heading east day after tomorrow, remember?"

Gail sobered. "No, I didn't remember. What was I thinking?"

"That's what started this conversation in

the first place, and I still don't know what we're talking about, except for stools, and just because I know the subject doesn't mean I know anything else about it."

"What?"

Catherine stood up slowly and walked toward Gail. She placed the backs of her fingers on Gail's forehead. "Nope, no fever. Perhaps the altitude is affecting you. Good thing we're leaving." She went to the mirror over a chest of drawers and started combing through her damp hair. "Yes, it's a damn good thing we're leaving," she said softly.

"What'd you say?" Gail came over to her.

"I said it's a good thing we're leaving," Catherine said resolutely.

Gail didn't respond for a long moment as the two looked at each other in the mirror. "I guess so," Gail said finally, and the excitement had left her voice.

"I can't watch Sheila's skirt spin by here another moment," Gail said to Prudie. They'd stood by the rough-hewn bar in the long barn, sipping glasses of wine and watching several sets of square dancing. "All those whirling flowers are making me motion sick."

Gail hadn't expected an array of skirts and

dresses to be paraded out for the bar-be-que and dance in the barn. Casual seemed to be the dress code for the days they'd been spending on the Triple or Nothing Ranch. She'd put on a clean pair of black Gloria Vanderbilt jeans, her silk teal tee shirt, and the gold sandals. Maybe all this finery was a part of the age-old ritual of courting. Even the men were decked out like strutting peacocks.

The music changed to something torchy with a hint of twang, and the lights were turned to dim.

"Check out Trey and Helene one time," Prudie whispered. "They're packed so tight you couldn't fit a whisper between them."

Gail turned a curious glance on Prudie. "Who have you been hanging out with, girl? Got yourself a bit of a drawl and some colorful prose there."

Prudie colored. "You know how it is. When in Rome . . ."

"This is Montana," Gail reminded her.

". . . do as the Montanans do, then," Prudie came back. She leaned toward Gail as if to share a secret. "And that's just what I intend to do."

"Prudie Chase!" Gail stepped back, a hand over her heart. "What's gotten into you?"

"Nothing . . . yet!"

Skeeter sauntered over then. His hair was slicked down with something that made it stiff. Gail noticed his Wrangler jeans looked as stiff and new as Prudie's had the morning of the breakfast trail ride. He wore a red plaid shirt with mother-of-pearl snaps and embroidered yoke that looked starched to within an inch of its life.

"Would you do me the honor of dancin' with me, pretty lady?" Skeeter bowed slightly.

Prudie looked down over the skirt of her pale green cotton sundress. "I'd be delighted, kind sir," she whispered in a girlish voice.

Prudie seemed to turn into a shy young girl in a matter of seconds, discarding her fifty-year-old spinster librarian look as a snake sheds its skin.

Sheila was locked in Wills's arms as they two-stepped by Gail, she with both arms around his neck, he with both arms around her waist, his thumb locked in the center belt loop on her jeans. With her eyes closed, she looked as if she were in heaven. Gail smiled. Sheila had wanted adventure. Maybe she hadn't gotten it exactly, but it looked like she had found romance, if only for another day.

The Minnesota man had found Bethanne and seemed to be bending her ear about something. Bethanne looked longingly toward the dance floor, but Minnesota droned on. Probably something about mining or manufacturing, Gail surmised.

"Is this where the wallflowers are planted?" Catherine whispered from behind.

Gail turned and stifled a yawn. "I did my dancing duty to the extent I have the energy to do it. I managed to elude two guys from Minnesota. One of the guys from our group, I never did get his name, hit on me big time, as the girls say. He asked me if I'd ever 'done it' in a pumpkin patch. I guess he's a fruit salesman or something. Seems to have a passion for Halloween, I guess."

"You danced with him?" Catherine turned incredulous eyes on Gail.

"God, no."

"Who, then?"

"Wrangler John. Twice. I think he likes me," Gail said, winking at Catherine. "Cute, isn't he?"

"He's all of twenty-two. Isn't that carrying the younger man thing a bit too far?"

"I know. I sensed tragedy in both our lives, so I declined his third request." Gail threw her forearm over her eyes in feigned drama.

"He was crushed, of course, and went off to drown his sorrow in a mug of beer."

168

"No. He bought an orange pop and took the young receptionist out on the veranda. So much for the depression of unrequited love. I think the old days must have been better."

Catherine ordered a glass of wine and watched the dancers. "I feel like a voyeur, now that I know all of the little secrets among the group from Prudie."

"I like to think of it as merely observing another part of life. It should make me a better photographer . . . or something," Gail said.

"You certainly are waxing poetic tonight. I don't think I understand. But then, my brain was subjected to something earlier that I can't determine, and all powers of reasoning and understanding seem to have departed. Not a good thing for a supposedly intelligent teacher, is it?"

"Ah yes, you never did explain how you happened to return to the house so foul-smelling and filthy. Care to elaborate now?"

"Bedtime story," Catherine said. "I'm still trying to figure out for myself what happened."

"What happened? I mean, what did you do today?"

"Well, I went on the calf roundup with Jerrie, as you know and . . ."

"Speak of the subject, and she appears," Gail said, her eyes fixed on the far side of the room.

"Where?" Catherine's voice took on a hushed quality that made Gail's head turn toward her.

She turned back. "Over by the far door."

Catherine strained through the dim light and crowd of dancers. "Where? I don't see her?"

"See the peach colored dress on the tanned woman with the long black hair?"

"Yes."

"That's Jerrie."

Catherine stared. "No-o-o."

"Yes-s-s."

"She's . . . beautiful," Catherine breathed.

Gail nodded. "A knockout. And every man in the place has just noticed her."

Gail and Catherine watched as several of the couples slowed or faltered in their dancing. Some of the men came almost to a stop, while the women stared first at Jerrie and glared second at their partners.

"Which one do you think she'll dance with?" Gail asked.

"I wouldn't want to bet on that one," Catherine replied.

Gail looked at her friend. "What's the matter? Did you and Jerrie have a disagreement today?"

"I wouldn't know," Catherine snapped, never taking her eyes off Jerrie.

"Well, what are you so mad about?".

"You wouldn't think a woman who looked like that could have been out wallowing in horseshit and snapping the heads off rattlesnakes, now would you?" Catherine sputtered.

"What is up with you, Cath?"

"Well, would you?"

Gail studied Catherine in her above-the-knee pale yellow linen chemise. Her hair was blown off her face, and showed off a few freckles and a healthy glow.

"As a matter of fact, I would," Gail mused, "except for the rattlesnake head snapping part. You look pretty great yourself, for someone who I'm certain was doing that very same thing this afternoon. Wallowing, I mean." She put her hand on Catherine's arm, and ventured a question. "I'm beginning to figure out that you might have been wallowing together. Were you?"

While Gail scrutinized her friend, Catherine held her gaze pinned on Jerrie. Then Catherine's face changed.

"Well, who would have bet on *that?*"

"What?"

"Look." Catherine's eyes never wavered.

Gail followed her gaze. Her surprise was even greater than Catherine's. Jerrie was now floating across the dance floor in the arms of Hawk. Gone were the paint specks and splattered coveralls. He was back in indigo jeans and dark ruby cotton shirt, open at the neck and with the sleeves rolled under to the forearms. She'd never known anyone who rolled his sleeves that way.

"He . . . dances?" Gail asked in wonder.

"Quite well, by the looks of it. Why are you so surprised?"

"I didn't think Hawk Kincaid ever had any fun."

"I think it runs in the family," Catherine said.

Jerrie and Hawk danced by Gail and Catherine. Hawk's black hair gleamed under the ceiling-hung lamps that were shaped like oxen yokes. His obsidian eyes swung around with his body and connected with Gail's blue ones, in the same moment Jerrie's did with Catherine's.

"He looks strangely at you," Catherine said to Gail. "Just what did you do today? Besides play in the war paint, I mean."

"Very funny. We didn't do anything. And he didn't look any more strangely at me than

Jerrie did at you. What happened in the horse muck?"

"Nothing. I guess she doesn't have a sense of humor is all." Catherine's voice carried a hint of sadness.

"Do you think he'll dance with anyone else?" Gail asked softly.

"Do you think she will?" Catherine came back.

"There's no man in this room who'd have the nerve to ask Jerrie to dance. Except Hawk. And he's her brother."

"I'll bet he doesn't let himself get near any of the guests tonight. You remember what Jerrie told us at breakfast trail ride."

"I remember. Then what's he doing at this shindig? Even if he is dancing with his sister, he's bound to rub butts or elbows with the tourists, or God forbid, have one of them speak to him. Not to mention he's the best looking and most masculine guy in the place. He exudes earthy magnetism." Gail set her glass on the bar with a thud.

Catherine looked at her. "My, my, you seem a bit testy about Hawk. Just how much 'nothing' went on between you?"

"None." Gail headed for the side door of the barn. Suddenly she needed a big breath of fresh air.

"I gather that's the problem," Catherine said to no one, and followed her out. She came up behind Gail who stood near a tree in the moonlight. "Want to talk about it?"

"If I knew what there was to talk about, I'd tell you, my dearest friend." She was silent a long moment. "Remember that discussion we had by the pool?"

"Mm-hm."

"Well, I'm feeling like that all the more. Or, I guess I should say since we're out West, that I'm losing my seat in the saddle."

Catherine laughed weakly. "I know what you mean. Come on, let's finish this conversation up in our room. I'm fading fast."

They walked back to the house. "I don't know, Cath. I don't know what's wrong. It's almost time for school to start again, and I don't feel ready. I don't want to go back and simply get through another year while I face the retirement wall."

"I know," Catherine sympathized. "And you probably don't want to face Chelsea Gotter either, since you never did report the theft of her bag."

"Oh, Chelsea Gotter," Gail dismissed it as they climbed the stairs. "What about you? You chomping at the bit to be back at Riverview?"

Catherine sighed. "I've been teaching for almost twenty-five years. I'm at a point where I don't know if I've taught the same thing twenty-five times, or if I've taught it differently every year for twenty-five years. And that didn't make a bit of sense, did it?"

Gail yawned. "Strangely enough, it did. That could be pretty depressing, if you let it."

"I know."

"Don't you wish something would happen that would force you to do something else entirely? Something so different, and so compelling, that you never, never had to teach the same thing for twenty-five years, or twenty-five times, whichever comes first?" Gail grew breathless at the top of the stairs.

"I don't know. I guess I never let myself think like that. I'd be too scared."

"Well, I wish something would. I really do. I wish something would happen so I wouldn't have to face retirement, so I wouldn't have to wonder what the hell I'm going to do with the rest of my life."

"Be careful what you wish for," Catherine warned with good nature, "you might get it."

Gail put the key in the door lock. "Question is, what?"

She opened the door, and they walked into the room. Gail threw the keys on the dresser, and Catherine snapped on the light.

They both sucked in sharp breaths.

Weeping Willow was in Gail's bed, covered up to her chin in the quilt, her big dark eyes wide with fright, her little brown face on the white pillowcase looking like a walnut in a snowbank.

Chapter Seven

Willow threw the quilt up over her face.

A cautious glance passed between Gail and Catherine before Gail walked slowly toward the bed.

"Willow?" she said gently.

No answer. Gail reached out and laid a hand on the little mound under the quilt. The mound jumped and moved away.

"Willow, please look at me."

There was no movement under the covers. Gail slid her hand up and took hold of the top edge of the quilt. She tried to lower it slowly, but a little dark brown hand, dirt embedded in the knuckles making them look almost black, grabbed it and held it fast. Gail made a firm but gentle tug and loosened the child's grasp. She slid the quilt slowly down over Willow's face.

A head of dark matted hair emerged, then a dark forehead, and finally Willow's enormous dark brown eyes. The eyes bored into Gail's, then darted to Catherine, then back. They were the eyes of a frightened fawn.

And those eyes held the same fear in them Gail would have seen in her own ten-year-old eyes, for Gail had run away from home, too. More than once. Only to be brought back by neighbors, or the police, or some so-called helpful relative who couldn't understand why a child would run away from such a wonderful mother. Mother was wonderful, when she didn't drink. Mother was wonderful before Daddy left home. Daddy didn't come home because he didn't like ugly little girls, Mother said. Mother said . . .

Gail swallowed dry tears. She shook her head and sent the awful vision flying. She'd had Aunt Adelaide and Uncle John to rescue her. Though they weren't blood related, those two kind people had taken her in, given her a home and love. Willow had no aunt and uncle to do that for her.

"Hello, Willow," she said softly. "I'm very glad to see you again."

The child was silent, her eyes shifting from Gail to Catherine and back again.

Catherine gathered her bath things. "I'll just head down the hall for a little while, okay? If you need me, just call."

Gail nodded, and Catherine left the room.

"I'd like to sit down on the bed next to you now. Would that be all right?" Gail asked.

Willow did not respond, but she never took her eyes from Gail's face. Gail pulled the quilt a little lower, and saw a clutched hand around the rolled magazine.

"I'm glad to see you have your magazine," Gail went on carefully, quietly. "I wanted to return it to you, but I couldn't find you. I can see it means a lot to you. And thank you for returning my brush."

Willow shifted her eyes away for a split second, then refixed her gaze on Gail's face.

"I'll let you borrow it again, but you must ask me first, all right?" The eyes remained steady. "Maybe you'd like *me* to brush your hair sometime." The eyelids moved toward closed almost imperceptibly. Gail took that to mean she'd touched the child somehow. "I could do that for you now."

Willow's eyes shifted toward the window. She moved under the quilt, and Gail thought she was seeking escape. For a moment she couldn't swallow, didn't dare to breathe. She didn't want the child to run.

"Maybe we could do it another time, if you're too tired tonight. Would you rather just go to sleep now?"

Willow didn't move. She didn't close her eyes. She didn't speak. She kept her gaze locked on Gail's face so intently that Gail grew a little uncomfortable. Those eyes seemed to bore right through her and touch an old, and then a new fragment of her soul. She wasn't sure what to do next. She'd never been in this situation with a child like Willow. A hurt baby inside a hurting little girl. Gail could understand that. She could *feel* it.

Gail stood up, and decided to just keep talking and getting ready for bed as if it was just another night for her.

"I don't blame you. I'm tired, too. I worked hard today." She kept talking as she went to the closet, removed her clothes. "Wait till you see all the new things happening at Medicine Wheel School. You'll be very surprised when you go back. What grade will you be in, Willow?"

The child didn't answer. She watched every move Gail made.

"The teachers are very excited about the new library and all the wonderful new books. And it's so bright now that the room has been painted. Did you know Hawk painted a beautiful picture on the wall? It has mountains, and sky, and Cheyennes riding horses, and . . . oh, but I won't tell you everything about it. I don't

180

want to spoil your surprise. If you want to see it before school starts you can go over there with us tomorrow if you'd like."

Gail stopped. Maybe she was talking too much, confusing Willow. It was difficult to know. At Riverview she had to second guess the students and speak before they did in order to stay ahead of them.

Gail took a flowered cotton nightgown from a bureau drawer, slipped it on and added a pale blue robe.

"I have to go down to the bathroom to brush my teeth and wash my face. Do you need to use the bathroom? You can come with me if you'd like to." She held out her hand. Willow clutched the quilt closer around her neck. "No? That's okay. I'll be back in a few minutes."

She took her toiletries case and left the bedroom, purposely leaving the door open slightly. She didn't want Willow to feel she was trapping her in the room. The feeling of being trapped could send panic careening inside a little body with the frailness of Willow's. Gail knew that feeling first hand.

Outside the bathroom she knocked on the door.

Catherine opened it to her. "What happened?" she asked, wiping the steamed mirror with a towel and leaving a trail of lint.

"Not much. I don't know. She's still there. Hasn't spoken a word."

"What do you make of it?"

"I don't know. This has never happened to me. I don't know what to do, how to handle it. And I call myself a guidance counsellor." Gail rummaged in her bag for her toothbrush and toothpaste.

"Well, guidance counsellor," Catherine said, laying a hand on Gail's shoulder, "you'll have to guide yourself in this one, and me, too, if I'm to be of any help to you. This is different from anything I've ever been through. Even when Tiffany Shor wanted to carry her baby to term at age fifteen and wanted me to help her raise it. At least I could finally reason with her and her family. This poor child . . ."

Gail finished her teeth. "We'll have to tread very lightly. I'm not even sure she'll be in the room when we get back there. She didn't seem to want to leave right away, and I took that as a good sign. God, my heart breaks for her."

"She seems so alone in the world," Catherine observed. "How does a child survive this long being so alone? She's got to be tough as nails."

"Yes, on the outside. That's how to survive in a world full of terrifying adults. But she's all cream puff inside, and that's what will destroy her, if someone doesn't help turn her around."

Catherine gave Gail a curious glance. "I thought you didn't know any kids like Willow."

Gail washed her face carefully, and patted it dry. She smoothed on night cream that cost forty-five dollars at one of Bloomingdale's cosmetic counters.

"I might have, once."

"Well, you've seen street kids in New York who are iron and steel through and through. Sometimes there's no turning around for most of them, no matter how hard people may try."

"I know. I hope it hasn't gone that far with Willow. This is a different environment."

"No less hard and abusive," Catherine said. "Be careful."

"I will. I won't do anything to knowingly hurt her."

"I didn't mean just the child," Catherine said. "Hurt goes both ways." She followed Gail out of the bathroom.

At the bedroom door, Gail took a small breath and pushed it open, not knowing whether she'd find Willow still hiding under the bed quilt or not. She wasn't prepared for what she did find. Willow stood next to the nightstand holding Gail's hairbrush, her filthy shirt and pants lying in a pile in the corner.

And she was wearing one of Gail's other night-gowns, a satiny flowered mini with a black background from Victoria's Secret. One dirty finger was poised against her mouth.

"I think she wants me to brush her hair," Gail whispered to Catherine.

"Before or after you talk to her about stealing other people's things?" Catherine returned. She smiled and slipped into her bed, snapped on the bedside lamp, and took out a novel. "I think I'll let you work this out on your own tonight. Say something if you want help. I only hope I hear you. I'm half asleep as it is."

Gail walked toward Willow and sat on the bed near where she stood. The child did not move. Her finger stayed clamped against her little mouth, and her other hand clutched the hairbrush.

"May I brush your hair, Willow?" Gail waited. The child's eyes blinked slightly. "Will you give me the hairbrush, please?" Willow's hand came out tentatively, then stopped. Gail reached slowly for the brush. The little fingers reluctantly released the handle. "Thank you," Gail said.

She touched the child's hair. It was unspeakably dirty. With a hand on the thin shoulder, she turned Willow around so she could begin at the back of her head. The tangles in her hair were impossible. Gail separated as many of them as she could, and brushed the strands smooth. Much of them were too matted, and she knew cutting was going to be the only way to remove them. And Willow needed a good bath and shampoo.

"You have very pretty hair, Willow." The head turned and big brown eyes looked up with something in them Gail began to understand. Was this the first nice thing ever said to this child? She turned her around to face her. "It's the color of the night sky before the stars come out." She kept brushing, though it wasn't doing a bit of good. She just didn't want to let the moment go yet. "Maybe tomorrow I could wash your hair for you with a sweet soap. My aunt used to do that for me."

Willow stepped back, a tiny frown settling between her brows. Her eyes narrowed. Gail worked at not letting the child's reaction unsettle her. She reached toward her again and brushed one strand down the side of her face.

"It's the same shampoo I use on my hair. Here, would you like to touch my hair and see how soft it is?"

Willow's eyes grew round as chocolate cookies. Gail took her little hand in hers. The fingers were thin and delicate, but the skin was rough and cut in places. She raised Willow's hand and put it to her hair. She held it there a moment, then slowly lowered her own. Willow didn't move a muscle in her body. She didn't drop her hand. She stared at it where it lay against Gail's blonde hair. Then suddenly she pulled it back and put the tips of her first two fingers between her little clenched lips. Gail saw deep emotions at work in her eyes and in the quivering around her jaws and forehead. But Willow quickly quelled them, no doubt adept at it from years of practice in her young life.

"See?" Gail said, wanting to soothe the child in some small way. "I think you'll like the soap. If you do, I'll let you keep the bottle so you can use it whenever you want to."

Willow relaxed, and Gail thought she saw the hint of a smile quivering now at the corners of her lips.

Gail yawned and stretched. "Well, it's bedtime for me. If you'd like to stay the night here in this room, it's fine with me." She put the brush down on the nightstand, took off her robe and slipped into bed.

Willow turned around toward the corner of the room where her dirty clothes lay in a heap. Gail caught it, and her heart suffered another small break. This child must be used to sleeping in dirty places every night.

Gail settled down on the pillow, pulled the covers back and patted the sheet.

"You can sleep next to me, if you like."

Willow watched her, fingers still against her lips.

"If you don't want to stay, it's all right. You can go whenever you want to. But would you please be sure to close the door when you leave?" She watched Willow's little stoic face, a face that had learned far too young how to conceal emotion.

Gail slipped under the covers farther. "Oh, and you can just put the nightgown back in the drawer where you got it before you leave. It won't be warm enough for you when you go outside. I'm going to turn the light out now, all right?"

Willow didn't say anything, nor did she move. Gail turned out the lamp on the nightstand, and the room went dark except for a shaft of light from the hallway streaming through the door. She waited, hardly breathing.

The child stood there for a long time. Gail let her breathing go even. Then Willow, apparently thinking Gail was asleep, closed the bedroom door. Gail clamped her eyes tightly and held back the wetness that had formed in them. Then she felt the bed move slightly. Willow quietly crept into the bed and slipped the quilt up over her thin shoulders.

Gail smiled in the dark, sighed, then went to sleep.

"Good thing your hair is light, and short. They can't hide in it so well as dark hair," Ada said knowingly.

Gail sat on a back porch step in the early morning sun, her head bent over a red and white enamel basin balanced on her knees. Ada sat on the step above her with Catherine. A similar basin filled with kerosene, a bag of cotton balls and a fine-toothed comb was spread out between them.

"How could this happen so fast?" Gail's voice was muffled by the towel she'd draped around her neck.

"That's how they are," Ada said as a matter of fact.

She parted Gail's hair and dabbed it with a cotton ball dipped in the kerosene. Then she parted a quarter of an inch over her head and repeated the procedure. When a quarter of her head had been parted and dabbed, and the kerosene was dripping into the basin on Gail's knees, Ada took the comb and drew a few small strands at a time, trapping head lice in the teeth.

"Better not get too close to the pow wow fire tonight," Catherine teased. "You'll give a whole new meaning to the term hot head!" She handed Ada a clean cotton ball dipped in the kerosene.

"Very funny."

"What time did Willow leave?" Catherine asked. "I never heard a thing."

"Neither did I," Gail said. "I woke up, just about sunup I think, and looked over on the pillow and she was gone. Then I sat up and started itching. At least I knew I hadn't just dreamed she'd been in the room last night wearing a Victoria's Secret nightgown."

Ada kept working over Gail's head, saying nothing. Her hands were sure and fast, making Gail think she'd performed this operation on many occasions. But Gail felt more than that. An intimacy, she guessed she might say. Strange to feel that. Maybe it had something to do with Ada's hands on her head performing duty a mother might be called on to do for a child. Suddenly she wished Willow could be sitting here experiencing this motherly intimate moment. The knowledge of why she had to be sitting here with Ada dabbing kerosene in her hair didn't detract from the feelings traveling between them. At least from her. She wished Willow could experience Ada's touch

. . . or maybe her own.

"I gave Willow every option to leave if she wanted to," Gail went on. "I thought that would make her feel secure enough to stay, thought I was doing the right thing so she wouldn't feel I was trapping her. I guess that reverse psychology didn't work on her."

"She seemed so tough," Catherine said, "but those big eyes betrayed the scared child inside."

"Why would she just get up and leave like that?" Gail wondered out loud, knowing there probably was no real answer.

"She's like that," Ada replied again as matter of fact.

"Hey, what happened?" Sheila came around the end of the porch.

"Oh Lord." Gail covered her face with her hands.

Sheila dropped a hand on Gail's shoulder. "At breakfast Wills told me he drew a basin of kerosene for Mrs. Kincaid to give you a shampoo."

Catherine explained as carefully as she could, barely concealing her difficulty in stifling a laugh.

"Lice?" Sheila stepped back. "For heaven's sake, Gail! You of all people. Ms. Clean with head lice! Wait till the others hear this one!"

"Oh Sheila, don't . . ."

It was too late. Prudie and Bethanne showed up. They, too, had met Wills at breakfast, and he'd shared with them as well his kerosene-drawing duties for Mrs. Kincaid.

"I'm not sitting next to you on the bus to-morrow," Bethanne said. "I certainly don't want to start out on a two thousand mile trip, my head itching, and nothing to kill the problems."

"Bethanne," Gail said wearily, "this isn't the plague, you know."

"My mother used to say it might as well be, to get something like that," Bethanne put in.

Gail worried where this conversation might lead. Bethanne's parents were well-to-do, as far as it went in a Philadelphia suburb in the forties and fifties. Bethanne attended public school just like the rest of them, and she re-membered as well as any of them how embar-rassed the poorer kids were when they came to school and the nurse found head lice. They were mortified, and the better-off kids whis-pered that's what you got when you were dirt poor.

"Your mother used to tell you she knew when you told lies to her because you ended up with white marks on your fingernails, too," Gail announced, "but you knew that was just an old wives' tale." She didn't want to embarrass Bethanne, but she didn't want Ada to think they were saying something derogatory about the little Indian child.

The women gathered around Gail on the porch while Ada worked, and they all chatted amiably then. Ada asked a few questions about their school, and about what each of them did. They all were happy to tell her about their jobs. Gail told them about the Medicine Wheel School, about the work, the clean-up, the lack of teachers, and the new library.

"Sounds dreadful," Prudie said, "but I'm pleased to hear of the emphasis on a library. When I get back home, I'll go through books we've discarded over the last year and send them out here, that is . . ." she looked in Ada's eyes, "if you think they would have any use for them."

"We would have use," Ada said evenly. She finished combing Gail's hair. "Mm-hm," she said, and nodded her head, satisfied she'd removed every louse.

Gail lifted her head and rubbed the towel through her hair and over her stinging scalp. She turned and looked up at Ada. "Thank you so much. I'm pretty clueless when it comes to something like this."

Catherine cleaned up the soiled cotton balls and the two basins of kerosene. "I'm afraid some of the history books Prudie will send you could still use a little rewriting, Mrs. Kincaid. You know what I mean."

"Yes. But we know how to teach around that." Ada smiled for the first time that morning.

Gail stood up. "I guess I'd better go wash this head so I don't go around smelling like fuel oil all day."

Then she noticed him. Hawk was standing near a shed not far from the back porch, holding the reins of his palomino. And he was smiling, too, the first time she'd seen that since the moment she'd set eyes on him. Or, she squinted, was he laughing at her in her predicament?

Catherine followed her gaze. "Looks like he knows how to have fun after all," she chided softly.

"What?" Sheila said, pushing herself up. "Who?"

"Nobody," Gail said.

"That nobody over there?" Bethanne was staring in Hawk's direction. "He's the best-looking nobody I've seen since he showed up last night at the dance."

"Who is he?" Sheila asked.

"My son," Ada said softly. She pushed herself up off the porch with some effort and went inside the house.

Hawk turned and leapt up onto the back of the horse and took off at a trot down a dirt trail that led toward a hilly range.

"Most beautiful sight I've ever seen," Sheila breathed.

Gail silently agreed.

"Oh, I don't know," Prudie said shyly. "I thought Skeeter looked particularly handsome last night, all duded up, as he said."

Gail caught a different note in Prudie's voice. She looked at her, totally, for the first time that morning.

"Prudie, I just noticed! You've let your hair down!" Gail said in surprise. "It's so long . . . and beautiful."

Prudie colored. "Skeeter said . . . he . . . well, actually he took it down last night. He said I looked . . . pretty. Can you imagine? Me?"

Gail hugged her. "Yes, I can believe it. You do look pretty."

Prudie smiled an enigmatic smile, and looked down at her feet.

"Wait a minute," Sheila drawled, "something else is going on with you, isn't it?" She leaned over and peered up at Prudie's bowed face.

The others waited a long tense moment. "Maybe she doesn't want to tell us," Bethanne

194

said, pouting. "And I don't know why not. We're her closest friends."

"Maybe she just wants to keep whatever it is to herself," Catherine put in. "Sometimes that's the best way."

Prudie looked up then, still holding a Mona Lisa smile on her lips. "I'd like to tell you."

"What? What?" Sheila wanted this secret so badly she looked as if she'd burst from the desire.

"Well, Skeeter and I . . . have become close."

"How close?" Sheila asked.

"He's been to my room in the house a couple of times." Prudie shifted her watch back and forth over the top of her wrist.

"Oh-h?" Bethanne drew it out.

"He's reckless," Prudie said with excitement, "wild. You know what he did?"

"That's what we're hoping to find out." Sheila again

Gail watched Prudie give out her story.

"He took all my pills and medicines, and he flushed them all down the toilet and threw the bottles out the window!"

"No!" Sheila breathed. "You must have gone berserk! What did you hit him with?"

"I couldn't do anything," Prudie hushed her voice. "I was flabbergasted. I just watched the

195

pills swirl away and the bottles go out the window."

"I'd say that was pretty daring of Skeeter," Catherine said. "Yes, sir, pretty daring. Did he know what he was risking?"

"I guess," Prudie said, coloring again. "Then he, he took my hair down, and threw the pins on the floor, and he kissed me. A real kiss."

"You're serious," Sheila said, only it came out as if she meant Prudie was kidding them.

"Yes, I am."

"What did you do?"

"I didn't know what to do at first. But then . . ."

"Then?" Sheila was fairly tipping over on her toes leaning in to Prudie's story.

"I guess kissing is something one simply is born knowing how to do. It was as if I was turned on like a light switch. And I kissed him back. A *real* kiss!"

"You were turned on, all right!" Sheila affirmed. "What did you think when you came up for air?"

"I thought I wanted more!" Prudie said, completely unabashed. "And I told him so!"

"Whoa," Sheila said, a new respect in her voice, "that took nerve."

"No it didn't. It was the easiest, most wonderful thing I ever did in my life."

Sheila looked away dreamy-eyed.

"Want to hear the rest?" Prudie whispered.

"There's more?" This time Bethanne was the excited one.

"Much more. He ... I ... we ... we made love."

"Prudie!" Her name went around all the lips almost in unison.

"Can you beat that?" Prudie said proudly. "Skeeter said he'd found a genuine, honest guaran-goddamn-teed antique. Fifty-year-old virginity! He told me after that he was the happiest man alive. And after the second time he said he died and gone to heaven. And after the third he said I was a precious . . ."

"Three times? You made love three times?" Sheila was almost dissolved.

"Yes, and if he didn't have to get up and do barn chores, we'd have done it again. It's really quite wonderful, you know."

"So I've heard, but I couldn't attest to that," Bethanne said.

"Amen," Sheila said.

"The main thing is you're happy about this," Gail said, hugging Prudie.

"Oh, I am. I truly am. I didn't think I would ever . . . I never thought it could ever

197

be that good . . ." For a librarian, Prudie seemed to have difficulty finding the right words.

"Will you be okay leaving now?" Catherine asked her with real concern.

"I don't know," Prudie answered honestly, "I've never been through this before, never felt this way before."

"You're in love," Sheila pronounced.

"Oh, heavens, I don't know about that. I'm not sure what that's supposed to feel like. But this, this making love stuff is spectacular!"

The group fell silent for a few moments, some remembering, some wishing, some simply understanding.

"That makes this vacation complete," Sheila said, hugging Prudie.

"So what's everybody doing today?" Bethanne asked, breaking the charged silence. "I don't think I want to take another tour of some museum or other. I'm saturated."

"Me, too," Sheila said, stretching and yawning. "I think I'll just hang out by the pool all day."

Catherine seemed restless. Gail saw her eyes slide toward the barn, then the range, then the house. She seemed to be looking for someone.

"I have an idea," Gail said. "This would be something different, something you wouldn't have expected to be doing out here."

"What?" Bethanne seemed truly interested.

"How about coming with me and Mrs. Kincaid over to the Medicine Wheel School and helping to put the library together? A couple of the classrooms need to be settled, too."

"A school?" Sheila was astounded at such a ridiculous suggestion. "You want us to go to a *school* and *work* on our vacation?"

Gail rocked her head slightly. "Well, what's so bad about that? It's not Riverview. And believe me, these teachers could use some extra hands right about now, even if you could stay only an hour or two. Besides, it would give you the chance to see another school."

"Thereby making part of this vacation tax deductible," Bethanne put in sensibly.

"I'd like to see their library," Prudie added. "Sure, I'll go with you. What time?"

Gail checked her watch. "In about an hour. Ada has to pack the lunch first."

"She has to take their lunch?" The notion that a matriarch of a family who owned a seventy thousand acre ranch would pack a lunch for a few teachers from a rural school seemed inconceivable to Sheila.

"She doesn't have to. She wants to," Gail said.

"All right," Sheila conceded, "count me in."

"Great! Meet us out front in the driveway!" Gail left then in a hurry. Her scalp was burning and she wanted to put her head under the shower for a long time.

At the end of two hours inside Medicine Wheel School, Gail noticed none of the women seemed anxious to get away. They chatted amiably with Carol and Ang and a couple of other teachers who'd come in to work. Even the Two Bulls brothers lingered wherever any one of the women were working.

Hesitantly Gail ambled toward the library room. She wondered if Hawk would be there finishing the walls or working on his mural. If he was, would she talk to him? What would she say? In polite circles most people sought and found a common ground on which to start a conversation. She hadn't found one with Hawk, and he hadn't given an inch of ground. Any exchange between them so far could hardly be called a complete conversation, unless the argument they'd had in the study that night could be counted as one. And their last encounter in this library had been . . . interesting.

With trepidation, Gail stepped through the open door into the library.

Prudie sat on the floor surrounded by short stacks of books, a square of three-quarter inch plywood resting on her knees. She picked up a book, opened past the front flyleaf, read, then made notations on a white index card, put the book on a shelf, and placed the card facedown on a pile. Then she picked up another book and repeated the reading, notation on another card, setting the book on a shelf. Gail noticed how contented she looked. And pretty. She knew now it wasn't just being among books that made this particular librarian happy.

Hawk was not in the library, and if he had been he left no signs. Gail didn't ask Prudie.

She decided to make further exploration of the school, and started down another hallway. At the end was a gray steel fire door. She pushed the bar and opened it to the back yard. Then she stopped, preventing the door from slamming shut behind her.

Hawk sat on a rusty bench swing cradling Willow in one arm. Her feet hung off the seat and she swung them slightly. Hawk propped one booted foot on his knee, the other was flat on the ground, and with that one he pushed the swing idly back and forth in a short journey over the sand beneath it. Willow's coffee-colored face was turned up toward him, and he dipped his dark head down. He was talking quietly to her, now and then using a descriptive hand gesture.

Gail shut the door as quietly as she could, seconds later realizing she was now locked out of the building. She stepped softly through the grass to a stand of cottonwoods not far from the swing. Though hushed, she could hear Hawk's voice clearly. He was speaking first in Cheyenne, then in English and she could tell it was a story he was entrancing Willow with. Gail saw that she was caught up in it, too. Willow was entranced by the way Hawk spoke the words, his inflections, his emphasis on some, first soft to build drama, then crescendoing to a surprise that made her laugh and clap her little hands. Gail had never seen the child so happy, and she delighted in it.

And then in a heartbeat, Willow jumped from the swing and ran down a dirt path, disappearing behind a rise. The swing stopped moving, and Gail's delight dissolved with Willow's footfalls.

"You can come out of hiding, now," Hawk's voice raised. Not looking over his shoulder, he sat very still in the swing.

Gail's pulse escalated and her hands started to shake. He'd known she was there from the start!

"I'm sorry. I didn't mean to frighten her

202

away." She walked with faltering steps toward him.

"You didn't frighten her," Hawk said, again without looking at her. "She knew you were there."

"Why didn't she run right away, then?" Gail kept advancing toward him, her shoulders tense, wondering if at any moment that he would pick up and run away from her, too.

"It is possible she was testing you."

Was he testing her, too?

"Testing? In what way?" Gail was abreast of him now. Still he did not move, nor did he look at her.

"To see what you would do."

"What should I have done?"

"Just what you did."

"What did she think I would do?"

Hawk turned then, and gave her the full force of his granite-hard gaze. "Trap her. Stop her. Change her."

Gail's shoulders dropped. "I don't want to trap her," she said softly.

"But you do want to stop her, you do want to change her, don't you?" His voice was stern.

"Only to help her. She seems so alone. I thought I could be of help to her."

"Help her? How? Just what do you think you can do for her? Give her a few things, clean her up, be her friend for a few days, show her a little of the white world?" He gave her a last scoffing look before he turned his head, uncocked his knee and stood up. The swing banged against the back of his calves.

"Yes! But not in the shallow way you're describing." Gail's voice took on the edge she was feeling inside.

He spun back, fire igniting in the black granite of his eyes. "Is that right? Then what way, what deep and abiding way did you mean? No matter what few breaths out of your supremely important life you give her, you will hurt her. There is nothing you can do for her. The fact remains you will soon get on a bus and ride out of her life. You'll go back to your safe, secure world, soothing your soul that you've done something charitable for a poor Indian kid. And she," he pointed in the direction of Willow's flight, "she will have had yet another person snatched from her."

Gail thought she heard a choke break in Hawk's voice. She must have been mistaken, she snapped at herself. This man had his own prejudices, and she was somehow a part of them.

"And won't you be glad," she growled at him. "You don't want me to do anything for Willow because I'm non-Native. You'd rather have her live dirty and wild than let somebody white, me in particular, although it escapes me just why you've singled me out, show her there are other ways. Not," she put up her hand as he started to open his mouth to speak, "not *white* ways. That's not what I mean. I mean kindness, caring, teaching her she has to care for herself, has to let other people care for her, has to love herself to get on in the world. You'd rather let her be a wild animal than to even encourage her to let people close to her! In my mind you're as bad as you think I am, or white people are, or whoever you're carrying a grudge against!"

The moment the speech ended on her lips, Gail was sorry she'd spoken the words. She'd never said anything that awful to anyone in her life. She'd wanted to many times, but she'd never allowed her decorum the privilege of slipping. And now look what she'd done.

Hawk stepped close to her. His features did not move, his mouth stayed even, though she could see it was taking some effort for him to keep it tightly shut. But the anger in his eyes was unmistakable. He towered above her. She didn't move, didn't blink her eyes as she gave him the same even gaze.

Then he turned and walked away, the high heels of his boots at the end of his long strides connecting heavily with the ground.

Gail watched him disappear around the corner of the school building. Only then did she let out a shaky breath. She knew he was powerful enough to have reduced her to a quivering mess, verbally as well as physically.

Only then did she realize that not once had she felt fear during their confrontation.

Chapter Eight

Under a circular wooden arbor, Gail stood among the scattered group of America's Adventure Tourists waiting to observe the Grand Entry of Nations at the Crow Fair pow wow. The tour company had provided a brochure about this, the oldest Indian pow wow in America. The Crow Fair annually drew hundreds of Native Americans from across the United States and Canada, it said, to dance in traditional costumes, to compete in rodeo and dance contests, to sell their arts and crafts, to gather together to express and confirm their heritage.

Gail had been looking forward to attending the event. Her mind seemed a sponge of curiosity these days, eager to soak up all she could learn about Native Americans, the Northern Cheyenne in particular. If anyone asked her why that was, she'd have no reply that would truly provide an answer. But she knew she was experiencing this quest for knowledge as if some other force were controlling her mind and senses.

From babies to grandparents, the people gathered at the Crow Fair. Behind Gail and the crowd stood a campground billed as the Teepee Capital of the World. Native visitors and participants in the Fair activities arrived with their families in trucks and cars, bringing their own huge canvas teepees, accompanied by dogs, and hauling horse trailers. At the entrance to the campground, Gail had noticed a sign, "lodge poles for sale," propped next to what was left of a huge pile of stripped lodgepole pine poles used to construct the braces and hold the teepees in place. Families lived in these teepees while they attended the Fair.

Under a cook arbor shaded with leafed tree branches, Gail saw Indian women making tacos and stirring deep pots of aromatic meat and sauce. She watched them lift fresh frybread from grease kettles then drain it on paper towels.

Before they entered the spectator arbor, the tour group was instructed to stay together and to strictly observe the rule that prohibited alcohol on the grounds. They walked among the stalls and stands of both native and nonnative people selling jewelry, tee shirts, belts, watch bands, and the like.

"This reminds me of the carnivals we used to go to when we were kids," Sheila said, picking up a beaded necklace.

"This isn't carny stuff," a potbellied Indian man with a pock-marked face told her. He stood behind the stall counter spreading out his jewelry, and rattlesnake belts and hatbands on a sheet. "This is my living."

"Oh, I didn't mean anything by that," Sheila came back quickly. "It's just that the atmosphere reminded me of the carnivals." She picked out a particularly colorful narrow beaded necklace and purchased it from him.

"The life of many modern Indian people living on today's reservations," Helene was reading now from one of her notebooks, "is one of joblessness, or of low-paying work off the reservation when they can get it. Many Indian people fight daily battles against the effects of alcoholism, poverty, and low self-esteem."

Gail looked around as Helene's voice carried outside their group. The typical tour guide reading made it sound as if these people were in a sideshow, on view for the paying customers. The idea disgusted her. A young Indian man stumbled into her, drunk beyond reason, and someone grabbed him and took him away. Gail felt a sadness inside, and a helpless feeling. This was no sideshow. This was life.

The air was still hot, dry enough to pull the moisture out of skin. Dust swirled up from everywhere and filled the air with tiny black particles that clung to her clothes and her face. Gail had found it increasingly difficult to keep up her beauty routine in this climate. She always worked hard to keep her usual fresh and neat appearance, but on this vacation it had turned into a major production. Her eyes burned from the dryness in the daytime, and her skin seemed to drink her moisturizer in gulps. And her hair. It was limp. She didn't know how to handle it. Tonight she'd worn a black beaver western hat to hide it. Her white Karan shirt and Vanderbilt jeans over black western boots were the right thing for this event, she'd assumed.

Now, when she looked around at members of the crowd not part of the tour group, she realized she probably looked more like a model out of *Vogue's* special spread on western wear. The thought made her uncomfortable. That was not the image she wanted to project at all. She was completely out of her element, out of her own easy way of life, yet, she felt a sharp jab of desire to know more and more about this way of life, to understand it.

She'd bought and wore this evening a pair of earrings, handmade by a Cheyenne friend of Ada's who brought her jewelry to the ranch once a week during tourist season. These were of porcupine quills and black beads fashioned into long airy loops and strung from silver earwires. She would treasure them among her few good pieces of jewelry, including her grandmother's cameo brooch.

Under the spectator arbor now, Gail stood at the entrance that opened into an expansive grass circle centered by a towering floodlight pole amid native and nonnative tourists and locals. People settled in the folding chairs they'd brought with them, or scrambled for seats on two-tiered wooden bleachers at the back of the arbor.

The speaker announced the start of the Grand Entry. The first to enter was an honor guard of Indian military veterans, some carrying flags of the country and of their own native nation. In various uniforms of the American military, veteran women and men circled the field. Spectators stood to show their respect and honor. The host drum group, the Black Pipe Singers, sat around a huge drum, each member poising his drum stick above it. As the drumming sounded, followed by the blended wails of the group, The Grand Entry of Nations began. First the oldest men outfitted in colorful regalia, feathers, moccasins, elaborate eagle feather headdresses, entered, accompanied by the sounds of bells jingling on their leggings or ankles as they walked. Honored old men and old women were flanked by the younger, and they began a rhythmic shuffle and tapping with their feet, moving slowly around the circle.

"Look!" Gail said in hushed excitement to Catherine. She pointed into a group of costumed men and women who passed close to them at the entrance. "It's Hawk!" She hadn't expected to see him among the dancers, and the revelation thrilled her.

"Where? How can you possibly pick him out?"

"Right there. Third one over, the tallest man in that group. See the three black and white eagle feathers on . . ."

"Yes! I see him!" Catherine was as excited as Gail.

Shoulders bobbing, head writhing from one side to the other, Hawk was easy for her to spot. He was several inches taller than the men he danced near, but it was more than that. Hawk wore the look of someone who had unmistakable command of who he was and where he was. He was proud of his Cheyenne heritage, and proud to show it.

He is spectacular! A shiver went up Gail's spine as the singers' voices went into a shrill crescendo.

"Look around the other side of him. See?" Catherine said.

"Ada . . . isn't it?" Gail breathed.

"Yes. Where is . . . ?" Catherine let the question die on her lips.

"Where is who?"

Catherine didn't answer.

"You're not looking for Trey, are you?" Gail turned and gave a frown to Catherine. "I can't believe he's even here, let alone out there dancing."

"He's the last one I'd look for."

"Oh, look," Gail said, pointing toward the entrance to the dance circle, "isn't that Jerrie?"

"Where?" Catherine's question was quick and anticipatory.

"Right over there, just going out onto the field. And she's got a child with her . . . Willow?"

Catherine pushed around the crowd for a better look. "It *is,* it's both of them."

213

Gail saw Catherine fix her gaze on the swaying backs of Jerrie and Willow. Then she turned back quickly so she would be sure to recognize them in the crowd of dancers when they circled and came back toward them. Jerrie's long straight dress was of deerskin, heavily beaded in brilliant colors. Her hair was pulled back in a long braid down the middle of her shoulders. Willow's dress was of red cotton and had tobacco lids rolled into cones sewn over it in tiers. With her hand in Jerrie's, she looked down at her moccasin-clad feet, seeming to study the way they moved next to Jerrie's.

Gail felt a pang of something. *Jealousy?* She wished Willow would put her little hand in her own, trustingly, the way she did with Jerrie. Willow seemed to belong to every person, and to no one in particular, a child of the People, a child of nature. Just like Hawk.

Was that all right with . . . the gods, or whoever? That Willow should be alone? That Hawk should at least appear to be alone? Why did it always seem to her that everyone should be connected to someone else, somehow, some way? Did Willow have real freedom? Did Hawk? Gail's mind was a whirling sea of questions, becoming as much a blur as the gyrating costume colors that passed before her.

The parade continued as the next younger, and on and on down to little children walked through the arbor opening and out onto the field, circling within their circles until there must have been well over two hundred moving, wailing, jingling, traditional costume-clad Native Americans from all over North America under the floodlight. And the relentless drums pounded the ancient rhythms, erasing the difficult life of modern day with the blood heat and glory of yesterday.

After about an hour, as the sun was leaving a dusky mauve and gray wash on the horizon, some of the dancers left the field to sit with families or walk among the stalls of food and souvenirs and crafts. Jerrie, Willow's hand still tightly locked in hers, approached Gail and Catherine.

"We could see all of you as we came around the circle," Jerrie said, a little breathless, "couldn't we, Willow?" She looked down at the child whose great doelike eyes were raised to Gail's.

Gail smiled down at her. The child stayed silent. "You two are very beautiful in your dresses. How did you learn to dance so well, Willow?"

Willow looked up at Jerrie then back to

215

Gail. "Hawk," she said shyly.

That was the first word Gail had heard her speak.

"And where did you learn?" Catherine asked Jerrie.

Jerrie lifted her long black braid from her shoulder and let it fall down her back. "Ah, you know how it is. We're born knowing how to dance!" Her blue eyes sparkled with mischief. "Comes in handy during the dry season, you know, when we need rain in a hurry. Things like that. You ought to try it. Dancing is very useful."

"Next time we need rain I'll give it a go," Catherine said, her brown eyes dancing at the moment.

"You two must be hungry after all that exercise," Gail said. "Would you like something to eat, Willow?" She hoped she might get the child to speak again.

Willow nodded, but said nothing.

"What do you like?" Again Gail tried, this time not giving the opportunity for a yes or a no answer.

Willow just looked up at Jerrie.

"She's rather partial to turnip greens and boiled rattlesnake, as I recall." Jerrie made a big gesture of squinting her eyes and putting a finger to her temple. Willow grimaced and shook her head. "Yes, that's it," Jerrie said, ignoring her purposely. "I know the man who makes the best boiled rattlesnake at the fair. Let's go get some!"

"Bread!" Willow said very loud so no one could make any mistake about what she wanted.

"Frybread, right, Willow?" Gail asked.

The little girl nodded. Gail held out her hand to her. She looked up at Jerrie who turned immediately to make conversation with Catherine. Willow fidgeted with her fingers, twining them in and out between each other, clutched them tightly, then looked up at Gail. Gail didn't take back her hand.

Willow wrenched one of her little grimy hands out of the other and stuck it into Gail's. Gail took it warmly, not squeezing too tightly, although she wanted to hold onto the little girl for dear life.

"I never thought that would happen," Catherine said to Jerrie, watching the two hands entwined as they followed behind Gail and Willow.

"Don't expect too much," Jerrie warned. "Willow is here today and gone tomorrow." She looked over at Catherine. "Just like you."

Catherine snapped her head around. "Yes . . . the bus leaves tomorrow. The group starts back East."

Jerrie nodded, then moved around a couple of men who pushed their way through the crowd of people in front of the stalls, before coming back to Catherine's side. "The group, yes. I'll miss you. You, not the group. I think we could have been friends."

Catherine said nothing, but she watched Jerrie thoughtfully as they came up behind Willow and Gail at a frybread stall.

"How many do we need?" Gail turned and asked them.

"Frybread all around," Jerrie ordered.

"Four, then," Gail said to the perspiring dark woman behind the counter.

The woman slid four paper plates onto the counter, and then with long tongs lifted two puffy frybread rounds out of a kettle of oil and drained them, then plopped them on the plates. She took two more out of another kettle. Gail lifted one plate down for Willow. Jerrie reached around her and picked up two, and handed one to Catherine.

"Remember at the old carnivals, Gail? We used to get that fried dough and sprinkle powdered sugar all over them. If you breathed out through your nose when you took a bite, sugar went flying all over the next person, or on your clothes!" Catherine laughed.

Gail and Jerrie laughed, too. "It was better than breathing in through your nose!" Gail added, then made a sneezing noise for Willow's benefit.

The little girl gave a tenuous smile, then peered up over the stall counter at the woman doing the cooking. The beefy hand pushed a pot of honey toward her.

"We use honey sometimes instead of that powdered sugar, which sounds to me like a hazard," Jerrie said.

Gail brought the pot down to Willow's level. "Would you show me the proper way to eat real Indian frybread, please?"

Willow looked at Jerrie, then back at Gail. She dipped the sticky spoon into the honey then poured it over Gail's frybread, smearing it with the spoon.

Gail took a bite of the bread, and got honey on her face. When she tried to wipe it with a flimsy napkin, white pieces of the paper clung to it. Catherine started to laugh. Then Willow's smile became brighter, and Jerrie chuckled.

"What's the matter?" Gail asked, feigning innocence for Willow's benefit.

"Oh, nothing," Catherine said. "You just look kinda funny. Right, Jerrie?"

"Right. Funny, yes. Right, Willow?"

Gail dropped down on her haunches and looked at Willow on her level. "What do you think, Willow? Do I look funny?"

Willow said nothing. She stood still a long time just looking at Gail's face. Then with one tentative small hand, she reached out and took first one piece and then the other of the clinging napkin from Gail's cheek. Then she shook her head.

"Thank you, Willow," Gail whispered. "I knew I could trust you to tell me the truth."

They finished their bread and Jerrie took the plates to a trash receptacle. Willow followed her. Gail watched them, and then the crowd grew thick in her line of sight. When they thinned, Jerrie came back to them, but Willow was not with her.

"Where is she?" Gail strained past Jerrie, her eyes frantic.

"She's gone. I think she's tired."

"But where will she go to sleep?"

"Wherever." Jerrie shrugged. "I should get back to the dancing. I promised Mother I'd go around with her once before she goes home. She tires easily these days."

Gail swallowed hard. Everyone seemed so nonchalant about Willow. She's survived this far, hadn't she? Why worry about a kid who was wiser, it seemed, than any of those brash students back at Riverview?

"Gail says your mother has been working pretty hard at the school," Catherine was saying.

"I know," Jerrie said. "And if you remind her she'll be seventy-six on her next birthday, she'll probably throw you to the ground like a roped calf!" She peered out toward the sounds from the dance ground. When she turned back, her eyes held a different look, her face showed a guarded countenance. "I might not see you tomorrow before you leave," she said evenly. "I won't say goodbye." She took hold of one of Catherine's hands and one of Gail's. "Until we walk again side by side."

And then she glided through the crowd toward the dancing.

"Is everything all right with her?" Gail asked.

Catherine seemed to be bewildered. She couldn't seem to find an answer for Gail.

Darkness had settled around them when Helene and Trey rounded up the group to start them toward the bus and the ride back to the ranch. Gail was reluctant to leave. She lingered near the arbor opening, hoping for a last glimpse of Willow. Catherine stood beside her and seemed to be hoping for a last glimpse as well.

And then, on the outside of the circling

221

group, Hawk came around. Gail watched him dance, watched the subtle movement of his feet and legs, the lines of large brass bells lining his deerskin leggings move below his hips. But it was the look on his face that disturbed her, abandoned to another time, lost in his own inner path.

And then his eyes shot toward her as if he'd felt her gaze on him. Her shoulders jerked. This time that black gaze seemed to summon her, beckon her into a heretofore closed sacred land.

"Come on," Catherine interrupted Gail's thoughts. "The others are getting too far away from us. We'll get lost if we don't go now."

Gail let Catherine pull her away, yet she could still feel those disturbing eyes on her back. And she already felt lost.

It was long after midnight when Gail turned over in bed and curled on her right side, her favorite sleeping position. Sleep didn't come easy, and when it did even in its lightest form, her mind churned images of whirling dancers, feathers, doeskin moccasins, brown-red faces, black, black unreadable eyes. She heard jingles, wails, trilling, drumming, drumming, drumming.

She saw school children in a classroom

without a teacher, Willow alone on a swing in a dirty nightgown, Ada's gnarly hands making hundreds of sandwiches, Hawk with a roller of white paint slashing across his mural on the library wall, three eagle feathers in a half circle atop his head of straight black hair.

Gail bolted upright in bed. "I'm not leaving tomorrow," she whispered. "I'm not leaving tomorrow," she said louder, and made it an affirmation.

Catherine rolled over. "Did you say something?" she asked sleepily.

"I'm not leaving tomorrow."

Catherine sat up and turned on the light. She stared at her friend. "Gail? Are you talking in your sleep?"

"I'm not sleeping."

"I thought I heard you say . . ."

"I'm not leaving tomorrow." Gail swung her legs out of the bed on Catherine's side. "I've made up my mind. I'm not going to spend two weeks driving back across country in that bus."

Catherine plumped her pillow against the headboard. "Well, I admit I'm not looking forward to that ordeal either, but how else are you going to get back home?"

"I'll fly."

"On what? A buzzard? In case you haven't

noticed, trucks barely get in and out of here."

"There's an airport in Billings. I'll just get someone to drive me there. I want to stay, Cath. I need time to get close to Willow. No matter what Hawk says, I can do something good for her, I can help her toward a better life."

"What did Hawk say? And when, for that matter?"

"Today." Gail stood up and walked to the window. She pulled the lace curtain aside and looked out over the moonlit back range. "At the school. He told me I wouldn't be good for Willow, that I'd only be one more person who walked out of her life. It's only because I'm white that he's saying that. I want to prove to him that I'm different."

Catherine leaned on her elbow. "I don't know Hawk, but Gail . . . my dear friend, he's right. In the end, you *will* walk out of Willow's life. Better sooner than later."

Gail looked over her shoulder at Catherine. "You didn't hear him. He cut me to the bone. I could see the contempt he held for me. Since he doesn't know me at all, what else could I think? It has to be because I'm white."

"All right, maybe. Unless he's speaking

from a personal standpoint."

"What do you mean?" Gail turned full face to Catherine, interested.

"Maybe somebody he cared about walked out on him, and he's not over it."

Gail thought a moment, then shook her head. "Too romantic. That would mean he let someone get close to him. And I can't believe he ever lets that happen. If I didn't know better I'd think he was just a granite escapee from Mount Rushmore."

"It was just a thought. But he has a point. You're going to be leaving here, leaving Willow, whether it's tomorrow or in a week or in two weeks. How much good can you do in that time?"

"Give her something to think about, something to remember." Gail's voice escalated.

"Where is this coming from? Gail, what she'll remember is that somebody was nice to her and then abandoned her."

Gail stood stockstill for several long moments, her breath locked in her lungs. She let it out in a long, sigh, her hands clenching and unclenching. "You're right," she whispered, and dropped down on the bed. "But I'm not leaving tomorrow, regardless."

Catherine came around and sat down next to her on the bed. "Would you like me to stay with you?"

Gail looked up at her dearest friend. "I couldn't ask that. You have to get on with your vacation, and then start preparing to go back to school. I know you have a lot of work to do before the semester begins."

"So do you. You do remember Riverview, don't you?"

Gail gave a wan smile. "Yes, I remember."

"So . . . do you want me to stay with you?"

"What would you think about that?"

"I think if I stayed it would save me from two excruciating weeks on that covered wagon they call a luxury motor coach."

Gail hugged her. "You are some friend."

Catherine hugged back. "Mutual, I'm sure."

Lone Hawk Kincaid pushed his Palomino, Morning Star, hard along the ground, speeding through post-dawn light shining on buckthorn, and prickly pear, and blue sage. His insides churned. His restless nature had taken hold of him again, and he couldn't ride hard enough or fast enough to settle it inside him. And he could never ride far enough away from himself.

He knew he looked like a wild savage, but he didn't care. He rode in deerskin fringed leggings and moccasins, naked from the waist up. He loved the feel of the wind whipping over his skin, revelled in it whistling through his hair past his ears. It was wild, free, that wind. Nothing had ever tamed it the way his ancestors had been tamed. Nothing had caged it the way he felt caged inside.

He'd been riding since before sunup, and he knew better than anyone that Star needed rest, water, food, and a rubdown. Hell, he needed the same things himself, but the most he could get were food and water. He felt hungover, sick the way he used to in the old days, though he hadn't touched a drop of alcohol. He'd been sober for five years, two months, and three days, and he was damned if he'd ever go through that again.

He crossed the dirt road and slowed Star. The horse sensed they were headed back now, and he shook his head and blew through his nose. Hawk spotted a roiling cloud of dust from below the hill. It was the tour bus pulling away from the house, leaving at last. His jaw flexed.

He hated this whole scenario that Trey had cooked up. They could have held the ranch together without having to play this tourist game. That is, if Trey would have done his share of the work. He always thought he was too good to get his hands soiled. Hawk's upper lip curled in a sneer. *Let the dirty Indians do it, right Trey?*

Hawk tried not to watch the dust cloud as it came nearer on the road. It galled him to think these tourists would pay up to a thousand dollars each for two weeks on a "real working ranch." Grudgingly he had to admit Trey's scheme was bringing in significant money. And of course, Trey got to play with that scatter-brained guide, Helene, every summer.

The bus came into view just as Star started down the hill toward the corral. The horse picked up his gait, sensing his rewards at the end of this difficult ride. Hawk patted his neck, speaking low in Cheyenne, apologizing for pushing him so hard.

He saw the top of the bus pass, saw arms waving out of windows, and he knew they were waving at him. He didn't give them so much as a look. He wouldn't give Gail Bricker the idea that he even acknowledged she was leaving. He was glad he'd never have to see her again. He knew her kind, all right. She came on strong as if she was different, as if she was honest. But he knew otherwise.

He'd never have to see her again, and he was damned glad of that. The rest of his evening at the pow wow had been ruined from the moment he saw her under the arbor. He could still see those porcupine quill earrings swinging below her cropped hair. She probably thought of them as souvenirs of her vacation out West. Never mind that Beaulah Yellow Bird had spent hours in the dim light of her trailer house, her arthritic fingers working the delicate beads into the jewelry art she prided herself in making. And never mind that those sales were part of what helped to feed her five fatherless children. That's not the kind of thing women like Gail Bricker would think about.

At the corral Hawk dismounted, and carefully took the bit from Star's mouth and slid the bridle off over his ears. He went into the barn for an old towel to wipe the horse down, and picked up a currycomb and brush. When he came out, Star wasn't there. Thinking the horse had gone around to the other side for the water trough and hay manger, Hawk went back through the barn toward the other door. He stopped in his tracks in the opening.

Star was at the watering trough, but he wasn't drinking. He seemed to be thoroughly enjoying having his ears massaged by a blonde woman straddling the top fence rail.

Hawk's skin burned in the late morning

sun. Or was it from something else? Anger? He wasn't certain. But one thing was certain — Gail Bricker hadn't been on the departing tour bus.

Chapter Nine

"Good morning," Gail greeted Hawk softly, and hoped he couldn't sense the strange apprehension she was feeling now that she was in his presence.

Hawk came up behind Star, approaching his left side, and started rubbing him down with the towel. *What the hell is she still doing here?*

"I decided to stay an extra week." She felt the need to explain her presence, even though he hadn't asked. He hadn't even acknowledged that she was there. "Catherine, too. We're going to lend a hand at Medicine Wheel School."

Hawk didn't respond, just kept rubbing Star, showing what she guessed was indifference.

"We've made an arrangement with Trey, and your mother gave her permission also. We would have asked for yours, too," she rushed on, "but you weren't around, and the bus had to leave."

Hawk didn't respond. He curried Star so hard, the horse moved away from the comb and brush. *Trey! So she's his next conquest!*

"Just thought you'd like to know," she said. When Hawk didn't even look up, Gail stepped down from the fence and started to walk away.

"How much help do you think you'll be?" His gruff voice startled her, and she stopped and turned back to him. She took a deep breath.

"A lot, as a matter of fact. We know how to set up classrooms and such."

"Maybe in a fancy eastern white school you do."

Gail flared. "Classrooms are for children. Period. Regardless of the distinction you seem to want to make."

"Who are you really doing it for? Those *Indian* children? Or yourself? Do you need your guilt diluted?" Throwing the brush over by the fence, he combed Star harder, leaning down to get the horse's underbelly.

Gail stomped back to the fence, climbed over the middle rail and stepped inside the corral. The man infuriated her. She picked up the brush and worked on Star's right side. She bent and worked the dirt and stick-tight weeds from Star's fetlock, then moved up his leg.

Satisfied with that, she then moved toward his right underbelly.

Hawk peered down at the top of Gail's head as she leaned into her work. Her hair was shining in the morning light like a cloud. His hand on the currycomb moved slower. *What would it feel like to touch that hair?* He worked on Star again, faster than ever.

Gail started brushing out Star's mane on his right side, and Hawk began on the left. Star danced between them as the brushing grew even more intense. Gail tried in her mind to add up everything she'd been thinking thus far, but nothing seemed despicable enough to spit out at him right now. She felt defeated by his bitterness, his implication that she felt guilty. Who did he think he was?

Gail didn't make eye contact with Hawk. She put down the brush and walked away.

Hawk gathered everything up and walked back to the barn.

"Did you see what I think I just saw?" Catherine asked from her fence perch at the far end of the corral.

"Yep," Jerrie answered, leaning both arms over the top rail, her boots resting on the bot-

233

tom one. "Two people who think they're different as night and day, but are very much alike and very attracted to each other and can't admit it."

"Yep," Catherine concurred, looking over at Jerrie. "Happens all the time."

"Yep, it sure does," Jerrie said softly, looking straight into Catherine's eyes.

Catherine abruptly drew her gaze back to Gail's retreating back.

"Know what else I see?" Jerrie lifted her voice.

"What?" Catherine looked back to her face.

Jerrie paused a long moment. Then she broke into a wide grin. "One fine Palomino who's relieved he hadn't been curried right down to his ribcage!"

Star whickered and kicked up his back hooves.

Gail's remaining week in Montana sped by in a blur of travel between the ranch and the school. She and Catherine scrubbed, vacuumed, washed windows, and painted a bathroom beside the Two Bulls brothers. With Carol they rearranged her classroom and decorated the bulletin boards with letters spelling welcome cut from leftover construction paper. Gail had time now to develop an idea she'd had about seats for the library tables; she got Skeeter and Wills to slice thick circles from the logs they were cutting down by the bar-be-que pavilion, and mount them on sturdy shortened cedar posts to make child-height tripod stools. She sanded the tops smooth, and put a coat of polyurethane on them. That project made her proud.

And she took photographs of the continuing progress of the work right up to the first day of school when the children arrived. As they trooped into the library she was there with her camera and spent the day photographing them. She charmed John, one of the young wranglers, into taking her to Billings where she found a fast photo developing shop and waited while they processed her film. Then she went back to the school at the end of the day and made a collage of the school's transformation which she mounted on an old corkboard she'd covered with a discarded white pillow case from Ada. On another she made a display of the photographs of the children, and painted the words, "Have a Happy Year" on the bottom.

And she took long looks at Hawk's mural

each day of the week, and each day she saw something new in it—an expression on a face, a tree with intricately drawn leaves, a buffalo running past a buffalo-hide teepee. And she marvelled at his talent and the sensitivity in his work.

On the second day of school, Gail rode in with Ada while Catherine stayed behind. She ambled down the hall past Joe Bearpath's classroom, filled now with extra desks, ladders, paint cans, and a partially constructed bookcase the Two Bulls were working on. It was a little before lunch break, and the halls were empty. But she could feel the energy in them, the excitement, the newness they imparted, at least to her. She smiled, and wondered if she had ever felt this way when the semesters started at Riverview. She couldn't remember. It would be another two weeks before the fall semester would begin there. The usual problems would reappear during the first week, and she'd spend the rest of the semester doing what she'd always done. And counting the days until retirement. Her smile faded.

She peeked into Ang's class. Ang was a dynamic teacher, that was obvious. She immersed herself in her subject, then gave it to the children as if she'd just discovered it and wanted them to be as excited about it as she was. Her voice and her body language were infectious. Gail felt excited watching her and watching some of the faces in rapt attention.

And then she saw her. In a far corner, behind the tallest boy in the room, closed in to make herself as inconspicuous as possible, Willow sat watching Ang. Clutched in her two hands was the ragged magazine rolled into a cylinder. She rested her little chin on the top of it.

As if she sensed Gail's presence, Willow's gaze shifted from the teacher to the doorway. Gail smiled, then moved away so as not to distract her.

What had happened to bring that little girl back to school? The answer didn't matter. All that mattered was that she was there. Gail wished she could have put Willow's picture in the library with the rest of the children who'd arrived on the first day, but she didn't have one. She stepped back into the doorway, lifted her camera, focused on Willow and snapped the photo. She'd mail a copy to Ang to pin up in the picture gallery.

Ang invited Gail and Catherine for dinner at

her house the night before they were to leave. Carol was there, too. After polishing off the biggest bowl of spaghetti marinara Gail had ever remembered seeing in her life, and consuming at least one glass too many of Chianti, the four women sat on the floor in Ang's tiny living room, lounging against the couch and a couple of chairs. They all had wine except Catherine, who'd drunk water at dinner, and had made herself tea.

"Well, I never thought I'd be saying this," Ang said in her direct way, "but you two aren't bad for a couple of eastern gals."

Carol put one finger up in the air. "I think what she means is," she drawled, more from the wine than a western inflection, "you did a hell of a job at the school, and . . . and, oh yes, you were fun. She's . . . we're gonna miss you."

"We have had a great time out here," Catherine said. "I never thought when I got on that so-called luxury coach, heading out on a glorious vacation away from the daily grind of school, that I'd end up scrubbing floors in another school!" They all laughed. "I always did like surprises, and this one was one of the best."

"These kids are lucky they have teachers like

you and the others," Gail said. "You seem to care so very much about them."

"Too much, sometimes," Carol said.

Ang patted her shoulder. "Some of us are more soft-hearted than others. If you get too involved you either get your heart broken or your ass in a sling."

Gail watched as Carol lowered her eyes. "Which part of it got you?" she asked her.

Carol drained her glass. "A little of both. I left for a couple of years. Went home, got a job as a waitress, made a lot more money than I ever did here. But, I came back, thanks, or no thanks, to Ang."

"Hey, we were shorthanded, and you were the best one for the job. Didn't take a genius to figure that out."

"You're shorthanded now," Gail pointed out. "Got any other teachers out there you can coerce to come back here?"

"Fresh out. Unless you know some." Ang gave her a level stare.

"Ha!" Catherine put in. "The differences in the lives of teachers at Riverview and Medicine Wheel are solar systems apart. None of our teachers would survive out here, let alone even consider teaching here for a moment. Don't get me wrong, they're very good teachers. But, this is a whole different atmosphere. I'd love to compare notes with the president of your teachers' association sometime."

"What teachers' association?" Ang came back. "We all just plug away, teachers, principals, everybody. Once in awhile we get a clunk of a principal or somebody like that, but if we hang on long enough they'll be gone, and somebody good will come in."

"Yeah," Carol said. "It sounds bleak, but teaching at Medicine Wheel has enormous rewards. At least for me. I was so pleased to see Willow there today. I'm going to do my darnedest to keep her there this year."

"How will you do that?" Gail asked.

"I don't know. It seems as if I've tried everything. But I'll think of something else."

"She sure seemed taken with you today," Ang said. "Couldn't keep her eyes off you when you were standing in the doorway."

"You knew I was there?" When Ang nodded, Gail grinned. "You're really good! A teacher who doesn't miss anything. I'm impressed!"

"You should be," Ang said, mocking smug pride. "I'm also good enough to know that Willow probably would have no trouble staying in school if you were there every day."

Gail stared at her. Ang's words sounded more like a suggestion than an idea.

"Too bad you don't live closer," Ang said, not skipping a beat in the conversation. Ang went to the kitchen for another bottle of wine. She came back with it and a fresh supply of breadsticks from supper.

Gail nibbled on a breadstick, her thoughts drifting. "Yes, isn't it? But then, there are no guarantees I could have any influence on Willow. From what I understand, she comes and goes with the wind, whenever she wants to. And no one seems to want to hold her, teach her some self-discipline. People she seems to care for, like Ada, and Jerrie, and . . ."

"Hawk," Carol said. "She lets him get close to her. But only recently, as far as I can tell. For a long time she wouldn't let any man near her. She seemed frightened of them."

"Why doesn't he take more interest in her, then?" Gail said. "It's possible he could be a big influence over her."

Ang shrugged. "Maybe he's too busy. Or maybe he doesn't care enough. Who knows?"

"I think he does care," Gail said.

"Then you know more than anybody else." Carol grabbed a breadstick and passed the plate to Catherine. "He's only come over to the

241

school in the last year. I think he does it to help his mother. Anyway, even in that year nobody got to know him. He seems guarded."

"Probably got a deep, dark secret," Ang said. She made her words sound mysterious for fun, and poured more wine.

"All men like to think they have deep, dark secrets," Carol scoffed. "Or at least they like to make women think they do, but we can see right through that every time. Is that what eastern men do, too?"

"Ask someone who's had a date in the last five years!" Gail said.

"I don't know anyone like that!" Catherine laughed.

"You mean, even in the East women still don't have dates on a Saturday night?" Ang's jaw dropped.

"Got that right," Gail said.

"And I thought it was only because we live out here in the wide open spaces where there's lots of wide open space between one man to the next!"

Gail leaned back against the couch and sipped her wine. "Do you . . . ever go out with . . . Indian men?"

"Sometimes," Carol said. "I dated a Cheyenne man for almost a year."

"Was it all right?" Catherine asked, her voice sincerely interested. "I mean, did your family object? Or did his family object?"

"Mine didn't know, and his didn't care. Some of these men have reputations for, well, to be blunt, screwing around. Divorce is as prevalent here as it is off the reservation."

"What did you do on your dates?" Gail asked. "Go out to dinner? Or to the movies or something?"

Carol laughed. "Mostly he came over to my apartment and I'd cook dinner and we'd watch television, when the set was working which it wasn't most of the time."

"What ended your relationship?" Catherine asked. "Don't tell me if that was too personal a question," she added quickly.

Carol made a face as if to say it was inconsequential. "Like I said, these men like to screw around."

"So," Ang said, sitting cross-legged on the threadbare rug, "haven't we painted a lovely picture for you? Doesn't this make you want to come work with us? You, too, can have a hard job with low pay, live in a cracker box of an apartment that's beastly hot in the summer, and freezing cold in the winter, and once in a while date a man who will screw around on

243

you, to put it as delicately as my friend, here, and know that at the end of the day you may not have gotten through enough to touch even one of these kids where it will give them some reason to care about themselves? How's that for a pitch?" She leaned over and flipped an imaginary cigar, a la Groucho Marx. "And if you fall for that one, I've got some prime commercial swampland I'll sell you!"

Catherine dissolved in laughter, with Gail chuckling along with her. "And here we thought trying to solve the problems of a squabbling faculty over salary and time off, keeping boys and girls with raging hormones from conducting sex marathons in the dorms, and losing sleep over stolen leather bags that cost more than two weeks' groceries were the best of good times! Right, Cath?"

"Right. Come on, friend, I'm taking you home." She stood up and pulled Gail to her feet. "Ladies," she said, turning to Ang and Carol, "I wish we did live closer. We had a wonderful time being with you, and next time we're on vacation, feel free to call us if you have any floors to scrub or toilets to clean. We're feeling exceptionally brilliant in that area."

Carol and Ang walked them to the door.

"I don't know what to say," Gail started. "I've enjoyed being with you both, and being at the school. I hope we'll see each other again one day. And I . . ." Tears started to form in her eyes.

"She hopes we'll all keep in touch," Catherine said. "And we both mean that."

The four women hugged and said their goodbyes, and Catherine and Gail got into the pickup truck.

"Nobody ever means it when they say that," Gail said.

Gail's head pounded with each downward step on the stairway she took, dragging her suitcase behind. Packing at seven in the morning had been an exercise in unproductivity, resulting in Catherine's making a sweep of the bureau drawers coming up with Gail's silk tee shirt, the nightgown Willow had worn, and several pieces of underwear. Gail would not admit to being hungover. What was a couple of social glasses of wine among friends? It couldn't have been that. It must be she was just tired from working so hard at the school, and from trail rides, and bus rides, and truck rides.

And emotional roller coaster rides.

She didn't admit the last to Catherine. It was enough her best friend believed all the first.

At the foot of the stairs Gail saw Ada going into the study. With some effort she set down her suitcase and followed her.

"Ada?"

The older woman turned slowly. "You're leaving now." Her voice was low, even.

"Yes. Thank you for everything."

"It's all part of your tour package," Ada replied, and the words sounded alien to Gail's ears.

Gail smiled. "I suppose so. The lodgings, the food, the trail rides, all of that. But . . . I received so much more than I signed up for."

Ada walked slowly toward Gail, her shoulders bent forward more than Gail had realized. She lifted her gray head and scrutinized Gail's eyes for a long time. At last she spoke, so far down to a whisper Gail had to turn her head to catch the words.

"I believe you. You are honest. Your deeds came from the heart."

Gail didn't understand the words at first. Then she seemed to grasp the meaning. "You mean at the school." Ada nodded. Gail closed her eyes and let out a long breath. "Yes, they did. I wish so much I could . . ."

Ada took Gail's hands in her rough ones. "Wishes are dreams set to words from the heart."

Was it only that she felt so groggy this morning that Ada seemed to be speaking in riddles? Gail gave her a questioning look.

"The heart knows and understands more than the mind."

Catherine passed the study door. She stopped and poked her head around. "I'll be down by the corral. Just come find me or send somebody when you're ready. No hurry. We have plenty of time."

Gail waved acknowledgment to her. "I have something I'd like to leave for Willow. Would you give it to her?"

Ada scrutinized Gail's face so completely, she felt uneasy. "Best you give the gift to her."

"But I won't see her. She's in school, and I'm glad of it. I'd rather you gave it to her. Would you, please?"

"Best you do." Ada started past her toward the study door. "We will meet again." She kept walking without looking over her bent shoulder.

Gail's eyes filled. "Yes, we will, Ada. I will

plan my vacation for next year and come out here. I hope that will be . . . all right." Her voice drifted away as Ada disappeared down the hallway.

Gail stepped out into the hallway, her eyes tracing the path Ada had just walked. *She's seventy-five years old. Is it possible she won't be here next year?*

Suddenly she was feeling more tired than she had when she first arose this morning. What was happening to her? It couldn't be just the effects of the chianti. She picked up her suitcase and went out onto the porch. Where had Catherine said she was going? Down to the corral. Gail guessed it was to say goodbye to Jerrie.

She decided she'd walk down to the corral and say goodbye to Jerrie, too, and to Wills and Skeeter if they were around. She set down her suitcase and started down the steps.

Willow was crouching in shrubs at the end of the porch and stepped out.

"Oh my God," Gail breathed, a hand over her heart. "You startled me, Willow."

The little girl said nothing. She stood in her ragged green cotton pants and a long white tee shirt. Her ever-present magazine was rolled tightly in one little fist. In the other was something Gail couldn't quite see. It was a hand-crafted item of some sort with feathers and twine suspended from a circular frame.

"You're going away," Willow said.

The halting words struck Gail hard. This was the first Willow had truly spoken directly to her, and her voice held an almost accusing tone.

"Yes, I am. But I'll be back." She started toward the child, but Willow backed up making Gail stop.

"No you won't."

"I will, I promise."

"When?"

"Next year. I told Ada I would come back." Gail tried to get nearer the child, but again she stepped back. Gail stopped.

"I don't believe . . . you." Willow's eyes filled, but she bit her lower lip until the emotion subsided.

Gail's chest felt constricted. She'd wished to have a conversation with Willow, and now she was having it and it was excruciating. She longed to embrace the child, hold her close, feel her little heart beating against her own, tell her she meant it, she'd be back.

"A year isn't so long. And you'll be busy with school and you won't even know I'm gone. Next thing you know I'll be back." She tried to keep her voice light, keep the mood light. If she didn't, she knew there would be a flood of tears. Her own. The thought scared the hell out of her.

"I'm not going to school." Willow rested her teeth on the rolled magazine pages and gave Gail a look from those big eyes that held a challenge in it.

"I'm very sad to hear that, Willow. The teachers like you and want you to stay. And you could have good times with the other children."

"No I won't."

Gail backed up and sat down on the porch steps.

"I'll show you that you can believe me when I tell you I'll be back." She opened her bag and took out her hair brush. "I want you to take care of this for me until I come back, all right? Would you have the time to do that for me?"

Willow gazed longingly at the hair brush. Gail saw her small lips twitch at the corners as she suppressed a smile. Gail held the brush out to her, but Willow would not come near.

"Oh, and you know what?" She rummaged in a carry-on bag until she came up with a black nylon zippered fanny pack. It was long with a waist belt. "I have this case for you to carry your things in." She unzipped it, felt inside for anything that may have been left in it, and showed the interior to Willow. "See? You can put your magazine in here, and the hair brush, and anything else you might like to take to school with you. Here's a pen with red ink you can use. Be sure to ask the teacher if it's all right with her if you use red ink." She leaned down conspiratorially. "Some teachers don't like red ink, but I have a feeling your teacher is special and your work in red ink will make her happy."

Willow inched closer, never taking her eyes off Gail's face. Gail kept talking. "Looks like I'll have to adjust the waist belt for you, but I think I can make it snug enough to fit. If you have a problem with it, when I come back I'll fix it for you. Would you like to try it on to see if it fits?"

Willow came near, nodding her head. Her face was gritty, and had some streaks down it. Gail knew she'd been crying at some time, but was tough enough not to show it now. Her hair was matted again, and Gail knew the lice must still be there.

Gail looped the fanny pack belt around Willow's waist twice, and tightened it through its keeper with the open pack in front. She took the hairbrush and settled it inside.

"There. Is that too heavy?" When Willow shook her head, Gail went further. "Would you like me to put your magazine inside, too?" Willow clutched it closer. "Or maybe you'd like to do that."

Willow slowly released her clutch on the magazine and held it out to Gail. Gail took it carefully, placed it inside the pack, then ran the zipper closed.

"There," she said through a tight throat, "I think it all fits quite nicely, don't you?"

Willow held out the handmade item.

"Oh, what is this?" Gail took it and looked it over. She didn't quite know how to hold it.

Willow took it from her hands. "It's a dream catcher." Her voice was a low monotone. She turned it in Gail's hands so that the woven and knotted twine was horizontal, and the three brown feathers hung straight down and moved slightly like dry leaves in a breeze. "Only good dreams," she said in her low, quiet voice.

"It's beautiful," Gail said, touching the twine, the feathers, and letting her fingers trace the circle of the light willow wood frame.

"Shall I put it in this bag with hairbrush and your magazine?"

Willow's eyes grew bigger and wetter. She fought against the tears with her mighty little strength, but they started down her cheeks in a steady stream. She turned and began to run. Gail dropped the dream catcher and caught Willow, sweeping her slight body into her arms and hanging on for dear life.

Willow stiffened, but Gail wouldn't let her go. She rubbed her back, pressed her cheek to the matted hair, and whispered soothingly to her, rocking her back and forth. At last the little body relaxed slightly. Her hands grasped the sleeves of Gail's white shirt.

"I will come back to you, Willow, I promise. And I'll write letters to you while I'm away, and you can write to me, too. And I'll send you some pictures."

Willow pushed with a new burst of strength out of Gail's arms.

"No!" she screamed, and ran away.

"Willow, no! Come back!" Gail started after her, but she disappeared into one of her hiding places. "Damn!" Gail muttered. "Damn it to hell!"

This was a vacation like no one had ever had, she was positive about that. She'd have to go home to rest up from it. Bring on the wealthy and privileged Chelsea Gotters of the world, and all their fathers. They'd be much easier to handle than one little Cheyenne girl named Willow.

Chapter Ten

Gail could think of one thing only: she wanted to find Catherine and get out of this place fast.

She headed toward the corral, barely seeing where she was walking through the tears in her eyes. Catherine wasn't visible outside so she went inside the barn.

"Catherine? Jerrie?" No one seemed to be there.

Morning Star was in his stall, and he did a little dance with his hind feet at the sound of her voice.

"Hello, Star," she said walking up to the half door. She reached up and scratched one golden ear. "Don't worry, I'm not going to brush you to death today. I apologize for going a little overboard before. You forgive me, don't you?" Star snorted. "Thanks. I'm glad I can count on somebody around here."

"Leaving?"

The low voice behind her startled Gail and

she spun around to see Hawk coiling a rope at the end of the barn. She could feel that dark searing gaze from where she stood. There was no mistaking it; he was glad she was leaving. And she couldn't get away from him fast enough. He frustrated her, he disturbed her. He was unreachable.

And when he walked toward her, as he was doing right now, he also made her aware in her basic animal instincts how potently virile and blatantly earthy he was.

"Something tells me it isn't soon enough to suit you, Mr. Kincaid," she said with a haughty tone she couldn't remember ever using with anyone else, ever. She didn't feel that way inside at all.

"That sounds uncivilized." He was right in front of her now. "Let me just say my goodbye will not be as long as it appears your earlier ones have been." He dropped his eyes to her chest.

She looked down and saw what he meant. The remnants of Willow's dirty hands remained printed against the sleeves of her white shirt, and gritty spots from her tear-wet cheeks left stains above the pocket. The sight caused a knot of emotion to swell inside her again. She swallowed it back.

"Mr. Kincaid . . . Hawk, for some reason

you have a totally wrong, unfounded opinion of me. I've learned I can't change your mind. I don't know why I should feel this way, but I'm sorry about that. I came to say goodbye to Jerrie. If you see her, would you tell her, please, that I'm leaving?" She turned away from him.

He laughed lightly. "America's Adventure Tour taking you to some even more exotic place than an Indian reservation in Montana?"

She stopped and fisted her hands. "I wish we could part on friendly, or *civilized,* if you prefer, terms. But it appears we can not." She turned back. "I'm sorry you don't like tourists, and I'm sorry I had to be one. After a while I forgot I was one. I thought I could make a difference with some people here, just because I felt it in my heart. You, somehow, had preconceived notions that I had some ulterior motives, some guilt to assuage. I haven't. I don't know what else I can say to make you believe me."

He relaxed his squared shoulders. "Why should it be important that I believe you?" He dropped his head toward her.

"I wish I knew. I'm certain it's just a figure of speech, since you seem to be unfeeling, unemotional."

He squared his shoulders again. "That's how

we Indians are, aren't we? Stoic, inscrutable, guarded."

She searched his eyes for something. What? A flicker of humor? But he might have been carved from the very mountain rock upon which they stood. Hard, unyielding rock, thirsty, yet too unwilling to receive the gift of water.

"Oh, please," she scoffed, "not the noble savage routine."

"Why not?" he scoffed back. "Isn't that the way we're portrayed in *your* history books?"

"Oh, for heaven's sake. Even most of *us* know enough these days to understand how distorted those things are. Things are changing, slowly I admit, but they are changing. Give us . . . me . . . a little credit, will you? I admit prejudices abound in this world, but we're not all like the stereotype you enjoy portraying!"

"Neither are we. And you can't change things fast enough to rectify the injustices done to three generations of my people."

"No, I can't," she whispered, "no one can. And you can't make life the way it was three generations ago. No one can do that. Neither side can ever pay back. We can only start where we are, and get on with it. There isn't world or time enough."

He gave her a hard stare for an uncomfortable moment, then turned his back on her and started down the center of the barn. She watched him take a few steps.

She turned her back on him and started down the barn the other way. Where in hell was Catherine?

"Gail!"

It was the first time he'd ever used her name. The impact of it was so great, she stopped abruptly. She turned to see him coming toward her with long purposeful strides, straw flaying out from under his feet with the impact of his boots. She was so startled by his voice and the picture he made coming toward her, she couldn't move.

He stopped in front of her, silent.

She waited.

Tension crackled between them like dry lightning in a summer sky.

Hawk's hands raised and he caught her by both upper arms, his fingers digging into her flesh through her shirt sleeves. His dark eyes bored into hers.

He dropped one hand and turned her roughly toward the door.

"Come with me." He headed for his pickup parked the other side of the corral.

"Where? I don't have enough time to go anywhere."

"You have time for this," he rasped, "and then you'll never have to make time for it again."

He pushed her into the pickup and slammed the door, then got in on the driver's side and started the engine. He threw the gears and the truck lurched forward along a tire-rutted two-path dirt road away from the barn and toward a craggy canyon.

Gail couldn't tell how far they'd traveled into the canyon. Speed wasn't a factor owing to the rocks and dips and winding nature of the vehicle path they were on. She hung onto the door handle and braced one hand against the dashboard and stared straight ahead. Every few minutes she stole a glance at Hawk's face, but she couldn't read his expression, unless it was one of determination.

The road narrowed and finally disappeared into grass. Hawk brought the truck to a lurching stop at the base of hill strewn with buckthorn clumps, prickly pear cacti, and stands of blue sage.

"Get out," he ordered.

"Why?"

He jumped out, slammed the door, came around and opened hers. He gave her less than a second to react before he grabbed her arm and pulled her out of her seat. She complied as fast as she could coordinate her feet and legs.

"Why are we here?" she asked, working to cover the trepidation she was beginning to feel.

"Don't talk now," he commanded.

He took her hand and pulled her along behind him. She had no choice but to follow him, stepping as carefully as she could over rocks and past cactus. Then a chilling thought gripped her.

"Shouldn't we be watching for rattlesnakes?" Her eyes darted like a mine sweeper back and forth over the path in front of her.

"Yes."

Gail knew that was all she would get out of Hawk right now. He kept walking, pulling her along behind him. At last he stopped on a ledge overlooking a narrow running creek edged by thick green shrubs and tall grasses.

Still gripping her hand in his, he shaded his eyes and peered along the rim of the canyon.

"There." He pointed high and to his right.

"What?" Gail squinted and looked beyond his tall body in the direction he pointed.

"See the two white rocks side by side? The rounded ones that look like a woman's breasts?"

Gail gave him a sidelong look to see if this was a trick of some kind, but she could see he was dead serious and intent upon her seeing whatever it was he saw. She tried harder, then spotted the two rocks. They did indeed look like large matronly breasts.

She shaded her eyes as he was doing. "Yes, okay, I do see them."

"Look between them, and a little up on the right one. See the ledge in it?"

"Yes."

"Now wait just a moment. Don't take your eyes from that ledge. And don't speak."

Gail couldn't fathom for one moment what he wanted her to see. Then it happened. Something, she realized now, that he knew would happen.

A golden eagle with a rabbit in its claws came from behind them in the brilliant blue sky, and landed on the ledge. Now she could see why. There was a nest on that ledge.

"I see it!" she said in awe.

"No you don't, not yet. Keep watching, and don't say anything."

Gail's breathing seemed to stop and she kept her gaze pinned to the nest. The eagle seemed to be doing something with the rabbit, and then she saw bits of fur flying away. Then she saw what Hawk wanted her to see. A baby eagle lifted its head above the nest, beak wide open. The mother eagle fed her offspring the prey she'd hunted and caught.

Then another golden eagle, larger than the first, landed near the ledge. Another young beak appeared above the nest rim, open, demanding. The large eagle dropped something into the wide open beak, waited a moment. Then the pair flew off together.

Gail's heart swelled in her chest. "Oh," she breathed audibly. "How wonderful to see such a thing."

"Yes," he said, and there was an element of awe in his voice, something she hadn't heard from him before. "Freedom, ancient freedom. They still have it, but there are fewer of them now. They are alone in the wilderness of civilization."

Gail looked up at him, at the chiseled bronze face burnished by the brilliant sun. The mask he usually wore, the mask of defense to block anyone from reading his real feelings, was gone. His jaw relaxed, his shoulders released. He watched the eagles, envious of their freedom, of their simple mission in life — to live, to care for their own, to send their offspring flying on their own life, and then to die and return to the earth from which they'd sprung.

"I understand," she said, and she meant it. When he didn't challenge her, for once, she

263

felt he might believe her for the first time.

Suddenly a rustle of leaves below the ledge on which they stood startled her. She stepped back. Three coyotes gave furtive looks over their shoulders as they slunk quickly away through the thick brush. Now Gail's heart pounded with the surprise of it. She and Hawk stood side by side and watched as the three creatures wound their way up along the craggy canyon wall to walk along the rim. They stopped, looked down for a moment, then disappeared behind some rocks.

"Oh," Gail let out a relieved sigh. "Why didn't they attack us? Didn't they know we were here?"

"They knew. They knew from the moment the truck left the road. We disturbed their nap in the cool green shade."

"Why didn't they come after us?" Gail realized Hawk still held onto her hand in a firm grip. She didn't try to wrench it free.

He turned and looked down at her. "Man is the enemy of the coyote, the only enemy. The coyote can master any animal or bird, large or small on this earth. He can even threaten the freedom of the eagles. But he is powerless against treacherous man."

Gail was caught in the all-encompassing breadth of Hawk's dark gaze. She read it now.

White society is the only enemy of red society.
That was what he was trying to tell her. That
warred inside him in a way she knew now she'd
never feel. He had a foot in both worlds, and
he could not find sure footing in either of
them. He saw things she didn't. His native
senses knew things hers didn't, born of the
generations of his ancestors.

For a long moment they gazed deeply into
one another's eyes, not saying anything, yet
communicating an understanding they'd never
reached before. Finally Gail slipped her hand
from his grasp and slid both arms up over his
and grasped the back of his shoulders. Then
she pulled him close to her, resting her head
against his chest. *I'm so sorry, I'm so sorry,*
echoed in her head, but she didn't say the
words. They would be meaningless.

She felt him stiffen, then slowly his hands
came up to rest on her waist. Then his arms
came around her in a hard circle, pressing
against her ribs. His head dropped down
against hers. His body emanated heat along
hers and through his arms and hands and the
side of his face. His breathing came from a
deep well. They stood thus for a time, communicating on the deepest level. No words were
needed. No words could have been adequate to
express the feeling that passed between them.

The faint drone of a jet plane from high above the earth intruded into the natural aura around the two people locked in an embrace on a rocky ledge in a canyon. The two stepped back from each other, shyly, tentatively, but not embarrassed. Gail looked up toward the plane.

Out of the blue sky, hazed over from the intensifying heat of the sun, she watched a hawk swoop on its quest after a little bird. Her heart leapt into her throat as she hoped the bird would manage to escape. It did escape several times, but then its sharp turns grew slower. *It's tiring,* she thought. A moment later the hawk snatched the little bird from its freedom.

"It's gone forever," she whispered.

"No," Hawk said, watching his namesake soar away with its prize. "The spirit never dies. The little bird will live again and again, always. And so will the hawk. They are born and reborn to live together again."

"But does it always have to be that way? The same hunters, the same hunted?"

"Until new lessons are learned."

"Then," Gail said, and almost didn't recognize her own voice, "humans might do the very same thing as eagles, and coyotes . . . and hawks."

Hawk hadn't taken his eyes from her since

they'd broken their embrace. "But they must have the courage, the tenacity of the eagle, the coyote, and the hawk, or they will never understand their own uniqueness."

He leaned over her. She lifted her face to him, and closed her eyes. Their lips met and clung, but neither of them began an embrace. They stood with sun and air around them and between them. Only the lips through which their words had passed sealed what had transpired between them.

Hawk drew away first. "You must go," he said, his eyes, as always, searing directly into hers.

She waited a moment, a moment of frenzied wonder and conflict. Then, "Yes, I must go."

On the plane, Gail and Catherine were silent. Now and then they made eye contact, but quickly turned away. There was so much to be said, yet if the words came, tears would come with them.

Gail reached into her carry-on bag for some throat lozenges. Her throat ached from holding back emotion. Her hand closed over something foreign. She pulled it out. It was the dream catcher Willow had made. Gail felt the work in it, touched the intricate weaving of the twine, cupped the feathers and felt their silkiness. She traced her finger around the circle of the willow branch the frame was constructed of. It was so much like the child, Willow, bending to the will of other hands, becoming what it had not been born to.

Or was it? Willow trees grew everywhere, served several functions outside their basic purpose of shade and soil preservation. They became the framework for sweat lodges, holding in the cleansing warmth, the spiritual reawakening of those who chose to sit among them. They became dream catchers to preserve only the kindest of dreams, to filter only the most beneficial of spirits to bless and keep the holder safe.

The child Willow seemed buffeted by the winds of outside forces, bending as a weeping willow tree might in a wild storm. Yet she caught and held her own dreams, seemed alive with a spirituality that only the most discerning eye could catch a glimpse of. The revelation struck Gail. *She* had that discerning eye, she believed that now. Willow had shown her, Ada had opened her heart, and Hawk had helped her see what she was looking at for the first time in her life.

Now what was she going to do with it? Save it for retirement?

* * *

In her office at the Riverview School the first week of the semester, Gail listened while Chelsea Gotter's father harangued her over the telephone. Life was just the way it had been before summer vacation.

Her Gloria Vanderbilt jeans were at the cleaners, so she took to wearing her cowboy-cut Wranglers she had purchased in Montana. They'd broken down to a comfortable softness that she enjoyed wearing around her apartment. Her boots were at the cobblers being re-heeled, but she'd taken to wearing beaded moccasins she'd purchased from Ada's friend the day she left the ranch. Her nails were beautiful once again, although her manicurist admonished her for letting them get in such terrible condition. Gail hadn't wanted to tell her that's what happens when one scrubs school floors, paints school walls, and curries ranch horses.

Her hair, once her crowning glory and pride, had been the worst to deal with. Getting it back into the crisp style she'd worn had been horrendous. It was as if her hair, too, had loved the freedom of fresh air, and once it had broken out of the constraints of styling gels and hair sprays, it rebelled against going back to confinement. But it had surrendered, just as Gail had.

Catherine came into the office and sat down opposite Gail's desk. Gail mimed that Mr. Gotter had been going on and on for what seemed like hours.

"I understand completely, Mr. Gotter, that you think Chelsea is a problem. You've asked what I thought, and I'll tell you. Chelsea is pleading for attention."

Gail clamped her eyes shut while Mr. Gotter told her the people at school shouldn't indulge her then, shouldn't keep giving in to her every whim. He certainly didn't have the time to keep calling the school and straightening out the latest insignificant problems with his daughter's classmates. If the school couldn't end the thievery of Chelsea's things, including her homework and exam papers, he would simply take legal action.

"Mr. Gotter, that's not the kind of attention Chelsea needs. In fact, that would be the worst thing you could do. Chelsea's things aren't really gone. She knows where they are, knows no one stole them."

The man came back with more. Who was she, *just* a guidance counsellor, to tell him what he shouldn't do? Why would Chelsea tell him she'd been robbed if she hadn't been?

That was ludicrous to suggest. If things needed to be shaken up at that school, then he was, by God, just the one to do the shaking. He'd check his calendar and see just when he could fit in an attorney to begin the case.

"Chelsea needs *your* attention, Mr. Gotter, her father's attention. She needs to feel loved. She's a child, she needs . . ."

Gotter interrupted her with a declaration of how he'd given Chelsea everything she'd ever asked for from the minute she could talk. He was a busy man, with important work to do. Her mother should be the one providing her with all that female pap, but he didn't even know where she was. Nor did he care. Chelsea was smart and she knew he was busy. But make no mistake, he would fit in a lawsuit against Riverview School if things didn't get better. And another thing . . .

"I don't want to hear another thing from you, Mr. Gotter," Gail interrupted him. "You're neglecting your child. She lies, she cheats, she steals her own things and reports them so that we'll call you. She's smart, you're right about that. But she purposely doesn't do her homework, and deliberately fails her exams. What she wants is for you to get yourself over here *personally,* or take her out of here to live with you, not send some lawyer to act on behalf of an arrogant absentee father!"

Gotter jumped in with a threat about Gail's job.

"Go ahead! Have me fired if that makes you feel better about what a rotten job you're doing as a parent. You're damned lucky to have a daughter. She's really a good person inside, but she's scared. There are wonderful children out in the world who don't have parents and need them desperately, need them to love and protect them before something horrible happens to them. I warn you, you'd better protect the offspring in your nest or the predators out there will take care of them for you."

Gotter sputtered that her superiors would hear from him regarding her rude manners. He'd cut off his contributions from this moment on if she didn't apologize.

"Your money would go for much better use if you brought your daughter into your home and acted as a parent to her. She's lost, she's alone, and she's vulnerable. You and whatever number wife you're on right now had better wake up, or you'll have a runaway on your hands, or worse!"

Gail slammed down the phone.

"You never should have said any of that," Catherine said evenly. "But you know that."

"Yes, I know it," Gail said wearily, leaning

back and rubbing her eyes. "I'm just so sick of the Gotters of the world. Their lives revolve around money and personal pursuits of happiness. Never mind the people and the planet they're responsible for."

"What's really bothering you?"

"Nothing. Everything." Gail stood up and looked out over the Hudson River. "I don't know. I feel caged for some reason. And that's ridiculous. I'm freer than most of the people I know. I have no strings attached, no husband, no children, no family. Free as a bird . . ."

"You may be freer than you think, if Gotter gets his way. He'll probably make trouble." Catherine stood up and walked to stand next to her friend in front of the big windows.

"Let him. Maybe it will shake this lethargy I seem to be in." Gail rubbed her temples.

"It will be hard to get another job."

Catherine was always honest, if depressing at times, Gail thought. "Well, I have been thinking about early retirement." She tried a half-hearted laugh.

"There goes that fabulous retirement package you expected." Catherine tried a return laugh that fell flat. "Ever since Montana you've not been yourself."

Gail shook her head. "I figured that out within twenty-four hours. That vacation did things to me. Think it was in the air?"

"Something sure was," Catherine said, and her voice held an edge. "I've had a devil of a time getting back into the routine of things this semester."

"Maybe that's the problem. It's routine."

"Well, that's what vacations are supposed to be for, aren't they? They're supposed to break the routine, shake things up, make one come back to work refreshed with renewed vigor for the job, right?"

"That's what the profoundly intelligent know-it-all 'they' always say." Gail turned and grasped the back of her chair with both hands. "I don't know, Cath. I don't feel refreshed, renewed. I feel no vigor for this job. What happened?"

Catherine sighed. "I wish I knew. The pop psychologists would love this, I know, but I'm not even sure who I am anymore."

"Well, you look great, you know. There's something different about you."

"Sheila says I'm not perfect anymore."

"Hurray for you!"

Catherine bowed. "I'll accept that graciously from one imperfect soul to another."

"Let's make a pact, all right?" Gail turned back to her friend. "We don't go on any more vacations unless they're to some tacky resort where we can look at the other tourists and be glad we're not them. Okay?"

Catherine laughed and turned around. "You got it! I don't ever want to feel this . . . I don't know, groundless I guess, ever again."

A knock sounded on the door, and it opened to Sheila. "I've got a great idea!" she shouted, stepping into the room.

"Quick! Get my shield and trusty sword!" Gail said to Catherine.

"What?" Sheila asked, looking bewildered. That was soon replaced by an enthusiastic rush of words. "There's a Christmas trip being organized by America's Adventure Tours to Mexico! Interested? Bethanne is all set to go. Can't wait to meet those dark and hot-blooded Spanish men. Olé! What do you say? Spicy food and spicy fun for the holidays?"

"And Montezuma's revenge!" Gail groaned. "No thanks, Sheila. I'm still recuperating from our summer 'vacation.' Count me out of this one."

"Goes for me, too," Catherine said. "I'm weary."

"Prudie's almost as bad. I suspect Skeeter had a lot to do with that. Have you seen her this week? She's taken to wearing red, and letting her hair fall loose. The kids don't know what to do. They haven't got anything to buzz about behind her back now!"

"Well, at least something has changed around here," Gail said.

"What did you two do when you stayed that extra week on the ranch?" Sheila eyed them, shifting her suspicious gaze from one to the other and back again.

"Nothing," said Catherine, quickly.

"Nothing much," said Gail.

"Well, then, 'nothing' sure has got the both of you in a funk. You haven't been the same since school started. Us, we're raring to go!"

Gail watched Sheila's face. She looked raring to go indeed. Did nothing earth-shattering happen to her while she was in Montana? She knew there'd been a bit of romance between Sheila and Wills. And it was true about Prudie. She walked around on cloud nine every day. Gail hoped it wouldn't disintegrate under her feet for a long while. Every woman could use that flush of love that gave a buoyancy to her physical life, and a giddiness to her mind.

"I'm begging off this time," Gail told Sheila.

"Me, too," Catherine added. "But you two have fun and tell us all about it afterward."

"You can count on that!" Sheila said, and in her excitement nearly bounced out of the room.

"A vacation in Mexico for Christmas," Catherine muttered.

"Bah, humbug," Gail muttered back.

The phone rang. Gail answered and then was quiet for a long time. Someone was giving her an earful of something, Catherine figured. She didn't figure what Gail would say when the speaker was quiet.

"Don't worry about that. You won't have to. Just tell the board I will submit my resignation this afternoon." She hung up.

"Gail?" Catherine said, tentatively. "Did what I think just happened, just happen?"

Gail turned around, her shoulders slumped. "If you think I just quit this job, then you're right."

"Oh my God." Catherine leaned against the desk. "You didn't."

"I did."

"Gotter made trouble, didn't he?"

"He did."

"Well, call back. You can tell the board you will issue a public apology and do everything you can to smooth things over with him. They'll ignore your resignation."

Gail turned and looked out the window, watching the Hudson rushing by below. Her life had been rushing right along with it, going nowhere but into a sedate life of retirement.

She'd suddenly built an instant dam, and the rushing came to a halt.

Why was it she didn't feel depressed? Didn't feel scared? God, she was now out of a job, out of a salary, and her retirement benefits were back to the pittance stage.

"I will call them back," Gail said slowly. "Only I don't want them to ignore my resignation." She turned around and faced Catherine. Her face broke into a grin. "In fact, I want them to believe me whole-heartedly! I'll call them back and tell them my resignation is effective immediately, now, today, this minute!"

"Be reasonable, my friend. Think. You have to make a living. You have a mortgage on your condo apartment. It's nice to eat now and then. And there's the little matter of things like health insurance, and gas for the car. What are you going to do for work? Who will hire a fifty-two-year-old woman for anything? Who would be desperate enough to take a chance on you? Think."

"I am thinking."

"Then why don't you look worried?"

"Because I'm not."

"Gail . . . what are you planning?"

Chapter Eleven

Gail made the move to Montana in late September.

She'd called the principal, James Black Feather, at the Medicine Wheel School and asked if they could use her, and received a resounding yes. There would be some routine paperwork to obtain accreditation from the state for her, but he assured her that could be handled quickly. She could have Joe Bearpath's room, and would teach high school English. They'd find ways of fitting an orientation into her schedule bit by bit. He knew of a small apartment available in a house not far from the apartment building occupied by Carol and Ang, about four miles from the school. He'd put a hold on it pending her arrival.

Gail packed her car with as many of her belongings as she thought she'd need, and arranged for it to go out by train in time for it to be in Montana to coincide with her arrival by plane. She sublet her apartment to Prudie, who was thrilled at the prospect of having her own place for the first time in her life. She bid a tearful goodbye to her friends who said they'd come out next summer with America's Adventure Tours. And she spent a particularly emotional evening with Catherine as they reminisced about the friendship that had sustained them for so much of their lives. Promises were extracted, each from the other, to visit before a year had passed.

The length of time between her departure from Montana in August and her return in September had been only four weeks, yet seemed as long as some of the worst semesters she'd spent at Riverview School.

On the plane she thought about the drastic turn her life was about to take, and wondered if, now that she'd more than passed the half century mark she was being courageous or foolhardy. As she toted the elements of this move, she began to believe the result indicated foolhardiness in spades. Her income would be slashed in half; her precious retirement package that she'd worked so hard to construct would adjust back to its less than adequate support; she'd be living in half the space she'd occupied before with none of the amenities like air conditioning and a view of the river; no more leisurely trips to the manicurist for silk wraps, no more afternoons in the beauty salon for herb facials and having her hair colored and trimmed while an attendant served tea and small cakes; no more stopping off at a trendy little cafe for capuccino with friends.

On the drive in to Lodgepole after she'd picked up her car, she constantly shifted her eyes from side to side as she drove along. It was as if she was seeing Montana for the first time. She saw the trailer homes of the Indians, convenience stores with parking areas jammed with pickup trucks and twenty-year-old cars with broken windshields and dented fenders; she saw fenced rangeland, dirt devils gusting in the distance against the stark blue sky, and cattle grazing. She saw buffalo, muledeer, the flirtatious antelope; she noticed the windmills again, some still turning, some idle for what looked like decades, and now and then a working oil well.

And she felt an overwhelming sense she was driving into a familiar, yet foreign land.

Near the town of Lodgepole a locomotive came into view, and she pulled over to the side of the road and stopped to watch it pass, its tenders brimming with coal. She was fascinated by this, a train so long she stopped counting the cars when she reached a hundred twenty, excluding the three engines pulling it. Somehow she liked the forlorn sound of the whistle, three shorts and one long, as if it were calling and hoping for another train to meet it. She waited then, and simply watched for the red caboose to come into sight as she had when she was child. Finally the caboose arrived. It was purple.

A purple caboose! Windmills! This Montana was quite a place, and she was about to become part of it! At least she hoped she would. As she watched the caboose disappear around a bend, she felt a rush of anxiety for the first time since she'd made her decision to move to Montana. What if she couldn't stand it, the teaching, the living? What if she'd just set herself up to take the biggest test of her life, and she failed it miserably? What if she just didn't have what it took to survive out here? What if she made big mistakes?

Gail started the car again and pulled out onto the highway. She had to ignore these naggings in her head. They reminded her too much of all that she'd heard and felt and sustained as a very young child before she'd moved in with Uncle John and Aunt Addie and they took on the enormous job of teaching her self-confidence and self-worth. She wondered now if anyone ever got over mental, emotional, and physical abuse that began at the same time as their human memory. Was she able enough to help these Indian children here who suffered from similar abuses? Could she really make any difference? If she couldn't, then she'd just have to leave and go back to New York and try to find work. Why was she doing this, anyway? For whom?

Hawk's challenging eyes came back to her, and his biting words stung her mind. He'd predicted she'd leave, he'd told her she could only cause more harm than good. He'd accused her of wanting to help only out of being driven by her own guilt. She knew that wasn't true. It wasn't guilt that drove her to abandon a comfortable life and pick up a harsh one. And it wasn't pity. And she was certainly no evangelical do-gooder trying to chalk up points for the entrance exam into heaven.

And Willow. Gail knew the child hadn't believed she'd come back. It gave her a certain amount of pleasure knowing she was proving something to Willow. For some reason she had to show that little girl she could be trusted, she could be relied upon. She'd felt a thread of connection with Willow before she'd left in August. Granted it was thin as a spider web, but she felt it was just as strong as one.

The only answer she knew in her head was that she wanted to do this, wanted to be here, wanted to help these children. Did there have to be an answer to *why?*

Gail pulled into the Medicine Wheel School yard and parked the car. She got out and stretched her back and legs and arms. Then she took in a full breath of the dry air before she went inside, hoping that new courage would fill all the places where she was now feeling scared to death. The cafeteria was full and buzzing with voices.

"Gail!" Ang was the first to spot her, and she came running over. "God, is it good to see you! Welcome back!" She threw her arms around Gail and gave her a hearty hug.

"It's good to be here," Gail said honestly, when she caught her breath and extracted herself from Ang's hug. She scanned the dark heads of the children sitting at the long cafeteria tables.

"She's not here," Ang told her. "Hasn't been here since you left."

"I was afraid of that," Gail said. "I hoped she might want to stay in school this time. Did you put up the picture of her that I sent with all the others?"

"Of course."

"Did she see it?"

Ang looked down, then back up to Gail's face. "We can't be sure. It was gone the next morning. It's possible she came in here at night and took it down."

"That would be something she'd do," Gail agreed. She saw Carol coming toward her, arms outstretched.

"Gail, am I glad to see you!" Carol gave her a hug, too. "Have you had lunch?"

"Not yet. I didn't want to waste time stopping."

"Well, come on. This is a lunch you'll learn to become very accustomed to."

Carol and Ang took Gail through the line and watched while two Indian women dished up lunch on a plastic tray for her. Chicken nuggets and french fries taken directly from their frozen state and popped into an oven, canned peach halves, white dinner rolls, and apple juice. Gail gave her two new friends a wry grin.

"Don't worry," Ang said, "we'll make up for it with pasta at my place very often."

"I can feel my clothes fitting tighter already!" Gail whispered.

James Black Feather introduced himself and welcomed her to Medicine Wheel School. He was young for a principal, Gail thought, maybe mid-thirties, and she was a full head taller than he. A full-blood Cheyenne, James dressed professionally in a navy blue suit and white shirt with a black bolo tie, and kept his hair cropped close. Gail liked him immediately. They made an appointment for early the next morning for her to fill out the necessary forms, and begin orientation.

She had the afternoon to make her new

classroom ready for students. Thanks to the Two Bulls brothers it had been cleaned out of everything stored there, and the carpet and windows had been cleaned, and the desks and chairs set out. Paper and other supplies were at a premium, she could see that. Maybe she could get Sheila and Bethanne to send her a care package to help out. She was just sitting down at her new desk at the end of the day getting the feeling of being in a classroom again, when Carol and Ang came by.

"We're here to take you to your new palatial home," Ang said. "Unfortunately neither one of us can help you settle in tonight. We both have meetings. But this weekend we can do more."

"That's all right. I'm not sure how much I'll accomplish tonight anyway. I'm exhausted." Gail gathered up her bag and followed them out of the school.

In her new living quarters, Gail sat down on the edge of the bed. Ang and Carol had spent an hour with her before their meetings making up the bed, putting away a few things in the kitchen, and sharing frozen dinners with her. It was a good thing they had. There was no microwave oven in the place, and she hadn't the foggiest notion how to start the old gas oven.

Now, giving in to her exhaustion, Gail sat

motionless. She was too tired to read, there was no television set, and she'd neglected to bring a radio with her. The two rooms and kitchenette were a jumble of boxes of hers and donated things from Carol and Ang. There wasn't a dishwasher or a washer and dryer, and her new landlady, a plump woman in her early sixties whose wrinkled dark face looked as if she'd been sucking lemons since she was old enough to eat solid food, didn't offer the use of her own if she had them. In the bedroom there was one shabby lamp made from a wooden spool topped with a paper shade so yellowed with age that hardly any light shone through it. As she sat there, the light suddenly went out.

She sighed, pushed herself off the bed and went over to snap the switch. The light did not come on. She peered out into the living room and noticed that the light she'd had on in there was still burning. The bulb must be out in the bedroom lamp. She scuffed to the kitchen in her chenille slippers and searched the cabinets and drawers for a spare bulb. None was existent. She scuffed back to the bedroom, sat down on the edge of the bed again, then dropped her head and sobbed out all the anxiety and tension she'd felt since the last time she was in Montana.

And she cried in her loneliness. Even with

the familiar faces of two of the teachers at Medicine Wheel, she still felt lonely, desolate, cut off from personal civilization. It was as if everything she'd ever known, every shred of support she'd been shown from the friends she'd made, the career she'd chosen, and the place in which she'd lived, had somehow vanished into thin air and she was floating in a disconnected state.

At the end of her first full day of teaching school, Gail stood by one of the windows of her classroom, and watched children playing on a set of rickety swings suspended over a sandy patch in the dry lawn. It had been a frustrating day, and Gail didn't know if it was because of her own apprehension at being here and teaching again, or if it was the students.

They didn't seem to care one way or the other that she was there to teach them. That wasn't fair. There were a couple of teenagers who seemed bright and eager to learn. So many of the others either stared at her with blank looks on their faces, or didn't pay attention at all. They fidgeted with papers or other books, or couldn't keep their hands off the student in the next seat. And she couldn't seem to control what was happening. It was worse in the afternoon than in the morning. Some of them appeared sleepy and bored, and others seemed to be possessed by nervous energy that kept them squirming in their seats or whispering among each other.

Now at the swings, they ran and chased each other and giggled and screeched just like the younger kids at Riverview. Only these kids weren't wearing designer jeans and polo shirts or had perfect haircuts. They rolled in the sand, roughly pushed each other off the swings, and generally scrapped over who had use of the only swing that was sturdy enough for the bigger kids to use.

And once again, Willow was not among them.

Time to do something she'd been wanting to do since the moment she touched down in Montana. It was the same thing she'd been dreading to do—go out to the Triple or Nothing Ranch and see the Kincaids. Maybe they'd know something about Willow, she told herself. Maybe they knew where she was. She wanted very much to see Ada again, and Jerrie, of course. She was carrying greetings from Catherine to them as well. It would be fun to see Skeeter and Wills again, too, and the other wranglers. Even Trey. She wondered if Morning Star remembered her, and if he'd let her brush him ever again.

As she went over everyone at the ranch, she finally let herself think about Hawk. At least think about him now that she was back. She'd thought about him every afternoon when she left her office at Riverview and started for her apartment. She thought about him during the evening. And she thought about him at night when she was in bed. She thought about their last day together in the canyon at the end of her vacation, remembered his words, remembered their kiss.

Did he know she was back? How could he? Would he believe that she was back to stay? How could he, when she couldn't answer that question herself? Would he want to see her? Only he knew the answer to that, and she wouldn't even try to second guess him.

The hallway was empty as she closed and locked the door to her classroom. She hadn't been to the library since she'd been back. It's not that she couldn't have gone during a break between classes, but she hadn't for some reason. Maybe she was concerned about her feelings once she got there, memories of fixing up the room, memories of Hawk painting his mural and measuring her with his inscrutable black eyes.

She didn't have to ask why she felt that way. She knew. And she'd been denying it. Maybe if she admitted nothing to herself, the intensity of what had happened inside her would subside.

She reached the library and stood in the doorway. It was still bright as a new penny, but now there was a little dullness to the shine from use. She was glad of that. The tripod stools were stored neatly under the spool tables which had recent crayon marks on them. There were more books on the shelves, and Gail recognized some that had come from Prudie's library at Riverview. She smiled, feeling the connection to old friends in a new place

And there was Hawk's mural. She went over to it. More figures had been added, and some buildings. And she could smell fresh paint. She looked it over carefully, mentally noting what she'd seen in it before, and what was new. She inclined her head in one area. There was a square gray building with the word "school" painted on the front. And on the front step was a woman waving her arm overhead. She must be a teacher, Gail thought. Upon closer look, she noticed that the teacher had short blonde hair. She stared at it. Did that mean . . . ?

He knows!

"It is good you have returned," a female voice said low and even from behind her.

Gail snapped out of her concentration on Hawk's mural, and turned around quickly. Ada Kincaid stood at the doorway.

"Ada! I'm so glad to see you."

Gail rushed toward her, arms outstretched. Ada did not reach hers out to embrace Gail. Instead she held out both hands, palms up. Gail grasped them both in hers and stopped herself from hugging the older woman. Ada searched Gail's eyes without saying anything.

"I'm glad to be back here, Ada. Have you seen Willow?"

Ada nodded. "Twice."

"They tell me she hasn't been back at school since . . ."

Ada nodded again. "Maybe now. Who knows?"

"I guess no one truly knows Willow at all." Gail squared her shoulders and released Ada's hands. "How is . . . everyone else at the ranch? Jerrie? And Skeeter and Wills?"

"Everyone is well. They were glad to hear you'd come back."

"They know?"

"Yes. Come to supper tonight. The last tour group of the season is there now. What they call senior citizens." Ada's eyes twinkled now, and she seemed to relax.

Gail picked up on it, and smiled. "Of which you are not one."

"They think I am." Ada turned to the door.

"But we know better, don't we?" Gail followed her.

"Yes."

"Thanks. I'd like to have supper with you, all of you."

In the back parking lot, Ada motioned for Gail to ride with her in the pickup.

"I'd better drive and follow you, Ada. I don't want anyone to have to drive me all the way back here tonight."

"And I won't want you to drive all the way back here alone tonight. You will please ride with me. We will leave your car at your apartment." Ada summoned Gail to lead her to her apartment, and Gail obeyed.

The bar-be-que pavilion was indeed filled with a group of senior citizens when Gail arrived, and a spirited bunch they were. Dressed in various expressions of western wear, they laughed and slapped each other on the backs. Even the oldest of old ladies was walking around with a can of light beer in her hand. Gail smiled at their fun, glad to feel that Montana high spirit around her, glad to be a part of it.

She was glad she'd taken a moment at her apartment to change from her school teacher sensible dark skirt and white blouse into the cowboy cut Wranglers she'd purchased on vacation. They felt good, like being close to an old friend. She'd put on a black tee shirt that was printed with green, red, and white teepees across the front, and the word *Montana* printed in white on the vertical next to them. That was a last minute souvenir she'd picked up at the airport. She supposed it had been a tacky thing to do at the time, but in the rush of leaving she'd been overcome with the sense that she simply had to have that tee shirt.

She moved her way deeper into the crowd. Smoke went up in great clouds from the pits where long-hinged grates with double rows of beef steaks between them were being turned by two young lean wranglers wearing thick gloves. The aroma carried in the air made Gail's stomach growl reminding her that she was as hungry as those baby eagles she and Hawk had watched together on her last day here. Funny that incident should come back to her right now.

And then she saw him at the far end of the pavilion. Hawk was standing in the same spot she'd seen him the first bar-be-que supper she'd attended on her vacation.

That was the night they'd met Jerrie as well. Gail started to walk slowly into the pavilion, allowing herself to think she would make her way to him without looking as if she was on a direct run.

"Gail! There you are!" Jerrie rushed through the crowd and grabbed her into a warm hug. She leaned back and looked into her face. "Mother said you came out with her. You look great! How've you been?"

"Thanks! You, too! Crazy, that's how I've been. What am I doing here?" Gail let her eyes go heavenward.

"The right thing, pard!" Jerrie released her. "I think it's great, and I hear the school is very pleased you've joined them."

"God, I hope so. I've never done anything this rash before."

Jerrie laughed and pushed her arm through Gail's and drew her to a table near the back. "I suppose you've seen my brother, the tall, dark, silent one?"

"I've seen him. I was just going to talk to him when you came over." Gail turned her head to the direction in which Hawk had been standing. He wasn't there.

"I think you surprised him."

"By coming back, you mean?"

"Uh-huh. You may have noticed he doesn't trust people, especially those with light skin and blue eyes."

"Starting with Trey, no doubt."

"You really are pretty astute about these things, aren't you?" Jerrie said, tilting her head toward Gail.

"Not very. Hawk *tries* to be inscrutable."

"He's not trying to, he just is."

"But sometimes I can read him clearly."

"That's because he wants you to . . . sometimes. It's the Cheyenne way. They don't like to be at the front of the parade."

Gail gave Jerrie a long look.

"Cheyenne people are quiet for the most part. They keep things to themselves," Jerrie tried to explain. "This is from the ancient teachings that the Cheyenne are the special people, the chosen people, they who stand above all men and animals."

Nothing was what it seemed to be with Hawk, ever, Gail sensed it, and his sister had just underscored it.

"How're your friends?" Jerrie asked, changing the subject.

"They all seem to be doing just fine without me," Gail told her. She explained how the school had hired a new guidance counsellor almost the moment she resigned, a man, of course, and how Sheila was planning next year's vacation, and how Prudie and Bethanne were planning on coming back here, and how Catherine had been upset when she'd left, but she hadn't heard from her since she arrived.

"She misses you," Jerrie said evenly. She turned her head and seemed to let her words trail out and beyond the range to the ridge of mountains growing purple in the twilight.

"I miss her," Gail replied, watching Jerrie.

"Do you think she'll come for a visit someday?" Jerrie kept her eyes on the mountains.

"I think so. But not on that luxury motor coach again! We both hated that."

"Neither of you are right for that sort of thing." Jerrie's voice seemed as far away as her thoughts appeared to be. She stood up quickly. "You hold the table and I'll get us some supper."

"You don't have to do that. I can get it. There's a long line, anyway."

"Don't worry about the line. I know the cook. I'll sneak around in back and no one will ever know." She winked and walked away.

Gail watched her move through the crowd, lithe as a sleek cat, trim in her soft jeans and rose shirt. Her hair, worn loose and long down her back tonight, shone blue-black in the light of the swinging lanterns strung through the pavilion. Jerrie looked the same, still strikingly attractive, still causing heads to turn. But she didn't seem the same upbeat person she'd been when they first met her in August. Gail wondered what had happened to make her change so.

She was glad to see Jerrie again. Something about her made Gail feel as if they'd been friends for much longer than the short reality of their acquaintance. If she'd let her, Gail would try to get Jerrie to talk about what was bothering her. She felt they were friends, and friends talked to each other, shared their feelings, everything, just the way she and Catherine had always done. She missed Catherine terribly. Her eyes stung with tears when she thought of her friend.

Someone tapped her on the shoulder, and she jumped.

"Skeeter! Oh, I'm so glad to see you!" She jumped up and the wiry man scraped his Stetson off his head and gave her a bear hug.

"Wal, ma'am you're sure a sight for these jaded eyes! This has been a week full of wrinkled prunes and flat behinds. It's good to see a soft round woman again!" Skeeter's eyes glinted with mischief.

Gail surveyed the crowd of people, and noticed that some of the women were pretty attractive, even if they were of a certain age. "I see some rather nice looking women here, Skeeter. Certainly you can find at least one to flirt with."

"It's this light. Don't look too close," Skeeter warned. "There's more rotten apples in this barrel than there are winterkeepers!"

Gail laughed heartily for the first time in a long time. "You sure know how to turn a phrase, Skeeter. I've missed you.

"And you've been missed," Skeeter assured her. "By everybody."

Gail thought about asking him to identify "everybody," but she didn't.

"How's everybody back in your neck of the woods?" Skeeter asked.

"Just fine. Incidentally, Prudie sends her best." If Gail didn't think Skeeter was a jaded old cowboy, she'd have thought she saw a blush color his already ruddy complexion.

"How is Miss Prudence?" he asked her, twisting his hat around in his hands.

"She's fine. Best she's ever been."

"Not taken sick since she went back east?"

"Not a bit. She's put on a few healthy pounds, and she's even taking riding lessons and learning about horses. Bought a whole new wardrobe, too. Not a gray item in it! Funny, how one vacation can change a person. How do you suppose that happened?" Gail peered into his eyes, purposely injecting an insinuation into her voice.

"Wal, now, I wouldn't know about things like that, ma'am," Skeeter choked, still twisting his hat. "Do you think she'll come back here next year?"

"Wild horses couldn't keep her away, Skeeter!"

"Bless my tailfeathers," Skeeter said, smiling big as the all outdoors.

"Hers, too, I'll bet," Gail said, reaching over and planting a kiss on his cheek.

Skeeter reddened again, plopped his hat on his head, pulled his torso up out of his jeans and adjusted his belt, and strutted out of the pavilion like a rooster on a hen hunt.

"Gail?" Jerrie called from behind her. "I've brought someone to see you."

Gail turned around to see Willow standing next to Jerrie, one of her little fingers looped through Jerrie's belt.

"Willow," Gail breathed. She walked over and dropped down on her haunches in front of the child. "I'm so glad to see you again."

Willow gave her a shy smile that lit up her dirt stained face. She was wearing her green cotton pants, but they were dirtier than ever and wet with a recent stain.

"Willow's going to have supper with us. Wills is bringing more food to our table."

Jerrie set down a pitcher of lemonade and three glasses on the table, then lifted Willow up so she could drop her legs over the bench. Gail sat down next to the little girl. She noticed Willow was wearing the nylon pack she'd fitted to her little waist the day she'd left. Her curiosity made her want to look inside to see if the magazine and hairbrush were still there, but she didn't.

Wills arrived with a tray of filled plates and set them down on the table. He greeted Gail with a hearty handshake and asked about Sheila. Gail assured him she'd be coming back next summer. What had happened on this vacation that had missed touching her and Catherine? Everyone in her group seemed to have someone from this ranch smitten with her, except for the two of them. Maybe they'd been Skeeter's description of the rotten apples in the bottom of the barrel of winterkeepers.

Gail turned her attention toward Willow. "I promised you I'd come back, Willow, and I did," she whispered to her. "Now, are you going to come back to school again?"

Willow drank a whole glass of lemonade without coming up for air. Then she picked up a baked potato, pulled it apart and dropped it quickly as the steam came out over her hands. She blew on it and picked it up again. All the while she seemed to ignore Gail.

"Please use your fork," Jerrie said, handing one to the child.

Willow took it dutifully and speared the potato. Someone had already cut the meat in small pieces so she could just pick them up and eat it from her hands. At Jerrie's admonishing look, she used the fork.

"Willow?" Gail pressed quietly. "Will you? For me?"

"Hawk told me to go," Willow said without looking up.

Gail sent a glance to Jerrie, then lowered her eyes to Willow again. "He did?" She couldn't keep the surprise out of her voice.

301

Willow nodded, and speared another chunk of baked potato. "He said I should go to school. I told him no. He said yes 'cuz you were back."

Jerrie raised her eyebrows in Gail's direction, an unspoken wonder in her eyes.

Gail swallowed her own wonder about Hawk's remarks. "Hawk's right, you should go to school. But not just because I'm there."

"I saw my picture." Willow sounded almost proud.

"You did?" Willow nodded to Gail with a brief glance. "I didn't see it there today. One of the teachers told me it disappeared."

Willow stopped chewing. She looked down at her nylon pack. So she had taken it.

"When you come in to school tomorrow, maybe some magic will have brought it back and put it up there again. At least I hope so. I want to see it there every day." Gail picked at her food. She was starving for it, but she seemed to be starving more for reaction from this dirty child sitting next to her on a picnic bench, swinging her legs under the table.

"If I come back, can I learn to take pictures like you?" Willow pointed to the lemonade pitcher. She wanted more to drink.

"If you'd like more lemonade, Willow," Jerrie said, "just ask for it." When Willow pointed again, Jerrie added, "And say please."

302

"Please," Willow said, giving in only that much. She pointed at the pitcher again.

"Yes," Gail interjected, "when you come back to school I'll teach you how to use a camera. But you have to promise you'll come to school every day and you'll keep coming until the end of the term."

Willow thought a long time. "Other kids want to take pictures, too."

"I'll teach them, too, if they stay. Will you promise me you'll come to school and you'll stay, Willow?" Gail pushed her carefully. She didn't know how far she could go with this.

Willow sent her a look that could only be described as disdainful.

"I promised you I'd come back. Well, here I am. I kept my promise to you. Will you promise me?"

Willow shrugged her little shoulders.

Gail started eating supper for real. "Well, if you won't promise me, then I guess I can't teach you how to take pictures."

Willow set down her fork, and dropped her hands in her lap. She kept her head lowered. Gail didn't say anything. Neither did Jerrie.

"Okay," came a thin voice.

"Pardon?" Gail said. "I thought I heard something. Did you, Jerrie?"

"No," Jerrie said, studiously eating her supper.

303

"Oh," Gail said. "I thought I did. Must have been the wind."

"Must be," Jerrie agreed.

They kept eating. Willow loosened her hands, reached up and tapped Gail's shoulder. Gail turned her face toward her.

"Do you want to tell me something, Willow?"

"Yes," came the faint answer.

"I'm listening very closely," Gail said. "Go ahead."

"Okay," came the timid voice.

"Okay, what?" Gail pressed.

"I'll come to school," Willow said quietly.

"What did you say?" Gail asked.

"I'll come to school," Willow said loudly, and some people from the next table looked up sharply.

"And you'll come every day?" Willow nodded to Gail. "And you'll stay the whole term?" Willow nodded again. "Then I will be very happy to teach you how to take pictures. We'll have a lot of fun doing it!"

Willow grinned, swung her legs faster, then picked up her fork and started eating with renewed enthusiasm. Gail started eating again, too. Her next step would be to find suitable living arrangements for the child. She knew she couldn't push that too soon. But the nights were growing cold, and maybe that would make her argument that more effective when the time came.

"I'm glad you've come back," Jerrie said to her between bites of corn on the cob.

"I think I am, too." Gail answered.

"Do you think any of your friends might ever have the same idea? I mean, the school can always use good people," Jerrie rushed on.

"I don't know that anyone is as impetuous as I've been over this move," Gail said. "I never was like this until now."

A shadow filled the lantern glow from over Gail's head.

"Maybe you've never known anything that would move you in quite the same way," a deep even voice came from behind her.

Gail's hand froze part way toward her mouth. She turned to look up over her shoulder.

Hawk towered above her, a look in his eyes that she could not have read if her life depended on the knowledge.

Chapter Twelve

In the fleeting moment their eyes met, Gail knew she was glad to see Hawk again. She'd wondered about that in the back of her mind, but hadn't wanted to think about it lest the energy it took distracted her from her momentous decision to move to Montana. The moment of eye contact was there and gone in less than a blink, yet in it she also recalled their kiss on her last day of vacation. She wondered if he'd thought about it as often as she had, puzzled about the kind of kiss it had been and how they hadn't touched anywhere but their lips, and speculated if he was as embarrassed as she'd felt, over and over, that it had happened.

As usual, there was no comprehending his thoughts by looking into his obsidian eyes. They were a black mirror that reflected not even the image he might hold of her. Taking in his whole dark image, long and sleek in black jeans, black shirt vertically striped with muted earthy clay and evergreen, and his jet hair loose and moving slightly in the whispering wind, she was reminded of a cat. A panther. Seen, possibly even touched with a courageous hand, yet separate, detached by choice from anything and anyone.

"Hello, Hawk," she managed to get out.

He nodded to her. "Hello, Willow," he said to the child. It wasn't that he ignored her greeting, Gail noticed. It seemed a deliberate act of moving his attention away from her.

"Hello," Willow said shyly.

Turning back toward Jerrie, Gail suddenly felt the strangest thought pass through her mind. *Did Hawk ever sit down?* The only time she remembered him sitting was astride Morning Star. She held back a giddy laugh, and knew now she was more embarrassed deep down about their kiss and the pleasure she felt at seeing him again than she could have imagined.

"Hey, big brother, come join us," Jerrie interjected, her voice light with a sincere invitation.

"I've had supper," Hawk responded.

"Then don't eat. Just be sociable."

Trey strutted up to the table then, his expanding girth straining a purple silk shirt over a wide snakeskin belt that circled perfectly

307

creased tan trousers. Gail noticed he seemed to be letting his blond hair grow. It was below his collar now, flaring out in uneven ends. His moustache was longer, dark, and streaked with gray hairs so light they looked white. He bore an unfortunate resemblance to George Armstrong Custer, and she wondered if he did that on purpose.

"Well, well, well," Trey's loud voice resounded around them.

Gail felt Willow shrink next to her.

"What's this? A welcome back party for the lovely Miss Bricker?" Trey held out his right hand to Gail. "Let me extend the warmest of the welcome wishes to you. I didn't realize how much you were impressed with the Triple or Nothing. But, to find you back here so soon is indeed a rare pleasure."

"Thank you," Gail said, and added an *I think* silently. She extended her right hand to shake his in welcome, and was taken aback by his capturing of it in both of his and raising the back of it to his lips.

"I'm certain we'll be seeing a great deal of each other." Trey gave her an obvious wink.

Gail slipped her hand out of his grip. "Actually I think we probably won't. I'm back here because of work, not an extended vacation."

Trey walked around behind her and placed both hands on her shoulders. She felt his fingers trailing up and down the back of her neck.

"Well," he said, leaning down close to her ear, "all work and no play will stunt your growth. And I've heard lack of a social life dulls your senses. I can assure you *all* of my senses are very sharp. Let me take you out and show you some of our more entertaining sights one evening soon."

Gail carefully maneuvered her shoulders and neck out from under Trey's grip. "I'm afraid I'll have to take my chances on the dulled senses," she said without looking at him. "I will have no time for a social life for a long while. My off hours from the school will be spent reading and learning about my students and about teaching methods different from what I've known. Thank you, Mr. Kincaid, for your offer, but I must decline."

It was then that she noticed Hawk was no longer standing near their table. She'd never know now if he would have been sociable, as Jerrie suggested, and sat down with them. But one thing she was certain of, there was no love lost between these two men of different heritages, forced to be brothers, each loathing the prospect. But there was one thing she began to suspect they had in common, and that was that neither one of them appeared to know much about love of any kind.

But who was Gail Bricker to judge that?

Gail spent hours devising lesson plans, ways to teach English grammar and literature to high school students at Medicine Wheel. She wanted to expose them to the classics, help them learn about life through writers who poetically and sensitively expressed life lessons throughout the ages. She was excited arranging her classroom, decorating the bulletin boards with cheerful pictures of high school students participating in social or sports activities.

She saw Ada twice early in the semester. On the first visit they talked about the ranch, and Ada told her everyone was very busy moving the herds, and fixing up the house and buildings for the winter. Trey had been away a lot, but Ada didn't elaborate on whether his trips were for business or pleasure.

"How's Jerrie?" Gail asked.

"She works too hard," Ada replied. "Up early, to bed late. She has the women's center open now. It's very busy. Too busy."

"Women's center?"

Ada nodded. "For abused women and girls. Women with problems. Gives them a safe place to go. She's working all by herself there. I help when I can. It's too much sometimes, but the need is great."

"I understand. I wish I had time to help.

Maybe later I can lend a hand," Gail told her, and she meant it. "And how is Hawk?" she asked with a small measure of reluctance. She felt apprehensive about asking for some reason, yet she wanted to know.

"Working all the time. Work is good, but not all the time." Ada didn't offer anything more and Gail didn't ask anything more about him. "It's good you're here," Ada told her. She'd made a thorough inspection of Gail's room, scrutinized the bulletin board displays, and looked at her lesson plans.

"Yes, I know it is," Gail had agreed that first time she'd spoken with Ada. "It's good for me, too. I hope I can give these kids as much as they will give to me just by being themselves."

But her students seemed to have everything else but learning on their minds. The last thing they cared about was why an adjective modified a noun, what good learning punctuation would do for them in life, and why they had to read boring things written by dead foreigners like Shakespeare and Austen.

When Gail explained how a solid high school education would serve them well in getting good jobs or entrance into college, she was met with more cutting laughter than she could bear after several days. She knew why they laughed. What jobs were they going to find on or off the reservation? Where would the money come from to pay for a college education? And as many of them had pointed out, the moment they could get out of school, they would be history to Medicine Wheel School.

The second time Ada came to the school, once again she inspected Gail's classroom. She pointed to the bulletin boards and suggested Gail take down the pictures of high school students having fun. They were, after all, pictures and posters she'd brought from Riverview, and the fun-loving students where white, suburban teen-agers. How could reservation Indians relate to them?

At the beginning of every day Gail peeked into Ang's room to see if Willow was there. Seeing the little girl at her back row desk every morning gave her a bright moment, a hopeful note on which to begin her day.

At the end of every day she felt drained and had to fight a feeling of uselessness. And at the end of every day she'd walk down to the library and just stand there for a few minutes, sensing the excitement she'd felt in being a part of creating the upbeat room. One by one her mounted photographs on the library bulletin board had been taken down. She hoped they'd been taken by the students to show their parents. She knew that was probably an eastern suburban school way of thinking, but maybe at least a small percentage of these students would do that. She wanted to feel heartened by the notion.

By the time the semester was half over, Gail knew a deep-to-the-bones exhaustion she never remembered feeling in her teaching career. She felt ineffective, and battled to keep away the nagging sense that she was making no tangible difference in any of her students' lives.

Her paychecks went for rent, utilities and, heat, and at last a telephone. Food, gas for her car, and the usual insurance had to be supported. She was forced to forgo her formerly crisp and stylish appearance for more subdued skirts, blouses, and sweaters. She was making do with what little was left of her cosmetics and elegant creams, and hadn't the glimmer of a clue how, or even if she was to replace them.

Once the snow started coming, Ada didn't visit the school anymore, and Gail had no more news about anyone at the ranch. Telephone calls between the ranch and her apartment were few, and usually restricted to conversations with Jerrie whenever she was in, which wasn't often. Jerrie spent more and more time away from her work at the ranch as the numbers increased at the women's center.

Social life for Gail became centered around a weak black and white television set she'd borrowed from Carol after her family sent her a color set for her birthday. Reception was terrible, only one channel was watchable, but Gail soon found herself addicted to game shows, justifying the time she spent watching them as doing something to keep her mind active.

Carol and Ang did their best to include her in what little activity they engaged in, and Gail had invited them over for supper on a few occasions. But they were all tired most of the time, and just wanted to settle inside during the evenings. Carol did charity work when she could, so her social life revolved around that at times. Ang had a new man in her life. Not a new one exactly. She knew him slightly, he drove the UPS truck and made deliveries to the school a couple of times a month. Turned out he was newly divorced. Ang invited him for a home-cooked meal as only Ang could prepare it, and he'd practically been a fixture at her place ever since. He was about it as far as single men went. That much was no different than back East.

At her usually empty post office box, Gail picked up a letter from Catherine the end of October. Unlike the cheerful one she received in September, full of news of Riverview and all the fun things Sheila and Bethanne were doing since they'd joined a support group called

Savvy Singles, this one carried a decidedly more somber tone. Chelsea Gotter's father had dumped his fourth wife, the Coach leather goods distributor, and taken off to Europe with a French woman who owned a chain of expensive lingerie boutiques.

Chelsea took the news badly, but shrugged it off in her typical smart woman-of-the-world attitude saying now she'd have the sexiest and most expensive underwear on the campus. She flirted with the boys outrageously, making overt promises she had no intention of keeping. She'd latched onto Catherine, hovering near her at school whenever she wasn't in class, and showing up evenings at Catherine's apartment unannounced. Catherine was troubled by a suspicion she was forming of Chelsea. The girl was hinting she might be more interested in a female love relationship than one with a boy. Catherine wished Gail were there for support because she didn't know how to counsel Chelsea with honesty and clarity.

Before she even took her coat off, Gail called Catherine that night after she got to her apartment. "Cath? Hi, I just got your letter. You all right?"

"Gail! God, I'm so glad you called. How are you?"

"I'll keep. Too cold up here to spoil any flesh and blood thing. Forget that. How are *you?* You sounded pretty down. Anything new with Chelsea?"

"Well, I think so, and it's not good. She just left here about a half-hour ago."

"What happened?" Gail settled onto the bench where the phone and its short cord sat.

"I . . . I don't think I'm mistaken about this, but she . . . God . . ."

"What?!" Gail sat up, a myriad of scenes racing through her head, not the least of which involved a suicide attempt.

Catherine sighed wearily into the phone. "She said she's been fantasizing about making love with women. And she cried like a baby and got down on her knees and begged me to help her."

"Oh, Cath." Gail's heart ached to help her friend. But she was a frozen tundra away and could only listen. "What, how did you handle it?"

"Not well, I suppose. I told her she didn't mean it, she was just projecting her disappointment with her father, and men or boys in general, into other feelings. She accused me of being a cold fish, of not knowing what feelings were anyway, love or sexual. Imagine a kid, all of sixteen now, saying a thing like that."

"Yeah."

"Maybe she's right."

"Oh, Cath, don't say that. She's wrong, and you know it."

Catherine was silent a long moment, and Gail knew she was swallowing her emotion, her deepest thoughts, as she'd always done. Catherine was the best at that in school. She left her problems, her hurts, if she allowed herself to have any, in the parking lot when she arrived at school. She never brought them inside or caused them to interfere with her teaching or with her relationship with her colleagues. Very professional, that was Catherine.

"Maybe," Catherine said finally. "What would you have done, Gail?"

Now it was Gail's turn to be silent. Then she finally answered the only answer she could think of. "The same thing."

"I wish you were here, friend," Catherine said.

"I wish you were *here,* friend," Gail said.

They hung up, and Gail knew their emotions, shaped by a long time friendship and mutual understanding, were heavy at the same time for each other.

Just before Thanksgiving when the cold wind and snow had whipped and frozen her too often and too long, when she'd shovelled her car out of daily morning drifts and risked

317

life and limb on treacherous roads to get to the school, Gail almost succumbed to a written invitation she'd received from Trey, between his many trips, to go out to dinner. Recognizing that as the lowest point of her existence, Gail distracted herself with adjusting every knob and button on the television set, and moving it to different locations around the apartment until she was able to receive faintly a second channel with as much snow in the picture as was falling outside.

Every night she wondered where Willow was sleeping, and every morning when she checked Ang's room as the winter closed in around them, she half expected to find the child missing. But she was always there, and always in the same clothes. Gail was determined she would buy Willow some clothes the minute she had a little extra money and could afford to drive to a bigger town to shop. Even a discount store in a mall would look good to her.

And every night Gail let Hawk's former presence slip into her fatigued mind. She hadn't seen him, not even a glimpse. Once when she probed Willow for information on how she was getting to the school, Willow said, "Hawk brought me."

"He did?" Gail had said, and knew she felt a heightened sense of warmth at the thought she might see him. "When?"

"Early," Willow had said.

"Is he coming back to pick you up today?"

"No."

"Is he going to bring you tomorrow?"

Willow had shrugged.

For two weeks after that conversation, Gail had made a point of getting to the school before anyone else. Willow was always there in the classroom, but she never saw Hawk.

At the close of the semester, Gail wondered if she'd made a huge mistake in moving to Montana. She'd been naive in thinking that one person could make a difference in many people's lives when the problems had been mounting and chinking themselves into place for years piled upon years. She knew that now. She and her Indian students had nothing in common. They didn't pay attention to her, and she knew she was boring them to distraction.

All her enthusiasm about coming to Montana, teaching in a reservation school, inspiring these kids toward a better life and a hopeful future was nothing more than dry leaves swept up on a cold November wind to dry and disintegrate in the winter of truth—one person made no difference whatsoever. Life on the rez, as the kids called the reservation, went on as always, as it always had and as it always would, and one more non-Indian couldn't make any more variation than one more quill could in a porcupine's back.

Besides that, Gail was plagued by constant sinus headaches, and culminated her total misery by starting December recess with a hell of a cold.

On Saturday night, bundled up in blankets, layered in baggy sweatpants, turtleneck and sweatshirt, and the only two pair of warm socks she owned stretched over her feet, Gail sat shivering on her lumpy couch. Drinking hot tea with lemon, she watched for at least the twentieth time in her life the antics of Bing Crosby and Danny Kaye in the ever hopeful Fifties rerun movie, *White Christmas*. Oh, it would be a white Christmas for her, all right, and snowy monochromatic gray on her television set. Rosemary Clooney was sitting by a fireplace drinking buttermilk and singing, "Count Your Blessings," and Gail was muttering through her shivering that she couldn't find a blessing to count, and wondering who in hell ever drinks buttermilk anyway, when her telephone rang.

The apartment was small, and the phone's low bench was no more than a few feet away from her, but getting to it while keeping the blankets wrapped securely around her was an exercise in creative dexterity that challenged

Gail's flagging energy. She caught it on the first ding of the seventh ring.

"Hed-do," she croaked. She could hear a rustle, as if someone was about to hang up at the other end. "Heddo!" she forced louder through a sore throat. Even a wrong number would be welcome right now, or with any luck a political survey questioner, or magazine salesperson.

"Gail," the male voice said, matter of fact, not a question.

"Jes," she managed.

"You're sick."

Her ears were ringing from the clogged sinuses and she had difficulty hearing. The man didn't identify himself, and Gail considered it might be a burglar determining if she was alone and weakened from illness. She dismissed it. Even if he was, at least it would be company. ·

"Jes. Got a code id my head or da flu. Who is dis?"

"Hawk."

Hawk. If Gail could have coughed, she would have, but her throat was too sore to allow it, and her head too packed with mucus for it to move. She had a million questions. To what did she owe this untimely and altogether unanticipated telephone call? Did he still live in Montana? In the United States? On the planet Earth, for God's sake? Didn't he care if she was alive, or in this case, almost dead? Of course he didn't. Why did she even consider such a notion?

"Hed-do, Hawk," she managed to croak again.

"I'm calling to ask if it's convenient for me to visit you," he said in that rich voice with the unidentifiable accent she'd grown to love to listen to in the rare moments when he had spoken.

"Visit? Me?" She fumbled through the blankets toward the tissue box. She knew her very sore nose was red and chapped, and in an insanely ridiculous moment she wanted to cover it up so he wouldn't see it. "I don't tink dat's a good idea. You could catch my code."

"I don't catch colds."

Gail plopped onto the bench and sighed. "Of course you don't catch codes."

"I'll be there in half an hour. Thanks." He hung up the phone following his announcement.

Half an hour! Gail knew panic almost as gut-wrenching as she'd felt the morning after she'd decided to move to Montana. Was that an omen?

A thought dropped into her clogged mind and was suspended for the minute amount of space there was left among her swollen sinuses:

there was nothing more unattractive and un-sexy than a woman with a miserable cold.

He was punctual, thereby making a lie out of what some of the teachers had referred to as "Cheyenne time," defined as usually a half-hour to forty-five minutes past any time agreed upon. They didn't say it insultingly, they merely imparted the knowledge as a fact to live with and take into consideration. She'd barely had time to fold her blanket, straighten her sweat clothes, try to get a brush through her matted hair, and dab some tinted moisturizer on her red nose.

When she opened her door to Hawk, a diffi-cult act owing to its ill-fit, a gust of snow blew in along with him. He held a canvas bag filled with groceries, it looked like, in one arm. In the other, wrapped in a blanket and perched over his forearm bench-fashion, sat Willow. He stepped in quickly, forcing Gail to back up, then backed up and forced the door shut with the bottom of his boot. He transferred Willow into her arms.

"Found her living in the school. She won't stay at the ranch. Says she has to stay with you. I told her it was all right, that you wouldn't mind." Hawk sent a message into Gail's scratchy eyes that told her he expected she wouldn't argue about this arrangement.

"You're right," she rasped, and adjusted the

little girl in her arms.

He peered around and spotted the kitchen, then headed for it, setting the grocery bag on the wood table. She followed him, still holding Willow, and watched as he took out a plastic covered tub of something, a towel-wrapped block of something, a half-full bottle of brandy, some small paper bags, a larger flat paper bag, and a six or seven inch square brown metal box with an electrical cord attached to it. When she frowned a question, he turned it around for her to see.

"Portable furnace," he told her.

Then he walked past her on his way down a short hall carrying the furnace and one of the small paper bags. He looked in the two open doors and disappeared into the bathroom. Gail felt like a lump just standing there holding the silent Willow, but she was stunned by his call and his arrival at her door, and knew she would be whether her head was clear of the cold or not. She heard water running. Then Hawk came out of the bathroom empty-handed and closed the door behind him.

He passed her on his way back to the kitchen. Then he came to her, holding the flat paper bag. He took Willow out of her arms and handed her the bag.

"Go take a bath and put this on," he commanded. She started to protest, and he stopped her. "Do it. And leave the furnace on and the door closed when you come out."

Gail dutifully went down the hall carrying the bag.

While Gail was in the bathroom, Hawk took Willow and ensconced her on the couch wrapping Gail's blankets around her. He went around the apartment checking to see that the heat ducts were all open and producing heat. There wasn't much coming from them, and he made a mental note to check further another time, and to inspect the windows for air leaks as well.

Then he went into the kitchen, opened the covered tub, searched for and found a pot, then emptied the homemade soup into it and set it over a low flame on the stove. He lit the gas oven, opened the towel-wrapped bundle and set a square of cornbread inside. He put a tea kettle on to boil water, got out three mugs after opening the doors and looking into the only two cupboards in her kitchen. Then he went in and sat with Willow.

Gail came down the hall from the bathroom and entered the tiny living room wearing a white heavyweight cotton long-johns suit extracted from the flat paper bag Hawk had given her, her own white socks and pale blue chenille slippers, and a yellow towel wrapped turban-fashion around her head. She held one hand over the rear trap door of the long-johns since she noticed the button holes on one side seemed a bit large for the buttons and threatened to slip open with the least provocation.

Hawk grinned. "What do you think, Willow?" he said, bending close to the child's ear. "Is that what all the best-dressed teachers at Medicine Wheel are wearing these days?"

If Willow had an opinion about such lofty matters, she kept it in check.

"I know it would be polite of me to thank you for such a . . . a . . . the words escape me," Gail said, shaking her head, and noticing that the steam had helped relieve the pressure in her sinuses.

"How about 'fashionable item'?" Hawk urged.

"No, those weren't the words I had in mind."

"Well, sit down here and think about it awhile," Hawk said, motioning toward the couch. "I've made some tea for you."

Gail's eyebrows went up, but she held back the words that came up with them. Hawk was actually behaving in a most . . . *civilized* manner. He was actually being nice to her.

Hawk came back with two saucers and mugs of steaming fragrant tea. He handed one to Willow, and then to Gail, who took a deep breath of the aromatic steam.

"Mm, what is it?"

"My mother's concoction of cold tea, as she calls it."

"But it's hot."

"But it's medicine for a cold."

"Of course." Gail sniffed and took a sip. "Spicy. What's in it?"

"Wild ginger and elm bark. And a shot of brandy. That ingredient is only in yours." He bent down and carefully lifted Willow in his arms. "Come on. You're about to have a bath and shampoo for the first time this year I think." Willow protested silently with a stubborn set to her little chin, and the bracing of her feet against his thighs. "Oh yes you are, and you know it."

He swept her down the hallway, Willow stiff in his arms and holding the mug of tea. Gail heard him open and close the bathroom door. She pulled the blanket up around her and cupped her palms around the warm tea mug. What a curious sensation this was—to be taken care of. Even more curious was the knowledge that she, and Willow, were being taken care of by the usually silent and stoic Lone Hawk Kincaid. What had blown in on that wild Montana wind?

Something smelled wonderful coming from the direction of the kitchen. Gail rose and went in search of her bathrobe in her bedroom. She slipped into the velvety sweep of midnight blue that touched the top of her slippers, and hugged her throat and wrists with narrow velvet ruffles. A bit dressy for an impromptu supper somewhere in the lonely wilds of the west in the middle of a raging snowstorm, but it was the only robe she owned. She couldn't keep walking around in front of Hawk wearing long-johns with a temperamental rear trap door.

She finished drying her hair and styled it as best she could by slicking it back with the aid of setting gel, then finger loosening it in waves all over her head. It was getting longer. She hadn't worn her hair long in years, but her intuitions told her she'd need more hair just to keep her head warm this winter.

In the kitchen she lifted the pot lid and sniffed the simmering soup. Whatever it was, it, too, smelled divine. And for the first time in several days she actually felt hunger pangs. She decided she'd go down to the bathroom and see if she might hurry Willow's bath along in order to make supper happen that much sooner.

"Ow!" Willow's pained voice came through the bathroom door.

Gail knocked. "Okay if I come in and supervise?"

"No!" came Willow's voice again.

"Definitely!" came Hawk's. "Hold still and it won't hurt so much!"

Gail went in and closed the door behind her. The bathroom was warm and steamy from their baths and the hard-working little furnace. Willow was in the tub up to her neck in expensive rose-scented bubble bath from Gail's dwindling supply, while Hawk, kneeling on the floor, bent over her scrubbing her head with a homemade mix that held a pungent aroma in sharp contrast to the bubbles.

Willow played with the tea mug in the bath, dipping under the water and holding it up like a foamy mug of beer, then letting it pour like a waterfall back into the tub, giggling while splashes of bubbles flew all over. She ducked and bobbed away from Hawk's hands, causing his fingers to get tangled in her hair.

"Ow!" she bellowed again.

"Here now. The teacher will think I'm beheading you if you don't hush."

Gail dropped down on the closed commode, and wrinkled her nose. "What are you putting on her head?"

"Shampoo. Pine tar based. Mother made it. She gave her the kerosene treatment, and now I'm cleaning it up."

Gail watched Hawk, and smiled to herself. He had iridescent bubbles in his hair and on the pushed-up sleeves and one shoulder of his dark green turtleneck sweater. Pine tar shampoo was splattered on his chest, and dotted the planes of his high cheekbones and his nose. But the look of concentration that moved around his face with every twitch of his full lips and crinkle of his eyes gave an endearing comical look to him that Gail never would have thought she'd see. She liked it. It made him feel human to her, not a piece of chiseled granite carved out of history.

"If you'll dry her off, I'll get some soup dished up for you," Hawk said, pushing himself up and drying his hands.

"I'd like that," Gail said.

She caught his eyes and noticed that they, too, had softened. If he wasn't more guarded, she might be able to see something of the man in them, something . . . well, sensitive and caring. She supposed that sounded too much like the modern buzz phrase regarding men that had been evident for the last few years in magazine articles and discussed in women's groups, but there was no other way to describe his actions this evening, especially the way he cared for the little girl.

Hawk was sensitive to Willow's needs, in spite of her resistance, and it was obvious to Gail he cared enough about the child to break down that resistance. And while she wondered about his showing up at her doorstep stating his intention to drop the child into her life, Gail suspected Hawk was at the very least sensitive to her own plight as well. She was alone and ill in a strange place in treacherous weather. Yes, he definitely seemed sensitive to her needs and Willow's in a natural earthy way by providing the basic human needs of food, covering, warmth, and communication.

Gail spent time drying Willow's body and fluffing it with powder. Then she dressed her in clothing from the pile of things Hawk had set in the bathroom, and set about attempting to do something with her tangled hair. She rubbed some conditioner into it, and searched among her things for a large-toothed comb with which to start the detangling process. Willow scrambled for her pack under her pile of dirty clothes and extracted the hair brush Gail had given her last summer. Gail noticed the tattered magazine was still carefully stashed away in the bottom of the pack.

"I think a comb would be better at first," she told Willow, concerned about the presence of lice in the filthy hair brush. "Let's clean that brush right now while we're working on your hair." She ran hot water in the sink and added some of Hawk's pine tar shampoo, and submerged the brush. "You must always use only a clean brush on your hair from now on, Willow, and you must have your hair washed often," Gail instructed softly while she worked on the tangled mass of black hair.

"It hurts," Willow said, wrinkling her nose.

"I'm sorry if I'm hurting you," Gail said, stopping the comb and rubbing the little head with gentle fingers.

"Not that. Shampoo hurts."

Gail held back a laugh. "Well, it won't from now on. It's just that it had been a long time since anyone cared for your hair. I promise you'll like it."

"Don't let Hawk do it. He hurts." Willow rubbed the crown of her head.

"He didn't mean to. He just wanted to be sure he got all the bad things out so you're head would feel better. He would never hurt you, you know," Gail assured her.

Willow looked down. "Hawk's good, isn't he." It was more a statement than a question.

Gail wasn't certain she could respond with any real knowledge, but she tried. "I think he is. He's a good man. And I think he really loves you."

Willow looked up at her with a pleased grin lighting her small features. Then she looked down again. "Some men are bad. They hurt."

Gail's stomach clutched. Was Willow trying to tell her she'd been abused by someone? Her father perhaps? Or someone else? She wasn't certain how to handle it. Should she question the child more thoroughly, or just let it go? She felt helpless to know what to do. And then it came to her. When she'd felt the despair of abuse herself as a child, all she wanted was for someone who truly loved her to pull her into warm arms and soothe away the hurt.

Gail dropped to her knees and pulled Willow's thin body into her arms. Willow's slight arms slid up slowly and encircled Gail's neck, and she laid her cheek against Gail's breast.

Gail rocked her, gently rubbing her back, lovingly stroking her hair. And hiding her own tears against the pajama-clad thin shoulder of a small human being who had, she sensed, suffered more in her short lifetime than many aged adults.

Chapter Thirteen

Gail took Willow, clean and shining and smiling, by the hand and led her to the kitchen.

"Are you as hungry as I am?" she asked on the way down the hallway.

"More," Willow said looking up at her, and there was an engaging smile showing a row of remarkably straight white teeth. Gail enjoyed the sight.

"Sit down," Hawk commanded warmly when they found him in the kitchen.

He'd set bowls of steaming soup at three places, a plate of cornbread in the middle, milk for Willow, water for himself, and another mug of tea for Gail. The television had been turned off, and her tiny radio, a recent purchase, was sitting on the kitchen counter, soothing classical music floating from it into the air fragrant from cooking food.

"Mm, this is wonderful," Gail exclaimed,

tasting the soup, savoring a blend of meat and onions, tomatoes, cloves, cinnamon, and even apple. "What kind is it?"

"Turtle," Willow told her knowingly.

Gail held her spoon mid-air and a mouthful mid-swallow. Her eyes shifted to Hawk who was busy spooning from his bowl and eating with vigor. He paused and cut some squares of warm cornbread and passed them to Gail and Willow.

"Right," he said. "Best thing to cure a cold if you've got one or ward one off if you haven't."

Gail swallowed hard. "Where do you get turtles in the winter?"

"The freezer," Willow told her in a tone of voice that said it was dumb not to know the answer. After all, the lakes were frozen and the turtles were hibernating now.

Gail laughed out loud for the first time. She relaxed, feeling better than she had even before she caught the cold. Maybe it was the bath, the food, even the tea laced with brandy. She knew better than that. It was the company that gave as much or more to her renewed strength and cheerfulness.

"This was very nice of you," she told Hawk, "and your mother," she quickly added. "It makes us feel good to know people care about us, doesn't it, Willow?"

335

Willow was too busy eating to do more than vigorously nod her head in agreement.

Gail spotted a half empty bottle of brandy on the sideboard. "That brandy certainly does do wonders for the tea. I'll have to get some next time I'm near a town."

"Don't bother. You can keep that," Hawk told her, cutting more cornbread.

"That's very generous of you, but you should take it home with you. You'll need it. Something tells me the winter gets pretty long in these parts."

Hawk shook his head. "I used to need it. I don't anymore. Keep it here." His voice was lower and quieter than it had been all evening.

Gail knew there was something more beneath his answer, but she didn't press it. "I guess your legend of the healing qualities of turtle soup is accurate," she said, lifting the mood back to where it had started. "My head is clearing, my throat is soothed, and I actually feel pretty good."

"Mother will be glad to hear it," he said. "But you should take better care of yourself, treat yourself better. You don't have to be sick, you know. Just don't accept the evil spirits, don't allow them."

Gail watched Hawk's face. As guarded as this man kept himself, right now his features seemed open, welcoming real interaction. She felt freer to be herself with him than ever before.

"I didn't ask for these evil cold spirits," she said, spooning the last morsel of turtle meat from her soup bowl. "They arrived unannounced and I seemed forced to extend them some kind of hospitality."

"You created space for them," Hawk said.

"How? Cold and flu germs just float in the air. The only way to prevent infection I guess is to get a flu shot, and I don't believe in getting those yet."

Hawk set down his spoon and pushed his bowl out of his way. "Well, Willow, looks like we'll have to teach the teacher, won't we?"

Willow shrugged, took a long drink of milk, and left a white moustache over her upper lip. Gail reached out with her napkin and gently wiped it away, ending with a playful tap on the end of Willow's nose.

"If you don't take care of your body and mind, the good spirits will leave it," Hawk began. "The Cheyenne believe in harmony and balance with the seasons and the earth. If we aren't living right, our good spirits leave our body . . ."

". . . and bad spirits move in," Willow finished for him.

Gail was caught up in their tale, truly attentive and eager to know more.

"That's right," Hawk said. "Once we've let them in, we've enabled the bad spirits to dominate our souls. That's one of the many reasons to sweat."

"Sweat?" Gail asked.

"In a sweat lodge," Hawk continued. "There we can leave the bad spirits to the hanging man's road. The sweat, and other ceremonies, help us to learn and maintain that balance, to let go of those evils that ensnare us, and open to Maheo."

"What is . . . mah-hay-oh, did you say?"

"Yes, the creator of all things."

"Oh. I'm not really a church person anymore. I went to Sunday school in a Protestant church, and even tried to attend services when I became an adult. I think there are too many faces to what people call God, or too many gods. Something."

"We believe there is only one god, the Creator. No face. The Creator is the center of harmony and balance with earth and human."

Gail watched Hawk as he spoke with the rich voice and inflection of words and syllables that she'd grown to . . . love. Fascinated by a spiritual depth and expression she'd never found in herself or with any degree of honesty in anyone else, she took in every thought he communicated. And she wondered if he practiced in his own life the beliefs he expressed so succinctly and clearly.

Willow yawned.

Hawk laughed. "I think that must mean there's been enough teaching for one night."

"I believe you're right. Come with me, Willow, I think it's time for you to go to bed."

"No, I'm not tired," said this most stubborn child. Gail marveled at the strength of resistance she possessed.

"Hm," she said. "Something tells me we have the spirit of sleepy then, come to make your eyes heavy. But it's a good spirit and I think it will be all right if you allow it to rest in your body tonight."

Willow's eyes grew wide with the sound of Gail's own brand of tale. She looked at Hawk. "Is she right?"

Sensing control had just been passed to him, Hawk rose and started clearing the dishes away. He turned back to Willow. "I've just thought it over. She is a teacher, and she listens well and learns well. Yes, I believe she is right about this particular spirit."

Willow took that as gospel, and obediently slid off her chair and started into the living room to find a corner to sleep in.

"This way, Willow," Gail said, holding out her hand. "First I'll find you a toothbrush so you can clean your teeth, and then you can crawl into my bed if you would like to. It will be much warmer, I think."

Willow stopped and looked toward Hawk again. Hawk appeared deep in thought. He spoke with the voice of a seer of ages. "That is true," he pronounced.

Willow grinned, and Gail sensed she'd just got what she wanted anyway. Except maybe the tooth brushing.

By the time Gail came back to the kitchen after tucking Willow in and leaving a small light on for her, Hawk had cleaned up the kitchen. He'd been out and started his truck engine to warm, and cleaned off the snow that had accumulated while he'd been inside. She could hear the engine running, and felt a small sinking inside. She didn't want him to leave yet. He stood near the front door, and an awkward tension filled the space between them.

"Thank you," she said, "you've brought me so much tonight."

His eyes were cast down toward his boots. "Willow has been given more." He raised his eyes and looked deeply into hers. "Thank you for taking her in. Although I didn't give you much choice, did I?"

"No, but you wouldn't have had to insist. I've wanted to take her in with me, but she always seemed to keep a distance." *Just like you do,* she added silently.

340

"She is a child of the wind, a gift of nature. She belongs to herself and the earth."

Gail let his softened gaze, his poetic words, and rich voice settle over her. He seemed to have closed some of the distance between them, a distance she confessed to herself they'd both created. She was drawn to him with all her senses, almost bewitched by her own unpredictable emotions. She swallowed hard.

"And is that how you see yourself, too?" she whispered, and almost wished she could take back the question.

He stepped back, and the softness in his eyes immediately hardened. "I would have no answer to that," he said, the richness in his voice also hardened around the edges.

Maybe it was the tea and the brandy, or maybe it was the elevation out of her misery, the entrance of Willow and Hawk into her home, or any number of things, but Gail felt no restraint on pressing him further with personal questions.

"Have no answer, or will not give one? Or worse, will not admit the truth even to yourself?" She didn't let her gaze waver, but held his by the sheer force of her own will. "Do you see yourself as belonging to the wind, the earth, but to no human being, not even to yourself?"

"Don't try to analyze me, Miss Bricker, you

are not equipped to attempt it. We are very different." His gaze narrowed, and he shot out an arm behind him and grasped the door handle.

Gail shot out her own hand and placed a restraining hand on his. "I wouldn't dream of attempting to analyze you," she said, her own gaze just as open as before. "I have enough trouble with myself. And that is where you and I are the same. We both keep up invisible barriers to ensure that no one gets too close. We don't want to get hurt. I'm right, and you know it."

Hawk released the door handle and slowly dropped his arm out from under her hand. His eyes relaxed to the point of losing their narrow hardness, yet they took on another look Gail couldn't define. She saw his jaw tense and relax, and tense again, felt the tautness of his nerves as he seemed to be holding himself in check. Had she angered him, stepped over a line of personal boundary? For a fleet moment she wished she could have swallowed her words. Her throat was starting to constrict.

And then he did something she never would have dreamed he was thinking about. He reached out with both arms and encircled her shoulders, crushing her against his chest. He let out a long sigh and she felt the electric tension in him release, then felt her own mount.

And then he leaned down and caught her mouth in his lips and kissed her softly first, then powerfully, engulfing her in the completeness of the kiss.

Gail's spine seemed to be made of a maple sapling, for she curved into his body with the grasp of his arms, the bending of his back over her. And she gave him back in her kiss as much as he was giving her, more mutually physical in its revelation because they both were recognizing fully the attraction they felt for one another. Yet it was deeply emotional, and in a blinding flash Gail sensed that the searing need, underlying the communion of their lips, arose from each of their own passion-barren years.

Hawk released his hold on Gail before she was ready to let him go.

"I'm sorry. I . . . shouldn't have done that." He backed away from her.

"I'm not sorry. And I'm glad *we* did that." She took a step closer.

"Good night." He replied and turned quickly and left the apartment.

Gail felt the chill wind blow around her. She closed the door tightly behind him, then watched out the window as he hunched against the driving snow and got into his truck. She regretted nothing. She did not feel lonely, did not feel he'd deserted her.

By the time he drove away, Gail was too filled with warmth and positive feelings for any evil spirits to get even close to her.

Willow was still sleeping and Gail was having her first cup of breakfast coffee when she heard a truck drive into her driveway. Her pulse quickened. She went to the front window. Hawk's pickup. She wasn't expecting him, and once again she knew she looked like death warmed over. She was dressed in sweat clothes and hadn't even washed her face yet. She ran to the bathroom to fix up a little, then stopped still in the hallway.

Other feelings eclipsed her image worries. Hawk was back! That meant he wanted to see her as much as she wanted to see him. Her mind reeled with the sheer joy of it!

She turned back toward the door to answer his knock, and flung it open ready to leap into his arms.

"Good morning," Ada said, standing in the snow and holding two double-handled large canvas bags. "I hope we are not too early. Are you feeling better?"

Stunned, Gail stepped back. "Uh, yes, I think so."

Hawk came around from behind his mother. "She was happy to hear of Willow's acceptance of you and wanted to come to see you," he told her. It was not an apology, just a statement.

"Um, oh, fine, yes, come in," Gail stammered. "Willow is still sleeping. I don't know how you managed to get her to school so early in the morning," she said to Hawk. He looked wonderful this morning, but he didn't look at Gail.

"I didn't bring her to school in the morning," Hawk said, negating what Willow had told her during the semester. He walked past her with a canvas bag of his own and started toward her living room. "She'd been living in the school all semester, that's why she was there so early."

Gail was even more stunned at that news. It never occurred to her that Willow might be sleeping in the school at night. She knew more than ever how much now she had to alter her conditioned thinking of what the "typical" student was.

"I have breakfast," Ada said, peering around corners in search of the kitchen. When she found it, she took over.

Willow padded down the hallway on bare feet, wiping sleep from her eyes with the back of her hands.

"Hawk still here?" she said with a raspy voice.

Gail felt her face warm at the child's innocent remark in front of Ada.

"No, honey. He and Ada came to surprise us with breakfast. Wasn't that nice?"

"I'm hungry," Willow said, and plopped her little behind in a chair at the table.

"I can't imagine how you could be after that supper you put away last night," Gail teased. "First you have to go brush your teeth and wash your hands. And put some socks on your feet. This floor is cold."

"I brushed my teeth last night," Willow said.

"I know, but you have to brush them in the morning, too," Gail said.

"I don't want to. It tastes bad." Willow pouted like any child would when told to do something she didn't want to.

"Hm," Gail said thoughtfully. "What do you think, Ada? Would bicarbonate of soda taste better than minty toothpaste first thing in the morning?"

"Elm bark," Ada said, nodding. "It's better."

"You think so?"

"I do."

Willow let the two older women discuss the differences in effectiveness of elm bark to sodium bicarbonate and ran down the hall to the bathroom to brush her teeth with minty toothpaste.

Gail slipped around to the living room to

find Hawk. "What are you doing?" she asked, watching his back and shoulders move as he bent into his work.

He straightened quickly, but didn't turn around. "Making these windows a little tighter. You're losing heat."

"Thank you."

"With a child in the house, it has to be warm."

Gail smiled slightly at his back. "Ah, I see. You're doing this for Willow of course."

Hawk moved to the next window. "Of course."

Well, if he couldn't admit he was working on those windows to make her apartment warmer for her as well as Willow, that was all right for now. He appeared to have constructed the barrier between them again as if the night before hadn't existed, as if they hadn't kissed with every ounce of their raging feelings. Gail wondered how long it would take for him to break it down again. Was it possible he might never break it down?

Ada summoned them all to a breakfast of orange juice, cured ham, and baked grits with grated cheese, and tea. Gail wanted more coffee, but Ada insisted on the tea. And when Ada insisted, Gail knew there was no dissuading her, no going against her commands.

Later, after Hawk and Ada had departed,

Gail went to the refrigerator for more juice. When she opened the door she found that Ada had stocked it with more milk, soups, meats, vegetables, and cheese. In the cabinet she found homemade breads, crackers, cereals, corn meal, and a small paper bag filled with tea.

She poured a glass of juice, leaned against the refrigerator and drank it, feeling better than she had in days.

Willow came around the corner carrying one of Gail's cameras. "I want to learn," she announced.

Gail smiled at her. "And I can teach you. We make a good team, don't we?"

Willow could only grin, wider than ever.

By the time Christmas arrived, Gail and Willow had become good friends. They went grocery shopping together, chose a television program to watch together several times a week. Their favorite pastime was when Gail would read stories to her after supper. Willow was curious, asked constant questions that Gail was only too happy to answer. Once in awhile Willow would tell Gail a Cheyenne story or legend that she'd heard some old people tell. Then it was Gail's turn to be the student to Willow's teacher. She was as fascinated by the legends as Willow was with the books.

It had become more than friendship to Gail, and she understood it more every day. She'd grown to love this little girl as much as she would have if she'd been her own daughter. Her feelings were as much maternal as they were of friendship, and they were at once joyous and confusing. How much could she truly act like the mother of Willow? Discipline, while a problem for this formerly wild child, was not difficult for Gail to achieve with her. After all, she'd been a teacher for many years and knew how to handle it and to give and expect mutual respect. There were the usual child-adult confrontations and resistance, but nothing they hadn't found ways to overcome.

But there were other things. How responsible should she be for this child? There was health care to worry about, and dental and eye examinations to schedule. What was she to do about religious experience, if any? She wasn't strong in that department herself, and she didn't know enough about the People's way to feel confident about teaching it to Willow.

There were more tensions at times than Gail wanted to admit to. She sensed resentment from native people whenever she and Willow were together in what appeared to be a mother-daughter situation. She knew many of the People opposed the placement of native children with nonnative caregivers.

Regardless of the questions in Gail's mind, regardless of the resentment from native people, Willow had made her choice of where and with whom she wanted to live. It wasn't at the ranch with the Kincaids, although it could have been. They'd wanted her. It wasn't with other native people. Perhaps it could have been, but either Willow chose not to, or she wasn't wanted. She wanted to live with Gail and Gail wanted Willow with her. It was as simple and as complex as that.

The two were invited to the Kincaid's home for Christmas. Gail and Willow had spent days making holiday preparations and gifts to take with them. Gail was as excited about doing it as Willow was. It didn't matter what the religious reason might be for celebrating Christmas, it was the good feelings that came with it, the love, the wanting to share.

"We're here!" Willow called as she burst into the front door of the ranch house the day before Christmas. "Look at me in my new clothes!" She carried a bag almost bigger than herself. Gail set down her bags, and helped Willow with hers.

Skeeter came down the hall from the kitchen and greeted them. "Hello, Miss Bricker. And who is this little snow princess you've brought with you? I don't b'lieve we've met, pretty lady." He bent down and thrust out his right hand toward Willow. "Name's Skeeter Davis, and I'm mighty proud to make the acquaintance of royalty."

"Aw, Skeeter," Willow said, grabbing his hand and swinging it back and forth, "it's me, Willow. You remember, don't you?" Since she'd been living with Gail for several weeks, Willow had blossomed, had become more talkative, more social.

"Willow?" Skeeter dropped his mouth open in mock surprise. "Why I never would have recognized you. You've growed right up into a beautiful young lady now, haven't you?"

"You think so?"

Willow sashayed back and forth showing off a bright red down-plumped jacket that grazed her knees, navy blue woolen pants, and black high-top insulated boots with a fleece cuff. She had on a pair of navy blue mountain mittens that were too big, and she clapped them together like flippers on an excited seal.

"Wal, I surely do know so. How'd you do that so fast?" Skeeter made it sound as if he wanted to get a secret out of her.

"Gail did it," Willow said, and she sounded proud.

"Nah," Gail said. "I just bought you some clothes."

"She makes me take baths all the time," Willow said, standing on tiptoes so Skeeter could hear her whisper. "And scrub my hair, and use toothpaste that stings."

"No!" Skeeter said leaning down.

"She does!"

"Is it really just terrible?"

"No. I'm glad!"

"But you don't want to tell her that, do you, for fear she'll make you take more baths and stuff, right?"

"Right."

Ada came down the hallway then. She smiled broadly at the sight of them. "We're very happy you could come," she said in her calm way.

"We're very happy to be here, Ada," Gail said, and she went over and hugged the older woman.

"Me, too!" Willow jumped up and down.

"Well, now," Ada said, "let me have a look at you, Willow." Willow turned around awkwardly for Ada's appraisal. "It's our same little Willow, all right. But better. You look very pretty, and healthy. Looks like living in a house agrees with you."

"Yep. We brought presents. There's something for everybody in here!" Willow dragged the big bag over to Ada. "And cookies. Me and Gail made cookies." She looked up at Gail with a face as shiny bright as a new angel. "I mean," she swallowed and spoke slowly, "Gail and I made some cookies."

Gail smiled approvingly down at her. She wouldn't have corrected her speech for anything, wouldn't have wanted to dampen her excitement in telling Ada about baking cookies. But she had to admit she felt very pleased when Willow knew she'd said it not quite right. The child was smart. All she'd needed was time, attention, discipline, and patience from someone who cared. And she had that someone now in Gail.

They hadn't put up a Christmas tree in the parlor, but they had brought in evergreens and twisted cornhusk boughs and set them around on tables and the mantel. A fire burned brightly in the fireplace, and the aroma from the kitchen was spicy and homey. Small trays of burning sage and cedar and sweet grass added to the fragrant warmth in the house. Gail felt good about Christmas for the first time in years, and she knew it was because of the Kincaids and Willow.

At a dinner of Indian chili made with venison meat and served with tortillas, squash, and tomatoes, Gail and Willow learned more about the ways of the People who didn't embrace the Christian manner of Christmas. It was more the thanking the Creator for the gifts of life and the earth and people, and then sharing those gifts with others, than it was the flash

353

and splash and spending that was so much a part of other Christmases.

Trey was away from the ranch once again. No one knew where, and it seemed to matter little to any of them. Hawk was quiet, distant, almost back to the way he was in the beginning when they first met. Gail wondered if she'd ever understand his moods, especially since he withheld any information about why he kept these barriers up.

After dinner, Jerrie took Gail out to the women's center she'd been so much a part of, taking clothing and blankets for the women and their children and huge boxes of food, all donated. Gail's heart filled for them as she felt their emotion of pain soothed by joy and warmth in the safety of the house developed by Jerrie. Gail made a promise to Jerrie that she would give as much of her own time to it as she could.

The exchanging of gifts the next morning after breakfast and in front of the fire was the most pleasurable Christmas experience Gail remembered. Very few things were purchased gifts, and Gail was glad of that and glad she'd taught Willow the value of making things with her own hands to give. Besides, the lack of money had forced her into it.

Willow displayed the cookies she'd cut out herself, and helped Gail to decorate. There were shapes of trees and stars, and some of animals like deer and rabbits. And they'd made gingerbread people and decorated them to look like everybody at the ranch, right down to Skeeter and Wills.

"Which one is this?" Hawk said, holding up a gingerbread man with colored stripes running from his head to his feet, and what looked like a loin cloth made from yellow icing.

"That's you," Willow said proudly.

Hawk held it out showing careful examination of all parts. "Are you sure? He's all painted up like a wild Indian. Have you been looking at too many of those ancient books in the school library?"

"No," Willow said with disgust. She went over to Hawk and took the cookie from his hand. "See this long stuff that looks like strings?" Hawk nodded. "That's your hair. We had to use chocolate frosting because Gail said we didn't have anything that would be as dark as the night the way your real hair is."

Gail felt her face grow warm at Willow's remark. Hawk sent a cursory glance, then studied the cookie with Willow's help.

"She said that?" When Willow nodded, Hawk added, "What else did she say? Is she the one who painted my face with chocolate warpaint?"

"I did that," Willow said proudly. "That's

not warpaint, that's your wrinkles!"

"Wrinkles! Well, I don't know if I like having those painted on cookies. I had to live a long time to get these wrinkles, and I'm pretty proud of them."

"Gail said you were proud."

"She did, did she? Is there a cookie in that box for her, too?" Hawk made a point of peering over the edge of the red tissue paper-lined cookie box.

"Uh-huh." Willow brought out a gingerbread lady with short streaky yellow hair. "See?"

Hawk examined it very closely. "Hm. I don't see any wrinkles on this cookie. And Gail has lived as long as I have."

Willow turned around quickly and looked at Gail, then back at Hawk. "I didn't know she was *that* old! She told me I didn't have to put the wrinkles on her cookie, too."

Jerrie stifled a laugh while Gail tried vainly to keep her cheeks from burning and her face turning Christmas cookie red.

"I'm not surprised," Hawk said with a lift of his eyebrows, and a smile playing around the corners of his full lips. He went back to his own cookie. "Now what's all this down my side, all these painted stripes?"

"That's your feather bonnet. I picked the colors, too. Gail said you were like the old

Cheyenne chiefs and warriors, strong and brave. So I gave you a chief's hat."

Hawk leaned closer to Willow. "She used the word *old*, did she?"

"Uh-huh."

"Willow," Gail interrupted this little interrogation before it went too far, "there's something over here for you to open. Look."

Willow handed the gingerbread man cookie to Hawk who promptly bit the head off and made a display of chewing and making savoring noises. She accepted the package from Gail and sat down on the braided rug in front of the fireplace and opened it. Her eyes grew wide.

"A camera!" she whispered in awe. "My own camera."

She extracted a small camera, the weight and size just right for a child with an insatiable curiosity and a good eye for composition and light. Gail was surprised at how good an eye Willow had for such things, how careful she was with Gail's equipment, and how interested she was in how it worked. She wished she had space in their tiny apartment for a dark room so Willow could see her pictures develop right before her own eyes.

"Can I give Ada her present now?" Willow asked. Gail nodded and she scrambled for a wide box wrapped in snow white paper and tied with an evergreen bow.

Ada unwrapped it slowly. "It's very heavy. What have you found for me?" She pulled away the tissue, and her eyes grew almost as wide as Willow's had at the sight of her camera.

"See?" Willow said, kneeling in front of Ada. "It's a photograph. I took the picture and Gail framed it. It's your house and the corral. And see right there? That's Hawk and Morning Star by the barn."

Ada studied the large color photograph using her finger to point out each new detail she spotted. She made long, low sounds of appreciation at each new discovery.

"Thank you," she said to Willow, giving her the full warm impact of her wise old eyes. She looked up at Gail, and slipped an arm around Willow's shoulders. "And thank you for this," she said to her.

Gail could only nod. Her eyes were dimmed with the tears of watching a grandmother and granddaughter side by side sharing a gift. It was possible. It was only by an act of nature that they were not blood related, any of them.

For Jerrie there was a long turquoise fringed wool scarf. Gail had embroidered her initials on it, and Willow had knotted the fringe with colored wooden beads. Willow received shirts and pants and socks from Ada and Jerrie, and

358

even a dress. She wrinkled her nose at that one, but Jerrie assured her it was not the frilly kind so she'd look very smart in it on teacher-parent night at the school.

"Hawk has one, too," Willow said, reaching for another flat box.

"I thought I had mine," Hawk teased. "And it was a delicious present, too. The wrinkles were very chocolatey."

Willow giggled, and handed him the box. Gail noticed how Hawk's interaction with the little girl changed him, softened him, dissolved any distance he constructed. He might keep that distance with her, but he seemed powerless against the charm of a little girl with eyes like chocolate kisses.

Willow watched Hawk taking care at untying the ribbon and the wrapping paper, exclaiming with each task how well done the package was. When he opened the tissue paper, Willow made a round mouth as if Hawk would soon say "Oh."

"Isn't this something?" he said instead, lifting out a pale blue chambray shirt with raw-hide whipstitching on the collar, cuffs, and decorating the chest pocket. The usual store buttons had been replaced with some made of horn in pale gold with black swirls. "Did you make this, too?" he asked Willow.

"Gail did all the work, but I handed her the

359

buttons and kept the rawhide from getting all messed up." Willow took the shirt out of the box and held it up against his jaw. "Do you like it? Gail said you would look very handsome in it."

"She certainly says a lot, doesn't she?" Hawk stood up, opened the shirt completely and held it up over his chest. "Well, what do you think, Willow?"

Willow grinned and turned around to Gail who was busy picking lint off the arm of her chair. "He does look handsome, doesn't he?"

Gail lifted her eyes. *Yes, he certainly does look handsome, with or without the shirt.* "Do you think it will fit all right?" she asked, lowering her gaze to the shirt.

"It's a great big thing," Willow answered for him, "it'll fit."

The gift-giving went on. Gail was given a beaded necklace made by Ada, and a belt made of rattlesnake skin fashioned by Jerrie.

"This is for you, too" Willow said, handing Gail a small box. "It's from me."

Gail was indeed surprised. She had helped Willow with all the gifts for the Kincaids, but she hadn't expected her to give something to her. She opened it carefully, and took out a long narrow piece of deerskin with colorfully beaded fringe at both ends.

"It's a bookmark," Willow said proudly, her

eyes shining into Gail's.

"I can see that it is, and a beautiful one, too. Did you make this yourself?"

"Yes, but Mr. Two Bulls—I forget which one—helped me with the deerskin. He made it soft and cut it for me."

"Well, it's just wonderful. I will treasure it always. We'll use it when we start our next book. I guess you didn't like the grocery store register slip I was using." Gail hugged the little girl closely. She couldn't have felt more like a mother if she'd birthed this child herself.

"That's all the presents," Willow said with a sigh.

"Are you sure of that?" Hawk asked her. "Did you search all the corners and behind the chairs?"

Willow gave him a questioning look. She scrambled up and crouched into corners and behind chairs. She was about to give up her search when she spotted something behind the door to the back hallway. She grabbed hold of the paper and slid it out.

"Now where did that come from?" Hawk asked, and went over to help her slide it out. "Let me see. There's a tag here. It says, 'to Gail and Willow from Hawk.' Well, now, and you almost missed it."

Willow's face registered delight as much as Gail's registered surprise. Hawk helped her carry the package to Gail. It was square and about twenty-four inches all around. Gail watched Hawk's face as Willow started the unwrapping. Gail had taught her not to simply tear into a present, but to admire the work of the wrapping and to open the package with care. Willow was doing such a patient and thorough job for a child, that Gail herself was almost frantic enough to rip the paper into shreds.

When the paper had been removed, it uncovered a painting in a frame constructed of aged barn wood. Gail knew Hawk had painted it. Her throat was too constricted to say anything, and her emotions were so intense they threatened to expose themselves through tears. Willow said it for both of them.

"Oh-h-h. That's me," she said breathlessly. "And that's you. Hawk painted us."

Gail blinked her eyes several times and gazed down at the faces of herself and Willow painted in a soft wash of watercolors, seated with the mountains as a backdrop, as if they'd posed at a photographer's studio for a mother and daughter portrait.

She looked up at him and sent her heartfelt thanks from her eyes. No words could ever tell him the depth of her emotions as she and Willow held the frame between them and touched their own feelings he'd captured on canvas.

Was he the one who had taken the photograph of Willow off the library photo collage wall? She realized something else more starkly—he had to have worked from memory when he painted her face since no photograph of herself would have been available to him.

Chapter Fourteen

The spring semester at Medicine Wheel School opened mid-January on a brittle cold, clear day. As Gail and Willow walked to the school together, Montana's big sky seemed bluer than ever, bright with sun, the air invigorating. Hard-packed snow squeaked under Willow's small rapid feet in her fleece-topped boots and crunched under Gail's in the first appropriate winter boots she'd owned in her life, a gift from herself for Christmas. They were big, dark brown, unfashionable as swim flippers at a cotillion, but they were high, and kept her feet warm and dry. And she loved them. And she loved walking to school with Willow.

Gail discovered she actually loved winter!

And she wondered where the old Gail Bricker had been spirited away to. But she didn't want to go looking very hard for her.

She and Willow were both looking forward to the new semester. Willow had a lot of catching up to do and it was hard work, but she seemed eager to try as long as Gail was there to help and support her. She looked to Gail for everything, and sometimes Gail felt weary with just keeping up with a child Willow's age. But Willow gave back to her twice as much as she demanded, and at the close of every tiring day Gail felt thankful and rewarded.

Late one evening in the opening days of February, Gail was relaxing with a novel after Willow had gone peacefully to bed. Jerrie had brought them an antique child's bed she'd found in the attic at the ranch, and Gail and Willow had fun fixing up a corner of the bedroom to accommodate it. Willow adored the bed and the big thick quilt Jerrie brought with it, and never made a fuss about going to bed at night. The ringing of the phone startled Gail. Late night calls usually meant trouble.

"Hi, my friend."

"Cath? Hi. Is anything wrong?"

"Now why would you ask that? Can't a friend call a friend anytime of the day or night? Within reason, that is. How are you? It seems ages since we've spoken. How is it going with the little girl, what was her name?"

"Willow. Everything is amazingly fine. You know me, I always wait for the other shoe to drop if things are going too well." Gail waited a moment. Catherine didn't say anything. She knew there was something wrong now. "So, you're sure there's nothing wrong, Cath?"

There was a long sigh at the other end of the line. Then, "Depends on how you define wrong. Got time for a long and involved story?"

"Of course, you're my best friend. I've got all night, if you need it."

Gail was growing worried about Catherine. Another long pause. She heard Catherine breathing, a raspy, ragged effort filled with emotion. Was she sick? Catherine cleared her voice as if trying to speak over something that choked and lodged in her throat. Finally Gail heard her settle her breathing.

"I think I've fallen in love, really in love," Catherine said at last, but her voice sounded sad and tormented, not joyful as Gail might have expected with so revealing a declaration.

"That's wonderful! But why do I get the idea you seem less than overjoyed about it? Unless . . . the person is totally off limits."

Silence hung between them for a long moment.

"I suppose some might think so," Catherine said, a heaviness in her voice.

"He's married, is that it?"

"Marriage has nothing to do with it."

"That's good," Gail said, relief evident. "You know how they are about that at Riverview." She waited for a response, but none was forthcoming. "Then what's the problem?" There was another long pause. And then the sounds of a flood of tears filled Gail's ear. "Cath, what's wrong? You haven't been infected with . . . who is this man?"

Catherine stemmed the flow of tears, and Gail heard her blowing her nose. "It's not a man—it's Jerrie."

Gail listened to her tortured friend, not comprehending what she'd heard at first, then tried to absorb the full meaning of her words.

"Wow," Gail managed at last.

"Yeah, wow. I finally allowed myself to accept who I am, what I am, but it seems others can't. I've lost my job over it."

"Oh, God, they found out? How?"

Catherine sighed. "Chelsea Gotter."

"Chelsea? What . . . how would she know anything about this?"

"Remember when I told you about Chelsea questioning her sexual orientation?"

"Yes, I do."

"And remember I said I wasn't certain how to address the problem? Well, I did what I hoped would help her the most, help her sort out her feelings and feel good about herself. I told her I'd wondered about my own sexual feelings, and that once I'd accepted the fact that I was more attracted to women than I was to men, I was much more comfortable with my life. Sounds good, doesn't it?"

It was Gail's turn to sigh. "It sounds sensitive to her needs, but risky as hell for you. I take it she told somebody about your conversation."

"You could say that. She threw herself into my arms and told me she had a crush on me. She asked me to . . . to make love to her." Gail waited, and Catherine started again. "I told her that we couldn't do that. I liked her as a student and wanted to help her work out her feelings, but that making love was reserved, in my view, strictly between two adults who understand that they love each other, are in love with each other. God, doesn't that sound sappy?"

"No, it sounds honest. How did she take that?"

"Quite well, I thought, until her father appeared at the director's office demanding my resignation for making homosexual overtures to his daughter."

"Oh my God!" Gail surmised the rest. Chelsea Gotter had made up yet another story to get her father's attention, and this time it cost a good teacher her job. "I take it the board believed him."

"Whether they did or didn't is neither here nor there. They accepted my resignation, and Gotter's hefty check, I might add, that afternoon."

"That is the most blatant display of discrimination I've ever heard of!" Gail was outraged at the entire scenario. "Take your case to an attorney!"

"I've made a statement about it to the board, to the local women's organization, and even to the papers. And now I don't care about it any longer. I'm glad to be out of that place. I'll miss Sheila and Prudie and Bethanne, but even they don't know how to deal with me now. It's as if the person I once was to them is now lost, so they don't know how to remain friends with me. They understand, or say they do, but I don't think they really do. Hell, I don't even know if I understand it all. I just hope I don't lose any more of my friends, especially you. I don't think I could bear that."

"Cath, for God's sake, you're the same woman I've known for more than twenty years. Nothing will ever change our friendship. I love you as I always have."

Catherine let out a relieved sigh. "I hope you mean that. We've been best friends for so long I've felt we've been connected in spirit. I don't know what I'd have done if you'd said we couldn't be friends anymore."

"Don't think about it. I'm concerned though. Isn't this a love from afar?"

"Only by distance. I think Jerrie's attracted to me, too."

"Are you sure?"

"No, not entirely. Shit, I don't know how I'm

supposed to know what I'm supposed to feel, or even how to act in a situation like this, for that matter. I've never given in to these feelings before. I've always suppressed them. They're supposed to be wrong, remember? Hell, I even got married once, so I'd be sure I wouldn't have those feelings ever again. Fat amount of good that did."

Gail knew that Catherine only used swear words when she was so upset inside she could barely breathe. She wished to high heaven she could respond with real understanding, say all the right words as Catherine had so often done for her.

"I guess I'll fail you as a friend with that one. I don't know how you're supposed to know either. But, it seems to me feelings are feelings, no matter who's feeling them for whom. Love is love, isn't it?"

"It feels like it ought to be. Do you feel it?"

Gail laughed. "I suppose I would if there was anyone to feel it from."

Catherine's voice lifted. "You're not serious!"

"Yeah, I am," Gail said hesitantly, "what are you thinking?"

"It's who I'm thinking about."

"Who?"

"Hawk Kincaid, of course."

"Hawk!"

"Yes. Jerrie and I had it figured out before

370

you and I left last summer. We thought you and he, I mean, I *know* you were attracted to him, and he sure acted as if he felt something for you, at least that was Jerrie's observation."

"Wrong!" Gail paused a moment, and grew quiet. "I shouldn't say that so finally. He has been very nice to me of late, understanding the difficult time I was going through and doing things to make it better. He's wonderful with Willow."

"Jerrie says she's noticed him following you with his eyes, those piercing black eyes, as I remember."

"I wouldn't know about that. He sends me mixed signals, smoke signals you could say, or maybe smoke screens. He seems friendly one day, and then the next I don't know what to make of him. I'm not certain of this, but I think he's built a stockade around him against women in general, and white women in particular. I have no basis in fact to say that, it's just my intuition. And maybe it's possible he's still fighting ancient wars."

"I understand about things like that. Anything left without resolution keeps the conflict from playing out."

"Very wise words. I think you're describing yourself as much as you are Hawk."

"And you."

"Me?" Gail was genuinely surprised at that.

"Yes. Have all your battles been resolved?"

"I don't battle them anymore. They're no longer important to me. It's you we have to think about now. What are you going to do? Try for a job at another school?"

Catherine laughed. "Are you kidding? You know how small the world of private and public schools is, how conservative they are. It won't be long before the news gets around about me and the brand I wear."

"Yeah," Gail said in musing softness. "I'm sorry about that, but it is true schools and organizations get around anti-discrimination laws. It's rotten, and it hurts good teachers, good people like you."

"And I know there are some teachers who have deserved to be fired. There are less then honorable people everywhere. I've never done anything to give them reason to even consider such action. But . . . I'm actually all right about that. Now that I have admitted to the world who I truly am, I don't want to work in the kind of arena where I and others like me are treated shabbily. I'll just have to think of something else to keep life and limb together."

Gail suddenly had what she thought was a mind-blinding idea. "Why don't you come out here and stay with me?"

There was a long pause at the other end of the line. "That's too simple."

"Simple? Why?"

"I'd feel like I was running away, like I was a coward."

"Catherine!" Gail dragged out the name like an exasperated mother. "You wouldn't be running away from anything, because there isn't anything there anymore for you to run from. You'd be going *to* something. Just come out here."

"And do what? Make Jerrie think I'm chasing her?" She let out a wry little laugh. "God, didn't that sound like a Nineteen Fifties high school sock hopper?"

Gail laughed. "At least we're having some fun over this. You could come out here and find a lot of things to do. People on the reservation need help. And besides, maybe Jerrie would like to feel chased, you know. We'd all like that in our lives now and then. And sometimes, if it's the right person, we slow down so we can be caught."

"Gail, be reasonable. I have to make a living. I've never been a kept woman and I don't intend to start now. Unless you consider the fact that I owe American Express my life's blood for all the trips I've taken as being a kept woman. Not to mention the fact that I owe on my car and my other credit cards, and . . ."

"And you at least have a house you could sell. That would bail you out and get you out. You could come out here, start a new life, and see what might happen with Jerrie. If you're right, you may have a wonderful new relationship out of all this turmoil."

Catherine was quiet. Then she sighed a long weary sigh. "What if I'm wrong?"

"You know in your gut you're not wrong, don't you?" Gail's voice was hushed.

Catherine cleared her tight throat. "What would Ada think? And Hawk?"

It was Gail's turn to be quiet. She had no idea what Ada or Hawk would think, how they would react. Every person and every culture had its own ideas and perceptions about homosexuality.

"I can't answer that for you. But maybe Jerrie can. Come on out here and find out. You can stay with me until you find a place of your own. Okay? Will you?"

"You make it hard for me to refuse."

"I mean to."

"It would give me a chance to think things through."

"It would. Believe me, once the winter socks in here there's nothing else to do but think."

"And, of course, the chances are I'd see Jerrie and that would tell me if I'm right or not."

"Bingo."

"Is next week all right?"

"If you really want to wait that long!"

"Gail, you're the best friend any woman ever had. I wish I could be there tonight! But, time for a reality check. It'll take me a while to get my act together. By early spring I should be able to make the move. Thanks, friend. I love you."

Gail swallowed back a hard knot of emotion. "You've been closer than a sister to me, Cath. I love you, too, my friend. See you in the spring."

Gail hung up the phone and dropped down on the couch with a new heaviness in her limbs. She drew a blanket around herself, pulled up her knees close to her chest and hugged them as if to keep her thoughts trapped inside.

Friends. She and Catherine were friends, and they did love each other. It would be a bleak life without the kind of friendship the two of them shared. And it was odd, but neither one of them shared as close a friendship with any of the other women they knew. Gail had just realized that this very moment. She'd never thought about what it meant to be a real friend to anyone before now. Why was that? Had she been taking their friendship for granted? She missed Catherine terribly, and even Carol and Ang who'd become new friends, weren't the kind of friends Catherine had always been.

No matter how foolish she'd ever acted, no matter how many mistakes she'd ever made, Catherine was the friend who stood by her in the act of being herself, and left her with her self-esteem intact. Had she ever told Catherine how much that meant to her, how she knew she was never diminished in her friend's eyes no matter how diminished she'd become in her own for doing some of the things she'd done?

She wondered now how she could call herself a best friend and never have known or at least sensed Catherine's turmoil, her handling of what was going on inside herself, struggling with a sexuality they'd all been taught was wrong. Why hadn't she seen any signs of that turmoil? God, what strength of character Catherine had if she could keep all her pain and wondering inside, all her questions, buffer the changes in the evolution of her person, handle it all on her own internally, projecting a calm, totally together exterior.

Gail pictured herself as average. No one truly unique or special. Just an average woman, doing a good job, being good at it, being a true friend. She was beginning to see just what being a true friend meant, just what reaching inside oneself and grasping something of one's own psyche could do. The wide open spaces were opening her eyes wider—and expanding her mind.

Her heart was another matter entirely. She should heed the advice she gave Catherine. She recognized what was going on in her emotions where Hawk was concerned, and she believed he was struggling with the same emotions regarding his own reluctant feelings for her. She was old enough, and she believed wise enough to know that. Yet, at the same time, she felt locked in a time frame of seventeen-years-old again, when love was so new and so powerful she was weak without the knowledge of how to act. It made no difference how old a person got, love and friendship would always cause growing pains.

In the barn Hawk sat astride a bench made from the trunk of a tree, a saddle thrown over it as if it were a horse. He dipped from a tin of saddle soap and rubbed the creamy emollient into the leather, working in small circles with the pads of his fingers. The saddle was old, too fancy for a working cowboy, but the workmanship in the intricate tooling was unique, one of a kind. It was never used now, and he'd built a glass-front cabinet for it, and kept it at the end of the horse barn where he'd also built a small room for himself. A haven, a place to go to if being outdoors in adverse weather became too difficult. Often he would spend his time thinking while he worked on the saddle, defusing explosive feelings of anger or frustration. And grief.

While he had no birthright to it, the saddle was a symbol of the continuance of life. It had belonged to Kenneth Kendrick Kincaid the first, who had commissioned its construction, and who had treated it, so Hawk had been told by his mother, as if it were a precious woman, the love of one's life.

When he died, the saddle was handed to the second Kincaid, husband of Hawk's mother. He hadn't used it very often, but kept it around as a reminder of his father, the founder of the Triple or Nothing Ranch, the man who had forged an empire in the wilds, and left his son a very rich man. Kincaid the second had a precious woman of his own. When she'd died of cancer, he was left with a young son. Trey. He needed a woman to care for the boy.

Kincaid had been trying to buy land from the Cheyenne. He had seen Woman Walks Far walking along a road carrying a sickly child, a boy of about five years. He'd picked her up in his car and taken her to his own doctor. The boy had blood poisoning and would have died if Kincaid had not come along when he did and driven them to the doctor. They had no home, no real home. The child had been born without a father. His mother had been married to a Crow man who died young, and she was left to raise the child on her own. Outcast from the few remaining members of her family because of her marriage to the Crow, without work, with small government assistance when she could get it from corrupt Indian agents, Woman Walks Far struggled every day of her life and her boy's life, to keep them together, to keep them alive.

Kincaid brought Woman Walks Far and her boy into his house, gave them a home in exchange for her care of the place and of his own son. After a time, the two married, and Kincaid adopted her son and raised him as a brother to his own son, Kenneth Kendrick Kincaid III, known as Trey. He took the boy and his mother to a church, had them baptized and gave them Christian names.

Woman Walks Far allowed herself to be called Ada after Kincaid's grandmother, but she refused to call her son anything but Lone Hawk. At the moment of his birth, alone, outside and protected by nothing more than a pile of sage and cedar she'd pulled together under a rock ledge, Ada had seen a lone hawk circling the mid-heaven above her in twilight. She took it to be an omen that her son would soar, but at the mid-point in his life he would be destined to live out his days alone. Hawk's Christian name was long forgotten and never used.

One day in Hawk's eighth year, Kincaid hoisted the boy up onto the back of his black stallion, Warrior, to sit astride the special saddle. He hoisted Trey up behind him, and the two sat high off the ground holding onto the tooled leather saddle skirts for dear life.

"This saddle will be yours someday, my sons,

as well as all the land you see around you. Guard the saddle well, care for it, remember that the man who made it provided all of this for you. He gave you this life you have, but you must be guardians of it or you will lose it all."

"Hawk can't have Grandfather's saddle, Father," young Trey had whined. "He's not blood. He's Indian. It's mine, and I don't want him to touch it." He grabbed Hawk's shirt by the back of the neck and pulled and pushed with his knees until he unseated Hawk and shoved him to the ground.

Kincaid grabbed for Hawk beneath the great stallion's prancing feet. He reprimanded the now petrified Trey. "You know better than to fool around on Warrior, boy! He's high-strung. And you remember this, Hawk is your brother, regardless of blood, and neither of you is ever to forget that."

But Trey had forgotten it, did his best to make certain Hawk forgot it, too, whenever they were not in the presence of their father. But Kincaid knew what was happening between them. He sent them away to school, thinking a change of scene would make them grow up, make them appreciate each other. But they never had. When Kincaid died, Trey took over the ranch and the finances, and took on a fancy-living life. When money got tight, he took the Kincaid saddle and sold it for a thousand dollars.

Hawk remembered that Kincaid and his mother had grown to love each other in an honest, settled love. He remembered how he took work on another ranch while he worked on the Triple or Nothing to make enough money to buy back the precious saddle.

Now as Hawk carefully worked the saddle soap into the leather, rubbed and polished it with chamois cloth, he was remembering much more than he meant to. He remembered how Laura, his young blonde wife, left them when Kenny was barely three to go east with a salesman she'd met in a bar. He'd signed the divorce papers as soon as they were in his hands. She'd asked for nothing. He was left with nothing. Nothing, and everything.

And he remembered the last morning he'd hoisted his own six-year-old son, Kenny, up onto the saddle on the back of the aging Warrior, and told him the story of the Kincaid saddle. Hawk never promised it would belong to Kenny someday, although he felt it rightfully should have. But if Trey had children, then the saddle would go to them. Trey never had children.

That day, with Kenny astride the Kincaid saddle looking down at his father with hero worship in his eyes, Hawk by his son's side holding him safely, they watched a lone hawk circling overhead on a lifting wind, searching, seeing something they couldn't see, and soaring away on silent wings.

That was almost twenty-five years ago, but the picture was still vivid in Hawk's mind. Hawk polished harder. A father believes he can protect his son all his life. Hawk never got over the one time he wasn't there to protect his.

Every man needed heroes. Kenneth Kendrick Kincaid the Second was Hawk's first hero. Kenny was his last.

He worked the chamois with fury. Maybe that would make the hurt go away at last. Maybe he could force the tears that dimmed his eyes back inside, and his vision would clear. Maybe. But he'd performed this ceremony hundreds of times and it had never worked before.

A hand touched his shoulder and he jumped.

"You're going to rub the nap right off that hide if you're not careful, big brother." Jerrie dropped down on a corner bench.

Hawk stopped rubbing. "Yeah. Forgot what I was doing. I was thinking."

Jerrie knew what Hawk had been thinking about, and she knew how melancholy he could get. She'd seen that melancholia, and she'd seen what he'd allowed alcohol to do to him. Those had been tough years on Ada, and tough on her, too. She loved Hawk deeply, and she didn't stop loving him through his addiction. She loved and respected him more when he beat it down like an ancient enemy.

"Sometimes I think you think too much," Jerrie said. The two understood each other completely.

Hawk got up and started putting his polishing things in a wood cupboard on the far wall. He genuinely liked Jerrie as much as he loved her. She was as much his friend as she was his sister, and he was grateful for her presence in his life.

"So, what are you up to today, baby sister?"

"I love it. Still a baby sister at forty! I'm the luckiest chick in the world!"

"Better than being an old hen, isn't it?"

Hawk picked up a handful of straw from the barn floor and flung it over Jerrie's head. That usually started a knock-down-drag-out that took them up one end of the barn and down the other until they both were rolling in straw convulsed with laughter. Not today. Jerrie picked up a handful of straw in retaliation, but let it filter through her fingers back onto the floor.

Hawk watched her out of the corner of his eye while he finished cleaning up. Maybe building a sweat lodge would be good for both of them today. He threw a woven blanket of muted reds and browns and greens over the gleaming Kincaid saddle, then went over to Jerrie and hunkered down in front of her.

"Want to sweat with me later?" he asked, his voice low and quiet.

"I don't think so."

"Why not? It will make you feel better. You'll cleanse yourself of whatever's bothering you. You've done it before."

"Not this time," Jerrie said, her eyes downcast, her fingers bending a long straw in an accordion shape.

"What's different about this time?" Hawk put out a hand and rubbed it gently up and down her forearm. He hated seeing Jerrie like this. She was the one who was always upbeat, always saw good in everything, always saw the silver beneath a tarnished coin.

Jerrie raised her eyes to the brother she adored. They shone glassy hard with tears. "What if I told you that what's happening to me right now is something I don't want to be cleansed of?"

Hawk listened to her anguished voice. His eyes held hers steady. "I'd understand and accept that. And I'd tell you that a sweat might make it easier for you to hold onto and live with whatever it is that's hurting you so much."

Jerrie held his understanding gaze a long time before she dropped hers. "I know. At least I think I do. My insides war with themselves, and nothing can bring peace this time."

"I know about things like that."

Hawk dropped to his knees and gathered his sister in his arms. Whatever she'd done, or thought she'd done was tearing at her and he couldn't stand seeing her in such turmoil. The blood of two vastly different cultures flowed in her veins, yet she'd somehow managed to emerge with the best of both. Unlike himself. The blood of his respected Cheyenne mother and the blood of the unseen Crow father flowed against each other like reverse magnets. His was involved in a daily war without the lull of peace at any time, not only of blood but of circumstance.

"Let me help carry your burden. I am the larger—I didn't say stronger," he added hastily when her challenging eyes came up swiftly to meet his. He knew how strong Jerrie was, not just in the back. "I am your brother. We share the same mother, but I am also your brother in the way the Creator meant for us all to be. Two minds and hearts can bear the heaviness evenly. You have already done that for me. You know you must honor me by letting me do the same for you."

"That was for Kenny. This is different," she said against his shoulder.

Hawk winced at the sound of his son's name. Then he rubbed her back. "It's hurting you. That's what matters." He hugged her hard. "Tell me," he whispered.

Jerrie clamped both hands against the muscles of his upper arms, and pushed herself back. She searched his eyes, knowing he would still love her no matter what she told him. She knew it in her gut, even if she were to tell him she'd murdered, he would still love her, stand by her, comfort her, help her. There was more strength in that knowledge and in the man before her than she had ever felt in her life from another living or spiritual thing except her mother. But this time she could not go to her mother. This would surpass her mother's vast ability to understand.

"I think I love somebody." She blurted it out and her voice sounded in her ears like that of a little girl's.

Hawk leaned back to get a clearer look at his sister's face. A small smile threatened to tilt the corner of his mouth. "You . . . think you love somebody?"

She nodded, and tears filled her eyes.

"Forgive me for saying this, baby sister at forty, but it's about time!"

Her tense laugh sent the tears spilling down her cheeks. "Why did I know you would say that?"

"Because we know each other very well," Hawk's voice was serious. "Why is loving this person causing so much pain?"

"Because no one will understand why it happened. I mean, I didn't ask for it, it just did. I wasn't looking for it, it just came to me."

"My dear sister, love in its various forms of

real and unreal manifestations has come looking for you from the moment you turned twelve and gorgeous! I've had to beat off the would-be admirers with a stone-headed tomahawk! Of course it came to you." He cocked his head. Her smile was only half-hearted. "Ah, I see. This time it caught you, or you let yourself get caught."

She nodded. "I was afraid to admit how much I wanted it."

"Everybody wants love," Hawk said, letting out a long breath and dropping down to sit in the straw in front of Jerrie.

"Everybody? Even you, my brother made of rock?" Jerrie cocked her head at him this time.

"Yes, everybody. Even me. I may want it, but that doesn't mean I'll let it happen."

"I see you haven't sweated away the sting of Laura's leaving you. Hawk, that was years ago. She had to go, and you know it. Laura was different to begin with. She wanted a different life."

Hawk picked up a piece of straw and carefully, drawing it out as if to extend the pain, shredded it in long thin strands. "Does this person not love you? Is that why you are so sad?" He closed the subject of his own life, and abruptly brought it back to Jerrie's.

"I don't know. I don't know what to think."

"If you don't know, then there isn't anything

to be sad about yet. Don't put a label on the feeling till you know the contents." Hawk brushed the heel of one boot with a handful of straw.

"You're very wise. And I'm afraid there's already a label that I had nothing to do with putting on it." She stood up and walked to the open window. "If I do anything about this, Hawk, I'll have to leave here. And that would break my heart."

"Why would you have to leave?" Hawk was alarmed at such a suggestion. "Why can't you and whoever it is stay here?"

"It would disgrace the family." Jerrie turned around to face him. "I could never do that to you or to mother."

Hawk rose. "You know that we will love you and want you with us no matter how bad you think things are. What is disgrace anyway? We don't care what other people think about us. Opinions are everywhere, wrong or right. All that matters is that you can rely on your family, trust us to support and love you."

"Trey won't!"

"Trey? How can you even suggest he'd have anything to condemn? Look at his life. And we've stuck by him through the hell he's given us, without so much as a shred of love and respect in return. You have given us more love than a human can expect in a lifetime." He went

388

closer to her, reached out and took her hand. "Now, tell me. Who is it? A criminal? A murderer? A welfare fraud artist?"

Hawk was out on a limb now, and he knew it. He wanted to tease her into telling him, or make her mad enough to blurt it out to him. Anything.

"No. It's worse."

"Well . . . ?"

"It's . . . she's a woman. Gail's friend, Catherine."

Hawk let out a long sigh. Jerrie watched his face cautiously, almost fearfully.

"At last," he said.

Jerrie looked at him incredulously. "What do you mean 'at last'?"

"The tension between you two when she was here on her vacation was thick as a good beefsteak. I wanted to lock the two of you together in a horse stall and make you stay there until you both admitted what was happening to you!"

Jerrie stood there, her mouth open, her eyes wide.

"I take it she's finally told you her feelings and so now you're just getting around to voicing yours."

Jerrie stood stiffly, not speaking.

"Sister, dear," Hawk said, letting go of her hand and cupping her chin, carefully closing her mouth. "There. Now open it and say something."

Jerrie swallowed. "You . . . ? I . . . You . . . knew? She . . . No, she . . . I . . ."

Hawk stroked his chin. "Ah, I see. You can't figure out how I knew, you thought you'd hid it well, you were hiding it from yourself so how could I know, she hasn't said a thing to you, but your sharp intuition tells you she feels the same way. Did I get it all?"

Jerrie nodded once, then shook her head.

"Oh," Hawk said, "I forgot to add that this doesn't change anything between us, and it won't with Mother either."

Jerrie swallowed again. "Hawk!" She threw herself into the shelter of his arms. "What about the People?"

He thought about that question a long time. "You matter very much to the ones who know you. Feel blessed. You love . . . and you are loved."

Jerrie hugged her brother closer. "You could feel as blessed yourself if you would admit it. And you know what I mean and who I mean. Let it happen, Hawk. Life isn't complete without it."

Chapter Fifteen

Hawk spent the better part of the afternoon building a sweat lodge in an isolated protected location along the Tongue River, far from the ranch. This rise along the river bank bordered the reservation and a small plot of land that had once belonged to his mother's family. A ramshackle cabin she'd shared with her parents rose in the advancing twilight, its black outline silhouetted like an eerie ghost against the darkening streaked sky.

He came here often to think, and to stay in the cabin for as many days as it took to rid his mind of the devils that occupied it. At those times he would build a lodge and partake in a sweat ceremony alone.

He built the lodge as if he were constructing a work of art, shaping and tying with twine the fourteen long thin willow saplings into a half-sphere, lifting the fifteenth willow branch up the middle to form the arrow, and lashing the canvas tarp around all sides, leaving an opening flap. He dug a firepit in the center, and selected forty-four rocks by their uniform shape and weight of around five pounds each. He could have used some of the rocks he'd used on previous sweat ceremonies, but this time the need in him was strong to get new ones. Perhaps their untapped energy would enter his body with the cleansing steam, rid him of his demons, and open his mind and emotions to help him feel strong again.

Today as he worked he became more aware of his body, his heart pounding from the exertion, his own breath making steam in the crisp air. Anticipation for his time in the sweat lodge mounted. He would find relief sitting among the cleansing steam, and giving over his roiled emotions, muddled thoughts, desperate questions to the primordial spirits who waited within the four directions.

Every year before the snows came he filled the storage shed behind the cabin with dried herbs and flowers, sage and cedar, and willow branches to be used only for *ema-ome,* his sweat lodge. He hauled out the fragrant bundles now and covered the floor of his lodge with a fragrant cushion. A few feet away from the lodge he started a fire in which to heat his stones and make coals to keep them hot. He brought a bucket of water and a dipper and set them inside the opening flap.

Hawk had known for two days he was going to sweat, and had begun his fast the afternoon before. He expected a lot from this duration, almost as much as he had when he'd sat with the elders nine times in sweat lodges, fasted, smoked the sacred pipe, made mental and emotional connection with the Creator, and, with the help of the holy men, willed himself out of the grip of depression and alcoholism.

When he knew he was ready, the elders had invited him to participate in Sun Dances. He remembered vividly the moments of his first piercing during a Sun Dance ceremony. Lying upon a bed of sage, he'd fixed his eyes on the great sky above, a blue arc surrounding him and the dancers and holy men, signifying oneness with Mother Earth. He'd watched the holy man set his jaw, and knew when he would begin to make the two parallel cuts across his chest. This was contrary to the holy man whose way of life was to heal and take away pain and hurt, not inflict it. Hawk had faced down the pain of the awl twice piercing the skin on his chest, and the greater pain, as intense as hot fire, as the pegs were inserted across the cuts. The gathered holy men and dancers had been deep in prayer. In the powerful moments of their coming together, the spiritual wind around them came in gale force. He closed his eyes now and visualized the completion of that Sun Dance and his first piercing.

The elders had often said that sun dancers understood more completely a woman's pain in childbirth. Hawk had been pierced three times in sun dances during his years of searching, connecting with his heritage, Maheo. He believed he knew in the core of his existence through his piercings what it had felt like for Laura to give birth to Kenny. Kenny's death had been the source of similar pain, for he felt his baby had been snatched from his own belly.

He remembered how, during his prayers with the sun dancers and holy men, he'd pledged bond and connection to Mother Earth and all her children, and he'd prayed for freedom from the bonds of his own devils. He believed he'd achieved that freedom, but now he wondered if he'd allowed his soul to be repossessed by the devils because he'd allowed another white woman to become important to him.

The rocks were now heated, and Hawk carried them inside and placed them in the pit. He closed the flap and allowed the darkness of the lodge to engulf him. Then he stripped to his undershorts and sat down cross-legged in the sage and cedar cushion of the floor, facing west. His eyes adjusted to the dark red glow from the stones and coals, and he took the first dipper of water and poured it over the rocks creating the steam to begin the first endurance. There would be four endurances in all, one made in each of the four directions.

Steam shot upward with a loud hiss, and with it the words of his first endurance toward the west, the direction of Father Sky and Mother Earth who provided this water. Hawk wished Jerrie had come with him to sweat. In her absence he offered a prayer for her, that her spirit would receive and benefit in healing and growth what this ceremony he conducted in the stark aloneness of his own spirit could provide.

Hawk spent the moments of the first endurance quietly chanting ancient words of appreciation for nature, creation, the oneness of all things with the Great One, the power of the water used to make the steam. He fastened his eyes on the glowing red-orange stones and images reflected from them that began to take shape. His son's laughing face appeared among the images of his spirit ancestors. Kenny looked happy, at peace, protected, not alone.

And then Hawk's own sweat became part of the mist rising with the steam, mingling with the life-giving water and falling back to the earth from which it had come. His shoulders wracked with the intensity of his pain and feeling. His arms ached to hold Kenny again, to protect him as he should have done as a father. He'd failed the boy, he believed, and he would never forgive himself for it. He had never allowed himself to weep for his son. Weeping was a sign of weakness, and he'd been weak enough as a father to last a lifetime.

Laboriously, Hawk rose and opened the flap for a moment to let in a breath of fresh crisp air.

Then he closed it and sat down, turning his body toward the north. In this second endurance he felt the cleansing steam penetrate his skin, and in the traditional way he chanted words that symbolized the recognition of courage, honesty, strength, cleanliness. He chanted them again, willing himself to believe the power of his ancient traditions would ease his pain again.

He poured another dipper of water over the rocks. Now the lodge was hot and steamy, darkly aglow from the orange-red rocks, and fragrant with the scent of healing sage and cedar. He closed his eyes and allowed himself to feel the weight of his life lift.

Before he could begin the third endurance, Hawk had to lift the flap and go outside for more hot stones. He was raising them with a pitchfork when he caught in his peripheral vision and was startled by a figure emerging out of the darkness. A more superstitious mind might have perceived the figure as the ghost of a lost spirit who had once walked beside him. Hawk, while holding on to the ceremonial traditions of his people, the ancient belief that the spirits of the departed live on in the air around, did not for a moment perceive the figure to be an apparition. When his eyes adjusted to the light from his fire, he recognized Gail.

"What are you doing here?" he muttered gruffly, hardly aware that he was standing barefoot in snow, naked except for his undershorts. "How did you find me?"

Gail shivered, trembled as much from the cold as from the effect his presence had on her, an effect she'd allowed herself at last to accept.

"Jerrie brought me." She shoved her gloved hands up the sleeves of her jacket.

"She shouldn't have." He entered the lodge and dropped the hot stones in the pit.

Gail came to the opening of the lodge and bent to look inside. "May I . . . come in, or is it unacceptable?" She watched as he struggled with his answer. "I don't mean to intrude. I know this is a sacred ceremony. I'll wait out here, if you prefer."

Hawk sat down, his body facing east. The ceremony was so ingrained in him, so much a part of him, that even interference from one of the reasons why he'd gone to sweat in the first place did not break the rhythm of his pattern.

"Come in, and close the flap."

She did as she was instructed, then stood waiting, not knowing exactly what she should do. Should she sit down, or wait to be invited? Should she speak, or stay silent unless asked to speak? Her eyes took their time adjusting to the dark glow.

"Take off your clothes and sit down," he ordered.

"Wh—What?"

"Take off your clothes and sit down, and be quick about it."

Gail took off her gloves and jacket, then her sweater. It was very warm inside the tarp and willow structure, warmer than she might have imagined. He wasn't watching her, seemed mesmerized by the hot coals and stones. She took off her boots and socks and waited. Still he said nothing. He sat motionless and silent before the firepit, his bronze body and jet hair gleaming in the low light like a comet hanging in a midnight sky.

"Is this enough?" she asked tentatively.

"No."

The abruptness of his answer startled her. All right. She knew this was a sacred ceremony. She couldn't stand here and be modest about this, yet taking off all her clothes in this kind of situation was alien to her sense of propriety. He lifted a dipper of water and held it above the stones, waiting, and she sensed his growing impatience disturbed his place in the ceremony more than her entrance had.

Quickly she began removing everything and was down to her bra and panties when he said evenly, "Enough. Sit down, facing that way." He pointed her toward the east.

She did exactly that, and he let the water flow over the stones that sent the steam rising.

"This is the third endurance," he said in that voice of varying pitches and resonance she'd come to love. "You have missed the first two. They are, first, the recognition of the spirit world, and second, the recognition of courage and the beginning of cleansing from the steam."

"I understand," she said, "I've read a lot about sweat ceremonies."

"That is nothing," he answered, reducing her to the level of pre-school education regarding her knowledge of Indian ceremonies. "The experience many times over is the only teacher. I did not want you here, but the sweat ceremony is one of bringing together of spirits, releasing the mist of one's body to mingle with the earth. This is a place of peace."

Gail stayed silent, watching Hawk intently scrutinizing the glowing rocks, their heat and hue washing over the chiseled planes of his face, his aquiline nose, his hooded eyes in the shadows. She listened to him as he closed his eyes and prayed out loud, speaking of the recognition of knowledge, both symbols of the third endurance.

"We are the people of the morning star," Hawk prayed, taking on the role of lodge leader as he might in a group ceremony. "The morning star is the symbol of awakening. In the awakening all people can gain wisdom, knowledge to overcome the fear of each other, to respect the naturalness of the earth. With the morning star we begin a new day, a new knowledge. With spirit and knowledge we can heal ourselves and heal our world."

Gail closed her eyes. Jerrie had told her once that she would someday learn about the morning star. She felt suddenly that she was rising from the earth, felt light, floating. The steam engulfed her with almost suffocating intensity, the fragrance of sage and cedar filled her senses, the heat pricked her skin. Hawk's voice in prayer filled her mind and soul.

"Now you," she heard him say from afar.

Her eyes opened with a jolt. Before her the coals undulated light and dark, images formed, shapeless yet somehow recognizable. And a naked bronze man with damp black hair pulled back away from his face and tied with a strip of rawhide sat next to her on a bed of aromatic greens like a fragment of primeval history at the beginning of time.

She opened her mouth to say something, but no words came. She was overcome with emotion and the sheer intensity of being swept into another space, another time, where none of the spirits of her life before her had ever been.

"Speak what's in your heart," he told her. "It will come without effort if you let go."

Gail hadn't prayed since Sunday school days when her whole class had learned the Lord's prayer by heart, and rattled it off the way kids of today could recite rap songs. But she'd walked away from organized religion at an early age. Later in her life she was nagged by questions about her own spirituality, about how to show appreciation for the gifts of the earth. She'd found no way to answer them or express her vague sensations.

"You can say whatever you like," he urged, and Gail thought he sensed her trepidation, the reasons for her hesitancy.

"Thank you," she whispered into the air. Her voice croaked, but the sound of it gave her courage. "Thank you for . . . the experiences in my life now. For bringing Willow to me. We are two souls of the same breath."

Her voice sounded to her as if it were coming from another's throat. She did not recognize it, was not prepared for the words. "Thank you for the present, thank you for memory of the past, both good and bad, for it makes me the person I am now. Thank you for the people in my life, the friends here, and there, the new friends. Thank you for this ceremony . . . this man . . . Hawk."

Without realizing it, Gail had moved within the ceremony in the traditional way, turning the prayer or next stage over to the person next to her.

Hawk stood, raised the flap and went out for more hot stones, bringing them in on a pitchfork so as not to bring the coals that would smoke. A gust of biting cold filled the dome and cleared the air making it easier for Gail to breathe. Her heightened senses seemed open and raw. She was amazed that her body in its semi-nakedness did not feel chilled.

Hawk closed the flap and instructed her to move facing south, and he sat down again. He lifted the dipper and poured water over the hot coals. The hiss of steam gave voice to the impact of Gail's moving experience inside the lodge with Hawk. Slowly he lifted the dipper and poured three more times. The steam built, filling the dome, and Gail was lifted higher by a buoyancy she did not have memory of before now.

Hawk spoke in prayerful reverence, and in his words Gail sensed he was teaching her. Whether consciously he meant to or not, his voice sounded as if he truly wanted her to know, to understand.

"The light and power of the Great Spirit surrounds and protects us. The fourth and last endurance to the south symbolizes healing and growth. The elders have taught us the meaning of the four directions. We must embrace them now as we pray for healing and the power to grow, first as a sapling in the gentle breeze, then as a mighty tree in the winds of change."

Gail knew it was probably not the traditional custom to hold hands in the sweat lodge ceremony, but she felt compelled to take Hawk's hands as they sat in peaceful communion. She reached out with both of hers and took both of his, and the moist heat of their mutual sweat blended upon impact.

Hawk's eyes shifted sharply from the glowing coals to her flushed face. For once she could read what was in them. The holding of hands was not his way. Yet in the sharing of the sweat ceremony with another, there was the voluntary acceptance of the other's way within the moments of prayer, an offering of peace and a wish for the other's healing and growth as much for one's own.

Hawk took Gail's hands and held them as she held his. Each turned back toward the center and the glow of the coals, and said their own silent prayers. Then he stood and assisted her to her feet. He led her toward the flap and outside into the snow. Barefoot, clad only in underwear as was Hawk, she stood by his side, her hand clasped in his, and raised her face to follow his gaze toward the black sky studded with the brilliance of countless stars. Wherever her mind and the senses of her flesh had been transported, she had no feeling of cold. There existed only a sensation of oneness with the universe.

Later in the cabin's big room, Hawk lit the fire he'd laid in the fireplace before building the sweat lodge. Gail had dressed and accepted the towel he'd given her to wrap around her damp hair. While she was in the privy, he brought in more logs for the fireplace.

Gail stepped back into the cabin from the rear door. She stopped at the entrance of the big room and looked around at the sparse furnishings. A table and three chairs, a bench, a pile of blankets on a log-framed bed, a threadbare rug. Hawk stood in front of the fieldstone mantel holding a log, staring into the fire, lost in his own thoughts. She looked at his back bent slightly toward the fire, his shoulders rounded. He looked more vulnerable to her than she'd ever suspected he could. He seemed always to be a rock of detached strength, imperturbable, impenetrable.

"Thank you," she said at last, letting him know of her presence in the room.

Startled, Hawk dropped the log into the blaze and when he spun around it appeared he'd done so mystically in a shower of sparks. Without speaking he stared at her as the fire behind him burst into higher crackling flames, illuminating him in a red-hot incandescence.

Struck by his phantomlike vision, Gail was unable to move. She shivered audibly. The sound moved him and he stepped toward her, seeming at the same time to step out of the glow that briefly surrounded him. She accepted his outstretched hand, and he led her to the fire and a long low bench drawn up in front of it. She sat down facing the blaze, warming her feet and hands, removing the towel from her hair and fluffing it with her fingers in the growing warmth.

She smelled something cooking, something delicious and aromatic with herbs.

She turned to look over her shoulder to where

he was stirring a pot over a portable gas stove. He picked up two glasses and walked toward her.

"Mineral water," he said, handing one to her. "You need to drink a lot of water and juice after a sweat."

She accepted the glass gratefully. "What are you cooking? It smells wonderful."

"Vegetable stew. I have been fasting for more than twenty-four hours. This meal is made from the fruits of the earth. I have bread as well. Will you have some supper?"

"If you have enough. You weren't expecting me."

"I have enough."

He went back to the pot and turned off the gas, then dished up three bowls of the steaming stew. He brought two and handed one to her, then took the other and went outside the cabin. Gail wondered if he meant to eat out there, as if that might be part of the ceremony, but he returned empty-handed. He brought the third bowl and a plate of bread and sat down next to her in front of the fire.

She watched his face a long moment as he stirred the stew and breathed in the aromatic steam it made.

"Why did you take the other bowl outside?" she asked.

"It is an offering to any spirits who may have entered the ceremony." He said it as if that were common practice.

"Thank you," she said again. "I feel . . . refreshed. Yet, the feeling is much greater, much deeper. I can't explain."

"Don't try. Just feel."

She ate the stew and bread as if she, too, had been fasting for twenty-four hours. "Do you come to the sweat lodge often?"

He shook his head. "Not enough." His voice was oddly thick, almost tremulous. He cleaned his bowl, refilled it, and brought the last ladleful to her.

"What do you mean?"

He sighed. "It is a ceremony of truth, of purification."

She puzzled over his words. Setting her bowl on the floor behind the bench, she turned to him. "Is there a truth you are afraid to face?" She knew that was prying into personal thoughts, but the moments they were sharing now seemed rife with electricity, as if every word said would have an impact.

"I face them," he said bitterly.

"But you can't accept them, and they've become demons you can't exorcise, is that it?"

He stood and took the bowls to the cooking area, returned with the bottle of mineral water and refilled their glasses.

"Truths or demons, they don't concern you," he said with a hard edge in his cracking voice.

Gail knew she'd somehow struck both. Jerrie

had told her a little about Hawk's personal wars, but she sensed now they didn't all have to do with his mixed heritage or his adopted siblings.

"If we are friends, and I believe we are," she pressed, "then I am concerned. What hurts you upsets me. Would you like to tell me about it?"

"You wouldn't understand, so stop prying," he snapped.

"How do you know I wouldn't?" Gail kept her voice quiet and even.

"I know. You haven't the experience."

"You don't know me or my experiences. You haven't let yourself know me, or let me know you. But I believe you want to. And I want to know you."

Gail knew she was out on a limb now, saying as much as she was, pressing him the way she was. If he threw her out of this cabin, she was stranded in the snow and cold wind. Jerrie had driven back to the ranch. Willow was spending the night there. They'd just assumed Hawk would drive Gail back to her apartment.

He set down the glass and turned his back to the fireplace. She could see the blaze in his eyes now, and regretted pushing him.

"What is the point of people knowing each other beyond a passing nod?" His voice was almost at growl level. "We are two nighthawks passing in the darkness, on our own selfish quests for food. Then we are all gone. That's all. In that flight we may encounter our own perils, our own soaring heights, but they are that only. Our own. No one else's. No one else's experience. Our own. There is no understanding from another, for another is not in your skin nor in your wings, whether they are broken or whole. We birth our own. We bury our own." He turned around and leaned against the mantel, staring into the fire, leaving his back to her.

Gail was stunned. In the sweat lodge his prayers, or his spoken thoughts if they weren't prayers, were so spiritual, so hopeful, as if beyond the notches of hell that dotted the landscape of life there were at least the hopes and dreams of opposite heavens, no final endings, only constant beginnings. These words seemed so final, so hopeless.

His shoulders slumped. She rose and was about to touch him when he turned abruptly.

"It's time we got back. Gather your things."

He started to walk away, but she grasped his upper arms and stopped him. "Talk to me, Hawk. I can see you're troubled. Let me help you."

A wry smile, almost a sneer tipped one corner of his mouth. "One sweat lodge ceremony and you think you are a healer." He jerked his shoulders away from her grip.

She didn't let go of him. "I didn't mean to imply that. We're friends. Friends help each other."

"You can't help me."

"How do you know that?"

He wrenched away from her and shouted, "Because nobody can!"

"Because you won't let them!" she shouted back.

"All right! All right! You have a perverted desire to know about me, know all about me. Well, I hope you've got all night, because you're going to get it all. Then, when you leave Montana and go back East where it's safe, you'll be the center of attention when you tell the story of the stupid reservation Indian you met."

"Hawk, don't say things like that and don't judge me!"

"Sit down, and listen, then."

She did sit down. He started out angrily, biting off his words, telling the story of his mother, his resultant Cheyenne-Crow mixture. He talked of Kincaid, his stepfather, Trey, Jerrie, the school he and Trey were sent to, the ranch. Only when he told her about the Kincaid saddle did his voice soften.

And then he told her about Laura and their son Kenny. His voice thickened. He swallowed. Gail swallowed with him and waited. He picked up the story again, this time with a vengeance, as if he wanted to hurt her with his words as much as he harbored his pain every day of his life.

He told her about Kenny, about their relationship and she sensed the boy was the complete joy and light of his life, an all-consuming love. Laura was a sometime mother. He'd met her in a bar in his drinking days, and he married her when she told him she was pregnant. He believed her when she said the child was his, even though he knew she'd been with many other men.

Kenny had problems, problems that weren't his fault. His parents were both alcoholics. Laura never stopped drinking during her pregnancy, and Kenny's learning disabilities were the result of it. Laura couldn't handle him, didn't have the patience. She came and went in and out of their lives. Sometimes he wanted her to stay for the sake of the boy, and sometimes he couldn't stand the sight of her and wanted her to leave for the same reason. She'd leave and be gone weeks, sometimes months at a time. By the time the boy was three, Laura had left for good.

Gail sensed as he spoke that Hawk changed with the impact of becoming a father, knowing that this helpless infant relied on him. Ada helped with her patience, her knowledge. But Kenny adored his father. Kenny wanted to be like his father. That's why he climbed up on the fence and scrambled onto the back of Kincaid's prize stallion when Hawk had left the animal saddled in the corral. He wanted to ride like his father.

Then something happened. Hawk saw Kenny on the stallion, knew the magnificent animal was temperamental, knew he responded only to the strength and gentleness combined in Hawk's voice and in his stepfather's before him. A rider the size of Kenny who giggled and squirmed annoyed and frightened him. Hawk advanced, telling Kenny strongly to sit still. But Kenny's sometimes shaky concentration and understanding eluded him. The horse started to buck. Kenny hung on. Hawk raced toward him. The horse gave a mighty pitch. Kenny flew up in the air, came down in an arc, and landed facedown in the corral dirt, followed by the sharp hooves of the stallion.

"There, are you satisfied now?" Hawk shouted thickly at Gail, and turned back to drop his head on his hands against the mantel. "Does it make you happy to know I killed my own son?"

Her breath caught in her throat, her stomach churned. Gail could not speak. She became aware that she'd locked the fingers of both hands, and as she stared at them her mind seemed paralyzed and couldn't send the message on how to unlock them.

She saw his shoulders shake, his back give a shudder.

Oh God! What have I done? The silent cry within her seemed the impetus for her fingers to unlock. She stood up and tried to touch him, but something stopped her. She went over to the bed and picked up some blankets and brought them back. Dropping all but one on the floor she draped the other one over his wracking shoulders.

On impulse she stood behind him and circled his waist with her arms.

And then gut-wrenching sobs exploded from him. She held him then, and rested her cheek on his back.

"You didn't kill Kenny, Hawk, you didn't kill him," she whispered over and over.

He shrugged her off. "Don't tell me that! I killed him with my carelessness. I knew how he liked being up in the saddle. I never should have left him alone in the corral, never should have left the horse saddled. Don't tell me it isn't my fault. It is!"

"All right, all right," she soothed. "Keep talking. Tell me the rest."

"Why?" he shouted, turning to face her, tears streaming down his face.

"Because you need to! Because you need to get it out!" she shouted at him.

"Why don't you just shut up!"

"Because you've shut yourself up too long. Whether you know it or not I'm being the best friend you've ever had. You think I have some sick need to hear about other people's tragedy? I don't. I'd love for life to be filled with nothing but flowers and good times. But the fact is it isn't. Now you talk about it, do you hear me? You talk about the fact that your father's horse stomped your beloved son to death. Go ahead, say it in all it's terrible fury! Say it, dammit, say it!"

He grabbed her shoulders. "All right. Yes, the horse trampled him, crushed his head, tore away his face. I gathered all of him, all I could get into my arms, held him, my baby, against my heart, but he couldn't feel it anymore could he? He was dead, never to be alive again. He never had a real father, never had a real mother, never had a real family. But I loved him, and look what that love got him."

He shook Gail hard so her head almost snapped on her neck.

"And what did you do then?" she hissed in a thick whisper.

Hawk dropped her shoulders, and turned back to the fireplace. He started to speak, and his voice had turned cold and hard and even.

"I laid him down. Stripped off my shirt and wrapped all the bits of his flesh I could find inside it." He took in a long, sharp breath. "Then I walked to the barn and got a rifle and a knife. I walked back. I raised the rifle. All the while the horse was watching me, trusting me. I pulled the trigger. I shot him. I cut his throat and tore his head off. Then I gathered up my son and took him to the elders. I left him with them. They would take care of him."

Gail's stomach turned over. The supper stew came up with a brackish aftertaste she had to force back. She waited, sensing more, although she wasn't certain she could take any more. But she knew Hawk had taken more, much more, and he still carried it.

He leaned his head against his hands braced on the mantel, and spoke into the fire. "And then I went away and drank. But I couldn't kill myself. I was already dead inside, but my outside refused to die."

Hawk slumped against the fireplace, then his knees buckled and he dropped to the floor. His arm hit the bench and it tipped back and fell over. Sobbing, he crawled to the blankets and curled into a fetal position, and let out a long low moan.

Gail dropped down to her knees beside him and pulled a blanket over him. He shivered and sobbed, then started trembling. She rubbed his shoulders, his back, swept his hair off his damp face, but he wouldn't calm. She stretched out beside him then, gathered his rigid body into her arms, and rocked him, whispering soothing words to him, stroking his hair, continuing to rub his shoulders.

Suddenly he let loose of the grip on his own arms and grabbed her roughly, slamming her chest against his. He held onto her as if she were the last breath to take on earth, and sobbed against her neck. He strained his long hard body next to hers desperately wanting, she thought, to be connected to someone, to her since she was all there was at the moment, from his feet to his head.

And she responded, clung to him and held him against her, wanting as much to be connected to him.

Sometime after midnight they both fell asleep. And sometime before dawn Hawk roused. Gail opened her eyes and watched him slip out the back door. All her senses were alerted. She heard him enter the privy, heard the door spring shut when he came out. She waited, hardly breathing. What would he do? She couldn't be certain. She shivered. The fire had gone out. She was cold, stiff and sore, and emotionally drained.

Then she heard the back door open again. He came inside carrying logs and kindling. Without looking at her he got the fire going, and worked at it until it was blazing. Then he turned back to her.

Their eyes met and held. Neither of them felt the need to speak. The silence between them was laden with emotion from both of them.

Never taking her eyes from his, Gail moved slightly, pulled the blanket away from her body and held out her arms to him. His eyes blazed with reflection from the fire. Silently, he removed his boots. Looking at her again, there was a question in his eyes, in the expression on his face. Holding his gaze she gave him his answer.

He slipped down beside her on the blankets, pulled the top one over them both, slowly lowered his head and touched her lips with his own. She wrapped her arms around his back and drew him against her. He sighed and relaxed his taut body against hers and gathered her close.

Then, in natural response to primitive rhythms newly reborn in them both, their minds, their emotions, their hearts, and finally their bodies taught the friends how to be lovers.

Chapter Sixteen

Gail stirred, stretched and, suddenly missing the warmth generated by Hawk's body, pulled the blankets over her naked body as a bone-chilling cold swept around her. Every muscle was sore, her shoulder blades felt rubbed raw, her neck ached, and her head throbbed. Yet she felt an odd sense of well-being!

Hawk came in the back door with an armload of firewood, stopped when he saw her zipping up her jeans and slipping on her sweater, then continued to the fireplace. He hunkered down, and started working on the fire.

"Good morning," she said softly. "I've missed you."

He turned toward her. His face was drawn and somber, his eyes held clouded messages.

"I owe you my thanks first," he said without greeting, "and my apology next."

She inclined her head toward him. "For what . . . in both cases?"

He looked down and stirred the wood chips on the floor near his feet. "Thanks for making me talk. I haven't talked about . . . Kenny to anyone, since it happened." He swallowed hard. "I guess you knew, and I knew it, too, that I needed to . . . should have . . ." He struggled for words, and Gail stopped him with a hand on his arm.

"You don't have to thank me. I'm glad we were together when you were ready to let it out. There's no need to apologize for that."

"I wasn't going to apologize for that. I'm not sorry about telling you. I meant to apologize for . . . the other." He looked back down at the wood chips and stirred rapidly.

Gail looked down at her own hands. She supposed she ought to feel embarrassed or something about the intense lovemaking they'd shared among these blankets she was calmly sitting on now. But she wasn't. Should she be concerned that she took advantage of him while he was feeling so vulnerable? Her friends would say that would be a typical male thing to do, and hurray for the female side when a woman did it. But she didn't feel that way at all.

Gail looked up at him until he met her eyes. "Please don't apologize for that. We both came together out of need. And . . . I wanted you." When his eyes widened, she smiled a little, almost shyly. "I have wanted you for a long time. I just hope the fact that we . . . made love, I mean, I

418

hope that doesn't change our friendship. I know now why you haven't been in a real relationship since your marriage, and I hope that just because I'm blonde, or used to be, doesn't mean you can't . . ."

This time Hawk stopped her, but not with a hand on her arm. He leaned over and kissed her mouth closed, then pushed her back onto the blankets.

"Would it be impolite of me to take all of your clothes off and make love to you before breakfast?" he asked, his voice morning husky.

"Not where I come from," she whispered.

"Good, because there's something you should know." He unzipped her jeans and started to inch them down over her hips.

"And what is that?" she asked, helping by pulling off her sweater and turtleneck.

"I've wanted you for a very long time, in spite of the fact that you're blonde . . . or used to be." He slid the fingers of both hands into her hair to cup her head. "I did need you last night, I admit that. Desperately, if you want the truth. It came as much from the release of telling the story to you as it was from wanting you, and resisting it. I didn't want to want you, if you can make sense of that."

"Yes, I can make sense of that."

He leaned down and kissed the pulsing hollow of her throat. "I want you now."

"I take it you've overcome your resistance," she

said against his mouth. When he gave a light small laugh, she said, "You're thinking something nasty, aren't you?"

"The best nasty there is." He kissed her deeply.

She waited.

Quiet.

The night before had seemed an explosion of shared raw senses. They'd slammed against each other again and again as in a primitive ritual where the drumming of their bodies drowned out the sound of their voices, his painful memories, her sleeping sensuality. They'd clawed at each other, demanding, giving, demanding all over again, inexhaustible in their lust. Feeling drunk with desire, Gail did not remember falling asleep.

Now Hawk moved and spread the blankets wide, removed his clothes, and lay down beside her, both naked in the firelight. The mounting sensations of what they were about to do, this time premeditated, piled on them like the falling snow on the roof. Chest against chest, pelvis against pelvis, they were purposely delaying the inevitable, savoring the exquisite tension. It was almost as if this were the first moment their bodies had touched, as if the night before had happened between their two spirits, making them ready for their flesh to be fused together with melding heat.

He began a trail of kisses beginning with her hair and down her jawline to her throat, following every line and hollow of her outstretched form until he reached her feet. He lifted each foot and kissed her insteps, tracing the underside of each with firm thumbs.

He was taking his time with every inch of her skin, and when he reached sensitive places, Gail cradled his head and pressed his face against her, holding him, letting her senses absorb the essence of him. As much as the night before was wild and furious, this morning was filled with long, slow lovemaking with visual as well as touching exploration of one another's body. And when he was deep inside her again, bracing himself on hands set on either side of her shoulders and looking down at her with lust-filled hooded eyes, their mating came as naturally to both of them as breathing.

They napped in the cocoon of their own heat, then awoke simultaneously to fulfill their mutual desire yet again. This time was marked by a sort of teaching, one to the other. His, an earthier side of lovemaking that, coupled with the emotional intensity between them, was an unforgettable sensual learning experience for Gail. Hers, a romantic way that gentled his cultural impetus to be a dominant male. She showed him how a woman could convey to her man what she wanted, what power he possessed to give her the ultimate sensual experience. And she displayed her own newly awakened power to bring him to the soaring heights his name implied.

"I didn't want this to happen," he said at last, after they'd lain silently side-by-side for a long time, exhausted from the total immersion in one another of mind, emotions, and body.

Gail shifted her head toward him. "I thought you said you wanted me."

"I did, I do," Hawk answered quickly. "I meant the rest of it."

"What rest of it?"

"I didn't want to . . . to love you," Hawk said thickly.

Gail didn't, couldn't, say anything for a long time. "And do you love me?" she whispered at last.

"I think so. I've never been in love. I expected, that is, I meant to make a life with a Cheyenne woman, if I made a life with a woman at all. I didn't want to be with a . . ." His voice trailed away.

"A white woman again," she finished for him. "Once burned, twice learned, is that it?" She let her fingers lazily trace the ridges of his chest.

"No. I hope you can understand this, but I never thought of it as being any other way. I mean, I expected that if it ever happened that I met a woman to marry, I wanted her to be Cheyenne. I wanted to keep my heritage strong."

"What if the woman you met was Crow?" she asked, knowing how he felt about the Crow people of his biological father.

Hawk shrugged. "I would not have allowed it."

"Have you met other women?"

"Many."

She wasn't certain she was happy about that response for a moment. A twinge of jealousy perhaps? Her powers of intellectual reasoning kicked in and reminded her that anyone prior to this moment when the two of them came together was ancient history.

"Anyone of them in particular you wished to be with?"

"No."

"Did you want to be married again?"

"Yes."

"Did you intend to have more children?"

He turned his head and stared at the ceiling. "No. I never wanted another child after Kenny. I had my chance at being a father, and I . . ."

"Wouldn't it have been possible for you to have more children so that you could have a second chance?"

"I did not deserve a second chance."

"Everyone deserves a second chance. And now you've met another white woman, and you think you love her."

He was silent a long time. Then, "Are you . . . have you ever been married?"

"No to both. I lived with someone once. He wanted to get married. I didn't want to then. And so we parted and he found someone else almost right away. They got married and had children."

"Did that hurt you?" he asked with concern.

"No, at least not the way you were hurt."

"Did you ever think about being married after that?"

"No."

"Didn't you ever want children?"

"Yes, sometimes. Sometimes no."

"Did you meet other men?"

"A few. I never minded being alone, really. At least not much. When I did have bouts of loneliness they were very painful."

"Were you in love with any of those men?"

He was certainly being inquisitive, Gail thought. But, then, turnabout was fair play, wasn't it? He seemed to truly want to know what happened to her, what she felt, and she wanted him to know.

"No. I know that I haven't genuinely loved any man since then. I'm not even sure if I was in love with him. But . . . I know I love you."

He shifted his head back toward her. "You do?" He sounded incredulous that such a thing could happen.

"Yes, I do." She reached up and kissed him.

He kissed her, then pulled back and looked into her eyes. "What should we do about this?"

"Let it happen," Gail whispered.

He seemed to be taking his time pondering that notion. "All right," he whispered back at last. He kissed the top of her hair, and held her. They seemed locked in the sheer pleasure of feeling each other breathe.

Hawk was the first to break the spell. "Now, so that I'll have strength enough to let something as monumental as falling in love happen, you'd better get up and make my breakfast."

She lurched up to rest on the backs of her elbows. "What?"

"Aren't you the little woman of this teepee?"

"In a pig's eye!"

"You know, of course, that it's against the natural order of things with the Cheyenne for the *man* to do the cooking and the cleaning." He folded his arms over his chest. "I have spoken."

"You will starve. I haven't a clue how to use anything in this cabin that remotely resembles kitchen appliances. I read somewhere that it was also the way of the Cheyenne to provide shelter and food for their sacred women. Whatever happened to that ancient tradition?"

"It went the way of the buffalo. Now our women just go to the supermarket and pick up something lying limp on a plastic tray covered with plastic film, both of which are environmental plagues."

"I see. Perhaps we can meet in the middle somewhere."

"We have been and I've enjoyed it very much!" She leaned down and nipped his rib. He lurched and messed up her hair more than it was.

"I thought you big tough Cheyenne men wouldn't have a sense of humor."

"How wrong can you white women be? The Cheyenne are noted for their humor, their clever tricks."

"You've got some clever tricks, I'll grant you that." He hugged her hard to his chest. She kissed the flexing muscle above his breast. "What I meant was, if you'll drive us to a town I'll buy your breakfast. That suits my white feminist side. Does that meet with approval with your Cheyenne macho side?"

He thought a long moment making an over-acted display of mutual concession. "It's a battle won by both. Let's go!"

Later that day in her apartment Gail marvelled over their lovemaking. She was not particularly experienced physically, at least not in numbers of partners, so it was not out of practiced knowledge that she'd shown Hawk how to pleasure her, and had revelled in giving pleasure to him. Rather it was more a natural event unto itself, as if the chemistry that was individual in both became explosive when mixed with the other's, and caused the resultant knowledge to be transmitted to hands, mouth, and mingled bodies.

To Gail the aura that surrounded them as they lay in the blankets on the cabin floor making love, talking, making love, learning about each other, falling in love, seemed as sensually spiritual as had the sweat lodge ceremony and the following moments when they'd stood barefoot in the snow, half-naked, making communion with the night sky.

For the rest of the day Gail smiled like a girl enthralled in the first flush of womanhood, experiencing the intensity of a burgeoning libido. Her mind dwelled on erotic thoughts, and she fantasized about the next time she and Hawk would be together.

Jerrie brought Willow back that afternoon before supper, and Gail invited her to stay and eat with them.

"From the look on your face I'd say my leaving you at Hawk's sweat lodge was not a bad idea," Jerrie observed as she helped Gail cut up carrots and peel potatoes.

Gail smiled. "At first, he was pretty angry with both of us. I interrupted his meditation for one thing. But, then, he generously included me in the rest of it."

"And what did you think of the sweat lodge ceremony?"

"I was actually moved by it. It made me wish I'd gone through it from the beginning." Gail's voice held a note of awe.

"The sweat can be very refreshing and uplifting if you go into it expecting to stay open and let go and let what will happen, happen. But you have to want to do it." Jerrie's voice sounded wistful.

"I didn't have any idea what I should or could expect. I'm not a religious person. I don't feel comfortable in church buildings and I've met too many church-goers who didn't practice all the righteousness they preached," Gail said. "But I know I've been searching for a way to get in touch with the spiritual side of myself, if I have one." She put down the carrot peeler and gave Jerrie a concerned glance. "I hope that didn't sound corny."

"Of course it didn't. I think whether a person wants to admit it or not, everyone searches for their own way to connect with a force greater than ourselves. A lot of nonnative people search out the People's way of connectedness with the earth and nature and other humans." Jerrie picked up a knife and quartered the potatoes Gail had peeled.

"I suppose that bothers you. It's one more thing of yours that other people want. I'm sorry that happens. I know a lot of people get into the religion-of-the-month, or try to adopt as their own another culture's beliefs and practices. I'm not that way. I didn't seek this out. I went to the river bank, Hawk was there in the sweat lodge, and the rest . . . the rest just happened naturally. It's all almost too much for me to comprehend."

"I take it you and Hawk came to a new understanding?" Jerrie probed.

Gail smiled cryptically. "You could say that."

"I'm glad."

"So am I. Unless he has second thoughts."

"He may. He's moody. Did he tell you . . . everything?"

Gail nodded. "If you mean about Laura and Kenny, yes. If there's more than that, no. But, God, that would be enough to crush the spirit of a lesser man."

"It almost killed him," Jerrie said quietly.

Willow came out of the bedroom then, bringing a book that Jerrie had been reading with her. "Look at this," she said excitedly, holding it up for Gail to see. "Jerrie gave me this book with Indian stories in it, see? There's even some about Cheyennes. That's what I am," she said proudly, "at least half of me is."

"You sure are," Gail said, hugging the child. She noticed how Willow had stopped calling her by name. Willow seemed to have no difficulty in calling Jerrie or Hawk or anyone else by their given name, but lately she'd stopped using hers and Gail wondered about it.

Gail wiped her hands, and took the book. She flipped to the contents page and saw the various myths and legends listed with the tribal name in parentheses. Willow ran her finger down the page until she came to a Cheyenne legend.

"There's one," she said, "and there's another

one."

"You are certainly getting very good at reading aren't you? You're much faster than you used to be."

"Uh-huh," Willow said. "Jerrie's been helping me."

"Well, she's doing a very good job, I must say," Gail said, smiling at her.

"See this one?" Willow pointed her finger at a tale of two lovers. "That's like the play you read to me about the girl and the boy with the funny names. They die, and their tribes who were fighting make peace with each other."

Romeo and Juliet," Gail said.

"Yes, that one," Willow said. "I didn't understand it, all of it. But this Indian story is just like it, and now I know what was happening to them."

Gail flipped to the story, and read the synopsis at the top of the page. "You're right, it's a lot like it. That's very interesting."

"I'm going to tell the kids in my grade," Willow said to Gail. "Are you going to tell the kids in your grade?"

Gail thought for a moment, then smiled. She bent down and hugged Willow. "Honey, you've just given me a great idea! Maybe this is how I'll get those kids to read and understand classic literature. They can read their traditional legends and then see how they compare with other writers."

She went back to the contents. Other tribes

were represented among the legends and, as she scanned their synopses, elements of the stories of classic writers like Shakespeare and Ibsen, and even Ferber and Dickens jumped out at her. This may be the key she was looking for to get and hold her students' interest in what they were supposed to be learning! She had homework of her own to do.

After supper and Willow's bedtime, Gail and Jerrie went into the living room and sat down with cups of tea.

"I talked with Catherine recently," Gail said, opening the conversation and testing the waters to see if Jerrie wanted to talk about her.

"Oh? How is she doing?" Jerrie sounded mildly interested, but she did not look up from studiously stirring her tea.

"Well, she's had a difficult few months. And now things are very bad."

Jerrie's eyes then rose quickly to Gail's. "Is she sick?"

"No, she's not sick. Certain parts of our society are, but not Cath." Jerrie didn't say anything, and Gail wasn't certain she should press this subject further. She decided to give it one more shot. "She may be coming out here, probably in the spring."

Jerrie sipped her tea. "She wrote me a little about the tensions at school. Visiting you will be a nice break for her when school's out."

"It might not be just a visit, and it will be before

431

school's out."

Jerrie sucked in her bottom lip. "I see."

Gail leaned over. "Jerrie, I value our friendship I've come to care about you almost as much as I do about Cath. As you can imagine, I think, she's told me about . . . about her personal feelings And, well, her warm and caring personality has brought her trouble from Riverview School. She no longer teaches there."

Jerrie frowned then nodded her head in understanding, but still she didn't say anything.

"I hope you don't mind, but Cath and I have talked about you, about last summer, and . . . I also hope you don't think that's an invasion of your privacy. Cath didn't mean it to be that way, as I'm sure you can understand. And what she's told me would never change my feelings about her. I love her, have always loved her, and always will. She's my closest friend."

Jerrie moved uncomfortably in the chair. "And what you're saying is that your feelings have changed about me now, is that it?"

"Well, of course they have. Wait a minute!" Gail put her hand out as Jerrie looked as if she were about to get up and leave. "I feel closer to you than ever, that is, if you'll let me. Who knows what will happen? If something good does, I will be very happy for her, and for you. And I support you both. I just wanted to let you know that you don't have to pretend with me if you don't want to.

And I hope I haven't made you uncomfortable."

Jerrie leaned forward again. "I, uh, I don't know what to say exactly. I don't talk about . . ." She shrugged.

"That's all right. You don't have to talk about it. I just want you to know that you can if ever you want to."

"Thanks." Jerrie drained her cup and held it almost dangling over her knees. She let out a nervous breath. "Why did she let that controversy get out of hand at the school? She could have gotten around it. Lots of people do."

"Catherine is a woman of high principles, as I think you know. She doesn't like lies. Honesty is important to her, and it starts with herself. She tried to stay with the school, tough it out, and maybe make inroads with the administration and the board there, but they made it impossible for her. She didn't quit, but they forced resignation on her."

"One more shape of discrimination, but the school will get around that, won't they?"

"Probably."

"I'm sorry," Jerrie said with a sad note in her voice. "You never know, do you? I mean, you never really know from one day to the next what impact some little word or gesture is going to have on your life or someone else's life?"

"No," Gail agreed. "There are no guarantees about anything. But that's not all bad."

"Maybe not." Jerrie hugged her knees, a worried look on her face.

Gail wanted to relax Jerrie, and thought changing the subject to something else might do it. She did truly feel that she and Jerrie were friends. The fact that she was Hawk's sister made the friendship even more significant. She wasn't ready to share what had happened between her and Hawk with anyone yet, but when she was, she knew Jerrie would be the second person.

"I've been thinking a lot about something else, and I want to get your opinion and your advice," Gail said.

"Opinions I've got. Advice I never give," Jerrie said, visibly relaxing. "I'm the last one to shell out advice, but I listen well."

Gail set her cup down on the coffee table, leaned forward and clasped her hands. "I want to adopt Willow."

Jerrie slowly set her cup down on the coffee table, and straightened. "Why?"

Her response surprised Gail. She guessed she expected Jerrie to be excited, think it was a great idea, tell her how to set the wheels in motion. She didn't expect a one word question for an answer, one word that expressed a hundred meanings, all of them negative. Gail felt deflated.

"Because she's alone, she has no family." Jerrie said nothing. Gail continued, and even as she spoke she had the vague sense her words sounded like a salesman attempting to sell a product nobody wanted. "I know Willow likes me, and I've grown to love her. I give her a good home, she's clean and has warm clothes and healthy food. And she goes to school every day because she wants to. I'm making less money than I've ever made in my life, but it's enough for two."

Still Jerrie didn't respond. Gail's mind shifted and she felt as if she'd been fabricating a litany of reasons why she wanted to adopt this orphan child, all for someone else's benefit. There was really only one reason. She loved the little girl. And she felt, well, *motherly* with her. And that felt very right.

"Why, suddenly, do you want to do this?" Jerrie broke her silence.

"It's not sudden. I've been thinking about this for a long time. It was a well-thought-out conscious decision." Now Gail thought she sounded as if she were presenting her testimony to a biased jury.

"It's not from wanting to make some old wrongs right by assimilating . . ."

"No! You sound like Hawk did. I'm not trying to erase some ancestral guilt." Gail's voice was low and hard. "I simply want to adopt her." She watched Jerrie's face and the dark expression clouding her features. "Jerrie? What's the matter?"

"You're asking for trouble."

435

"Why?"

"The tribal court will not let you do it." Jerrie's voice carried a harsher tone than Gail ever remembered hearing from her.

"What does the tribal court have to do with this?" Gail was growing agitated. The idea that had sparked such excitement inside her before, was being doused before it had a chance to burn with real substance.

"Willow is Cheyenne."

"*Half* Cheyenne."

"Nevertheless, the tribal rules are explicit about adoption."

"Maybe they are, but from what I've observed the tribe doesn't know about Willow, or if they do they don't care about her. She's been alone since she was practically a baby. It's amazing something worse than malnutrition and head lice didn't happen to her. Nobody seems to care that she lives with me."

"They probably don't."

"Now here I am taking care of her, maybe the first person in her life to ever do that, and wanting to make a commitment to caring for her until she can care for herself, and you're telling me a bunch of dispassionate people are going to tell me I can't?"

"Gail, calm down. You don't have to sell me with your qualifications for becoming Willow's guardian. Personally, I'm all for it. I can see how you both care for each other. I'm just trying to warn you about the opposition you will most likely face with this."

Gail took a deep breath. "I'm sorry I snapped like that. I'm more emotional about this than I thought I was. I don't just want to be Willow's guardian, I want to be . . . her mother."

"But you're not her mother."

"And neither is anybody else who can be produced! The one who was her mother abandoned her. For God's sake, the welfare of a child is the important thing, isn't it?"

"Yes, it is. I believe that and you believe that. But . . ." Jerrie leaned forward and rested her forearms on her knees, looking intently at Gail. "The facts are these, you aren't Cheyenne, you're not married, you're over child-bearing age, and you're white."

"Just because I'm not married doesn't mean I can't be a good parent and provide a stable home for a child. Being older ought to be an asset in caring for a child."

"I know that. Even if you were married, if your husband wasn't Cheyenne the opposition would be there even more strongly. It's just the way it is."

Gail stared as intently as Jerrie. "Up until this moment I never thought there was a thing wrong with being a single white female."

Jerrie gave a wry laugh. "Yeah." She leaned back in her chair, and the laugh scaled down to an amused smile. "You know, of course, that you'd have a better case if you were married to a Cheyenne."

With growing surprise Gail looked at the woman who had become a closer friend this evening than either of them would have imagined, and the implied meaning behind her words began focusing clearer. It made her feel oddly uncomfortable, not wholly in a negative way.

She was searching for a response to Jerrie's remark when a knock came to the door. The two women moved visibly, shaken out of the intensity of their conversation.

"Saved . . . I think," Gail said with a smile, and rose to answer the door.

"My God, winter happens out here with a capital W!" Catherine was borne through the door on a gust of snow-filled wind.

"Cath!"

"I hope you meant it when you invited me to come, friend!" Catherine threw her arms around Gail and hugged her as if they hadn't seen each other in years.

Gail stepped back and looked at Catherine. "You look wonderful!" She hugged her again.

"You mean for someone who's been through the wringer."

"Why didn't you tell me when you were coming? Did you fly? You didn't drive the whole way, did you? How did you find me?"

Catherine held up a woolen gloved hand and ticked off the answers. "I didn't know myself until I did it. No. Yes, and it wasn't half as bad as last summer's bus ride from hell until winter descended like the wrath of heaven somewhere past a forlorn cornfield in Iowa. And you're a big hit at that little convenience store in Lodgepole. Everyone there knows where you live. You were serious about my coming, weren't you? Even in this storm the closer I knew I was getting to you the better I felt. Is this a bad time?"

"Of course I was serious! And it's never a bad time for you to be here. I'm so glad!" Gail remembered who was just around the corner in the living room, easily hearing the whole exchange between them. "Um, I do have company right now."

Catherine leaned over and whispered, "Hawk? Oh God, did I interrupt something?"

Gail leaned over and whispered back. "No, not Hawk, and how could you interrupt anything when I share this tiny place, not to mention my bedroom, with a child?"

Catherine's face showed relief. "Who then?" she whispered.

"Come in and find out," Gail whispered.

They walked around to the living room. Jerrie stood with her back to them looking out the window into the dark night.

"Jerrie? Look who's here."

Jerrie turned around slowly. "Hi," she said quietly.

Catherine couldn't speak for a few seconds. "Hi, Jerrie," she managed finally.

"So great out here you chose to get away from the East and come back, huh?" Jerrie's voice held a slight tremor.

"Yes and no. Part of it was by choice. The good part."

The air seemed charged with tension. Gail broke into it.

"You must be frozen. Have you eaten? How about a cup of tea? I can fix you a plate of roast beef from dinner. Get those cold things off, or do you have luggage to bring in from the car?"

Catherine pulled her coat around her tightly. "Tea sounds great, but no food, thanks." She started to shrug off her coat, turned toward the door and then back again, as if she didn't quite know what to do next. "I do have some unloading to do. I guess I should do that now. I'm sure I won't feel like bundling up again to go out in the blizzard and do it later."

Jerrie made a move past them toward the door. Her face seemed to relax as she slipped into her boots, wrapped her scarf around her neck and started getting into her jacket. "Blizzard? You call this a blizzard? This is just a few snow flurries. The real snow hasn't started yet. Come on, I'll help you unload the car." She zipped up her jacket and went outside.

"Gail, I . . ." Catherine held out her hands in a questioning gesture.

"Go!" Gail said to her. "The sooner you get settled in here, the sooner we can talk."

Catherine hugged Gail again. "Thanks, friend. I hope there's enough energy left in this weary mind to form words. I feel as if I've said all there is to be said to anybody."

"There's always enough left over to share with your friend, *friend*."

Catherine's eyes filled. "You are that, in spades." She fastened her jacket and followed Jerrie out to her car.

Gail dabbed at the corners of her eyes. Hadn't she and Catherine planned for their lives to become easier once they were in their fifties?

Chapter Seventeen

Gail was positive she'd never truly known what the season of winter was about at any other time in her life until her first winter in Montana. All her growing years, the snow people she'd built, the snowball wars from behind snow forts with the neighborhood kids, the sled rides, the ice skating, the winter parties, and even the picturesque New York countryside in winter all seemed now to have been preserved forever in a plastic bubble in her mind that she could turn upside down whenever she wanted to and watch snowflakes drift lazily down over a quaint village.

When she felt healthy again, she actually enjoyed walking in the crisp air. But after about three months of it she'd felt battered physically by the weather, which changed daily from bad to worse, then from worse to abominable. But more than that she was feeling the effects of being caught up in a storm, tossed around emotionally by the winds of change. And it was the dizzying impact on her life of one fragile little person named Willow and one resilient big person named Hawk around which the maelstrom revolved.

She'd started it all with her abrupt move from a comfortable career at an affluent school in New York to an uneasy settlement into a reservation school in Montana. Who could have predicted that turn of events in her life? Whatever happened to her carefully formulated plans for the future?

Then there had been Catherine's arrival.

"What's the best thing that's happened to you since you've moved out here?" Catherine asked Gail after dinner one Friday evening in late winter.

Every evening after Willow had gone to bed, they sat and talked as they used to in New York. Sometimes their conversations were one-sided, where one or the other would vent some feeling that required nothing more from a friend than a good listening ear. Other times they were two-sided discussions as they'd often been in the past where both let out their problems or questions without expecting the other to come up with solutions or answers. But lately they'd been conversations between two friends who were learning a new way of life at the same speed.

They talked as if just hearing one another's words would shed some light of clarity into the fog of their own evolution.

Gail leaned back against the couch and rested her wine glass on her waist. She smiled. "There isn't just one."

"Start with the school first," Catherine urged, "and we'll avoid the obvious other two for the time being." She stretched out on the living room floor resting her elbow on a pillow.

"Well, let's see," Gail began, "it's certainly been a time of introspection. Ang told me that out here a person learns either to like herself or hate herself, and there'd be plenty of time to figure it out. She was right. I've learned more about myself in these last few months than I have in years."

"And what's the verdict?"

"I like what I've learned." Gail grinned. "Conceited, aren't I?"

"Just sure of yourself, I think."

"I wasn't always so sure. I didn't think I could survive without the creature comforts I'd become accustomed to."

"I know what you mean. We lived a good life in a comfortable environment." Catherine laughed. "Remember that weekend we spent at the spa being pampered? All we wished for, as I remember, was to have peace and quiet, to get

444

away from students and other people, not hear the phone ring, be by ourselves."

Gail laughed. "I look back at that and wonder if it was me and not some other woman who'd done that! I sure got that wish to be alone out here, and more. God, I was lonely for a long time, really lonely. It was so *desolate,* miles from civilization, I thought. I begged the phone to ring. I kept thinking any moment I'd figure out that I'd made the biggest mistake of my life, and I'd just pack up and go back to Riverview where they'd welcome me with open arms into my warm and comfortable little office."

"But you didn't ever figure it that way, did you?"

Gail let out a long breath. "No, I didn't. Then Hawk brought Willow to stay, and two lonely souls got over being lonely. And we both seemed to have the same purpose after a while, to give one another a reason to try." Gail smiled, thinking about Willow. "It sounds corny, I suppose, but it's almost as if I've been dropped into the kindergarten of life, you know?"

Catherine turned a rattleskin bracelet around and around on her wrist, a late Christmas present from Jerrie. "No, it doesn't sound corny at all," she mused. "It sounds like every person's fantasy, to trade in one good life for an even better one."

Gail watched her friend, knowing she'd passed just as difficult a winter. She sat up straight and set her glass on the table. "I've come to understand why Hawk was so convinced I could do no good with Willow or any other child on the reservation. There's an inherent sense of distrust of white people. Who can blame them, what with the convoluted way the government works even now with regard to these people? Even the commodities and welfare systems seem to trap people rather than to help them get going again. Even the tribal government sometimes works against its own people."

"I can see that at the women's center," Catherine said. She'd been spending time between the center and the school every day since she arrived, and now she was a fixture at both places. "They've felt trapped. All those sad, yet hopeful faces on those women and children. They look toward Jerrie, and even me, as if we can solve their problems. I wish to heaven I could make things better for all of them."

"You are, just by being there and being understanding," Gail said.

"I love these Cheyenne people." Catherine sat up cross-legged on the other side of the coffee table from Gail. "They're subtle, creative. They don't waste words, but I get the feeling they're thinking all the time."

"I do, too. It takes a great deal of stamina to live straddling the border between two worlds." Gail held out her open palms, indicating a scale. "One world is traditional, based on communion with the earth and their Creator, and the other is a morass created by history and imposed alien religions. There's a general feeling of worthlessness among these kids—that's the thing I'm most frustrated about. I can't convince them of their own self-worth, especially the girls."

"Exactly. I feel like a paper boat on a turbulent sea. Why do you stay? What good can one woman do, or even two, to help to change now what happened generations ago?"

"Because I believe that one woman can make a difference," Gail answered quickly. "Even if it's only with one other woman or one child. And, to be honest, I stay for myself now as well as for them. There's Willow. I love her. I like taking care of her, being a mother to her. I wish I could be her real mother."

Catherine's eyes widened at her friend's confession. "You've become maternal?" When Gail's face warmed with color, she added, "You mean, legally you want to be her mother?"

"Mm-hm."

Catherine grinned. "As your best friend I feel I should be giving you a baby shower or something!"

"Don't start decorating yet. I've investigated adoption procedures a little, and it doesn't look good for me to be able to accomplish such an arrangement."

"Why not? You're a responsible, employed adult. I'll vouch for you."

Gail shook her head. "They have a tribal court structure that's as complex as any white government could devise. I understand what they're getting at. They want Cheyennes to bring up Cheyenne children. They'd put her in a foster home faster than they'd give her to me. Ada's too old to take on the responsibility, and Jerrie . . ."

Catherine gave her an understanding look. Everyone knew now that she and Jerrie were a couple. Recently they'd moved in together in a house near the women's center. There was a general feeling of acceptance among the People, but foster care and adoption of children would be as much a complex problem as it was for Gail.

"No one else wants her, and she doesn't want to be with anyone else," Gail said. "I do want her, and she seems to want to be with me. But Jerrie says the courts will never allow it. I'm afraid to even start anything for fear they'll take her away from me now."

"There must be some way you could . . ."

"Jerrie says if I marry a Cheyenne then the

448

court would at least consider the case."

"Gee," Catherine said, smiling, "what a terrible proposition for you, huh? I mean, you have this gorgeous Cheyenne man who . . ."

"I want to be a mother, Cath," Gail interrupted her friend with an amused quiver of her lower lip, "and that's no reason to get married."

"You've resisted marriage all your life, I know. But there are other fringe benefits here, aren't there? How is Hawk anyway? You two on speaking terms by now at least?"

Gail smiled cryptically. "We found a new way of communicating. You could call it sign language."

"Well, am I glad to hear that at last!" Catherine beamed.

"Don't get carried away with enthusiasm," Gail warned with good nature, "it was only one time. I don't know if there will be anything more or not."

"You're both cowards. You're in love, and you won't admit it. Jerrie and I had you figured out last summer."

"So she told me."

"Does she know about . . . you and Hawk now?"

"Even I don't know 'about' Hawk and me. Neither one of us has gone out of our way to pursue anything. It's too new and too complex

449

to think about anyway, let alone talk about."

"Being in love is always complex."

"Who said anything about being in love?"

"You didn't have to. I know you are, and he is, too, isn't he?"

Gail felt her face flush. She smiled. "We haven't been together enough to know if we're in love or not. We did confess feelings for each other, but beyond that . . ."

"Beyond that, what? Why not marriage?"

"Whoa! Slow down! God, Cath, we're not kids anymore. And we're very different. I've never been married. Hawk was married once a long time ago. He . . . had a child."

"And it was devastating to him, I know. Jerrie told me. But you said it yourself, you're not kids anymore. You're all grown up, better for it because of the slings and arrows of fortune, if you'll pardon the too obvious reference. You'd both start out marriage much differently than you would have when you were very young."

"Even so, I've never really wanted to be married. It's too confining, too restrictive. I just want to be who I am, single. Nobody gets hurt that way."

"Marriage isn't all bad."

"I've seen more that are than not. Things can get nasty when marriages break up. Even relationships without marriage can be complicated when they break up."

"Some don't break up."

"And the people in them are miserable."

"Not all of them, Gail. How do you know you couldn't make a good marriage with the right man?"

Gail laughed. "You said the magic phrase again, 'right man'! First you have to know you have the right person, and nobody is ever sure of that even if they say they are."

"Well, there are no guarantees in anything in life," Catherine said as matter of fact.

"Exactly. Maybe that's what I've wanted, a guarantee that nothing will ever go wrong between my partner and me. The thought of marrying anybody, even in the throes of biological urges, scares the hell out of me."

"Why? Face it kid, none of us has another fifty years left to live. In thirty or forty years you'll be dead, long before the glow of love in a marriage could have time to wear off. How much more guarantee do you need than the fact that you won't outlive the love?" When Gail gave her a skeptical grin, Catherine shrugged and opened her palms wide. "All I'm saying is, you have a chance of adopting Willow if, as Jerrie says, you marry a Cheyenne. Whether you and Hawk think you're too old or too jaded to admit it or not, you're in love. Marriage quite often follows love. Case closed. Go for it!"

"My dear Catherine, you of all people should know life just isn't that simple."

"No, but it ought to be, oughtn't it?"

Gail drained her wine glass. "It ought to be simple enough for any two people who want to be together, to simply be together. That's what ought to be."

"Yeah," Catherine agreed, "that's what ought to be."

Spring burst forth green and sunny yellow with more exuberance than Gail ever remembered a season change. Maybe it was because of the severity of the winter. Perhaps the earth was as ready as people and animals were for warmth and renewal, and that made their embrace of the new season all the more ardent.

And spring brought Ada back to Medicine Wheel School on the first Monday afternoon in May. Hawk had driven her out there with another delivery of books for the library. Willow and Gail were just leaving to walk home when they met them at the front door.

"Nesko," Willow said excitedly, calling Ada by a Cheyenne word for mother, "come see the new playground! All us kids have been building it ourselves!"

"All by yourselves?" Ada sounded properly impressed.

"Well," Willow drew out the word as if she were thinking of the next one, "Mister Two Bulls, both of them, helped. And Catherine and *her,* too," she said, looking up at Gail, giving her the little twinge inside every time Willow referred to her that way.

"They helped, too?" Hawk asked.

"Uh-huh," Willow said, nodding her head vigorously. "They drew it out on paper first. I told them what they should have. Even Jerrie helped. We told her it was a surprise, so she wouldn't tell you."

Hawk exchanged a questioning glance with Gail whose lips tilted with a secretive smile.

"Now why didn't you want Hawk and me to know about the playground?" Ada whispered, bending slowly toward Willow.

The little girl looked up at Gail. "We can tell them now, can't we?"

"Better than that," Gail said, smoothing the back of Willow's hair, "we can show them."

They led Ada and Hawk out the back door to the place where the old rusted swing set had straddled a sand pit. Mother and son stopped at the edge of the lawn and stared in disbelief.

"Would you look at that?" Hawk said with genuine delight.

In place of the swing set was the developing profile of a magic castle full of turns and levels and corners. It was constructed of sturdy square fence posts, rubber tires, sand boxes, wood and heavy rope swings, plenty of rungs and ladders for climbing or hanging upside down, and several barrels sanded and shaped into a tunnel for hiding. A turretlike structure at one end contained a curved stairway to a lookout perch at the top. The four-sided roof of it was topped with a mismatch of shingles in varying sizes and colors. Above that was a medicine wheel made of wood, decorated with strips of cloth in red, white, yellow and black that fluttered in the breeze. Flanking the imaginary kingdom were newly planted flowers in half-barrels brightly painted in primary colors.

"It's not finished yet," Gail told them. "We think of this as the nucleus of what can be with an addition every spring. Some of the kids are already working on a design for next year's addition. A stage. They're determined to have one so they can put on shows, and now they're figuring out how they can devise it so it can be used in the winter. One senior girl suggested a tepee. Isn't that a great idea?"

"Who gave you the money to build it?" Ada asked.

"Nobody," Gail told her. "The idea was that

nothing or no one is without worth or value. Anyone can look at something and think it's worthless and should be thrown away, and someone else will see a whole new purpose for it. The same with a person. Every person has value, every person is different, and has a different idea. So, they all began to look at things and people with different eyes and different minds, and the playground is one of the results."

Ada started to walk around it. Gail stepped around the outside of the structure and watched the older woman touching various parts of it.

"It was constructed of found objects," Gail said, "whatever they could beg, borrow . . . I'm hoping they didn't steal anything. Everybody got into the act. We worked on drawings all winter, and we held elections throughout the school to decide on the components. Then they had to figure out how the parts would all go together. Every class used it as a project, from math to art to English twelve."

"It's wonderful," Hawk said, walking around the structure, stepping into it and looking up toward the sky. "A place where a child could stretch his imagination, be anything he wanted to be." He walked around to one side and gazed out over the hills.

Willow followed him with Gail behind her.

"Tell Hawk what name was chosen for the new playground, Willow."

Willow placed a little hand on Hawk's shirt sleeve and tugged on it so as to garner his full attention. When he looked down at her, Gail saw tears glistening in his eyes.

Willow gazed up at Hawk with eyes full of adoration. "Kenny's Castle," she said proudly. "Everybody likes that name. Do you? *She* said you would."

Hawk swallowed, tried to speak, couldn't, cleared his throat, and tried again. "She did. How did you come up with the name?"

Willow watched his face, searching for Hawk's approval. *"She* said Kenny was a little boy you loved, only he's a spirit now. *She* said he has a place like this to play in where he lives now, and he wants the other kids to have one, too. It's really fun. You can come and play here, too, whenever you want to." When Hawk didn't respond, Willow asked with a tremulous voice, "Don't you like it?"

Hawk dropped to his knees and hugged the child close to him, burying his face in her hair. "I love Kenny's Castle," he choked. "And Kenny does, too." He stood up and his eyes met Gail's.

Gail just smiled at him. No words were needed.

Hawk took Willow's hand and led her around

to what appeared to be a drawbridge entrance to the castle playground. "What would you think," he began, "if I were to paint a sign to put over the castle door?" He made a high sweeping gesture with his other hand. "Kenny's and every kid's castle. Do you think that would be okay?" He looked down at her.

Willow squealed with delight. "That would be very okay! Can I tell the other kids? When will you do it?"

"I'll get started right away. You can tell the other kids whenever you want to."

"Oh boy! Did you hear that?" Willow looked up at Gail.

"Yes, I did. I think it's a wonderful idea. Then everyone who comes here will know about Kenny and all the great kids at the Medicine Wheel School."

"Yeah," Willow said, and ran off to find Ada.

Hawk watched her scamper off like a happy rabbit. "I was wrong," he said quietly to Gail. "You can make a difference, and you have."

"Thanks," she said, holding his gaze. "I needed to hear that." She started to go after Willow, then turned back. "I've missed seeing you these last few weeks."

He looked down where the toe of his boot was making swirls in the sand at the base of Kenny's Castle. He knew he'd been avoiding her, and it wasn't making him feel good. He remembered the evening they spent in the sweat lodge. She seemed genuinely to be interested in what he was doing and feeling in there, and she'd even participated whether she meant to or not. He did feel good about that.

And the night in the cabin. Hell, he'd cried like a baby and she'd held him like one in her arms. What had ever caused him to let his guard down like that? Telling her about Kenny and Laura. He'd never told that to anyone except one of the elders at his first sun dance. He loved Jerrie, but he'd never even truthfully told her how he felt about Kenny, about himself. What was it about Gail that he felt secure enough with her to bare his soul like that?

It was good with her, taking her body like he had that night. He hadn't even cared if he'd hurt her. He was brutal and he knew it. God, why did she take it? And she'd given back to him, and he'd let her do it, let himself feel . . . *loved.*

He didn't have to wonder what she was trying to prove anymore. Just looking at her now, her honest clear eyes, her open face, he knew who she was. Trouble was he was still trying to find out who he was. Sometimes he felt closer to it, and then he'd get scared. Him, scared. Imagine that. Descended from a long line of courageous warriors, and he was scared as a rabbit in the nderbrush. It was easier just to stay the way he'd been, wasn't it?

"I know this isn't probably the traditional way," she was saying when he heard her voice again, "but I'd like to ask you to go out with me next Saturday night, that is, if you haven't any other plans."

"Out?" Hawk inclined his head toward her.

"Yes, you know, like on a dreaded *date*."

"I've never been on a date in my life."

"I've rarely been on one I enjoyed." Gail laughed lightly. "What do you say we rectify both our records?"

Hawk looked down. He felt almost shy! What do you do on a date? Hold her chair out in some fancy dude restaurant? Is that what she would expect?

"Um, what would you want to do on this date, if I said I would go."

"Well, there's a dance over in Lodgepole, and since you only danced with Jerrie last time when I was here, I thought . . ."

"I wouldn't go to one of those things if you paid me!"

"Ouch!" Gail stepped back as if he'd tromped on her toes.

Hawk softened. A date. He supposed he'd have to do that at least once in his life. Although, what the hell for? Dates led to complications. He'd had enough complications to last the rest of his life. He looked in Gail's eyes. She didn't look as if she'd dissolve into a puddle because he'd reacted so badly to her suggestion. In fact, she looked as if she could take care of herself just fine. If she wanted a date, he supposed she could just go out and find some guy to go with her.

"What I meant was," he drawled, "I know of a much better place to go, one that wouldn't be smokey and filled with rowdies. If you think you'd be interested, I'd like to take you there."

Gail smiled. "Are you asking me out on a *date?*"

"It's all in the interpretation, I guess," he said, smiling back. "You probably think that's a Cheyenne macho thing, don't you?"

"It's all in the interpretation," she rejoined.

"Does that mean yes?"

"Yes, it does."

Hawk was pleased with himself for the rest of the week. The following Saturday he went to her place in his pickup.

Willow met him at the door. "You look very handsome," she said, giggling.

"Thank you, pretty lady," he said, making a sweeping bow. He'd dressed in a jacket, white shirt, bolo tie, pressed black jeans, and highly polished black boots.

"I'm not the pretty lady. Wait till you see *her!*"

"You mean Gail?"

"Yes. She's beautiful," she breathed.

"What do you call her, Willow? Do you call her by her name?"

Willow put a finger against her lips. "No."

"You used to, didn't you?"

"Yes," Willow whispered, rocking her shoulders back and forth.

"You like Gail, don't you?" Hawk pressed. There must be a reason why Willow had made some subtle changes in her relation to Gail, and he wondered about them. He didn't think she stayed with her against her will, but Willow was as changeable as the wind.

"Yes," Willow whispered again.

"Is anything wrong?" Willow looked down and rocked her shoulders again. Hawk hunkered down in front of her. "You know you can tell me anything, don't you?"

"I heard . . ." Willow's lower lip trembled.

"Heard what?"

"They want to put me in a foster home. I don't want to go. They can't make me, can they?" Her big dark eyes flashed the fear she felt, but for only a moment. That was the way Willow was, too, or had been. She'd always known how to mask her true feelings.

"Who is they? I don't think Gail would do

that. She cares for you very much. Who said these things to you?" Hawk's heart was growing heavy. This little girl had wormed her way in there somehow, and was firmly lodged. That gave her power over his feelings. How had he let that happen?

"Even if she wants me, they won't let her keep me because she's white." Willow sniffed, valiantly holding back tears. "I don't care if she's white. Do you?"

Hawk hugged her just as Gail came down the hallway. "Don't worry," he whispered in her ear. "Don't worry. I'll take care of it." He perched Willow on his arm and stood up, giving Gail a long, slow, approving sweep with his eyes. She was wearing a flowered rayon dress in muted shades of green, blue and mauve, and leather high-heeled sandals. With her hair grown out almost to her collar and feathered softly around her face, Hawk thought Gail looked beautiful. "Well, now, Willow," he said huskily, "it appears you were absolutely right."

Willow turned toward Gail, and the smile she gave her was so full of love Hawk marveled at her swift change in mood.

"Of course Willow was right. She's very smart," Gail said proudly. "What was she right about this time?"

"I said you were beautiful," Willow said, and

put her finger against her lips again.

Gail went up and kissed her nose. "Oh, I've taught you to say all the right words, haven't I?"

"Something tells me she thought that up all on her own," Hawk said.

Before Gail could find words to respond, Jerrie arrived to sit with Willow. "Now don't worry about anything," she sputtered like an old nanny, "the little one will be just fine. You two kids go out and have a good time. Now don't be late. You know how we worry."

"Brat!" Hawk said, and pulled his sister's braid. He took Gail's hand and escorted her out to his pickup.

"You know, of course, that I had a very ordered life," Gail said an hour later. "I knew where I was going to be every day, every evening, every year, and the year after. You've upset that order, you, and Willow, and Montana. I never expected to be where I am right now."

Hawk and Gail were doing their own version of a waltz to a country song popular a few years back.

"Aren't you having a good time?" he asked.

"You mean right here, right this minute, or overall?" she said, feeling flirtatious in the late spring air.

"Your entire time in Montana." He said it so it sounded like Mawn-tanha, and she loved it.

"Beginning with or after the America's Adventure Tour?"

"I think the whole story wouldn't be complete without mention of that tour. After all, the chances are you wouldn't be here right now if you hadn't come out here then."

He'd driven her to the canyon where they'd first seen the golden eagles, turned on the radio and escorted her out of the vehicle. He'd swept her into his arms and danced with her against a glowing burnt orange backdrop of the setting sun in the western sky.

"It's been an adventure, all right," Gail said. "Not all of it external." It was true what she'd read about the rhythms of earth's creatures. Cradled in Hawk's arms now, the smell of newly growing grass and earth-damp air floating around them, she felt her winter-drugged senses truly come alive again.

Gail dropped her head, and he let her cheek rest against his chest. She was reminded again and acutely aware of how easily they fit together now as well as that night in the cabin. He height, his even taller stature offered the hollow of his shoulder to the jut of hers, the curve of her hip along the arc of his thigh, the top of her hair under the roof of his chin.

Hawk looked above the rim of the canyon then down. He tilted up Gail's face so that he

464

could really see her in the rapidly darkening light. He gazed long and hard. She looked softer to him, not the menace he'd made of her when she first arrived with that crowd of tourists. Had she changed that much? Or had he?

He thought of Laura. She was a real party girl, and back then all he'd wanted was a party, a big party. He'd picked her up in the beginning of his love affair with the bottle. He'd danced with her, too, only not like this. His arm hadn't slipped around her the way it was around Gail's waist now. Her cool hand hadn't slid up over his shoulder and barely grazed the back of his neck like Gail's did now. He and Laura had danced madly, in smokey bars jam-packed with sweating bodies, native and white, and the overpowering stench of stale beer. They hadn't touched, but they'd seduced each other with their eyes and their writhing bodies, until they'd ended up scrambling in the back of her Chevy.

They were both devils then, but they'd produced an angel. And he'd continued his affair with the bottle long after they'd both gone.

He hadn't wanted to start that way with Gail. He'd wanted to be out beneath the big Montana sky, the air and trees all around them, no outside force. That was the way to start, at the real beginning of their own real time.

Start? Was he starting something with Gail?

Or had it begun last summer?

"Hawk?"

Gail's voice interrupted his thoughts. He was glad. She'd interrupted his thoughts at the precise moment he'd needed, now and that night in the sweat lodge. He was grateful for that. She'd helped him dig down in his guts and churn out all that he'd needed to cleanse himself of, and he'd be eternally grateful to her for that. But it was more than gratefulness, he knew that. He was afraid of that.

"Yes," he answered her.

"Are you feeling all right?"

"Yes, I'm feeling terrific. You?"

"Terrific. So, what do you think?"

"About what?"

"Dating, of course. I mean, that has been so much on our minds, hasn't it?" She laughed, and gazed happily into his eyes. "What do you think?"

"Oh, of course, of course it has been on both our minds." When she rested her cheek against his chest again, he noticed that the radio station had stopped playing music. A male voice was giving a weather report, and they were still dancing.

"Sunny and hot," Hawk said, resting the point of his chin against her hair.

"That's what you think about dating?" Gail's

muffled voice came against his shirt.

"What do you think?"

"No fair. I asked you first."

He pulled her closer. "I guess this one's all right. I wouldn't want to date all the time."

Gail slid her head out from under his chin and looked up at him. "Well, I wouldn't want to either. But I guess that's a good place for some people to start, isn't it?"

Hawk closed his eyes and took in a deep breath of the spring air and Gail's fresh, womanly scent. He was learning to live with himself again. And one of the first big steps was a dance with a special woman at sunset on the rim of a canyon.

Chapter Eighteen

The remnants of a long winter were still apparent around Medicine Wheel School as the month of May arrived. Gail delighted in walking to school again, breathing in the crisp, clean air, taking in the spectacular landscape. Snow was visible capping the Big Horn Mountains, and pockets of it still lay along stream beds and beneath stands of cottonwoods and cedar.

This spring she sensed more than ever its promise of freedom from the encumbrances of a hard winter that had kept her inside striving for warmth of body as well as spirit, and she'd become impatient for outward expression of the months of inward investigation. She'd grown more confident in her abilities as a survivor and as a teacher in an environment she never would have dreamed she'd be living in.

While her ideas for students to compare ancient Cheyenne legends with the legendary writers of literature proved brighter in theory than in practice and was only moderately successful, Gail was feeling buoyed by the new rapport between the students and herself. And she became their willing student as well. She learned how their literal frame of reference, life as they knew it now, in comparison with a literary frame of reference was the more useful jumping off place. Once they began to trust her and she allowed them to express their own thoughts, the mutual flow of ideas picked up at a livelier pace. Some days when she left the classroom she felt satisfied as deeply as she felt weary.

As for Willow, Gail no longer worried that the child would run away from her, disappear. As spring gained momentum, Gail knew there was a real bonding between them. She could feel it, and she knew Willow did, too, and she believed it couldn't have been stronger if they'd been together since the moment of birth.

The emergence of spring awakened the senses, exploded the blossoming emotions of youth, and showed up as weariness in the faces of the teachers, and rambunctiousness in the students' behavior. Everyone seemed ready for the school year to come to an end.

May also brought the reminder of Mother's Day and the announcement of a wedding that had everyone at Medicine Wheel School twittering as much as the spring birds. Ang Carinci and her UPS man, Albert Maxwell, had set their wedding date, the third Saturday in the month. Invitations went out to friends and family, and to all the students in Ang's sixth grade class. In the meantime, elementary grade students were at work making Mother's Day cards and gifts during the week preceding that special Sunday.

"It's a difficult time," Carol spoke to Gail about some of her students. "There are those kids who are all excited about making things for their mothers. But then there are the others who sit back and watch, and no amount of coaxing can get them to participate. One told me his mother wouldn't be interested in a Mother's Day card or anything else from him because she didn't care about him anyway."

"I think television doesn't help much either," Gail said. "I've seen a lot of perfect looking families celebrating these holidays with food and gifts and lots of people around them."

"I know. The ads are worse, though. You've got some famous man peddling special bouquets of flowers and saying that's the only thing Mother wants on her day. Or greeting card companies showing intimate moments between mothers and daughters and their expensive cards. I was told in no uncertain terms yesterday by this girl who said she wasn't going to make any dumb old card or present for her mother, and I couldn't make her."

Gail thought about Willow. How was she responding to the flurry of construction paper, and paste, and crayons, and cutouts? She asked Ang about her at lunch.

"Willow shows half-hearted interest in the project," Ang told her. "But she did help another girl in the class. The girl has hand-eye coordination difficulties, and couldn't cut the rose pictures out of a seed catalog neatly enough to paste on her card for her mother. It was frustrating for her. Willow showed remarkable patience. She carefully cut out six of the roses for her. Now the two have become fast friends."

At home when they talked about it, Gail could see that Willow found the prospect of attending her first wedding most exciting, and had even decided she'd wear a dress to her teacher's big day. But she found much less exciting, even depressing, the rapidly approaching Mother's Day holiday and the Father's Day that would follow a month later. A conflict of sensations warred against her burgeoning perception of herself, and she fought the battle internally.

Gail, too, had been feeling more acutely aware of holidays than ever, and would be glad when the next two had passed. It seemed everything within eye or ear contact was designed to make those who weren't parents, or who were parentless, guilty or sad about what they should think of as their missing parts. She pondered constantly what to do about it, how to make it more comfortable for both of them. By mid-week, Gail thought of something to help Willow, and herself, through the Mother's Day dilemma. At breakfast on Wednesday morning, she discussed it with her.

"You know it's Mother's Day this Sunday, and I have an idea for something to do."

"What?" Willow asked, glumly. She leaned her head on one hand while she toyed with the remaining oat cereal in her bowl.

"We'll have to get busy, though. We have two mothers to think about and not much time to prepare things."

Willow looked up. Gail smeared raspberry jam on a piece of wheat toast, cut it and handed one half to the child.

"Don't tell me you forgot," Gail said, smiling at her and biting into the toast. She waited the few seconds it took to chew and swallow. "Or maybe you're already planning something for Ada."

Willow brightened slightly. "She's not my mother. She's not your mother either."

"That doesn't matter. She doesn't have to be our mother to be honored by us on a special day. She's the mother of Jerrie and Hawk. And she's like a mother to us. She mothered us when we were sick by bringing," Gail swallowed some coffee, "turtle soup and orange juice. And she's a grand lady who cares about your school like a mother does, too. I think she deserves to have some handmade gifts and cards on Mother's Day from us, too." Gail tilted her head to get a look at Willow's downcast face. "Don't you?"

Willow stirred, then she smiled with a brightness Gail was hoping to see. "I can make her a card in school today," she said with more excitement than she'd shown in several days.

"That's wonderful. I thought I might find some pretty vines and flowers, and we could make a dish garden for the window in her bedroom. What do you think of that idea?"

"She likes things that grow. I can make a planter in school, too. Some of the other kids are making those."

"That's good. I'm so glad you thought of that," Gail said, sounding relieved. "I wasn't sure what to do for a planter. I have some pretty ribbon saved. We'll make a big bow to wrap around it."

Willow smiled and finished her cereal. She was halfway through her glass of milk when a thought came to her. "You said we had two mothers to think about. Who's the other one?"

"Mother Earth, of course. You didn't forget her."

Willow looked skeptical. "You can't give her any presents."

"Why not? She gives us presents all the time, doesn't she? Air, and sun, and rain, and vegetables, even the ones you don't like, and even snow that I've learned to live with. We ought to give her something back, don't you think?"

Willow thought long. "Mr. Black Feather makes us clean up everything we drop on the ground. He says we should do that for the earth. And he makes us re . . . re . . ."

"Recycle?"

"Yes, paper and cans. He says that's a good thing to do for the earth, too."

"He's right. But maybe we can think of something more special to do. We still have a few days. What do you say?"

"Okay. Maybe Jerrie will help us. And Catherine."

"Oh, yes. You're going over to the women's center today, aren't you?"

"Uh-huh. They told me I'm really good with the little kids. Kind of like a big sister."

Gail smiled. "I bet you are a wonderful big sister."

The air was brisk and clear on Mother's Day

Sunday when Gail and Willow drove over to see Ada.

"Just in time!" Jerrie said as they got out of the car in the horseshoe drive. "We've packed a picnic and we're going up to the cabin for the day."

The cabin! She hadn't been to the cabin since she and Hawk . . . "A picnic! What a great idea," Gail said.

Ada came down the stairs carrying her canvas bag bulging with food. Hawk was close behind carrying a rectangular red and white cooler. He made eye contact with Gail. She felt her stomach flutter and her pulse accelerate. It was a marvelous feeling knowing those physical sensations came just as unexpected and tipped her just as off-balance at her advanced age as they had when she was a teenager in the throes of her first crush.

Willow ran up to Ada and grabbed her hand. "Happy Mother's Day, *Nesko!*"

Ada slowly set down her bag and gave Willow a hug. "Thank you. It's good we can all be together today."

"Hi Hawk." She followed him to the back of his pickup.

"Hi Willow. You're growing up fast. Weren't you a foot shorter last week?" Hawk set the cooler in the truck bed.

Willow grinned at him and slipped her hand inside his as they walked toward the others. Gail could see the love in her eyes for him. He was her hero. And she could see in Hawk's eyes flashes of his feelings for the little girl. Perhaps he couldn't say it in words, but those feelings were love.

"Hello," he said to Gail, and she heard a dozen other meanings behind the simple word.

"Hello," she said to Hawk, and a paragraph of other words followed in her mind.

He went back into the house, and returned a moment later with another cooler.

"Did you bring extra clothes?" Jerrie asked. "Sometimes it gets chilly up there by the river."

"I think we're dressed warmly enough," Gail said straightening the turtleneck on Willow's shirt and feeling the thickness in her cotton jacket.

"I've got some extra sweatshirts," Catherine said. She bent down to Willow. "Hey, you were great the other day. You got Alice Little Horse to say her name."

"I did?" Willow's eyes widened and sparkled.

"You sure did." Catherine looked up at Gail. "There's a little girl who's been at the center with her mother off and on. They've had a very bad time. The child wouldn't talk no matter what we did to try to get her to. But she loves Willow, follows her with her eyes when she isn't toddling after her. Willow read three stories to her when she was there last, and wherever a girl's name was mentioned in it, Willow put Alice's name in there instead. After Willow left, little Alice came up to me and pointed at herself and said her own name. She giggled all over with her own accomplishment, and her mother was excited over something for the first time since I met her."

"And Catherine cried," Jerrie said, walking over to them. "It was a great moment." She smiled at Catherine.

"I knew you were a wonderful big sister," Gail said to the beaming Willow. She looked back at Catherine. "And you've always had a soft heart. I'm glad you're happy."

"I am," Catherine said. "What a difference a year can make, eh?"

Gail hugged Catherine. Her friend had changed from the perfectly groomed, impeccably dressed, cool, and introspective private school teacher into an open and warm woman with a breezy nature and healthy outdoor looks to match. Her natural skin glowed. Her eyes sparked with happiness and enjoyment, and reflected the satisfaction of a woman in love with her own new life and the people around her. And with one special person in particular.

At the cabin, the sun seemed to shine especially warmly on the gathered group. Gail took a leisurely glance at each face. In an odd but wonderful way, the bunch of them made a family unit for Willow and for themselves. Jerrie and Catherine were as much or more like aunts to Willow than any blood ones she could have. Ada was grandmotherly and enjoyed teaching Willow about her heritage, now and then throwing in a few lessons in courtesy and table manners. And Hawk was a substitute big brother, or an uncle, or . . . Gail hesitated even to think it . . . a *father* to her.

And, increasingly, Gail felt more like the mother she wished she could be.

She'd made preliminary inquiries with a legal counsel for the Northern Cheyenne, and what she heard from him about tribal laws scared her enough to stop asking. She didn't want to call attention to the fact that she was caring for this little half-Cheyenne girl in her home. The attorney had made it quite clear that Cheyenne foster homes were available for such children, and were the preferred choices of care. Gail knew if she allowed Willow to be taken from her and put into a foster home, the child would not stay. She'd most likely run away again and hide for good. All her strides forward would become a race backward, and she might never trust anyone again. Gail couldn't take that chance.

"When's it going to be time to give our presents?" Willow asked. They'd finished the last of the food spread out on a picnic table overlooking the river.

"How about now?" Gail said. She swung her legs over the end of the bench and went to produce a box from behind a tree. Willow took it and gave it to Ada along with a big smile full of love. She stood next to her while she opened the box.

When Ada lifted the dish garden out of the box, Willow watched her face carefully, waiting for the look of approval she sought in every person she cared about. Ada did not disappoint her.

"Oh, my," Ada breathed, "it looks to have been planted by the hand of the Creator. A fern here, an ivy there," she poked among the plants in the container Willow had made by tying small cedar logs into a circle with rawhide thong, "and even a bed of sage over the earth. It will always grow and become new." She lifted old dark eyes to the face of the beaming child in front of her, and touched Willow's cheek with a leathery hand. "You are truly a special daughter of the earth."

Gail's heart filled at the sight. She saw Hawk's face, saw the respect in it for his mother, and understood the enjoyment felt in Willow's gift.

Willow ran to the car and came back with flat thin package wrapped in white school drawing paper. Shyly she went to Gail and slowl held it out to her.

"For . . . for me?" Gail asked, her voice thic with emotion. She dropped down on the bench

Willow nodded.

With trembling hands, Gail opened the pack age carefully. She didn't want even the wrappin to sustain any tearing. She reached inside an felt a square of heavy construction paper, an lifted it out. It was pale blue and folded into card. On the front Willow had drawn an painted a border of yellow and pink flowers wit green leaves. In the center of the border was snapshot of Gail taken at Christmastime. Sh was holding the bookmark that Willow ha made for her then.

Gail opened the card. Inside was painted star sprinkled with gold glitter. In the middle o the star uneven letters in dark blue paint spelle out "Happy Mother's Day *Na-hko'eehe*." He throat constricted and tears moistened her eyes

"Do . . . do you like it?" Willow asked in thin voice.

Gail hugged the little girl close to her. Aroun them she felt the emotion of the others as the looked on. "I . . . love it. And I love you," sh whispered against Willow's hair.

When they parted, Jerrie leaned over and urged, "Explain to Gail what everything means, Willow."

Willow backed up and just watched her face. For a moment Gail wondered if she was she going to run off. Then the girl come slowly toward her.

She pointed to the glitter. "This is the morning star. It's the same color as your hair."

Gail thought of how her hair had been when she came to the Triple or Nothing Ranch the summer before. It had been a soft blonde created by an excellent colorist in New York. She wasn't doing that anymore. Her own dark blonde hair had emerged over the winter, and showed a sprinkling of light gray along the temples. How wonderful that this child hadn't noticed the change.

"The morning star," Gail said, and smiled.

Willow nodded. "Cheyennes say the morning star lights the sky and shines brighter than all the other stars."

"That's beautiful," Gail told her. "Happy Mother's Day," she read the card out loud. "That makes me very happy." Willow's lower lip quivered just a trace. "What does this mean?" Gail asked, pointing to the Cheyenne word.

Willow's eyes glistened. "Mother," she whispered.

The quiet that drifted around the family gathering then was one of comfort and warmth. No further words were needed from anyone. Willow had said everything in one from the Cheyenne.

Gail was still overcome with emotion from her Mother's Day gift as they drove ahead of Hawk's pickup on the way home.

"We didn't do anything for Mother Earth yet," Willow said in the seat next to her. "I couldn't think of anything."

"I did," Gail said, smiling.

"What?"

"You'll see. Hawk will be surprised, too."

She pulled into the drive at Medicine Wheel School and drove around to the playground. Hawk followed and got out of his truck.

"Bring the shovel," Gail called to him.

Hawk lifted a pointed-end shovel from the truck bed and walked up to them. "Are you putting me to work on my day off?"

"I don't think you'll mind just this once. At least I hope you won't." She walked toward the playground.

At the entrance gate she stopped next to the sign Hawk had painted for Kenny's Castle. A willow sapling, its roots balled and tied in a burlap sack was propped next to it.

"I found this little tree near one of the nice houses in town. The people had been doing some landscaping and they dug up this little tree and threw it on a pile. I asked them if I could have it. I thought we could plant it here and make it Kenny's gift to Mother Earth."

Hawk didn't move. He stood leaning on the shovel, just staring at her.

Gail's throat caught. "I . . . hope that's all right."

"That's a good present," Willow said, not looking at them. "It will keep growing and get real big right over the playground. Mother Earth will like that. Kenny will, too, won't he, Hawk?"

Hawk didn't answer. He turned his back abruptly, and started to dig a hole a few feet away from the sign. Gail wasn't certain what to think about his reaction. He wouldn't let her see his face and eyes.

She went to get a pail of water. When she returned, Hawk was unwrapping the twine and burlap, releasing the sapling's roots. Willow stood nearby just staring down into the ground. Hawk lifted the sapling, ready to place it into the hole. Willow stopped him.

"I want to give something else," she said in a barely audible whisper.

Gail watched her, but Willow did not look up. She unzipped her waist pack and took out the tattered old magazine, still rolled into a cylinder. She held it in both hands, but didn't unroll it.

Hesitating, she lifted it to her lips. Then she hunkered down and placed the magazine in the hole. With two small hands she covered it with some of the earth Hawk had dug, then stood up and looked at Hawk, who'd kept his gaze on her the entire time.

"Shall I plant this now?" he asked her.

Willow nodded, and two little tears spilled down her cheeks. Hawk carefully lowered the tree roots into the hole, then took Willow's hand and placed it on the trunk. He looked over at Gail then for the first time. She was shaken, and her tears fell unchecked. He took her hand and placed it on the trunk below and opposite Willow's. They held the little willow sapling upright while Hawk filled in the hole and tamped the earth closely around it. Then he watered it and the three stepped back and admired the stalwart little tree, its lacy young branches waving in the breeze, tapping gently against the welcome sign to Kenny's Castle.

Ang's wedding was the perfect spring event, from the earth-fragrant warm air to the spirit of love and fun that surrounded the event. Hawk hadn't ever been to a ceremony quite like this one. He and Laura had run off to a justice of the peace. He gave a wry inward laugh. Peace had nothing to do with his marriage to Laura.

Willow sat with other students in her grade opposite the church aisle from Hawk. Gail, Ada, Jerrie, and Catherine were on the other side of him. Hawk snatched moments out of the ceremony to watch Willow's reaction. She seemed to hang on every word from the minister and from Ang and Albert. When he tried to steal a look at Gail, he felt uncomfortable doing it. She, too, had been looking over at Willow, and he was afraid his eyes would meet hers and she would read something in them he wasn't even certain of himself.

These days he was having feelings that stirred his insides, and he couldn't put them to rest where they would stay put and not bother him. Family feelings, that's what they were. There, he'd admitted it. Not the usual family feelings he had for Ada and Jerrie. Definitely not ones for Trey who hadn't been at the ranch all winter long. These were family feelings like the ones he'd felt for Kenny.

Maybe it was just because of spring. Maybe he'd begun to mellow in his middle age, although a wildness still ran through his veins that he refused to tame. He never would tame that feeling that made him know where he came from. Lately he'd begun to question who he was and where he was going. He'd recognized that those questions had started right after he and

Gail had shared the sweat lodge, and shared more than just the night in his mother's cabin.

After the bride and groom had walked down the aisle to the front door to greet their guests, Gail caught up with Willow. "What did you think about that?" she asked.

"I liked it," Willow said. "Does that mean they can stay together now, and nobody can make them leave each other?"

"That's the idea," Gail told her.

"Is it like that for Cheyennes, too?" Willow asked Hawk and Ada.

"It's always the way we want it to be." Hawk didn't want to have to tell her that things didn't always work out as lovely as the wedding ceremony promised.

"Can you marry anybody you want to?"

"Well, yes," Hawk hesitated. "They should want to marry you, too, or it's kind of sticky." He laughed.

"How do you know if somebody wants to marry you?" Willow asked Gail.

"I guess you have to know first if . . . if the two people love each other." Gail seemed at a loss for the correct answer. The teacher in her had fled when the questions came from Willow.

"How do you know that?" Willow pressed. "Just because they say it? Do they mean it? How do you know?"

Gail hesitated even longer than Hawk had. He was glad Willow hadn't asked him that question. He was about as effective as a dry leaf against a windstorm when it came to explaining love to anybody, let alone himself. He had to simply trust his instincts. He'd trusted them in the cabin with Gail, and right after that he'd become terrified of his own feelings.

"You just know," Gail told Willow. "And you have to believe your feelings. Why all the questions?"

"Just wondering," Willow said with a lopsided grin.

At the end of the last day of school, Gail picked up her mail and walked home alone, realizing just how tired she truly was. Willow said she was going over to the women's center with Catherine. Without her chattering by her side on the way home, Gail had time to reflect as she walked.

It had been a difficult year, full of changes, a test of her energy and reserve. She'd forgotten what it had been like to be in a classroom day after day in constant contact with students. Now she knew. It was stimulating and energy-draining all at the same time.

The lazy days of summer were going to feel

good to her, no matter how beastly hot it be came. She hadn't forgotten her summer vacation of the year before. She hadn't been the same since that experience.

She got out her keys and came around by her front door. A long wrapped package leaned against it. She opened the door, then picked up the heavy package and carried it inside, curious about who had sent something to her. The only identification was her own name printed across the front.

She changed into jeans and a tee shirt and sandals, then went back to the living room. She tore the brown paper wrapper away and opened the long box. Under a layer of tissue was a white doeskin dress. Gail sucked in her breath and lifted it by the shoulders, letting it unfold slowly. She walked to a mirror and held it up in front of her body. It fell almost to her ankles. This was not a new garment, she could tell that. The doe-skin was soft, carefully stitched, fringed and studded with multi-colored beads. She recog-nized its style as a Cheyenne wedding dress from early in the century. She'd seen it portrayed in one of Willow's books given to her by Jerrie.

Gail searched among the tissue for a card or note, something that would identify the reason the box had been delivered to her, and the per-son who sent it. There was nothing. Perhaps

Willow knew. She'd ask her as soon as she came back from the women's center.

She sorted through her mail and came upon an envelope bearing the return address of the tribal legal counsel she'd spoken with. Her heart pounded. *Oh no! He's found out Willow is living with me!* Gail's mind raced. Her hands trembled as she tried to open the envelope. Would they take Willow away from her? She knew, as much as she'd survived a great deal since the moment she'd stepped foot in Montana, that she would not survive the loss of Willow now.

She opened the letter and reluctantly began to read it. Her eyes scanned the opening paragraph which mentioned something about his being grateful for the opportunity to meet her recently. There it was.

"We've learned you have been caring for a Cheyenne child of about twelve who is called Willow." Gail read the line and her eyes burned. Then her vision blurred as tears welled. This was it, the moment she'd dreaded. The tribal counsel was about to take Willow from her.

Gail clutched the letter, and her mind whirled. Should she take Willow and run away with her? After all, Willow was half-Cheyenne, not full blood. Didn't that account for something in her favor? Could they come after her? Have her arrested? She took a breath. Maybe there was a

way to appeal this decision. She had to be calm
She had to finish reading the letter, had to know
how long she had left with Willow.

". . . and I'm pleased to tell you that you ca
start legal proceedings to adopt this child pric
to the day of your wedding if you so choose. Pa
pers can be drawn and finalized on that day, an
henceforth you would be the child's legal guard
ian. Congratulations."

What wedding?

Gail panicked. Had they made a mistake
Could they be confusing her with someone else
No, how could they? Counsel said he'd me
Gail, and that was so. He'd said he knew Willo
lived with her, and that was true also. But
wedding?

Willow burst through the door then, startlin
Gail. She headed straight for the refrigerato
and poured herself a glass of orange juice. Sh
seemed unusually excited, Gail observed. Mayb
it was just the fact that school was out.

"Willow? Look at this." Gail brought the bo
with doeskin dress out to the kitchen and set
on the table.

"It's beautiful," Willow said, looking but nc
touching.

"Yes, it is. But I don't know where it cam
from."

"It's Ada's," Willow said with her increasin

Cheyenne inflection that reminded Gail of Hawk's voice more than ever.

"Ada's?"

Willow nodded. "Her wedding dress. She showed it to me once."

"Why would she send it to me?" Gail's wonderment was growing by leaps and bounds.

"For a surprise."

"Well, I am surprised, I can tell you that."

"We have to go to the cabin now," Willow said, picking up Gail's car keys from the sideboard and handing them to her.

"The cabin? Why?"

"I'll show you." Willow headed out the back door.

In a daze, Gail followed her.

When Gail drove her car up the small rise that led to the cabin, she saw Hawk's pickup parked near a stand of cottonwoods. He was standing next to it, looking long and lean in jeans and an open denim shirt, and leaning against the door chewing on a piece of new hay.

"What are we doing here?" Gail asked as she got out of her car and walked toward him. Willow ran ahead of her and threw her arms around Hawk's waist.

"I haven't any idea," he told her. "I'm here at the rather secretive summons of Willow."

"What are you up to, Willow?" Gail eyed the

child suspiciously.

With a cryptic smile, Willow took them both by the hands. She led them to the river bank and motioned for them to stand side by side. She picked up a slim willow tree branch from a flat rock. Gail looked at Hawk and they both knew the branch had been placed there previously. Willow's eyes darted up toward the cabin for a moment. Then she moved around them and stood in front of and facing them, took out a sheet of lined yellow paper from the back pocket of her jeans, and began to read.

"Miss Gail Bricker, will you have this girl Willow, to love and cherish as your daughter and never leave her?"

Gail's mouth dropped open.

"If so," Willow looked down at her paper, lost her place for a moment, then found it and read, "if so, answer by saying 'I will.'"

Gail looked at Hawk for a moment, and swallowed a lump in her throat. "I . . . will," she croaked, *if only she could.*

"Good," Willow said with a nod of her head.

"Mr. Lone Hawk Kincaid, will you have this girl, Willow, to love and cher . . . cherish as your daughter, and never leave her?" She gave a darting glance at Hawk, then went back to her paper. It trembled as if a breeze had caught the edges. "If so, say 'I will.'"

Hawk stared at the child for a minute, then at Gail. He seemed to be asking her to help him say the right thing. Gail looked back at him with a look of helplessness on her face.

Willow tugged his sleeve. "You have to do this quick, or it doesn't work."

"Oh, I didn't know," Hawk said, apologetically.

"So, will you?" Willow pressed impatiently.

"I will, yes, of course."

"Good." Willow turned her paper over and read carefully, pronouncing the words clearly. "Now, with the power ves . . . ves-ted in me by the fact that I'm half white like you," she looked at Gail sternly, "and half Cheyenne like you," she gave the same look to Hawk, "I now pronounce that you are my mother," she tapped Gail's head with the willow branch, "and you are my father," she tapped Hawk's head in kind, "and I am your daughter," she tapped her own head. "What I have joined together, don't let anybody break up."

Gail and Hawk could not take their eyes off this incredibly clever and intelligent girl in front of them.

"You may kiss your daughter," Willow urged.

They both laughed, hugged, and kissed her one at a time and then held her in their own embrace.

"How I wish it could be as easy as this," Gai[
whispered.

"I forgot something," Willow said, turning
her paper back to the front.

"Oh, dear, do you mean we have to start thi[
all over again?" Hawk asked, teasing her.

"I think it would be okay if we did just part o[
it," Willow said.

"All right. Did we forget to say something w[
were supposed to?" Gail asked.

"No, I did." Willow said.

She got down on her knees, read her pape[
one more time, then placed it on the grass. The[
she took Gail's hand in one of hers and Hawk'[
hand in the other. She brought their hands to[
gether and made them clasp them.

"I love you. Will you marry me?" she asked i[
her little voice, all her love and emotion ex[
pressed earnestly on her face and in her enor[
mous dark eyes. "Then we'll be the sam[
family." She pointed to Gail's heart, "white.[
She pointed to Hawk's heart, "Cheyenne." Sh[
pointed to her own heart. "Both."

Chapter Nineteen

Neither Gail nor Hawk could say anything, struck even more speechless by the second part of Willow's speech than they had been by the first.

"Then this is where I was supposed to do the stuff about being your daughter," Willow said, her big innocent eyes searching their faces. "Do you think it matters that I did it backwards?"

When Gail found her voice, she whispered huskily, "No I don't think it matters at all. It was a beautiful ceremony."

"So, do I get an answer now?" Willow's voice held a breathless note of anticipation.

How could her questions be answered honestly? Gail's rush of emotions clouded her mind, but Willow deserved directness, one answer, straight as an arrow. She sensed Hawk's collected calm, heard his breath sucked in and held like an opera singer at the moment before he hit the final high note in an aria. Gail let out her own breath in a rush as if she were releasing Hawk's anticipation.

"Sometimes," Gail started, "when a woman gets a proposal of marriage, she likes to think about it. She wants to be sure of what's in her heart before she answers."

"Does it take long?" Willow's impatience was being sorely tried.

"Sometimes. Sometimes weeks."

Willow frowned.

"Sometimes only a day or two," Gail said, smiling.

"Why can't the woman make up her mind faster?" Willow pouted.

"It's worse for a man," Hawk said. Gail could see he was troubled and was trying to save face for both of them. "Women are much better at answering than men. They are smarter, know themselves better in those areas."

"How long does it take for a man?" Willow looked hopeful.

"Oh, maybe years." When Willow's expression turned to shock, Hawk hastily added, "Or three or four days."

"That's too long." She looked down at her little fingers which were entwining and loosening, entwining and loosening.

"Well, it's a big decision to make," Hawk said, his voice sounding scratchy. "And sometimes the answer isn't what the other person, or people, want to hear. It's very complicated."

"Oh," Willow said, and her disappointment could be read on her face like the bold headlines on the front page of a newspaper. Then she brightened, holding out her hands as if she were handing them a simple solution. "It's easy," she said. "You're not married," she said to Hawk, "and you used to have a child, but now you don't. And you're not married, either," she said to Gail, "and you never had a child." She touched the fingers of both hands to her chest. "I don't have a mother or a father, and I'm a child. See?"

"It sounds very simple when you explain it like that," Gail told her. "But adults always make things complicated. We will think long and hard about this, and give our answer very soon. Right Hawk?" He nodded. "It's certainly the most beautiful question I've ever been asked."

"Really?" Willow said.

"Absolutely," Gail said, sniffing and searching her bag for a tissue.

"Then why are you crying?"

"Because I'm happy you asked that question."

"Oh."

"I promise I'll be faster than other men have been known to be," Hawk said, trying to reassure Willow. "It's a beautiful question for me, too." He rose, stroked the back of Willow's hair, then walked up the hill toward the cabin.

"How did you ever think of . . . ?" Gail started. She heard rustling footsteps from behind and turned, surprised to see Catherine and Jerrie coming toward her, smiling.

"Well?" Catherine asked, excitement lifting her voice. "When's the big day?"

"What big day?" Gail asked.

"Your wedding day, of course," Jerrie said. "This is great!"

"We haven't . . ." Gail looked at Willow's confused face. "Can I talk to you a minute alone, Catherine?"

"Come on, Willow." Jerrie took the little girl by the hand. "Let's see what wildflowers are blooming now."

When Willow was out of earshot, Gail turned to Catherine. "What is going on here? Did you know Willow was going to ask Hawk and me to marry her?"

Catherine nodded. "Yes. When she came over to the center today, she had the whole idea worked out in her head. She wanted us to help her write it out."

"Does Ada know about it, too?"

"Yes. Did you get the dress?"

"I did. I take it she approves of Willow's idea."

"Jerrie says she does."

Gail sighed, and ran a hand through her hair. Willow, and Ada, and Jerrie and Catherine had concocted a grand scheme, something they all figured was a surefire winner. But they forgot about the principal players. For any scheme to work, the main characters in the plot had to want to cooperate. Gail's mind kept shifting to the cabin where moments before Hawk had entered. This whole puzzle was becoming even more complex.

"Cath, I didn't know what to think now. Willow can be hurt, perhaps more than she ever was before. Did you have anything to do with a letter I received from the tribal legal counsel saying I can adopt Willow on my wedding day?"

"No, I don't. Jerrie never mentioned anything about that. But, that's perfect, isn't it? It's what you've wanted, isn't it? When you marry Hawk it fulfills one of the biggest requirements of the tribal council, a Cheyenne husband."

"What makes you think they had Hawk as the Cheyenne husband in mind?"

"It's a small town. Who else could they be thinking of?" Catherine smiled. "Great, huh?"

"I don't think so. You don't see the Cheyenne man in question, do you?"

"He went up to the cabin. I take it he wasn't keen on the whole idea." Catherine's eyebrows came together over the bridge of her nose.

"No, I think he wasn't. This whole thing was made much more difficult for him coming from Willow." Gail shook her head, trying to rid her mind of the darkening thoughts.

She struggled with what to do next. Surprised at the admission to herself, she thought the idea was actually quite wonderful. She and Hawk marrying and adopting Willow. Strange to be thinking that, she who had spent her life believing she never wanted to marry, never yearned to have children. Now she wanted both. And at her advanced age! These were the dreams of a teenager in the throes of her first crush, not those of a woman old enough to be a grandmother.

What Hawk wanted was something else entirely. Gail knew he wouldn't want to hurt Willow. That was the only thing she knew for certain. He'd once said he loved her, and she'd confessed she loved him. It had been as if they both understood that was all there was to be. Nothing more. They understood each other well. He had his own reasons for staying alone, and she had hers. And that's the way they both preferred it. Wasn't it?

"I'll go talk to him. Maybe together we can find a way of giving Willow an answer without hurting her." Gail started toward the cabin.

Jerrie came back to Catherine, leaving Willow

by the river bank. "Something went wrong, didn't it?"

Catherine looked perplexed. "Yes, but I'm not sure what. I thought you thought Hawk wanted to marry Gail."

"I did."

"Then why did he turn his back on her and Willow and go off to the cabin alone?"

"You have a lot to learn about us, my dear. It is our way to work out our problems alone. Besides, from what I got from Willow, Gail didn't say yes right away to her proposal, and knowing my brother, he thinks that means she said no."

Catherine nodded. "And from what I gather from Gail, Hawk's walking away from them shows his answer is no. Now what?"

"Well, this time I think we'd better let them figure it out for themselves."

Inside the cabin, Hawk stripped out of his jeans and boots and shirt, and pulled on a pair of doeskin leggings and his favorite softly worn moccasins. His Cheyenne mind could think better if his body was unencumbered by the restrictions those clothes had meant to him so often in his life.

He went around the place and opened the windows, letting in late spring breezes. He heard

Jerrie's truck start, looked out and saw Catherine getting in. He watched the truck until it disappeared over the hill. And he saw Willow sitting on the rise overlooking the river, hugging her knees and rocking back and forth.

What an unexpected turn of events!

He heard the cabin door open, and turned around. Gail stepped into the room and closed the door quietly behind her. "Well, that was quite a bombshell Willow dropped on us, wasn't it?" He didn't answer. "I think we have to talk about it," she pressed.

"What more is there to say?" He walked to the fireplace and began sweeping the hearth. Anything physical to distract the mental and emotional.

"Much more. I feel as if I've just had the wind knocked out of me." She did sound as if she were out of breath, as if she'd just raced up the hill to the cabin.

Hawk didn't speak.

Gail watched him, watched the muscles in his shoulders and back move subtly under his skin as his arms moved. He'd taken off the ranchman's clothes, and had stripped almost naked to those of his native world. He took his time in his task, and she became sharply aware of something she'd felt in the far reaches of her senses — his motion was smooth, fluid. He moved with the majesty of the monarch of a wild kingdom. He was beautiful to watch, and the sight took her breath away.

In that moment she felt like a tourist again, a strange person in a strange land, traveling in uncharted territory over the landscape of her own emotions. No telling what was over the next rise, or around the next curve in the road. She was careful to proceed, but not afraid.

"We can't leave Willow wondering what we're going to do," she said, knowing she herself was wondering what they were going to do. They. Were *they* in this predicament together? She sat down on the bench near the fireplace.

Hawk let out a breath. "You're right, of course. We have to tell her something. We can't let her be hurt because of us."

Silence. Gail entwined her fingers. Hawk rubbed the toe of his moccasin in the swept pile of hearth ashes.

"I've been a teacher half my life," she said, staring at her hands, "and I feel now as if the roles have been reversed. My student is trying to teach me a lesson, and she's much better at explaining her knowledge than I am."

"I know. She shocked me."

"And everything seemed so clear and simple to her child's mind."

"But we know differently, don't we?"

503

"Nothing is ever clear and simple to an adult," Gail said.

"I wonder why it can't be," Hawk said.

"We know too much."

He waited a long moment before speaking. "But I wonder if we have learned anything."

Gail could not respond.

"We said we loved each other, remember?" he said, not looking at her. He felt her start to rise then sit back down hard.

"I couldn't forget that," she said, after a long pause, not looking at him.

"Did you mean it then?" He was feeling more unsure of himself right now than he ever had, and a new kind of agitation unsettled him.

"Yes. Did you mean it then?"

"Yes." He meant that, he knew it. Imagine that. He'd just admitted to something he'd been positive would never happen to him, something he vowed never to let happen.

There was a long silence. What question should be asked next? And who should ask it? Hawk took the burden on himself. "Have you changed your mind?"

Gail lifted her head toward him. He could see questions in her eyes that now seemed as wide as the Montana sky. "No, I haven't. Hawk, what is going on here? Have I missed something?"

He turned toward her. "Well, I think we both

have. Willow kind of jumped a few steps, and I wasn't prepared for it."

"Well, neither was I." Gail stood up and faced him. "So what are you saying?"

"I'm saying, I think I love you."

"Think you love me?"

His confusion changed the configuration of his face. "I've never been in love before. My feelings have been battling like arch enemies."

Gail stared at him. "But your old wars are stronger, is that it? I'm not Cheyenne, and that holds you back."

"They're not wars. They are my life, and the life of my ancestors. I can't forget that."

"I'm not asking you to forget. Maybe I'm asking the impossible, asking you to walk a path in both worlds."

"I've been doing that all my life."

"But only with utter resistance."

"Isn't that what you've been doing? Resisting what you've been thrust into since you've come back to Montana?" His eyes bored into hers, and he thought he could see behind them, thought he could see her letting down the first wall of defense.

Gail felt his dark stare burning behind her eyes into her mind. He possessed the same uncanny knack as Willow for getting to the heart of the matter in someone else. They were alike in so many ways, Hawk and Willow, holding hurts inside, protecting themselves with a shell as tough as a turtle's. She wished then she possessed that same shell.

"You don't understand what I'm going through. I've never been dependent on anyone. I've learned to be capable, self-sufficient, to take care of myself because that's all anyone ever really has. At least that's what I used to believe. Now . . . now it seems everything in my life and in my future depends on two other people, a wild kid and a wild man. And frankly, I don't know how to act!" She spread her palms and shook her head with the futility she was feeling.

He gave her a level hard gaze. "I'm trying to understand what you're going through. Maybe you haven't understood me. I'm not dependent on anyone, either. I've made damned sure of that. I was dependent on Kenny for my happiness. He made life worth living. He was everything. When he was gone, everything was gone with him, and I swore no one would ever be that important to me again."

Gail's breath grew ragged. "What about Ada?"

"I love my mother, and the ranch, but they aren't dependent on me for their survival. In fact, Trey could take care of them very well, even with his ideas on how to get out of hard work."

He came around the bench and sat down next to her.

"Your mother needs you more than she could ever need Trey."

"That's not entirely so. I think she's wanted him to be like a son to her, mostly because he's the son of the man she married and came to love. And I think underneath of it all he wants he same thing. I've decided I will do what I can to make peace between us. I think he's still afraid. He hasn't learned what I now know that I have." He picked up her two hands and held them warmly in his own.

Gail felt his warmth go up her arms, creep over her shoulders and relax her a bit. "What have you learned?" she whispered.

He gave her a steady, honest gaze. "I've learned that I can keep my own world and share it with you. I've learned I don't have to embrace your whole world to share what's important in it with you. Willow's been teaching me, too, I guess, and she's allowed me to see what Kenny had to teach me as well. Loving another person is the only way to have real connection outside yourself. I'm not afraid anymore. And we are connected. And I know I love you with all that I am."

Gail's chest ached as if her heart had swelled to fill its cavity. She felt breathless, disoriented.

Then her thoughts gathered into one, and she didn't hide the fact that her pulse was racing out of control as her words spilled out between them.

"I've learned I'm better with you and Willow than alone, that no woman is an island unto herself. I know now how empty my life has been, even when I thought it was perfect. I never expected to ever feel totally in love with someone the way I do with you. I never knew that person even existed. But when you became part of my life I knew it was you I needed and wanted, you who filled that emptiness. I know you make me feel connected, too, complete, you and Willow. knew I loved you, and that was almost my undoing. I could barely hang on to my life as I knew it."

"Maybe you should have let go sooner," he said huskily.

"The same for you," she whispered, leaning closer to him.

His lips came down on hers at the same time his arms went around her back and her arms slid under his and up to clasp his shoulders.

"So what do you think?" he asked when their lips parted, and he'd drawn her to her feet. "Can we make a family out of the three of us?"

"I don't know. What do you think?"

"I asked you first."

"Is that a proposal to me, an answer for Willow, or one for you?" She eyed him skeptically.

"It's everything. What about you?"

Gail took in a deep breath, and let it out long and slow. "I never dreamed I'd be asking this question ever in my life, but, in the words of a smart little girl we both know and love, will you marry me, Mr. Lone Hawk Kincaid?"

Hawk watched her face, read her eyes, then lifted his head toward the top of the cabin and closed his eyes. "Yes, gladly, completely, if you will honor me by saying you wish to become my wife and Willow's mother."

Gail smiled with her whole face. "The answer is yes to both of you." They kissed deeply. She leaned back and looked up into his eyes. "I just wonder how the tribal counsel knew what my answer was going to be. Would you know anything about that?" She searched his face, smiling, tracing the planes of his cheekbones with her finger.

He looked down, almost shyly, then raised his eyes to her. "I know a little about that. They knew she was living with you, and even though they could see you were giving her excellent care, they did have their rules about adoption. I convinced them that you and I were going to get married and that we wanted to legally adopt Willow and make her our own."

"My great warrior." Gail kissed him tenderly.

"Some warrior. That part was easy. I was scared to death about having to convince you to marry me! I knew it would be tough, after all, you'd told the world you never wanted to be married. Then I knew I wanted to be married again, to you . . ."

"Little did you know what a piece of cake that would turn out to be." She kissed him again.

"Willow kind of pushed things along differently than I expected. She surprised me. I didn't know how to react because I didn't know how you were going to react to me, let alone to her proposal. It all got complicated in a very few minutes."

"Not anymore," she said.

"Not anymore," he agreed.

They held each other for a long moment blending their feelings. If there had truly been opposing worlds that set these two apart, those worlds collided in that moment of physical connection, dissolving any boundaries they'd believed existed between them.

Gail leaned back in the circle of his arms, and smiled up at him through a veil of jubilant tears. "I think we shouldn't let our daughter wait any longer for her answer."

Hawk smiled his agreement. Arm-in-arm they walked outside. Willow stood on the rise facing he cabin. They waved to her. Her face broke nto a grin that rivalled the sun's rays, and she an toward them, her dark head bobbing as she caled the hill toward the first parents she would ver truly know in her young life.

When she jumped into their outstretched arms nd the three clasped one another in their first mbrace as the family they'd created out of their wn individual selves, their different worlds became one.

And there was love at last for all three.